SAVING
the
RAIN

Elliott Rose

kensingtonbooks.com

KENSINGTON BOOKS are published by:

Kensington Publishing Corp.
900 Third Avenue
New York, NY 10022

kensingtonbooks.com

Copyright © 2025 by Elliott Rose

This book is a work of fiction. Names, characters, businesses, organizations, places, events, and incidents either are the product of the author's imagination or are used fictitiously. Any resemblance to actual persons, living or dead, events, or locales is entirely coincidental.

To the extent that the image or images on the cover of this book depict a person or persons, such person or persons are merely models, and are not intended to portray any character or characters featured in the book.

All rights reserved. No part of this book may be reproduced in any form or by any means without the prior written consent of the Publisher, excepting brief quotes used in reviews.

Without limiting the author's and publisher's exclusive rights, any unauthorized use of this publication to train generative artificial intelligence (AI) technologies is expressly prohibited.

All Kensington titles, imprints, and distributed lines are available at special quantity discounts for bulk purchases for sales promotions, premiums, fundraising, educational, or institutional use.

Special book excerpts or customized printings can also be created to fit specific needs. For details, write or phone the office of the Kensington sales manager: Kensington Publishing Corp., 900 Third Avenue, New York, NY 10022, attn: Sales Department; phone 1-800-221-2647.

The K with book logo Reg US Pat. & TM Off.

First Kensington Trade Paperback Printing: September 2025

ISBN 978-1-4967-6064-7 (trade paperback)

10 9 8 7 6 5 4 3 2 1

Printed in United States of America

Electronic edition: ISBN 978-1-4967-5898-9

Interior art by Cosmic Imprint Publishing
Author photograph by Elliott Rose

The authorized representative in the EU for product safety and compliance is eucomply OU, Parnu mnt 139b-14, Apt 123
Tallinn, Berlin 11317, hello@eucompliancepartner.com

For the readers ready for a pair of tattooed hands and a cowboy hat to make everything better

Introduction

Hello dear reader,

Welcome to Crimson Ridge...
For those of you who wish to go in to this book blind, please keep in mind this taboo romance is a work of fiction.
This is an interconnected-standalone, Forced Proximity, cowboy romance, with a happily ever after.

Please be aware that if you have triggers or content you prefer to avoid, this story may contain topics or subject matter that you might want to consider before proceeding.

Content Notes

Please scan the code below:

My website has a full list of Triggers, Content notes, including a chapter by chapter break down if required.
ELLIOTTROSEAUTHOR.COM

Please note, you can email elliottrose.pa@gmail.com for more information or clarification.

The Playlist

One Headlight • The Wallflowers
Devil You Know • Tyler Braden
SPAGHETTII • Beyoncé
Rodeo World Champion • Shaboozey
Strangers • Kameron Marlowe, Ella Langley
Guy For That • Post Malone, Luke Combs
Black Hole Sun • Soundgarden
Lost on You • LP
I Hate Myself For Loving You • Joan Jett & the Blackhearts
Cry • Benson Boone
Give Me One Reason • Tracy Chapman
Kaleidoscope • Chappell Roan
I Want Love • Elton John
BIRDS OF A FEATHER • Billie Eilish
Dancing With A Stranger • Sam Smith, Normani
Good News • Shaboozey
The End • Pearl Jam
Rushmere • Mumford & Sons
Troubled Waters • Alex Warren
Indigo • Sam Barber, Avery Anna
Do I Wanna Know? • Hozier
Sailor Song • Gigi Perez
Hello Whiskey • Kameron Marlowe
Where The Night Goes • Josh Ritter
Never Make A Move Too Soon • B.B. King
Good Horses • Lainey Wilson, Miranda Lambert
California Sober • Post Malone, Chris Stapleton
weren't for the wind • Ella Langley
Better Year • Sam Barber
Northern Attitude • Noah Kahan, Hozier
Cowboys Cry Too • Kelsea Ballerini, Noah Kahan
By My Side • INXS
Wanna Be Loved • The Red Clay Strays

SAVING THE RAIN

CHAPTER 1

Kayce

"Goddamn. That ass was sculpted to wear a pair of wranglers."

Tipping my gaze up, I'm met with the sight of uninhibited, glinting green mischief radiating from the eyes of the cowboy sitting opposite me. One of my closest friends who loves nothing better than to live up to his name—*Chaos* Hayes.

He blows out a low whistle then jerks his chin toward a group of other ranch hands, cowboys, and cowgirls hanging out across the other side of tonight's bonfire. Orange flames dance high into the crisp evening sky, keeping time with the music running low and relaxing through the stereo set up on the porch at our backs.

"Who are you perving at, so I can at least get a chance to warn them," Brad groans as he nears our table. "I really needed to add a warning when I put out the invite. Should've told everyone to bring a squirt bottle, knowing you'd be extra frisky after a win like that." As always, our host for tonight's post-rodeo BBQ at Rhodes Ranch is taking stellar care of us all, in the form of a mounded pile of food fresh off the grill delivered right to the table.

"Fuck yes. Thanks, babe." His boyfriend, Flinn, who is built like a linebacker but kinda looks like a nerd with his glasses, pounces on the food. "It's that new dude. Pretty sure he's just arrived and is working one of the local ranches. He's gonna eat up every guy *and* girl in this place." Reaching forward to help himself, he waves one hand, gesturing vaguely in the direction of whoever it is they're all drooling over.

I shake my head and let out a chuckle. "Trust you, Chaos. Eyeing up the fresh meat before you've even been back in Crimson Ridge for five minutes." We rolled through the main street of this sleepy little place we call home among the mountains at stupid o'clock this morning. After driving what felt like a thousand hours to get back from the latest stop on the rodeo circuit, my eyes were scratchy as fuck and damn near falling out of my head for those final miles.

All I've done since getting home is shower, pass out face down, then roll out my screaming muscles when I finally woke up this afternoon. My last ride was a bastard of a bronc who put me through my paces, thrashing me hard, but the horse scored highly because of it. I walked away with a good enough total to place second overall. Chaos took out the top spot in our bareback division. The smug fuck is still riding the high of his win.

As he should be.

I'm damn proud of him, but even still, it's always the goal to come first. No matter how graciously defeat might be accepted, the motivation to win a buckle pumps hot through your veins as a rough stock rider. *If only I'd scored a few points higher.* All that time driving gave me plenty of opportunity to stew on the tiny details of my ride—my form, the way the horse bucked—anything which might have made all the difference.

Lucky me. Take out second place, and I get to come home to a cold bed and a spine that feels like it's been greeted with a sledgehammer.

Oh, the glamor of pro rodeo behind the scenes.

Brad elbows my ribs, getting me to shuffle sideways and make more room at the outdoor table we're seated around. He huffs at Chaos, before wedging himself onto the bench seat at my side. "Didn't your dick get enough attention after that win, superstar? Christ. Who are you eyefucking now?"

Chaos flashes a wide, shit-eating grin. Giving off wave after wave of irredeemable asshole energy that acts as both a pussy *and* cock magnet wherever he goes. "What can I say? Us Hayes' have healthy appetites to keep satisfied." He chomps a large bite of steak, before swiping at the sauce running down his chin with a thumb.

Flinn waves his half-eaten burger in the direction of the fire, but all I can see are the climbing flames and shadowy outlines of individuals from where I'm sitting. "Over there in the red flannel. He's got that look about him. You know, the one that says he's bad for your health, and your heart."

As they keep talking about whoever this guy is, that uncomfortable sensation keeps creeping up on me. The one slinking into my awareness far too easily. Weaving around all my organs, it settles somewhere deep inside my stomach. An almost weightless sensation. An awkward feeling as if I'm quietly unspooling. The unsettling knowledge that I'm hiding a massive fucking secret from my closest friends.

I've hidden away the kind of revelation about myself that leaves me feeling as fluttery and nervous as a naive schoolgirl about to go to her first prom. Not at all like I'm in my late twenties, compete on a pro rodeo circuit, and have had more sexual encounters than I can count.

It's when they're talking about *this*—about hot guys—that I turn into a flushed-cheeked, tongue-tied disaster that I gotta do my best to hide.

My friends don't know what I did one night, when I was here for New Year's Eve, while hidden away in the garage. I never told them, not because any of them would treat me any differently . . . I guess, mainly because I don't understand my goddamn self anymore after that urge hit me outta the blue.

Turns out, getting myself sober in recent years lifted the haze on more things than just pulling my shit together and dragging my ass back in the arena in search of sponsors prepared to back my rodeo career.

"Anyone want another drink?" My knee bounces, and even though I was hungry earlier, now I'm not even interested in finishing my food. Any excuse to walk off this uneasy feeling will do at this stage. "I'm grabbing a soda. Who else wants something?"

"I'll take one." Brad looks my way, then squints thoughtfully.

"Pretty sure we're all out of what I had stocked in the kitchen. Everything is in the cooler over there."

Great. I follow his line of sight, my eyes tracking in the direction of this mysterious hot guy. Of course, that's where the drinks are.

"Go chat to what's-her-name while you're there, Wilder," Chaos says through a mouth full of food while giving me a wink. "Pretty sure she was hanging on your every word and move this week."

I know exactly who he's talking about. Jessie is one of the barrel racers who trains with us at Rhodes Ranch. She's cute and sweet, and at one point in time, I for sure would have flashed a smile her way in return. But now? I'm just all sorts of fucking flipped inside out.

Well, one thing I do know for certain is that I'm not worth anyone's time. They might think they're interested in Kayce Wilder, the cowboy package who looks the part to the rest of the world on the outside. Only, once they see the damage beneath the surface, they run a mile.

"C'mon man, you've gotta get back in the saddle. It's been ages since that disaster with the crazy pregnant bimbo. You can't let that overshadow your life."

There's nothing more to be done other than give Chaos my middle finger and let him think I'm taking him up on that challenge. Because, on one hand, he's right, but on the other, he's way off base with what he thinks he knows about me.

Hell, I don't even know about me.

"Game on, fuck face." I click my tongue at him.

If I don't at least *pretend* to be interested and go over there, talk to her for a few minutes . . . well, that potentially raises too many questions. The kind I have no interest in digging into right now.

If I stroll across to where Jessie's hanging out and put up with a bit of small talk, even if it's with the intention of taking it nowhere, at least it's an easy route to keeping everyone's noses out of my business.

I've spent years running from my own demons, and while it used to be much more convenient to do so while shitfaced, this is just one more night among hundreds of nights when I slap on a mask and be the good-time guy. Only problem is, doing it sober takes a hell of a lot more effort. It's exhausting being a former fuck up who's trying to sort his life out.

One day, and one conversation, at a time, I guess.

As I cross to the other side of the fire, weaving my way through the small crowd who have turned up for tonight's gathering, I nod at the familiar faces and say brief hellos as I go past. It's mostly ranchers, rodeo folks, and locals who have horses stabled here.

Shoving my hands in my pockets, I cast a quick glance at Jessie, taking in the sight of her from the side. I'm trying to figure out why I've never felt more attracted to her when she's literally a cowgirl-doll. Blonde hair. Petite. Cute style. Half the guys in Crimson Ridge have tried to get her number, I'm sure.

What I do realize, all a little too late, is that the group she had been surrounded by before seem to have all disappeared in the time it's taken me to circle the bonfire. Now that I'm a few paces away, I see there's only one guy standing to her side, covered in deeper shadow. Jessie has her head tilted back, smiling up at the spot where he towers over her, and as I get closer, my eyes are drawn to *him* more so than her.

I mean, I'm curious who she's so avidly talking to. I'm intrigued after hearing what was being said about this guy in a *moth-drawn-to-flame-about-to-burn-its-wings-off* kind of way.

Swallowing heavily, my eyes race about, trying to capture a quick glimpse without making it seem as though I'm outright staring. That would be hella fucking weird. To make matters worse, I'm about two seconds from crashing their intimate little moment for two, surrounded by a cloak of dark and orange firelight licking their skin. Jesus, this is already feeling like a goddamn disaster, and I'm cursing myself silently. Not only for leaping up to avoid my own bullshit, but also for snapping at Chaos' bait to come over here.

At a stolen glance I suppose, objectively, the guy isn't bad-looking. The lower half of his face is all I catch before my eyes slide lower. Scruffy, worn black jeans, faded along the thighs. Tattoos. Rust red check pattern shirt rolled at the elbows.

His palm is wrapped around a beer bottle, which reveals a map of veins on the back of his hand. They stand out, prominently highlighted by the warm glow of the fire. An inked design of a rose covers the skin there, and my breath catches as I take him in. His hands have got me stumbling, and I don't know what to do with the sensation. I've never even thought twice about what another man's hands look like. Let alone... *appreciated* the sight of them.

What the fuck? I'm feeling all sorts of prickly and clammy beneath my hoodie. Heat crawls up my neck and makes itself at home on my cheeks.

How can it be that I kiss one guy, one time, in a reckless fucking moment on New Year—which was months ago—and now I'm a jangled-up mess at the first sight of some random cowboy arriving in town?

My legs seem to keep moving of their own accord until I'm close enough now to hear them talking. Jessie lets out a breathy, flirtatious laugh before the guy speaks again, and I continue on my path, where I'm about to fumble headlong into disrupting their private fucking conversation. There's a magnetic pull on my body that I can't fight, drawing me closer and closer to encroach on the space where they stand.

"... I might not enjoy a crowd, but I know a lot about pleasing an audience." From the other side of her, the way his focus drags down her body is unmistakable.

"Do you now?" With drink in hand, she holds a straw to her lips and takes a slow sip. Followed by a playful tilt of her head.

I don't hear what he says in reply—with just a low rumble catching on the night air—but my heart is goddamn *pounding* for no good reason.

Another laugh comes from Jessie as she turns, all glossy lips and batting lashes, before her dark eyes flick my way. My presence registers, and an unreadable expression slides across her face for the briefest moment.

"Oh, hey, Kayce." As she takes me in, eyes widening slightly, she smiles. The kind of look that tells me she's more than pleased to show off the attention given by someone else since I haven't been reciprocating any of her hints.

And while I'm figuring out what to even say now that I'm standing here, she ducks her head while reaching up to hook a strand of hair behind her ear. That's the second I get my first proper sighting of the profile of the man at her side—at the same moment he lifts his chin to look toward the bonfire.

I stop dead.

My pulse spasms, heart jumping straight into the back of my throat, before my stomach plunges in the opposite direction and hits my boots.

"What—What the hell?" I croak.

Jessie's brow pinches together. She looks between me and the man at her shoulder, who I'm struggling to wrap my goddamn mind around seeing in the flesh after all this time.

"Do you guys know each other?" she asks. Hesitation evident in her expression.

"What the hell are you doing in Crimson Ridge?" I straight up ignore the girl between us. Jaw locked up tight, ice seeping into my veins.

His dark gaze meets mine and lingers for a drawn-out, weighted pause before speaking. "Got a job. I work here." The words prowl forward, languid, and gritty. No greeting. No acknowledgement. But I wouldn't expect anything less from this asshole.

With an indifferent shrug, his attention tracks up and down my frame. He always was so fucking infuriating with that cold, callous attitude he carries around.

"No. No, you don't. This isn't happening." My teeth grind. "I thought we agreed to stay outta each other's way."

"Gladly. Last I checked, this town ain't yours, snowflake." Lifting his beer, that motion reveals the slight glimpse of prime intolerable asshole settled on the corner of his lips before he takes a swig from the bottle.

"You can't be serious." *No.* There's no way this is real.

Another lift of his broad shoulder. "Dunno what you expect me to say. I'm working on one of the local ranches. So, run on back to your buddies."

I take a step toward him, bristling.

"You're not coming out here and entering events . . . you're . . .

you're too old." A protest splutters out of me. My stomach forms a churning mess, thrashing around to the point of seasickness.

"I'll do whatever the fuck I want." He chuckles. "And you know I would still win, too."

Fuck him. Fuck every single goddamn twist of fate that has brought him back into my life.

"This is bullshit. You could literally go anywhere else. Go base yourself on any other ranch." My throat struggles to work down a swallow.

"I could, but this little neck of the woods seems kind of sweet." His gaze slides down to Jessie, while giving her a wink. "I'll bet I can have Crimson Ridge eating out of the palm of my hand. All it'll take is a couple of wins, and that'll be enough."

"Fuck you. Cut the crap."

"Besides, you're almost aged out yourself. Twenty-nine, aren't you?"

My throat works. "I'm twenty-eight. You know that, dick."

"*Mmm*. So basically washed up." One of his tattooed hands rakes through his mess of dark curls.

"Screw you."

"Gonna melt if you stay too close to that fire, snowflake. I'd be careful where you stand." His eyes flicker over me once again, leaving my mouth filled with chalk. "And no, I'm not here to fool around with rodeo. I'm here for a job, but we both know I could still school your ass anytime I like, without even trying."

He leans down to say something in Jessie's ear, then guides her away by the elbow. She offers me an apologetic shrug, before the two of them head off in the direction of the grill, leaving me standing, staring out into the darkness of a fall evening. The kind of night that should be brimming with laughter and celebrating hitting the highs of placing in a competition event.

Instead, I'm numb from head to toe, trying to wrap my brain around what just happened. The gut punch of my past coming back to haunt me in the most unexpected of ways.

The last person I expected to see again.

My goddamn stepbrother.

CHAPTER 2
Kayce

I scrub a hand over my mouth while mid-yawn. A gallon of coffee and extra heaping of sugar have yet to fully kick in. Through bleary eyes, I scroll the messages in my Instagram inbox. Beyond the windows, it's the kind of morning where mist shrouds the ranch in a thick, morose cloak. Everything is painted in shades of bruised gray, and my mood suits the color palette up here.

Even Devil's Peak, which normally stands guard watching over the ranch, has decided today ain't worth her while to put in an appearance.

CHAOS
> You slunk off like a little bitch last night, Wilder.
> Irish goodbyes aren't usually your style.
> I'll see your ugly ass at Beau's tomorrow, yeah?

> Gotta get my beauty sleep if I'm gonna beat you next stop on the tour.

> But yeah, I'll be there. Should be down early-ish. I'll sort the horses and the cattle out first thing.

Leaving my phone on the kitchen counter to charge, I head out to make a start on the day. Literally no point carrying the damn thing around up here, since our only means of communication is via radio. Modern technology? Yeah, that's pretty much a running joke on this mountain. Good luck getting the internet to work anywhere beyond about three hotspots inside the house.

There's no pause for idle scrolling or wasting time on social media around here. Mornings start early as shit, and the animals don't appreciate their routine being fucked with. If there's one thing that a ranch demands, it's every ounce of your attention. Mother Nature never lets up, and the worst mistake you can make in a place like this is to assume you've got plenty of time in the day.

Fall basically translates to getting all your crap prepared for winter. That bitch is ruthless around these parts.

Shoving into my boots, I stifle another yawn while getting ready to face leaving the comfort of warmth inside the house. My first stop is the barn, seeing to the horses; then, I'll head down to the further parts of the ranch to check our herd of cattle. As I crunch my way across the gravel yard outside, plumes of white billow in front of me like dragon's breath. I'm fiddling with my brim and shrugging to pull my hoodie up over my entire cap against the chill.

Last night was . . . I don't even know what to make of it.

What I do know is that I slept fuck all, even though I'm dog-tired and still trying to recover after that last event.

Zeke Rainer. *Raine*. The colossal asshole I thought I'd long put behind me.

A face I honestly didn't think I'd see again . . . until he loomed out of the shadows beside the bonfire.

Jesus. I scratch at my day-old stubble, long strides carrying me into the barn in a half-asleep sort of haze. Hay and leather and the muskiness of the horses' scents all drift to fill my awareness. Their snorts tell me in no uncertain terms to hurry the hell up. I'd put money on the fact they're already impatiently waiting for breakfast. At least by spending the day running through the motions and generally being able to disappear into my own thoughts, I can attempt to sort through the whirlwind of memories long shoved down. Seeing my stepbrother for the first time in so many years has dredged up shit I'd rather forget from someplace mighty deep.

SAVING THE RAIN

Mom married his father when I was twelve years old. After bouncing between a revolving door of shitty boyfriends, it seemed like a good thing at first. Weddings and marriages and seeing your mom settle down equate to positives. Right? A permanent address. Staying in school and being able to maybe *this time* hang with the same group of friends until senior year. A roof over our heads, especially one that wasn't going to disappear if she missed rent . . . seemed like living the dream.

Except, when she married Ezekiel *Senior*, his package deal included a son who took one look at my ass and sneered like I was something foul he'd stepped in.

Raine has hated me since that first day we locked eyes. When I was nothing more than a scrawny little kid sat perched on an unfamiliar couch, running clammy hands up and down my jeans. Practicing my best manners while being introduced to the guy who was set to become my stepfather.

Life in the here and now is a million miles from the home I grew up in. My biological father, Colton Wilder, had no idea of the life my mom was leading. He didn't know about the pills. He didn't know about her shitty choices. And I didn't know him, either. For most of my life, I swore the guy was the worst piece of shit to ever exist.

The reality wasn't pretty, but I'd been fed lies about him by one parent who was bitter toward the other. A woman who projected her own mess onto me whenever possible.

If you grow up only ever hearing one side of the story—that he wasn't interested in being a father, or having anything to do with his unwanted kid—you form a pretty solid image of the heartless bastard who knocked up your mom as a teenager.

I spent twenty-five years cursing my father's name, because that was all I knew.

Well, turns out not even a decade living under the roof with a stepfather who was supposed to fill a role, to provide that security and steadfastness I'd never had, proved he was just another crap decision. One more poorly thought-out plan made by my mother to add to the laundry list of terrible choices she's intent on making in this life.

My girl Winnie pops her head over her stall to take a look at me when I walk through the doors to the barn, and I pause to give her a thorough scratch using both hands all around her long nose and ears.

"Did you miss me, girl?" I hum softly, placing a kiss on her forehead. She gives me a nudge with inquisitive, whiskery lips to tell me I'm running late with my attention and affection. The two things that make Winnie's world go round, followed closely by offerings of carrots or apples.

Standing in this barn is a stark reminder of everything my dad has worked his ass off to achieve. And he did so almost entirely on his own, literally bleeding and giving everything he's ever had for this ranch.

Could I be a jealous, petty dickhead about the fact that I didn't get the chance to grow up here? Sure. Or I could recognize that no one is perfect, and I sure as hell now understand why my dad allowed my mom to take me what felt like a million miles away. She left this place when I was a baby, and never looked back.

What I've learned since moving here to Crimson Ridge is that the man who, for the duration of my youth I was certain was the scum of the earth, is, in fact, anything but.

Sure, Colt Wilder is a man who absolutely made mistakes, but he dealt with surviving a shitty upbringing and physical abuse the only way he knew how. My dad was barely a kid himself when I came along. He thought he did the right thing by me. Who knows what my life might have looked like if my mom hadn't up and left Montana to go and settle in the Midwest, but I've gotta play the cards I've been dealt.

For too many years, that looked like getting wasted to avoid my shit.

For too many years, the easy option was to hide in any escape a bottle crudely provided.

For too many years, I coasted along, thinking that my rodeo career would suddenly take off because I had natural talent and the kind of smile that seemed to open doors for me.

Tumbling from the high-highs is one hell of a sucker punch when you plunge into the low-lows. The temptation to chase the rush that came with obliterating myself was all I lived for. I missed too many sponsor's calls. Too many times, I made promises I didn't keep. I fell off the tour with a brutal thud.

With a rueful whistle, I pat Winnie's neck. "No one's surprised I crash-landed on my ass in Crimson Ridge, huh?" My lips twist as she tries to crane further, attempting to ransack the front pocket of my hoodie. "Rocking up on my dad's doorstep begging for a place to stay at twenty-five with a red-line bank account and a fuck-ton of terrible decisions following after me. What a joke."

She snorts loudly. Probably agreeing. Mostly disgusted that I haven't got a stash of treats like Layla usually has.

Fucking hell. It makes me feel nauseous to think of that first year when I came to settle at Devil's Peak Ranch. By that stage, I'd already made a complete mess of my life and nearly got myself tangled up in even deeper shit.

I'm pregnant, Kayce. It's yours.

Those five words sent me into a goddamn blackout spiral. The girl I'd been messing around with at the time blew her stupid pink bubble of gum, popped it with a loud smack, and showed me a crumpled ultrasound she'd shoved down her bra.

After that, I don't think I was sober for months.

Jesus. My stomach knots. There are a lot of days when I try to avoid even thinking about it all. What kind of piss-head moron goes and fucks around without protection? Especially when I was drunk at every opportunity and ended up in bed with the worst kind of bad decisions. It was only thanks to my dad's influence—his unwavering help—I was able to screw my head on straight, get sober, and most importantly, have a goddamn paternity test done.

A life-altering step that proved I wasn't the father.

However . . . it still didn't erase all the shit leading up to that moment. It didn't go any way to changing the course I'd set myself on. I had to work doubly hard to even get back to competing in pro rodeo. Finding sponsors after you've already been ditched once? Yeah, I had to live on scraps and crumbs, busting my ass doing basically two full-time jobs on the side of training and traveling.

Blowing out a breath, I wander further, checking in on the horses before coming to a stop at Ollie's stall. She's super docile but will demand you stand there all day, giving her your undivided attention. Not that I mind. This is what I love more than anything. Being with the horses. Hanging out in these wide-open expanses where there's nothing but mountains and pines and cattle. Of course, it's soothing, and I'm blessed to be living in one of the most beautiful places on earth. But I need connection, too. Being around people gives me something; it's one of the biggest differences between me and my dad.

Colton Wilder has happily lived in isolation on this mountain for decades. When I first came here, it felt like being shackled into a prison sentence. I only did it because I needed the money. Now, I know that time spent with the horses fills that void for me. Whereas I used to chase that vibrant glow and sense of being *needed* somehow with partying and day drinking—sinking to the bottom surrounded by a group of people who were all equally as fucked up—I've figured out that ranching gives me that intangible thing I'd been searching for.

So now? Life revolves around managing Devil's Peak, taking care of the cattle, the horses, and running the property when my dad and Layla are away—like they are at present, off to Ireland for the fall and winter seasons. I'll also help out at the other ranches down in Crimson Ridge when they need extra trail guides.

Getting paid to ride a horse, flash a smile, and talk shit? Too easy.

I'm grateful to have found some kind of peaceful ground with my dad. He might not have been there for my childhood, but I can tell how much that eats at him. Regret is so often thinly disguised in the creases around his eyes . . . lined between his brows during brief moments when I catch him looking my way. He's a man of few words, but his actions make up for that. And the guy didn't let me carry on with the self-destruct mode I'd been committed to pursuing.

Even if our first months of being in each other's lives were anything but straightforward.

The first thought that crossed my mind when I found out my ex had hooked up with my father? *Relief.*

A bone-deep, lengthy, drawn-out exhale, knowing that Layla had found someone better than me. Because while my dad might be a self-professed grouchy asshole, I was nothing more than a cheater and an alcoholic. Kayce Wilder. Douchebag and endless screw-up.

SAVING THE RAIN

I messed around behind Layla's back. I used her. I made too many drunk decisions out of desperation. She didn't deserve any of the hell I put her through.

At least my dad was there to gather up the tattered pieces after I'd torn everything apart and treated someone who has such a good, kind heart like absolute shit.

While it ain't ideal for all of us to be living here, I'm away a lot with rodeo throughout the year, and the two of them are happiest when hermiting away from the world. They prefer to stay in a cabin my dad built up on one of the ridgelines if the weather allows. Then, at times like this, they're gone traveling overseas anyway. Strangely, it works. As bizarre as our circumstances are, it provides a cathartic sort of glimmer of hope. Like I'm somehow making it up to a good woman, someone to whom I was no better than an immature, foolish idiot.

What none of that self-reflection does, however, is resolve the fact I've now got to face my past again.

A childhood I've long tried to shake off. A mom who was never really a parent. A prick who seemed to get off on making my life even shittier than it already was once our homes were combined in the most unwanted of ways.

In all the years we spent under the same roof, Raine made it his business to prove just how much he hated my guts. Naive, stupid me. In all my prepubescent idiocy, I thought Mom getting married might have been a bright spot—a ray of hope in an otherwise pretty bleak life with her only ever scarcely holding her shit together.

I thought I might have been given the gift of an older brother, a mentor, someone I could grow close to . . . instead I was landed with a hot-headed jerk who loved to laugh at my mistakes.

Scrunching my eyes closed, I tilt my head back. What in the fresh hell was last night about anyway? Was I objectively looking at the guy's ass in a pair of jeans? Seeing his figure—before I caught a glimpse of his face—I felt more excitement thrumming in my veins than at the prospect of talking to Jessie.

And that leaves me all kind of churned up inside my head. I thought my own stepbrother was *hot*.

Fuck. My. Life.

Plenty of people go through an awkward phase. Everyone experiences confusing, conflicting sentiments at one time or another. An awakening or opening of their eyes where their sexuality is concerned. We're not always the same person we were twelve months ago, let alone five years. In theory, I know all that. I also know for certain I've got people I can talk to when the time is right—including one offer already from my friend, Sage, the perceptive little minx she is. Hell, if needed, I'd be able to talk to Brad, or Flinn, or even Chaos, right this second.

I blow out a long breath into the crisp air. Ironically, I've ended up surrounded by friends who wouldn't blink twice if I strolled up, leaned on a fence railing, and came out to them—seeing as some of the people closest to me are bisexual themselves, just all in different kinds of relationships. Or, in Chaos' case, being bi means enjoying the fact that it gives him a very *wide* playing field.

My friends would undoubtedly be there for me, but what do I deserve of their patience? After I've been nothing better than a man whore myself in recent years. After I've used numbing and avoiding as a way to run from my own damn self. Then all the effort it's taken to go about getting sober, getting my ass back on the competitive rodeo circuit... I barely deserve their support on top of it all.

All in all, my recent interactions, with either sex, include one scare about knocking someone up and one unexpected moment on New Year's Eve that toppled me into the territory of looking in the mirror and thinking *what the fuck.*

I've kissed exactly one guy, one time. I gave in to a flirtatious look and a moment standing so close I could taste the mint on his breath. When he shoved me backward, hands fisted in my shirt, and lips touching mine, something came alive inside me. I've never felt anything like those sparks replacing my blood, or that tingling sensation coating my mouth like sugar crystals. Of all times and places, in a darkened garage, between a deep freeze and a shelf full of tools, I learned more about myself than I had in two decades.

I still like women. I *think* there's a chance I might still even enjoy being with the right kind of woman ... hell, I don't know. But either way, I'm realizing there's a part of me that has been ignored my entire adult life so far, because it never once crossed my mind that it was something I might need.

"Kinda gotta figure my shit out, don't I?" Ollie's big liquidy eyes blink back at me. "But first, I better get you hungry assholes fed before you riot." From further down the line of twenty or so stalls we've got, hooves stamp as my words float on the morning air.

It's a stretch, but I can manage up here on my own. I've got a handful of competitive events left in the season before winter hits, and that's when I'll be stuck on this mountain for the better part of several months. Snow fronts roll in anytime from fall into spring, and during the darkest depths of winter, Devil's Peak Ranch is frequently cut off from the world, stranded for weeks on end. An isolated and bleak spot, while the roads shiver under layers of snow and ice, waiting to be cleared.

WiFi is shit at the house. There's no cellphone coverage anywhere. This place is, for all intents and purposes, severed from the world for long-ass stretches of time.

So, I'm bracing myself for when winter rolls up her sleeves. I gotta make the most of these next tour stops and then keep my fitness up so I can be back out there again come spring.

The years only seem to be going by quicker, and the injuries take longer to heal. Back when I first started out, it was like I was made from rubber, able to bounce back from anything. Nowadays, I fucking feel it jarring deep in my bones. The aches and pains are almost a full-time job to manage in their own right. A race against time before the next competition kicks off. Constantly trying to beat the ticking clock in order to be fit and ready to climb on the back of a bronc. Determinedly hanging on until that buzzer sounds.

Thoughts of my early rodeo years inevitably bring me back to the man I'm doing my best to shove from my mind.

Raine competed in the bareback bronc division, too. As I was coming into my own, still wet behind the ears— green as fuck, and only just getting myself out in the arena for the first time—he was the established name on our home circuit. Zeke Rainer was the guy to look up to, and the guy everyone was trying to beat.

At seventeen and anxious to learn, I should have relished the fact my own stepbrother was the star taking out first place. By all rights, it should have been a gift to have someone in my life to study, to learn the ropes from. Instead, I was left eating dirt and covered in shame wherever our interactions were concerned.

He was a cocky asshole. With five years between us, didn't he love to remind me of that fact. How could I compare with everything he had that I didn't? *Older. More experienced. More desired.* Everything from sponsorships to buckle bunnies, prize money to event invitations, success circled him at all times like a damn halo.

The smug prick never let me live it down. Reminding me just how easy it was to beat me any time he launched out of the bucking chute. The guy had the world and any horse he rode on a string, and I'd never been more relieved than when he took off for Canada.

But it stung like a bitch to realize the *only* reason I started to win was because he'd moved on from our region's competition. If he'd been there, I'd still have been stuck watching him walk away with the buckle, the top spot, and giving me that superior fucking look as he did so.

A raised eyebrow and tip of his lips. Always the silent promise that he could see straight through me.

No surprise, we haven't kept in touch. The guy is a jerk and a selfish dick.

I certainly don't need to spend any more time thinking about my stepbrother, or what he's doing in Crimson Ridge. I've got my own life to live, and my own future ahead of me.

He left me to survive those two assholes on my own.

And that's what I did.

CHAPTER 3
Raine

Gushing water fills my cupped palms beneath the tap. Bending forward, I splash a couple of handfuls over my face, digging callused fingers into the corners of my eyes in an effort to scrub away the fogginess of sleep.

When I straighten and dry off the droplets coating my skin, I'm greeted in the mirror by the sight of my stubble and scattering of early grays popping through. With the towel, I catch the rogue droplets that have flicked down onto my bare chest and upper arms. Rolling my neck, I blow out a heavy breath. My mind is already five steps ahead, starting to run through the list of shit I need to get done before the day is through.

Another ranch. Another job. Another place where I can keep to myself and do what I do best.

There's something goddamn cathartic about living this way. Rarely having to deal with *people* and getting to enjoy being left the fuck alone. It doesn't matter if it's here in Montana, or north of the border, or wherever you can find yourself a bed and a horse really.

Some might see it as a sort of fresh hell. Those are the kind of people who would think it's a punishment to be ripped away from the noise and thrum of a city that never sleeps. I couldn't give a crap about any of it. Being able to stay about as far away from that garbage is fine by me.

Although, now that I know what I know, I probably should've just stayed where I was in Canada.

Fucking Kayce Wilder.

Resting my hands on the edge of the vanity unit, I exhale a silent curse. That blue-eyed, blond-headed idiot really had to be here in Crimson Ridge, didn't he? With all his stupid smiles and jokes about every goddamn thing when it's plain to see that beneath that surface, he's a mess.

The dick has always been that way. Never wanting to take responsibility, or to face up to reality. It used to grate on my nerves back then, and it won't be any different now.

Man, it was always the most satisfying thing to see him eat shit and lose. The kid would always look about two seconds away from bursting into tears. For some reason, that used to give me a goddamn kick to have him realize there were actual consequences for not living up to his potential.

Kayce had a hard time, with a momma who popped pills? So fucking what. Some of us ate the broken glass life tossed at us, putting up and shutting up. He got it easy, but he was just too much of a weak little bitch to see that. I certainly didn't need to spend my time coddling him, or doing any more than was absolutely necessary where his ass was concerned.

His stupid, doe-eyed expression at the bonfire the other night was the last thing I was expecting and one heck of an unwelcome surprise. Watching him stutter and stammer his way through protests about me being here—hearing just how easily he freaked the hell out about me competing again—might've been satisfying, but left me in no mood to carry on with the girl I'd been chatting to.

Jamie? Jenny? Fuck. Who cares, it doesn't even matter. She gave me her number, but I'll come up with some reason to cut it off from turning into anything more. Even though she seemed cute and all, if I see her again I'll only end up thinking of Kayce, who she wouldn't shut up about anyway. There were too many stars in her eyes saying his name, and I'm not inclined to have anything to do with the guy. No thanks. I'd rather gnaw my own arm off than get tied up with a girl harboring a crush on that fucking princess.

My golden boy stepbrother. *Christ.* I wasn't to fucking know this was the backwater of Montana where his goddamn father's ranch is located.

Pushing off the edge of the vanity, I swipe up my shirt. This loft is small, a self-contained apartment really, perfect for what I need while I'm on contract here. I've got these quarters all to myself, right above the barn. Frankly, it's a breath of fresh air after how many ranches I've worked on where the cabins are cramped, shared between any number of men and women living on top of one another.

The space is compact—a simple bedroom, ensuite, and a single room with a kitchen and living all squeezed in—but hell, it might as well be a palace after the last place I stayed. Besides, the fact I don't have a whole house to take care of makes life easier on the seemingly unending days. When you're bone weary after herding cattle from dawn until dusk, all you feel capable of doing is to eat a hot meal, shower, and get some shut-eye.

As I button up the worn flannel shirt, movement snags my attention through the window. Bloody Tessa. That woman is up to her usual shit again. I jab one hand through my damp hair before crossing to the door in a few strides. Yanking on my cap and shoving into my boots, I head down the steps leading along the side of the barn, damn near two at a time, doing up the last buttons as I descend.

"What did I tell you?" Growling at her, my breath streams white in front of me, thanks to the crisp fall air this morning.

She straightens, cheeks flushed pink, pregnant belly sticking out more and more each day it seems now.

"Oh, hey, Raine." She instinctively holds her lower back as she stands upright. "God. Don't you give me that glare."

"Well, I told you to come and ask me for help. Not to keep trying to do shit on your own." I jog across the gravel and swipe the bag of laundry from her hands. Once again, she's attempting to heave crap into the back of the truck on her own.

"But . . ." Tessa whines, before I cut her off.

"But nothing. You're an exceedingly capable woman, yes? One who is growing a goddamn child." I jerk my chin in the direction of her jacket hanging open at the base, the point where buttons refuse to do up any longer. "So quit doing dumb shit when I'm right here to help."

Tessa's blue-gray eyes soften, and she leans against the back of the vehicle, absently rubbing the front of her rounded stomach.

"I'm sorry. You're busy and pulling extra-long hours without Beau here. I hate feeling like I can't do the simple stuff." With one hand, she waves dismissively in the direction of the laundry bags tied with a drawstring. Bundles of used linen that have come from the cabin accommodation for guests staying here at the ranch.

I hurl the sacks of sheets and towels into the truck bed, then slam the tailgate closed. The metal has an icy feel to it this morning beneath my fingers, and a chill seeps through the fabric of my shirt. I didn't even stop to put a jacket on, but I'll certainly need extra layers before I get started with the horses and stock. These mountains sure are beautiful, but it's cold as fuck at this time of year.

"Well, I'm pretty sure your brother will kill me if you get injured, and your husband will dig me up from my grave to do it all over again. It's purely selfish because I don't need either Beau Heartford or Oscar Diaz on my ass."

She smiles and pats my arm. "Anyone told you how cute you look when you're being all huffy?"

"No." I scowl.

That makes her eyes dance, an impish grin growing wider by the second. "Like a big grouchy teddy bear, aren't you? Had coffee yet, sunshine?"

"What do you think?" My brow creases. "I'm running out here, barely half-dressed, because I saw what you were trying to sneak out and do before anyone noticed."

"I just brewed a fresh pot." Tessa tilts her head toward the main house. The one the guests use as a communal kitchen and living area. "It's right there if you want some."

My lip curls. I can't think of anything worse at this time of the morning than being around the guests who are currently staying. Don't get me wrong, it's a big part of what we all work for here on this property, with visitors booking in to enjoy a taste of *ranch life*. But I'm just not interested in small talk at any time of day. Let alone when the sun has hardly gotten out of bed.

"I'm good, but thanks for the offer." I bang my fist on the top of the tailgate and move to head away, then pause. "How are you planning on unloading all this when you get into town?" My eyes narrow.

Tessa wets her top lip with a little peek of her tongue. "Uhhh . . . gravity?" She mimics pushing something off a ledge with both hands.

"Jesus, Tessa." Pulling out my phone, I fire off a quick text to Beau, letting him know that his sister needs to get in someone to start doing the heavy lifting when it comes to the accommodation side of the ranch.

"Oh. No." She swats at my hands, trying to steal my phone. "You're telling on me, aren't you?"

"Absolutely, ma'am." I lift my focus to meet her wide eyes.

A text pings back straight away, a thumbs up, and a couple of words telling me he's on it.

"Don't tell Oscar." She presses her palms together, playful pleading in her voice. "Bull riders are unbearably smug when they get to say *I told you so*."

I shake my head, and a tug pulls on the corner of my lips. "That's pretty much rough stock riders all over. We love to win."

Her husband competes at the top level in bull riding, and is currently away with the pro tour. I know he hates being on the road while his girl is pregnant, but he just came off the back of a season ruined by injury. We all want him to be out there doing what he does best, and that means rallying around Tessa to be there for her while he's gone.

I've only been at this job a couple of weeks, but I swear to god, this woman has managed to make it feel like we're family or some shit. I suppose you can count that as another glaring example of how my only blood relation is the worst son of a bitch you could ever have the misfortune to meet.

"What time does this shit need to be dropped into town?" I glance between my phone and the woman standing in front of me.

She volleys her head from side to side. "Sometime before they close at the end of the day is all. It's not urgent, but I wanted to get it outta the way before I plonk on my ass . . . and then struggle to get back up again." Her fingers wiggle a circle in front of her belly. "You know, with this extremely comfortable and not at all tiring situation I've got going on."

"Leave it to me. I'll have time to go into Crimson Ridge later."

"Oh, no, you really don't—"

"Tessa," I grunt. "I'm helping. End of story."

She gnaws on the inside of her cheek.

With both hands, I take her by the shoulders, spin her around, and give a gentle nudge in the direction of her office. "Now piss off, and go put your feet up. I'm freezing my nuts off out here the longer we dance about this."

Her huffs mixed with curses drift on the morning air, and she gives me a middle finger while trudging away from the vehicle. "Thank you. Being pregnant and useless sucks. I hate it here."

"That baby of yours will thank me," I call back over my shoulder as I set off in search of an extra strong coffee and my jacket.

Once I'm armed with both, I get into the regular routine around this place. Horses. Cattle. All the day-to-day rhythm of what it means to run this ranch. My boss, Beau Heartford, is away for the fall and early winter, helping his woman out with her work as a PR and marketing manager on the pro rodeo tour. After a glittering career and being a world champion bull rider himself, the guy now has this ranch to his name. His retirement dream come to life.

When the opportunity arose, it was a fucking easy *yes* to agree to come and work for a guy like him, to be based here in Crimson Ridge, even if it did mean learning the ropes at lightning speed to take on managing the property in his absence.

At least everything is set up to run like clockwork. There's the guest accommodation and activities side of things that Tessa handles. On top of that, the place is a working cattle ranch with a herd that falls to me to keep watch over. Sunset Skies Ranch has any number of strings to its bow, and beyond all that, there are also rescue horses, plus a budding equine therapy program.

One of Beau's long-time friends, Stôrmand Lane, and his girl Briar take care of all that. He's also the farrier employed here at Sunset Skies

—a former pro bull rider himself, which makes it even easier to get on with what I'm in charge of doing on the daily. The guy knows his shit; he's as natural as they come with stock and horses, like it's always been in his blood, so he helps out if I need extra hands where the cattle are concerned. We've got an arrangement while Beau is away that the two of them will step in and run things whenever I need to take some days off.

Not that many involved in ranching ever fucking know what a day off looks like. It's a life you live and breathe, which is why Beau has been the first one to order me to book some time away whenever I want and let Storm handle shit for me as necessary.

> **BEAU:**
> I've got a couple of guys who will cover the trail rides booked in this week.
>
> They're familiar with the horses. Know how the place runs, so you don't need to do anything.
>
> Between the two of them, they'll look after the groups.

> Got it. Thanks, boss.

Beau Heartford is a damn good man to work for. He might not have been a ranch owner for long, but it's clear he has poured everything into establishing this place. I know he's champing at the bit to be back, but where his heart is concerned, he needed to go after his woman.

They'll return once winter arrives, and that's about when I'm going to be hitting the road again. I'll find another ranch and carry on my way. Just like I've always done.

As I pass through the horse stalls, I hear vehicles approaching. The faint thud of music cuts out at the same time as the engine. Making my way over to the doors, I guess I gotta spend at least a few minutes to greet whoever Beau has brought in to run the trail rides.

Fuck, I'm grateful. Not that I couldn't do it myself if necessary; it's more that I can't be bothered. Having to deal with a whole lot of tourists yapping for hours and needing to make sure they don't fall off their horse sounds like a fresh sort of hell. I've got more than enough to do around here without that kind of hassle.

A rust bucket Bronco has pulled up, and as I reach the threshold to the barn, I see a younger guy jump out of the vehicle who I recognize straight away. We met briefly at the bonfire out on Rhodes Ranch and got to talking since he's a bareback bronc rider. A buck with natural talent to burn.

"Hayes, isn't it?" I readjust the brim of my cap.

He settles his cowboy hat over sandy hair, hanging a little long and roguish around his jaw. Green eyes give me a quick glance over as he strolls my way, closing the distance between us. He's got that air about him I know well enough, because I was that guy during the peak of my rodeo career, too.

"That's me." He reaches out to shake hands. Firm, all business. "Good to see a fellow bronc rider working hard out here. Raine? If I remember correctly?"

I dip my chin.

"You're here to run the trail ride this morning? Beau tells me you know your way around the place?"

As I say the words, another vehicle makes its way toward us down the long driveway leading into the property. There's only a faint cloud of dust kicking up under the tires thanks to the dampness hanging in the fall air.

Hayes leans a shoulder against the wall. "Yeah, we can pretty much do this shit with our eyes closed now, after how busy the summer was. This will be a breeze."

"Great, I'll be out checking on some fences that need fixing up. But I've got time to help get the horses ready before I go, if you need an extra set of hands?"

"Appreciate it, man." He flicks his gaze to the black truck that parks on the far side of his Bronco.

"Sup, pretty boy. You put your best lipstick on for today, or what?" Hayes calls out.

I'm turning around, ready to head inside the barn, when I hear it. The laugh and curse that floats over to us in reply is unmistakable. A voice that immediately makes me realize there's no possible way it could be anyone else who has just arrived.

Kayce looks up as he rounds the tailgate, just as he's shoving his phone into his back pocket, and falters. Blue eyes widen comically when he sees me standing there, and it feels like that fateful moment he appeared out of the darkness beside the bonfire all over again.

Like this kid is a bad smell I can't shake. He keeps turning up where I don't bloody well need him to be.

The air damn near crackles as he looks back at me, exactly like the same little kid who always wanted to run. I see it flicker in his eyes. That urge to bolt.

"No fucking way," he mutters.

I couldn't agree more.

Hayes' head is on a swivel, looking between the two of us, first gesturing to point a forefinger at Kayce, then at me.

"Have you guys met before, or what?"

CHAPTER 4

Kayce

Of all the fucking ranches.

As my shitty luck would have it, Raine works here. Today can go to hell already, because this was the last thing on my mind coming down from Devil's Peak. Promising Beau Heartford I'd always be available to help take guests out for rides when possible clearly wasn't enough of a good deed. I've gotta tolerate his grouchy ass now, too?

I mean, not that I've been able to shrug off how much seeing my stepbrother affected me the other night. The crappy memories were all waiting to burst forward once that bandage got ripped away without warning. Now that I'm *sober*, it's a hell of a thing to have to confront all of that history unexpectedly.

Right now, I feel like I'm crawling out of my skin as he gives me those judgmental, obsidian eyes. The fucker surveys my presence in silence, seeming to enjoy every second I have to fight to collect myself while rooted to the spot here in front of the barn.

Yeah, I fucking get it. I judge myself for my past and my mistakes, and my shitty decision-making, too. Except, seeing this prick for the first time in years—for the first time since he left the circuit where we'd been competing against each other on the regular—all it does is provoke me. His mere presence dumps me back on shaky ground.

It's bad enough I'm trying to figure out who I am and my sexuality. As if my world isn't already kinda flipped upside down, the memory of that night insists on boring into my brain. The sight of him smacked me sideways, and it's like my head is still spinning in an effort to recover my senses. The impact of the blast keeps ringing in my ears, and I feel like a prize idiot stumbling around trying to regather my bearings.

Raine, however, doesn't seem bothered in the slightest by the fact we've yet again been thrown together without warning. If anything, there's a look hidden behind his silence that tells me he'd love any excuse to watch me fail at this, too. He's standing there in a forest green flannel that has certainly seen better days, with the sleeves rolled to his elbows, and jeans wrapped around strong thighs. A faded cap pulled down over unruly dark locks reveals a few curls poking out at his nape—his hair is longer, wilder than I remember it being.

He shouldn't have this much power over me. Not now that we're both adults.

Not after all this time.

Then why am I stuck, boots cemented in place, while the back of my neck glows red hot, and I can't stop looking at his tattooed forearms?

I spend hours on end with Chaos in the close confines of a truck, driving to and from rodeo events. In all that time I've never so much as looked twice at the guy's arms or hands.

"You both know each other or something?" Chaos asks. One eyebrow lifts, and the expression he slides my way is one of *What the hell is wrong with you, Wilder?*

Good fucking question. I don't know either.

Swallowing to clear my throat of cobwebs, I nod. "Uh. Yeah. This is my stepbrother."

"Oh, shit... for real?" Chaos' eyes pinball between the two of us.

"For real," I grumble and scuff my boot in the gravel before jerking my head in the direction of the horses. We really need to get started on saddling up so that they're ready in time for this group. "Let's go and just get on with it, huh. I'm sure Raine's got plenty to do."

I know Chaos will be bursting at the seams, ready to put the blow torch on me with questions, but for now I'd rather focus on being busy and doing anything in my power to ignore this entire scenario.

Raine runs his tongue over his front teeth and doesn't budge. It's like he's purposely filling the barn entrance, challenging me to come closer, in some sort of weird game of chicken.

The sound of an incoming call slices the tension rippling across the several feet separating us. Chaos fishes in a pocket for his phone, takes a glance at the screen before looking over at me. "Gimme a minute, it's big bro. Probably with his panties in a wad about something." Flourishing an eye roll, he answers at the same time as wandering off inside the barn.

"I know you're old . . . but would it kill you to learn to send a text like a normal person instead of *calling*, asshole?" he grunts into the phone, his voice fading the further he walks away.

Leaving the two of us outside . . . alone.

I glare at Raine's stupid jaw. The guy has never been clean-shaven in all the time I've known him. My first impression was how he just seemed to be *grown* already. He was only a teenager himself, but to my naive eyes seemed like an adult. Even back then he was the guy with scruffy stubble and ink, who everyone wanted to either *be* or *be with*.

He was the scrapper who regularly sported a black eye or a split lip. Forever turning up looking like he'd chosen to waste his nights in a back alley bare-knuckle dust-up.

Now, he's the thicker set, more heavily tatted version of the stepbrother I was forced to become *family* with. Only the faintest hint of a silver strand or two in his stubble gives any real indication that Raine is in his thirties. He's got an ageless air about him, like a resident of Neverland, somehow youthful at the same time as being a miserable old fuck.

"How long have you been working here?" My teeth clench.

"Arrived a few weeks ago." He studies me, and it makes my nape prickle even more with each passing second.

"Planning to stick around?"

That draws a glint in his expression as he lifts his gaze and swings a leisurely look around at the ranch. "Dunno. Maybe? Beau's got a pretty sweet set up here."

God, he's impossible. It's like he's purposely trying to get a rise out of me, and I hate that it's working.

"Yeah, well, there are plenty of other properties. Other towns." He could literally be anywhere else in Montana, and I couldn't care less, but Crimson Ridge is far too small, too cramped with him being here.

He clicks his tongue. "No one else in this place seems to have a problem with me. It's just you bleating on and on, like a little lost lamb."

Darting my gaze around, I step closer, and the words tumble out in a hushed protest. I don't need Chaos, or anyone else hearing this. "You can't just barge into my life and make friends with all my friends." I seethe quietly.

"Jealous, are we?" His dark eyes glitter at the sight of how successfully he's gotten under my skin within a matter of minutes. "Worried I'll be better at that, too?"

"There are other people . . . other places . . . just, leave it alone, Raine." Adequate words feel out of my reach, which is never the case. I'm usually at ease with anyone or any situation. A *people person* to my core.

Until this bastard shreds all of that with just one look.

He shrugs. "Hayes seems like a good guy. Buckle winners tend to stick together."

My fists ball up as I fold my arms across my chest. "Oh, piss off. You're such an asshole with all that *winning* bullshit."

"Just calling it how it is." Lifting a hand to his jaw, he slides a thumb over his mouth. He's infuriating. Staring me down like I'll melt into my boots beneath the combined pressure of his intense scrutiny and crappy attitude.

"Well, *how it is* . . . is that you can go fuck yourself, Raine. Take your stupid goddamn power trip and shove it. This is childish." I've officially lost any sense of which way is up with him.

Right now, it feels like being straight back to a time and place where we shared a bedroom wall. This is a reminder of the arguments, the doors slamming, and the constant walking on eggshells around my mom. Was she having a good day? Was she on the up, or coming down? Would I get the apologies or the yelling for simply breathing wrong? I'm the trembling middle schooler, and he's the asshole high school dropout who loved nothing more than to push my buttons because he could.

His lip curls at the corner. "You're looking a little fried under the collar there, snowflake. Sure you don't need to run on home? Let the big boys handle things here today."

"Stop treating me like a little kid."

Another shrug is all I get. "When you quit bitching like one. Then, I'll consider it."

"Jesus. You're insufferable, you know that?" I lift my hat off my head and stab fingers through my hair.

"Don't trip over your big words, boy."

"Does Beau know you're out here being a prize assjacket?"

"Only for you. Now I know how it gets you all hot and bothered, I'll save it up especially." He chuckles, a deep noise that makes my guts do an uncomfortable flop. "Since it looks like we'll be running into each other more often..."

"Just stop." I shove my hat back on and level him with a glare. "I've got crap to do, and this is stupid."

"Quit turning up where you're not wanted." His dark gaze narrows on mine.

I can't help the wry laugh that bursts out. "That's mighty rich." I spread my arms and look around at the peaceful ranch and mountains—the sight of golden leaves fluttering on the breeze, a canvas of orange and burnt umber decorating the slopes of the hills and ridges surrounding us—and then turn back to him. "Coming from the guy who turned up in *my town*."

"*Hmmm*. Doesn't it just rub you all kinds of wrong that I've been here two minutes and already got myself a nice little warm welcome?" Raine stares at me, and then his tongue runs a slow line across his bottom lip. "She tasted pretty damn sweet too."

My blood turns white hot, but not with jealousy or any sort of sensation that I would normally expect to feel. No, there's something else lurking there. I'll be damned if I acknowledge what those words, uttered in that tone of voice, just elicited as a response in my body.

I can't tell if he's fucking with me.

His eyes pin mine, and my stomach does backflips and somersaults.

My mind's eye fills with sensual, illicit images and flashes. Glimpses of the veins popping on the back of his hands as they pin hers to the bed. Snapshots of his lips and stubbled beard grazing her exposed throat. His hips thrusting, pumping, rolling against her body. My chest tightens, and I'm struck down, voiceless, like always seems to happen around him.

Screw this guy.

I'm done with this hurricane of bad memories and twisted-up confusion brought about by his arrival. None of this is worth wasting my breath on, and I sure as hell don't need to spend any more precious time, or energy, engaging with my stepbrother's taunts.

"Whatever." This time, I shove my hands in the front pocket of my hoodie and make a definitive move. I grind my teeth, jaw clamped tight as the distance closes between us.

When I get near enough to have to sidestep his broad frame, I catch a sideways glance of him. I can't help but watch as his tongue pokes against the side of his cheek, indifference in that burnt coal gaze when he casts a sharp glance at my figure from head to toe.

"See you around, snowflake."

I huff and carry on, pushing past to enter the barn, ignoring the hint of spice and mint and coffee that hits me as we almost jostle elbows.

It's hard to know how much time has passed since arriving. Somehow, it feels like I've just been trapped in a void outside of time and space for endless minutes. Yet, in the same breath, it's also hardly been a flurry of pounding heartbeats—an interaction over and done with as quick as eight seconds in the arena.

Finally disentangling myself from his attention, I step into the barn, gladly swallowed up by the familiarity of the rows of waiting horses, the scent of leather, and the sweetness of hay hanging in the air. Down the far end of the stalls, I see Chaos already at work carrying a saddle from the tack room, and my feet carry me away from the goddamn headache at my back.

I've learned to cope. I've managed to turn shit around in my life.

This isn't anything that I need to spend time letting get to me. My stepbrother doesn't need to churn up brain space, and I definitely need to shake this weirdness that has been lingering since the bonfire.

There was no way to know it was him, so it's not like I first laid eyes on Raine with any intention to look at him in a certain way. It was a genuine mistake, one I'm gonna put out of my mind from now onward.

Kayce Wilder has turned over a new leaf, which means I'll be sure as hell to keep my focus lasered in on the important things. Namely, getting my ass on the top of the winning podium at the next event. That's my goal.

Train hard. Get my head on straight. Win that buckle.

I gotta protect my peace.

CHAPTER 5
Raine

Rapping my knuckles on the wooden doorframe, I hover outside Tessa's office while she finishes up a phone call. Through the glass of the ranch slider, she gives me a wave and holds up two fingers. *Gimme two minutes.* Simultaneously, she flashes me one of those endless smiles the woman seems to so generously hand out to anyone she encounters.

From the covered porch outside her office, there's an uninterrupted panoramic view of the mountains reaching into the sky. All purple-tipped, swirled with mist, and dusted with powdered sugar snowfall along the craggy tops. Carpeting the lower slopes, yellows and bronzes of the season crawl up from ground level. As my eyes drift across the landscape, they reach the spot over in the distance where the copper shard of Crimson Ridge itself climbs above the town, like a blade.

Further along the line of windows and doors of the main house, a group of guests occupy the outdoor furniture as they sit around drinking their afternoon coffee and chatting. Looks like a group of retirees vacationing together. This place is only getting more popular by the minute. It's no wonder Beau has plans to build additional cabins and extend the facilities to cater to the growing demand.

That's one of the things I make a mental note of needing to talk to him about—how many extra horses he's likely to need by the time next summer rolls around. At present, they have ten quarter horses suitable for taking on treks and letting novice riders loose on the ranch. With how busy the place is getting, it'd be a wise investment to look at adding to the stables sooner rather than later so the animals don't struggle physically with the workload.

It's different operating as a rancher, completely in tune with your horse's needs, rather than being a tourist unfamiliar with animals, merely hopping on for a novelty day trip. Part of what I do is to make sure none of them have picked up injuries that might have gone unnoticed by their rider. The kind that, if left unchecked, can become a massive fucking problem real quick. A stressed horse is the last thing any of us want to be dealing with.

There's a rolling, stuttered, creaking noise when the door at my back slides open. A gust of warm air hits as Tessa beckons me inside.

"Sorry to keep you waiting. Although, you don't need to hang about being an awkward duckling. You can just barge in here any time, you know." Tessa pokes at the shoulder of my jacket and then wanders back over to her desk, leaving me to follow behind.

I linger with one fist wrapped around the handle.

"Oh, god, this again? You and your cowboy manners. Stop worrying about your boots coming inside." She flaps a wrist at me. "Why do you think I chose the hardwood floor? Get your ass in here and shut that door to keep the heat in."

Giving her a raised eyebrow, I follow her orders, but even so, double-check to make sure I'm not about to track horse shit in with me. Tessa might be accommodating, but I'm not gonna be *that* asshole.

"Got paperwork to add to your collection." I hand over the stack of invoices and receipts and nod in the direction of the tray stacked with other similar pieces of paper.

It's enough to make me shudder, yet this woman isn't phased by any of it. Just takes it off my hands like the angel she is. Tessa Diaz is the type of person who can turn her hand to anything and make it successful, I'm sure of it. Pretty sure that's why she and Beau have worked so well together for as long as they have. They might be siblings, but without question support each other and operate as a rock-solid unit ... a team.

"So, when were you gonna tell me?" She swivels in her chair, scoots across the floorboards, and props her slippers up on the stool beside her desk. An immediate flood of relief settles on her face at having her feet elevated.

My brain is already composing a text to Beau to make sure he's underway with those plans to get in extra help, and ensure she's not overdoing it while running around the ranch unsupervised.

"And what might that be?" I scratch at my beard. My pulse does a stupid thing where it thuds a little harder, because this is a conversation I've been avoiding over the past week . . . well, until now, I'm guessing.

Her grin broadens. "Kayce is your brother? C'mon, I know you're a man of few words and all, but for the love of rodeo, how could you not tell me?" She feigns a pout and holds both hands over her heart. "I thought you said I was your favorite person on this ranch."

"You're basically the *only* person on this ranch." My palm wraps around the back of my neck.

"Don't go insinuating you prefer the horses to me. I know they're your only soft spot, but at least let me live in blissful ignorance." She teases, and I let out a sigh.

Tessa drops her palms to rest over the swell of her stomach, evident through the dress she's wearing.

"So ... you guys are family?"

"Stepbrothers." I bite out.

Her lips twist. "You never mentioned you knew each other."

"I didn't know." Shifting my weight, I'm already trying to figure out how to exit this conversation as quickly as possible. "Didn't know he lived here in Crimson Ridge, I mean."

"Oh?"

Her expression says it all. She's so damn close with Beau; I'm certain it's impossible for a family like theirs to understand all the ways I've tried to outrun my own.

Clearing my throat, I shove my hands in my pockets. "Look, we ain't close. Kayce and I? We're too different. We just never got on."

Shooting a firm glance at Tessa, I add. "But I won't let that affect how things run here, I can promise you."

She cocks her head to one side and gives me a thoughtful look. "Well, maybe things will be different now? Kayce really seems to have straightened himself out. I don't know firsthand or anything, but I heard he went through a rough patch. Now? He's a doll with the guests; they adore him as a guide, and he's been doing well since he cleaned himself up."

I sniff. "Good for him." Yeah, I'm about ready to be done with this conversation.

Tessa's eyes shine a little brighter as she smiles. "Maybe you two might have more in common now you're older? Wiser and more mellow and all that shit."

"Sure." If there's one thing I know about Kayce Wilder, it's that he might have changed on the outside, but I know the truth of him. There's no hiding what still lies beneath the surface, the reality behind that golden boy smile. "Anyway, I better get back out there." Jerking my head in the direction of the door, my exit is made that much easier when Tessa's phone rings again.

"Ok. Bye, grump." She laughs and, before she picks up the phone, calls after me. "Can you send Storm over here once he's finished up? I'm gonna pull the exhausted pregnant woman card. Hauling this bowling ball over to the barn today sounds way too tiring."

"Will do."

An uncomfortable feeling sits squarely on my chest. Walking away, Tessa's words are still ringing in my ears about Kayce and how she thinks he's sorted his life out. One thing I wasn't prepared for was how goddamn frequently the guy turns up.

This time of year is a boon for fall photographers, tourists, and visitors to Sunset Skies Ranch in general, which means that the demand for guided horse treks and trail rides is in peak swing. So it feels like every damn time I turn around, his black truck is rolling up outside the barn. Each day, while I'm trying to mind my business and get work done, he's there somewhere, laughing and smiling.

The boy with the blue eyes, blond head of hair, and boundless *charm*.

Of course, it's all for show. Inside, he's scared, and he's never been able to confront that part of himself, so he conceals it. Always damn well hiding away and expecting everyone around him to pick up the pieces.

It's easy enough to be busy, to keep my head down and focus on what I gotta do, but it pisses me off that we've been obliged to see so much of each other.

I take a few deep inhales, feeling the mountain air expand my lungs. A cool freshness laden with the added moisture that fall brings. It's one of those days when everything glistens with little pearls of water droplets, and low-lying mist shrouds the ranch like a shawl.

This is the kind of weather that swirls and hangs about, nipping at your heels. An ever-present reminder that winter is about to purse her lips and start blowing those first icy kisses our way any time she pleases.

Outside the barn, the Devil's Peak Farriers' truck is parked up, and it's easy to spot where Stôrmand Lane is currently working. A shower of orange sparks burst into the air above his head, and his welding mask reflects the red-hot glow of metal as he works.

He's got the usual pulse of thrumming music in the background, and one of the horses is hitched on the rail with a bag of feed hanging beside their head. As I get closer, I see a familiar spiked mane of white hair flash behind him.

Of course, the *Duchess* herself is glued to her boyfriend, supervising every move he makes from up close.

"Everything going ok over here?" I ask once I'm within earshot, and Storm's piercing blue gaze meets my own. He picks up a horseshoe and gives me a wink.

"You know me. Keeping out of trouble." The guy smirks, and strolls to the horse waiting for him. "How are you settling since we last spoke?" He keeps talking as he bends over and catches one hoof between his thighs to rest on his chaps. With all the fluent, practiced efficiency of a man who could do this in his sleep, he collects up a few nails in his mouth, whips out a hammer from his tool belt, and begins to quickly drive them in one by one to secure the horseshoe.

Storm works fast. Impressive. Smooth. His tattooed hands take excellent care of the horse, making sure that each nail protruding out the topside of the hoof is snipped off and filed down in a blink.

"No complaints. Got myself a comfy bed. And there's plenty to keep me busy." Leaning my ass on the back of his truck to watch him work, I'm quickly nudged in the thigh by a white muzzle and whiskers. The perfect height and vantage point to seek out any potential treats that might be lurking in my pockets.

The Duchess of this ranch is actually named Willow, and struts around like she damn well owns the place. A miniature pony with a planetary-sized attitude. Oh, and she's absolutely head-over-hooves in love with Storm. There's no need to tie her up; she'll trot around on his bootheels all day long like an obedient shadow while ignoring anyone else and generally being a menace whenever he's not here. Nothing in the world brings this horse more joy than to try and put her stable-mates in their place, even though they might be three times her size.

She snuffles and then snorts at me, shaking her head from side to side upon discovering that I'm not, in fact, the treat dispenser she was hoping for.

"Tessa asked if you could drop by when you're all done here."

Storm finishes checking over the base of the horse's hoof, sets it back down, and then straightens up. "No problem. I think she wants to chat about plans for winter."

"Yeah, I was going to suggest we aim to have all the horses fitted with their new shoes before then. That'd be best."

He dips his chin in agreement and sets to work on removing the old shoe from the other hind leg. "You just let me know when you need a break from everything you've taken on here. Me and Briar are happy to come down whenever, man."

"I think I'll be good. Work is work, ya know."

Storm laughs softly to himself as he starts to trim the hoof and clean up the underside. "Yeah, and the offer still stands." He double-checks the spot where that particular horse has been wearing the heel down quicker. "My girl fucking loves it here."

Using the tool in his hand, he gestures over toward one of the enclosures just off the barn. "As you can see, it's no chore if we end up staying for a few days at a time."

Inside I can see Briar along with a couple of kids who turn up once a week to help out with grooming the therapy horses they've got based here. She's got her boy Teddy out in the pen with them, and he's walking on a rope and halter with the two kids leading him, all under her close supervision.

I can't help but exhale a laugh beneath my breath. "That fucking turncoat. I swear he looks at me like I'm a punching bag, yet he's out there batting his eyelashes at your woman like he's a prizewinning show pony. I'll bet Briar could suggest putting ribbons in his mane, and the prick would flop over to show his belly."

"That's the way he rolls. Gets a kick outta knowing the likes of us aren't turning our backs on him for one second." Storm shakes his head.

"He's got a hell of a set of teeth on him; I'll give him that." My shoulder can still feel the sting where he got me real good on about my second day here. Beau had warned me, told me exactly how Teddy likes to greet newcomers—well, anyone who isn't Briar, more specifically—and yet he still managed to get a good nip in. A row of purple marks later, I'd officially had my branding and formal welcome to Sunset Skies Ranch.

Can I blame him? He's had a shitty life prior to being rescued and coming here. I know all about what it's like to trust no one.

"Gotta get my ass out there and check on the cattle." I laugh to myself, watching the Duchess try to angle her head in order to lean up against Storm, not giving a fuck whether he's working or if she's getting in his way. He absently reaches out to scratch behind her ears, and I swear the little thing goes knock-kneed, melting on the spot.

"I've already done Mist if you want to give him a run. Let him stretch his legs while Beau's not here."

"Will do." After we chat for a few more minutes, I leave him to it. Making my way inside the barn, I follow the line of stalls to where Beau's quarter horse is located. Mist is a gorgeous Blue Roan, and I can see exactly why he'd apparently had his eye on this particular guy for a long time.

"Wanna get outta here, huh?" I click my tongue his way, and his ears flick around at the sound of my voice. His long neck immediately bobs over the door to his stall, keenly watching my steps as I head for the tack room.

This ranch is fucking well-equipped. It's a pleasant change from some of the places I've worked, where everything is held together with duct tape and a prayer. There are too many landowners who refuse to invest in the stuff that matters most or haven't adapted to changing times in order to keep the cash flowing in.

Beau Heartford might've had a glittering pro career, been a god on the back of a bull, and walked away with world champion status, but that didn't guarantee shit where turning his hand to ranching was concerned. He bought this property and immediately put a plan in place to make sure business was going to flourish all year round.

To walk into a gleaming tack room with the smell of new leather and careful attention to detail is a refreshing notion indeed. A relief to find everything in its place. There's no worrying your equipment is gonna break on you mid-ride, and there sure as hell aren't any nagging concerns about saddling up. No matter whether the horse is one you've ridden day in, day out, or—like today, with Mist—one you're taking out for the first ride together.

It's the way I've always dreamt a property of my own might be.

The respect, passion, and thoughtfulness . . . caring for your animals is how I'd run things. If I ever had the luck to own a piece of land myself, that is.

Hardly likely. Guys who grew up out of the dirt like I did aren't ever gonna be the ones with their names hanging on a sign at the front gate.

As I'm carrying the saddle and blanket over to Mist's stall, I hear laughter pealing through the open window overlooking the western hills of the ranch. The trail horses are making their way back from today's ride. Front and center are Kayce and *Chaos* Hayes, their horses side-by-side at the head of the group.

My eyes flick their way quickly, then toward the main doors where Storm's heavy metal drifts in from. It's an odd sensation, almost feeling like I've been caught watching them when that's definitely not the goddamn case. I'm not fucking creeping on what they're doing; I'm just checking how the horses are looking after their long ride for the day.

I shift the weight of the saddle in my arms and can't seem to move from this spot right here, where it's easy to watch as they approach the barn. The two of them are busy cackling, honking like a pair of goddamn geese, and Chaos leans over to shove at Kayce's shoulder. Their knees bump as their horses walk in step, so close it would be nothing to reach out and take hold of the other's reins.

Something about seeing the two of them acting like idiots fucks me off. I can't explain it. They're technically doing their job. It's adequate enough, although if I was being a dickhead about it, I should really chew Kayce out for not making sure one of them was stationed at the rear, pulling up the last rider position. But I know from seeing them head out earlier this morning that they did, in fact, set out that way.

Nope. It's nothing I could give a crap about. The two of them are obviously obsessed with each other. They travel to pro events together, they ride together, and they're training partners. Being up each other's asses is how they live and compete.

I inhale deeply and make my way over to saddle Mist. They're going to be in here, filling up this barn any minute, and I'm not interested in hanging around listening to them crack jokes, thinking they're funny. It's none of my business. They can suck each other's dicks while they're at it, too. I've got work I need to get on with.

As I heave the saddle into place and thread the straps through their buckles, making sure nothing is too tight around Mist's belly, the pressure inside me refuses to dissipate. The frustration I've got rolling around my shoulders and chest is probably a sign I need to work this out of my system.

When I let Kayce think I'd hooked up with that girl from the bonfire, it was just to mess with him. I never did go there, and I certainly don't have any plans to. But hell, it was satisfying to see the look in his eyes when he thought his sweet little barrel racer had ditched him.

No prizes for guessing that I need to work out this tension somewhere and somehow. Between moving across the border and getting my head around managing this place, it's been a dry spell. Too much work isn't an issue, but I clearly need to break the drought—pussy or cock, doesn't worry me.

I've got phone numbers for both, and invitations I haven't taken up yet.

All I gotta do is get through this week, then when the weekend rolls round I can let Crimson Ridge find me a bit of hot-blooded, no-strings attached fun.

CHAPTER 6
Kayce

Wrapping and unwrapping my grip in the rope, I'm dialed in. My focus narrows, shrinking down with each pulsating thud of my heart. Beneath me is a horse I've ridden in the past. One that helped me walk away with a buckle-winning scoreline when I've been drawn with this bronc before. This is a routine I've done a thousand times, settling my weight, tightening my core, grounding myself with a steadying breath.

The brute strength of the animal is right there. An electric feeling of knowing we're about to do one hell of a dance. Guys leaning over the rails beside me. Pickup men ready and waiting. All that needs to happen now is for me to give the nod.

Readjusting my grip one final time, locking my glove in place, I dip my chin.

The metal gate to the chute is flung open, and my horse explodes into the arena, flying from the first dynamic kick. My heels mark out in perfect timing. I'm flung backward with the sheer force of the fifteen hundred pounds of muscle and athleticism beneath me.

Nothing interrupts my pinpoint focus. I don't even hear the roar of the crowd, or the announcer, or see anything outside of my intense concentration on the glossy mane and rippling shoulder muscle below me as our center of gravity lurches forward.

With my free hand stretched high in the air, my grip is secure, hella firm; there's no dislodging me despite the way the horse bucks over and over and over. We're in a tango that takes us deep into the arena—the kind of dynamic, pulsating ride judges fucking gobble up. One that will score the animal highly and add to my points tally.

Spine strong. Core powerful. Chin tucked.

We're in sync. I read every decision this horse is making, as if we sat down and poured over the playbook together. Only a couple more bucks remain in this ride. The millionths of a second trickle down like grains of sand until that buzzer sounds, and I'm done.

I fucking nailed it.

I fucking nailed it.

The transition to my pickup riders goes smooth as silk. I'm light, floating on the assurance that was the best score of the event, and will blitz the field tonight.

That buckle is mine.

My fist tightens around the smooth pebble, warm and comforting in the heart of my palm. From that point of soothing contact, I feel the *winning* energy seep into my veins. It drifts down to the soles of my boots in the dirt. Wind dances across my cheeks as I tilt my chin to the sky and take a deep inhale to lock this feeling in. To imprint it on my DNA, etch it onto my bones, to stamp the feeling of *success* indelibly on my psyche.

Eight seconds is all it takes. The kind of timeframe that—to ordinary people—is no more than a distracted thought, a blink, an inconsequential ticking of a clock. However, when that's all you're training for, you develop a unique relationship with *time*. Some rides feel like an eternity, when you're hanging in there and fighting tooth and nail to avoid being slammed into the dirt. With others, you're in total alignment with your horse, and there's a special kind of muscle memory that carries you into the stratosphere.

It's a feeling like nothing else. The type of sensation reverberating through your veins, luring all of us into forgetting the worst days, rehabbing injuries, chasing after another high. Rodeo isn't for the faint of heart, and rough stock riding will chew you up and spit you out without looking back.

"You're thinking hard over here, Wilder."

Cracking one eye open, I see Brad approaching me.

This is a spot I like to come to when I'm at Rhodes Ranch for training. A quiet space to visualize from. To play out the ride in my mind hundreds of times. To internally walk through the movements and the specifics. Witnessing success as it unfolds in slow motion.

Rolling my shoulders to loosen up some of the stiffness from standing out here so long, I tuck the stone back into my jeans pocket. We've all got our superstitions as rodeo riders; for me, it's this pebble I found just after I got sober. It's been my talisman ever since.

"Just running through it." I shrug and tap one side of my temple before flexing my grip around the metal railing to the training grounds. Looking out over the arena, I see the barrel racers gathered together, getting ready to start running some drills with their horses. Those of us based in Crimson Ridge train at this property together as much as possible. It's like having a family when you're on the road, and there's something a little bit special about being tight-knit when we're out there competing, no matter what part of the country that might be in.

"You were close last stop on the tour, man." Brad joins me and takes up a similar position, hooking one boot on the lower rail. "It's a game of millimeters."

"And yet, you eat dirt and feel like that buckle might as well be light years away."

"Chaos isn't god. He likes to think he is, but all it takes is for his hot streak to falter."

Blowing out a breath, I let his words hang in the air. We watch on as the first barrel racer takes to the course. Her horse flies across the ground, showering a great peacock tail of dirt as its hooves dig in, tightly rounding the first marker.

It's not until she hurtles toward the turn closest to us that I see a familiar gold braid, realizing it's Jessie that we're watching. She's dialed in, perfectly in tune with her horse, and doesn't have a care for anything outside of the course she's gunning to complete. I wouldn't expect anything less.

"She's looking confident," Brad says. "You two still talking?"

Out of the corner of my eye, I watch him adjust his hat. He's got a smirk on his face. I know it, even if I can't exactly see it.

There's a strange feeling occupying the space dead center in my chest. Like I've been shot with an arrow, right in the bull's eye of the target, and I'm about to be knocked on my ass. This right here is it. The fateful moment when I feel like I'm about to topple over at the side of this very arena, because everything has been too much lately.

I've been trying to shove it all into the corner, to sweep it all aside and ignore the reality that my world has tipped on its axis. Attempting to avoid the undeniable truth . . . that I don't know how to handle any of it.

Let alone how to even process what the fuck happened that first moment I saw Raine. A problem compounded by every single one of our tense interactions each time I've seen him at the ranch since.

Fuck. I feel the numbness building, climbing from my toes. A stormy tide rising fast and relentless, threatening to carry me away without warning. One that will, without doubt, leave me gasping for breath, dragged under, not knowing which way to kick and struggle for the surface.

"Hey, man. You good?" This time, Brad knocks my shoulder with his. My friend's face is drawn tight with obvious concern.

I swallow thickly. Words cling to the back of my tongue, refusing to pour forward.

"No matter what it is. I'm here for you . . . you gotta know that." He flickers a quick glance around, then lowers his voice. "If it's the drinking you're struggling with, or—"

"I think I'm into guys." It blurts out of me. The thing I don't know if I should say, but have no hope in hell of stopping. "I think I'm . . . I might be gay." Those words are echoing and distant to my ears, like they're down a tunnel, and it's not me saying them. My senses become drowned out with the aftershock of cannon fire, and even though it's only sixty out today, I'm a clammy, sweaty mess.

"Ok, then talk to me." Brad doesn't miss a beat. With a nod, he says it so reassuringly, so calmly. His quiet understanding permits my heart rate to ease ever so slightly after confessing the thing that has been on the tip of my tongue, but I didn't know if I was ready to admit it out loud to myself, let alone another soul.

He's been out to his dad, to others, for nearly his whole life. There wasn't ever any massive revelation for him. No big deal. No drama about *coming out*. It's just been who he is since forever. He told me once that he'd been certain since middle school that he was bisexual. If there's anyone I trust with this, it's him.

I just feel like such a shitty person that it's taken me so long to actually tell one of my closest friends.

"Back when you had the party here on New Year's . . ." Owning up to this is so unbelievably hard, I realize, as the words croak out. "I kissed someone. Well, more like he kissed me, and I had no interest in stopping it because I felt like I was going to climb outta my skin if he didn't put me out of my misery and do it."

"Holy shit. So, are you guys . . . together?" Brad lets out a low whistle while tilting his head. "Don't you dare tell me this the first I'm hearing that you've got some secret boyfriend. Are you gonna break my heart and reveal that you've been hiding a lover boy from me all year, you little bitch? I coulda been organizing cute double dates and dinners for the four of us, y'know?"

That playful scowl and side of scolding is what finally makes the pressure feel like it eases. A rusty chuckle makes its way past my lips, and I shove against his shoulder with my forearm.

"Nah." I exhale and scrub a hand over my jaw. "He did text me his number. But he's from out of town and left it open-ended. Kinda like if I was ever around and he was around, and we wanted to meet up."

"So?"

"So, nothing, cupid." My lips twitch, seeing the hopeless romantic flickering away behind Brad's eyes. "In case you missed the memo, I've gotta stay focused on rodeo, and manage the ranch. There ain't time to waste on navel-gazing and figuring out why I suddenly wanted a guy when I've never felt that way before."

"Oh, I bet you weren't gazing at your navel." He waggles his eyebrows.

A full-bodied laugh barks out of me, and I give him a harder push this time. "Shut up."

"Cool . . . so you played a little tonsil hockey with a dude . . . one time?"

I shrug. "Yeah. That's all it was." The more we talk about this, the less of a big deal it seems. One little kiss? And here I've been blowing it all out of proportion. It seems pathetic, laughable, really.

Brad taps on the railing, staring out into the arena as we watch the next horse and rider complete their cloverleaf pattern, circling the barrels. "So, then what happened? You put yourself on ice for months on end and clammed up like a high-security vault rather than talk to anyone about it—I'm not butt hurt, by the way. Not. At. All." Brad sticks out his bottom lip and proceeds to dramatically plunge an imaginary knife into his heart.

"God, you're a drama queen."

"Have you told other people? Or talked to anyone else about this?"

"Just you, man."

Brad clicks his tongue softly. "Ok, Wilder, you've officially gone a little way toward patching up that giant hole you just gouged in my heart. I'm honored you felt like you could tell me. Even if I'll never let you live it down that you were sneaking around sticking your tongue in a boy's mouth at *my own party* and didn't tell me."

I dig my heel into the dirt. "I was hardly shoving my tongue anywhere. It wasn't like I planned for it to happen or anything."

"Was he a good kisser, at least? For your first time and all."

"Fuck, you're really not making this easy." My ears singe, and I wrap one palm around the back of my neck. "Dunno. I guess so? Pretty sure I went from staring at his mouth, to blacking out when he grabbed hold of me. I think I only came back to earth when he walked away."

"Hot." Brad sighs wistfully. "So you think it's guys only for you, or are you still figuring things out? Which is totally normal, by the way." He's hasty to add.

Groaning, my head tips back between my shoulders. "Pretty sure I'm just broken."

"Dude. No way. You're not . . . maybe you're just needing a deeper connection?" Brad eye rolls me with a *quit being so pathetic* look. "Now that you haven't got booze to use as a crutch, you're probably in a better state of mind to realize what, or who, you're actually wanting. You should see if he still wants to meet up?"

He might be right, but it still feels awkward, like a pair of boots a size too small. I try to brush it off. "No promises—besides, I can't go for a *drink*, so it makes it kinda weird jumping straight in the deep end to ask a guy out for dinner, or some shit like that."

Brad laughs. "Kayce Wilder. Stage five clinger right out the gate."

"Fuck you." My lips tip up.

He grins broadly while digging out his phone, checking a message that has just arrived. "Crap, I gotta go help out my dad over at the stables." With a thoughtful, searching stare, he looks up from the phone, narrowing his eyes at me, and then lands a soft punch on my arm. "You're good? Need me to find an excuse to bunk work so we can go for a drive if you wanna chat more in private?"

"Nah, go see what old man Rhodes wants. I'm fine . . . but thanks for . . . you know . . . understanding."

He starts striding away, but calls back over his shoulder. "If you need anyone to talk to about how weird the heart is, I'm your guy. My best friend is dating my dad, and well, Flinn and I have got a story to tell you one of these days."

I chuckle and wave him off, deciding to stay and watch a couple more of the barrel racers before heading to my truck. Damn, it feels like a whole elephant has climbed off my chest by unloading some of that to Brad. Having him just *listen*. Even if it doesn't exactly solve the problem about the bonfire night or any of the messed up collision of thoughts I've had ever since.

Maybe it really is because I'm broken?

I've never felt close to anyone, certainly not enough to trust them, and definitely not to fall into something more involved than just chasing a rush. Drinking helped me pretend, be the guy who fucked around, nothing but a good time. The life of the motherfucking party, the last man standing at five a.m., all while dying on the inside.

As I decide to head home, to make my way back up Devil's Peak, my phone vibrates in my pocket. When I pull it out and catch a glimpse of my notifications, a plummeting sense of stone-cold dread hits out of the blue.

Mom.

Our non-existent relationship summarized in the series of red dots steadily piling up on my phone screen. Three Missed Calls. Two new voicemails. Five unread texts.

I've already ignored the attempted calls that came in earlier. Arriving in Crimson Ridge and being back in cell phone service always means picking up a whole slurry of notifications when they all bombard me at once.

In this case, I'm gladly going to overlook anything where her name is concerned. There's only one reason she ever tries to *talk*, and it's when she wants something.

Beneath that is another handful of attempted calls from an Unknown Number. Most likely her, too.

Mom has her own demons. She's always loved the pills over and above anything else. Still does to this day, even though she might try to claim she's really truly given them up for good this time.

We both know she's lying.

There are other texts waiting for me, mostly from Chaos. His recent ones rabbit on about an upcoming event at The Loaded Hog, Crimson Ridge's one and only place to find a hot meal and a cold drink. What had previously been a backcountry dive bar has remodeled itself, polishing up nicely since he and his brothers took over not too long ago.

Even though Chaos rides broncs, he still rolls up his sleeves and helps out the other *Chaos Twin*—as the two of them are affectionately known around here. A name that suits him down to the ground, but is more of an ironic nickname for Knox. The guy isn't even related to the Hayes' for a start, never mind the fact he's the ominous thundercloud to Chaos' eternal sunshine.

CHAOS:
> Come to the Hog on Saturday? We're putting on a thing for Oscar since he's back in town. You can be my bar bitch. Wash glasses and look pretty.

SAVING THE RAIN

I type out a reply while I'm still here and have cell coverage. After my chat with Brad and knowing all the shit I gotta keep on top of at Devil's Peak Ranch, I'm not feeling it.

> As tempting as that sounds . . . Nah, I don't think I can be bothered.

> C'mon. Do it for Knox?

> Apparently business is always way better when Crimson Ridge's star attraction turns up.

> It's me. I'm the star attraction.

Sighing and shaking my head with a wry smile, I start tapping at the keys. He loves nothing more than to flash a set of pearly whites and play up the starlet bareback bronc rider role. And he's not wrong; the nights when The Loaded Hog can advertise that they've got rodeo competitors in-house to take some photos with and sign some autographs, the place packs out.

> Your modesty is fucking breathtaking.

> I'll think about it. No promises.

A reply pings back quickly, but knowing Chaos, it'll be something dumb. So I slip my phone into my pocket and cut a path across the yard to my truck. Between opening up about what I'm feeling for the first time, to all the failed attempts at getting in touch from Mom, to worrying about how my next event is going to go, my head is a swirling mess circling the drainpipe.

Yeah, I'm just needing to cover some miles and blast some music, and not have to deal with any of it at present.

Once I'm behind the wheel and cruising down the long gravel drive, my head is dragged to another part of Crimson Ridge, to dwell on thoughts of the other ranch where I spend so much of my time at present. Maybe it's the lingering ghost of seeing my mom's name on my phone, but inevitably, my past with Raine lurches to the front of my mind as I bounce over a pothole.

It still stings like a bitch what he did. The way he just *left*.

To make it worse, even though we were still in each other's lives, he made it plainly obvious he didn't want to know me. The rodeo community does what it does and stays tight, but he couldn't have flashed a bigger *fuck off* sign my way. Once I was old enough to start competing, I still saw my stepbrother all the goddamn time, but now it was in the arena. It was only ever under the spotlight and glare of going up against one another.

We were permanently skating on thin ice, being in close proximity, a hair's breadth from a fiery standoff at every turn. Angst and rampaging testosterone that threatened to spill over whenever the jagged, torn edges of our worlds touched. Heap on top of that a rivalry in competition standings, constant points scoring, and the drive to come out as the one astride a podium . . . well, that soured our dynamic even more.

There wasn't ever a world where me and Raine were going to get along.

He set the tone from that very first day, when he might as well have spat in my face at the prospect of our parents getting married.

He made it abundantly clear he'd rather chew glass than get to know me as a person.

He was the one who sneered and told me to get the fuck out of his life.

And yet, the most wretched, starkly messed up part in all of this—the bit I can't seem to shake no matter how hard I try to ignore it—is how he stood in my way and blocked my entrance to the barn. He might have been slinging verbal barbs in my direction, but there's something about his presence, seeing him up close, that keeps nagging in my brain.

If I had to put a label on it, the fact he didn't ignore me and walk off without saying a word, was . . . different.

Why did having Raine's attention on me feel like a *welcome* thing? And more importantly, why the hell did it warm my blood, rather than causing it to boil?

CHAPTER 7
Kayce

A gainst my better judgment, I allow Chaos Hayes to do what he does best, and sweet-talk me. He successfully convinces me to turn up at The Loaded Hog tonight.

Some people in my situation might feel like a frog being boiled alive, having to spend time at a bar after giving up drinking. For me, frankly, I don't mind being here. It's a place I feel comfortable, even if there's a flurry of hazy memories that race through my mind every now and then. Flashes of a time when I was no better than a shit-faced cowboy stumbling around with a bottle in hand at every opportunity.

Though, the idiocy I got myself tangled up in magically disappeared once I stopped seeking out the type of people that attract nothing but trouble.

Funny how that works.

It helps that the Hog is run by friends now, I suppose. They look out for my ass and will be the first to let me know I don't have to stick around if I don't want to. But they also know me well enough. They understand my need for being around people, and how keeping that in balance is actually a helpful thing . . . even if I'm doing it all while staying sober in this shiny new era of *Kayce Wilder*.

Walking through the doors, a live band belts out a honky-tonk tune, and the booths are all packed. It's more or less a comfortable standing-room-only vibe tonight, with an area set up along one wall where Oscar looms larger than life. The guy is in *pro bull rider* mode, flashing a practiced smile while giving a thumbs up for a camera.

Close by his side sits the familiar face of his wife, Tessa, and in the next booth over from hers are the folks I spend most of my time with in Crimson Ridge; Storm and Briar, and the crew from Rhodes Ranch, including Brad and Flinn. A major difference is that my dad and Layla aren't here among them. This fall, it feels more noticeable, since they'd ordinarily stick around until winter before heading off overseas for her veterinary placement work.

Another unmistakably absent presence is Sage, without the vibrant spark she brings to every occasion and, conversely, the quiet steadiness of Beau. It seems odd not to have them around, either. Those two aren't going to be away much longer, but are currently wrapping up her gig as a marketing specialist for the pro rodeo tour. Who would have thought they had become a thing last summer, hushed up and right under all our noses?

No wonder the guy spent the year after she left town moping around like a bear with a sore head. He looked fucking miserable every time I saw him for months and months on end. Now we all know why . . . it was because Sage had gone, and he was dying on the inside every day without her.

A small crowd waits patiently for their turn to grab a selfie with Crimson Ridge's latest rodeo sensation. While Oscar might carve out windows of opportunity to travel home between events—maximizing the amount of time he can spend with Tessa through this stage of her pregnancy—the likes of Sage's work keeps her, and Beau, choosing to stay on the road, rather than going to the effort of flying back and forth.

For a night like tonight, Oscar's most recent win is an added benefit for the town, now that he and Tessa are officially residents and all.

When I make my way over and reach to the end of the booth I slap a palm on Storm's shoulder. "I heard there was a geriatric bull rider here tonight trying to relive his youth. Is this the storage unit where they park the museum exhibits?"

Storm grunts at me and curses something creative under his breath.

"Wilder." From the other end of the table, Lucas Rhodes—Brad's father—dips his chin. "Brad tells me nothing but good things about your last event. Training was looking smooth the other day, from what I saw."

"Yeah, well, someone has gotta topple Hayes off his perch." I jerk my head in the direction of where I can see his sandy-blond locks sticking out above the crowd as he talks to some of the patrons.

"Hey. You eaten yet?" Brad distractedly greets me, then looks up from something he's typing on his phone. "Flinn was just about to go to the bar and order for us." He affectionately bumps his shoulder against his man.

"Since when?" Flinn readjusts his weight to lean back in the booth seat, looking anything but ready to leave his spot.

Briar and Sky are seated between their two respective cowboys across the other side of the table, flanked by Storm and Lucas. The two girls send pleading eyes in Flinn's direction. He's at the end of the booth with the easiest path to slip out of his seat. "Pretty please." Two fluttering sets of eyelashes and coaxing looks are offered when they slide their menus across the table.

"Hi, Kayce," Briar adds, with a bright smile flashing my way. "How are things up on top of the Peak?"

"Same as usual. Hungry horses. Even hungrier cattle."

Her expression is soft. I know she loves coming up to spend time with Layla at the ranch. She and Storm are about the closest thing we've got to neighbors on the mountain, I'm sure she misses having her friend nearby.

"You're managing ok up there on your own?" Sky chimes in. Pink, bobbed hair catching the glint of festoon lights overhead as she takes a sip of her soda.

"Nothing I can't handle." I shrug. "Certainly ready to demolish a heap of food, though. You coming, Flinn, or want me to do the honors?" I hook my thumb in the direction of the bar.

"Fuck, yes. Please and thank you, kind sir." His face lights up, and he starts listing off on his fingers a multitude of meals and sides they want to order as the rest of the table descends into laughter.

Brad shoves at his shoulder. "You're such a shit."

"What? Wilder offered. Heard he was picking up the tab tonight, too." He feigns innocence.

"It's fine." Shaking my head, I snap my fingers and point at the table. "Though you're all gonna have to deal with getting what you're given... don't blame me if I can't remember and you all end up with a garden salad." With one hand, I scoop up the pile of menus before walking off.

"Six house burgers and fries. Don't fuck it up." Brad cups his mouth and calls after me.

I pause beside Tessa, and stoop to give her a quick peck on the cheek. She's in the middle of chatting with a group of people waiting to have their photo taken with Oscar. The guy is still busy signing autographs like a machine, but gives me a salute as I go past. We've met a handful of times since they moved to Sunset Skies Ranch. On the odd occasion our paths have crossed at rodeo events, too, less so over the past year while he's been working his way back from injury.

Crossing through the crowd, I spot Knox Hayes pouring drinks behind the bar. Dark hair, tattoos on nearly every visible patch of skin, requisite bad boy scowl fixed in place.

It never ceases to amaze me that the guy wanted to take on a venture like this when he's chronically averse to people. But then I guess we all do what we gotta do after surviving shitty upbringings. He's been running with the Hayes boys, taken in as part of their family, for a long fucking time. Knox hasn't ever said as much to me, but I figure he must have wanted to build some kind of legacy of his own, since the brothers have their family ranch. He might have taken on their surname instead of the one he was born with, but it's still never gonna quite be as solid as being blood related.

Knox doesn't even ask me what I want, just slides the usual soda order my way, and I leave our group's food order with the kitchen. After helping the Chaos Twins around here often enough, I've gotten to know just about all of their staff who work the bar with them. I'd never expect any of these people to run around after me like I'm a customer or some shit.

By the time I make my way back across the room to rejoin everyone at the booth, there's another figure filling the spot where I was standing a moment before. They're all staring at him like he's a piece of art they've been blessed with a private viewing of, or something equally as ridiculous.

Raine's broad shoulders and scruffy hair are unmissable. My throat tightens, fingers clench around my glass, and I can't goddamn wrestle my pulse to the ground. Instead of idling at a normal pace, the damn thing kicks up a gear and tries to take off on me.

Fuck this.

When I step up to the table, I kick Flinn's boot with my own, where he's sprawled over the edge of the booth. With a quick jerk of my chin, I silently tell him to shove over and make room. Sensing my arrival, Raine gives me a solitary flicker of his gaze, all heavy brow and firm planes of his cheekbones above that stubble he never tidies up and doesn't pay me any mind or acknowledgment. Those dark eyes slide off me as quickly as they flashed my way, before he excuses himself and moves on.

Asshole.

Though he doesn't go far. The back of my neck prickles, it would be just my luck . . . he's settled down at the booth right behind ours, joining Tessa and Oscar.

Raine being indifferent to my presence is nothing new. This was so often our dynamic when we competed against each other. In all our years as rivals in the rodeo arena, he'd give me a slight curl of his upper lip, maybe a snide remark, but more often than not, he was happy to ignore my existence.

It never used to bother me too much back then. Sure, it stung, but I got the fuck over it and learned to focus on my own game. Besides, I figured it was better if his venom was directed elsewhere.

So why am I left with a skin-crawling sensation in the here and now? Why are my ears straining for any hint of conversation to float across from their table? When he's a dickhead to me, he's talking to me at least.

This? When he pretends I don't exist at all, it feels like a murky, sticky tar in my stomach.

Even after all the crap with my mom, and the work I've done to repair the damage I caused more recently to those closest to me, this right here feels just as uncomfortable as any of that. A reaction I wasn't anticipating myself to have at all.

We're nothing to each other, that much I understand. But even so, this kind of situation puts doubt back in my head. Filling every corner of my mind with the white noise and scratching claws that remind me yet again of the fact that I'm an eternal fuck up.

I loathe feeling this way.

I hate feeling as if I'm so much of a terrible thing in his world that he'd rather ignore my presence completely.

Our meals fill the table, and conversation flows around me, a swirling pool of jokes and nonsense chatter. But I'm not in the mood for any of it. Where normally I'd be chowing down, and enthusiastically in the thick of the subject my friends are talking about, tonight feels like it's all too oppressive.

The company isn't the problem. No, it's got nothing to do with them and everything to do with my inner turmoil. For some reason, the intrusive thoughts are front and center, loud as fuck, fixated on the fact everyone here has got their shit together. It's too much like being smothered by a blanket of happy couples being mushy and in love to the point I can't breathe.

Yeah. That's enough to get rid of my appetite.

Shoving a few more mouthfuls down—I've forced myself to at least eat enough up until now so that I won't get dragged into talking if I'm not chewing—I mop up the last of my fries and sauce, then grab hold of my plate.

"I'm gonna drop this off to the kitchen," I mumble, and haul myself out of the booth before anyone can ask me a damn thing. If there's anywhere I want to be right now, it ain't sitting there, nor is it with the nagging pressure of knowing my stepbrother is only a few feet away. Without looking back, I fist my jacket in one hand and head in the direction of the bar.

My eyes scan the room for the sight of wild blond hair.

"Seen Chaos?" Raising my voice over the music, I catch Knox's attention as he's running the soda hose along a line of tumblers crammed with ice set out on the bar top.

He slopes his head toward the end of the room. "Pretty sure he went outside."

"Got it. Need any help with those?" I offer. At least if I've got something to keep my hands busy, I can try to ease this bullshit feeling bombarding me. My veins are burning up from the inside out, fizzing with something messy and uneasy that I can't wait to get rid of.

"Nah, man. Shit's under control tonight." He flips an extra glass up onto the counter, fills it, then slides it my way. As he does so, the guy gives me a curt nod. Knox's equivalent of telling me to kindly fuck off, quit bugging him, and leave him to it.

"Thanks." I dip my chin and keep my ass moving.

Swiping up the soda after offloading my plate to the kitchen, I'm pretty fucking relieved to wander outside, leaving the crowd and thump of music in my wake. If there's anything I need right now, it's fresh air. Maybe that's the thing eating away at me tonight? A packed room usually doesn't bother me in the slightest, but there's a first time for everything, I suppose.

The night air is sharp on my senses when I step outside. Fall has taken hold, dropping the temperature rapidly when the sun drifts out of sight behind the Peak. The garden area is scattered with people at outdoor tables and a courtyard set up with strings of bulbs crisscrossing overhead. A fancy fireplace, custom built, allows the night air to feel comfortable enough while being outside. Shrugging into my jacket, I let my gaze drift around the small clusters of folks enjoying the night air and the softer bass of music floating through the doors each time they open.

Looks like Chaos has disappeared. Knowing him, there's every chance he's already long vanished for the night. Or, more likely, he'll be hidden around the back somewhere with one of his fuck buddies.

He's never going to turn down an invitation if his dick is interested.

Letting out a long breath through my nose, I figure this is more the pace I'm happy to stick at for the moment. I'll hang here a while before deciding if I'll just dip out and make my way back up the mountain to my empty house and cold bed.

I stroll in the direction of the blazing fire and park my ass up on the ledge of the wall running around the perimeter of the garden. It's been built with a wide wooden rail on top to double as seating, and in the process of settling in, I put my glass down beside my hip while getting my phone out.

> You drag me down here, then ghost me?
>
> I'm out in the garden if you want to pull your dick out of someone's mouth and actually hang.
>
> Otherwise, pretty sure I'm gonna head off soon.

Swiping past all the other notifications sitting there, leaving them all unread, is easy business. I'm not in the mood for her crap at the best of times, especially not right now. Crossing my boots at the ankle, I scroll through Instagram for a bit. I'm right in the middle of watching a clip Sage has posted from the most recent pro tour event when I feel someone hovering.

Lifting my gaze from my phone, the face in front of me is not one I recognize, but he must be in his early twenties. He's sporting close-cropped dark hair and freckles, standing a foot or so away, offering a shy smile.

"Hey . . . uhh . . . you're Kayce Wilder, right?" He looks almost apologetic.

"That's me." I flash a grin in return and slip my phone into my jacket. Reaching out, I give the guy a brief handshake. Between the rodeo community, Devil's Peak Ranch, and the trail riding work I do for Beau, it's easy enough for people to know me, or know of me, even if we haven't properly met before.

His eyes brighten a little and he quickly rubs that same palm I just shook over the back of his neck, stepping a fraction closer as he does so.

"I saw you ride at the last event." His words rush out. "You were really good out there."

"Thanks." I shake my head a little with a grimace. "Although . . . not quite enough to walk away with the win, as you woulda seen."

"From where I was sitting, I thought you deserved it." There's something in the way he states those words, an earnestness that grabs my attention. Suddenly I realize, with a stronger thud in the side of my neck, this guy is looking at me with the sort of keen expression I've only ever picked up on when talking to girls in the past.

Holy shit. That subtle recognition scatters my brain cells like tiny marbles. I haven't ever looked at guys with *that* sort of awareness before, and right now, it feels like this is a whole new dance I gotta learn real fast.

In theory, do I find a guy like this . . . attractive? Am I into country dudes with his sort of clean-cut vibe? A neat white button-down paired with pale jeans. He's about my height but has a much leaner frame, almost lanky. Shit. I don't even know. This is all so brand new for me that I'm still trying to awkwardly determine the lay of the land. Still working out which way is up where my newly discovered, rather confusing, interest in *men* is concerned.

I sniff and take a sip of my soda, trying to collect my thoughts. Do I dare say something that pushes into the kind of territory that might be considered flirting? Do I let him take the lead with where this conversation might head? Christ, I've seen Chaos fuck around with teasing and playing the field from up close plenty of times. It's not goddamn rocket science. I just need to chat to the guy. So why do my words feel like they're stumbling over themselves before even making it halfway to my mouth?

"Sorry. That sounds a bit stalkerish." He laughs, a nervous flutter that fills my awkward silence. "I swear it's not like I usually rock straight up to someone and blurt shit like that out of the blue."

That makes my lips curve up a bit. Ok, at least he's making a joke, being kinda endearing about it.

"Nah, it's ok. I can talk rodeo all day." I rub my now very clammy palms over my thighs. Still not quite sure whether I want this guy to get the idea that I'm interested. Right now, in a normal situation like this, I'd happily sit down and chat about ranching and broncs and generally shoot the shit. I'd do it without a second thought, because I never once assumed a man might be interested in anything else.

I never once considered that I might be looking for *more*. Maybe the kind of conversation leading to a night chasing desire and exploring a physical attraction.

But something nags at me, a voice of warning immediately announces itself. Clarity drops in with a thud that I don't want to lead this guy on. Most importantly, not when I'm unsure if I'd even want anything more than a friendly chat with him.

Shit. *Shit.* This is way harder than I ever imagined.

"Have you ever competed?" I ask. Pushing to my feet, I step closer to the fire, needing to do something with my hands. Leading me to bend over and lift one of the stacked logs.

"No way. I couldn't do what you do." He chuckles softly. "You've got the gift of making it look effortless . . . when the rest of us mere mortals know it's anything but."

Shrugging one shoulder, I toss the wood into the flames, then reach for another. "Comes with practice, I guess."

I hear him rustling for something in his pocket. "Man, you're way too modest . . . practice, sure, but add having a fuck load of talent to that list."

As I crouch down, that's when I definitely feel the guy's eyes all over me. Heat races up the back of my neck, knowing he's absolutely, undoubtedly checking me out while I'm not looking his way. The flames build higher as I linger, not exactly knowing what to do in this situation, and my mouth feels more than a little dry.

"Thanks . . ." I add the next piece of wood to the fireplace, then slowly straighten up.

I haven't quite turned around, when I see it out of the corner of my eye. With both hands cupped to his mouth, a click is followed by a flare of orange as he lights a cigarette.

He sucks in a long draw as he pockets the pack and lighter. That keen look reconnects with my gaze just as his lips purse and curve around the filter. It's a crooked little smile that reaches up to his eyes with layers of hopefulness written there. Subtext I'd recognize from a mile away.

The kind of expression I've shared with any number of girls late at night, before going on to make terrible goddamn decisions. A question hovering in the subtle tip up at the corner of his lips, one that asks . . . *what do you think?*

Just as I'm opening my mouth, unsure how to reply, my shoulder gets jostled from behind. A hand covered in ink shoots out. My jaw hangs wide as I watch the glowing cigarette get ripped from the guy's mouth.

Followed by a heavy boot coming down to stomp it into the dirt.

CHAPTER 8
Raine

Tessa goddamn Diaz talked me into coming tonight. She kept on at me until I caved and agreed to put in an appearance.

In my head, there's an unending list of things I'm well aware will need to get done in the morning, so I'm here for one drink max. No rolling out of bed foggy-headed and thick-skulled—no nursing the lingering thud of a hangover and cottonmouth. Those options are off the table where managing a ranch is concerned.

Before even walking in the door tonight I felt on edge. Not that I've been able to put my finger on why exactly, but there isn't any point dwelling on it. Coming here tonight could at least be a useful distraction. Another small town bar in cowboy country. Just like countless others I've lost track of wasting nights in.

After spending enough time chatting with Tessa to keep her out of my hair about *having a life*, or some shit, I can see she's starting to fade. Fatigue draws her expression tight, energy flatlining as her social battery runs out. It's the look of someone who would much rather be at home curled up in bed. So I excuse myself and choose to escape outside. No way am I gonna risk getting stuck at that table with Kayce and all his buddies when she inevitably turns to Oscar any second now, giving him the word, and they bail for the night.

Which is how I've wound up with this spitfire of a redhead eyeing me over the top of her vodka mixer. She's funny enough and doesn't seem all that fussed with knowing much about me beyond the basics. As in my name, and I'm not even sure she cares too much about that, either.

"I'm only here for two more days." She lifts an eyebrow, while fiddling with the chain around her neck.

"Is that so, red?" I take a sip of my beer. I'm still nursing the one drink tonight, which is probably why I'm even less interested in hanging around. In years gone by, I might've done so if I had a bit more liquor on board, but truly can't be fucked with that sort of carry on anymore.

She scoffs at me on hearing the nickname that I'm sure has been tossed her way thousands of times, in thousands of different variations. Who cares? I'm not really into this, but I suppose it could just be a meaningless hookup. That chance to blow off some steam I'd been planning on, or at least considering.

"What do you cowboys do for fun around here when you're not hanging out at a bar?" Her tongue swipes a line across the swell of her bottom lip. At least she doesn't appear rolling drunk like some of her friends seem to be on the other side of the garden. They keep letting out loud, high-pitched squeals of laughter, and one of the girls she's here with has almost slipped straight off her stool about three times.

"You wanna know?" I chuckle, and watch as her eyes flare in the glow of the hanging lights overhead. She's pretty, and self-assured. Certainly comfortable in her own skin from what I can tell the longer we chat. I'm guessing this girl would quite like the full *Crimson Ridge cowboy* experience, which is why I imagine she walked straight over to me and boldly struck up a conversation in the first place.

She says something in reply, but I don't catch it. Just at the same second, I lift my eyes, only to witness the golden boy himself walking outside. Fuck, the whole reason I came out here was to avoid his ass. He looks around, but fortunately not over this way, before cutting a path directly toward the fire.

The girl in front of me keeps on talking—something about her friend's birthday being the reason she's here in town—but my focus continues to be drawn to him in a way that grates like I can't fucking explain. Just knowing he's there has a muscle pulsing in the side of my jaw. Kayce sits down and is straight onto his phone; of course he is. Scrolling and texting, fully focused on the screen in his hands before a young buck pretty much climbs onto his lap in an effort to catch his eye.

Jesus. It's painful watching this idiot virtually start humping his leg from the outset.

"... I mean, if I'm reading the signs right, and you're interested in getting out of here, or something?" The girl's sleeve brushes over mine when she reaches up to drag her long hair over one shoulder, twirling the strands.

That pulls my attention back down to her heavily lined lashes. She blinks at me expectantly, a cheeky sparkle to her brazenness.

My grip tightens around the nearly empty bottle. It would take all of two seconds for me to swallow the last mouthful, and agree to scratch that itch she's got a hankering to satisfy. Drape an arm around her shoulder, whisper something dirty in her ear, make a hasty exit to my truck—the role of the perfect playboy cowpoke. A version of events that have played out almost to this exact script far too many times to count. Too many meaningless goddamn hookups over the years.

Yet, the sight of Kayce standing up draws my line of sight away from her again for the briefest second. I see him toss some wood on the fire, then straighten just as the asshole beside him cups his hands. There's a distinctive spark, followed by the flicker of a flame as it illuminates the lower half of his face.

My brows knit together, and teeth grind. What a fucking moron.

I'm moving within a beat, discarding my beer bottle onto an empty table, closing the space with determined strides. I don't even care that I bloody well almost shoulder charge Kayce out of the way. He's such a goddamn idiot for standing there doing nothing and saying nothing. I yank the freshly lit cigarette straight out of the prick's mouth and grind it under my heel with a snarl.

This skinny little runt, a fucking wannabe buckaroo with pimples on his forehead, frowns at me. Mouth gaping wide, he stares at the ground, then back up to meet my scowl. "What the hell, man?"

Balling my fists in an effort not to shove this twiggy-looking motherfucker out of the way, my grunt comes out gritty and forceful. "He's got asthma, you shit for brains."

He coughs out a wry laugh that brings remnants of smoke gusting from his nose. "Like I would know that? Who are you, his dad?"

Christ. This isn't the place to get my ass arrested for breaking his jaw. But I'm sure as hell tempted to send him packing with a bloodied nose and a pair of black eyes.

Shoving my hands in the front pockets of my jeans to keep them safely tucked away—to not reach out with the intent of fisting the front of his preppy starched shirt so I can headbutt him—I lean closer, keeping my voice measured. "You want me to kick your ass in front of all your snot-face friends, huh?" My lip curls.

His eyebrows shoot up, glance darting over to Kayce, then back again. Raising both palms, he shakes his head while stepping back. "Dude. Chill out. *Psycho*." As the guy walks off, a quiet mutter drifts back.

Kayce's death glare bores into my skull. "What the *fuck* is your problem?" he snaps.

"Clearly, you are." Turning his way, as I take in the sight of him up close, my jaw pulses. A dusting of stubble lines his chin, but he's still the same fresh-faced golden boy. Standing there in his hoodie, jacket, and jeans, the kid looks like he's walked straight off a fucking photo shoot. It's annoying as hell because he's all flushed lips, razor-sharp cheekbones, and a slight curl to his hair. Acting all innocent.

As if he doesn't have a clue that he's gonna have jerks like that panting after him wherever he goes.

Pretending like he doesn't give a shit that he's got all the charisma, the looks, and the talent. He couldn't give a fuck about any of it. Spent his life flushing it all down the toilet when he had everything handed to him.

"You think you know me or something? Think you know *anything* about my life?" he snarls, dangling a quiet threat between us. Those big blue eyes of his jump around to make sure no one else is close enough to hear.

I look him up and down, my top lip curling in disdain. "You can say thank you anytime. I know you can't even take care of yourself . . .

clearly . . . if that's the kind of limp dicks you're hanging around with. Letting them blow smoke straight in your face, Christ, you're more of an idiot than I thought."

He threads his fingers into his blond locks, tugging on the roots. "God. You're unbelievable. Imagining you're rushing in to save the day, or what?"

A cold laugh escapes me. "Save your dumb ass? No. Didn't do that for you, snowflake." I scoff. This kid has always thought everything should revolve around him. Always wanting me to give him attention and to treat him like he was something, or someone, important to my life. When he and his mom were anything but. A giant fucking pain in my neck was all they were. A constant headache I didn't need.

They have no idea what trouble they caused by showing up and sticking around.

Kayce folds his arms, a muscle in the side of his jaw flexing. "Sure seemed like you were ready to sprint over here real quick." His stupidly blue eyes glint a more vivid turquoise color with the soft glow of lights strung out above us. "Looks like your date wasn't prepared to stick around after a performance like that."

Tipping my head to one side, that old familiar sense of being constantly infuriated with him—for no real reason other than him *existing*—has boiled up. "Like I said, I didn't do that for you. I did that for *me*, so I don't have to haul your ass to a medical center at this time of night." I step closer. "All because you're too much of a loser to make good decisions." With a click of my tongue, I take in the way his eyes narrow in response, his chest rising and falling faster now.

"Don't fucking flatter yourself. I wouldn't ask for your help if you were the last person on earth." He spits the words out.

"You can't even make a good choice while sober. Doubt anything's changed. Like you'd know how to get through a single day without relying on everyone else to pick up the pieces for you."

His face hardens. "Screw you. Prick."

Tension hangs thick in the air between the two of us, with the fire cracking and popping to fill the momentary silence.

"Take your sorry ass home, Wilder." I back up, shaking my head at him as I prepare to walk away. "Unless your goal is to come last the next time you compete, then by all means, hang out here choking on a lungful of smoke. I bet Chaos will be laughing all the way to that next winner's podium."

I can't be fucked with this guy, or this conversation any longer. He's just gonna throw everything away all over again, and I certainly won't give a shit if he ruins his life.

Turning away from his stupid, pouty expression and feeble excuses, I see the group of drunk girls still occupying the same corner as before. The redhead glances up at me from where she's now surrounded by her friends. I don't pause, striding back over there, and as I get closer, her eyes flicker up and down my frame appreciatively.

"Hey, you." She twists her lips and swings around to lean over the back of her chair when I reach the group. There's a chorus of feminine giggles and a couple of hiccups from one particular friend—presumably the birthday girl, judging by the glazed look in her eyes and the fact she's swaying to her own beat.

"So, I heard a rumor you're the cowboy to ask for a private tour at Sunset Skies Ranch?" She leans on one palm, staring up at me with a look that says she's more than ready to leave, all I gotta do is give the word.

"Might be." I cock my head to one side.

"I bet you know all the best places to explore after dark."

Leaning down, I bend low enough for my mouth to graze the shell of her ear. "Let me buy you a drink and steal you away from your friends for a little bit first, *hmm?*" I whisper.

A little shiver roams through her frame, and she dips her chin while making a noise of agreement.

Lingering there for an extra second, my gaze drifts back to the spot where I was just a moment ago. Immediately, my eyes lock with Kayce's. He glances up from typing on his phone, and I see his focus bounce from me, to the girl with flame-color hair as she hops up from her seat.

Fuck it. Drawing a scowl out of him shouldn't feel this satisfying, but it does. When I walk into the bar with my palm guiding her by the small of her back, the whole way, I feel it.

Those wide eyes of his drill into the back of my head.

Turning to look over my shoulder, I give him a wink. And to my black-hearted satisfaction, the golden boy who oozes charm has been thoroughly ruffled.

I'm met with a thundercloud glare, rather than bright blues in return.

CHAPTER 9

Kayce

Today has been a shit show.

Half of the cattle were out when I got down to their paddock to check on them and feed out. By the time I'd rounded up the last of them, made sure they were secured, and then fixed the broken fence post, my patience was just about worn through.

It's fucking freezing today. Knifelike winds, straight off Devil's Peak, slice across any bit of exposed skin. The kind of buffeting icy gale that leaves you aching down to the bone and exhausted from constantly fighting against it to do even the smallest of tasks.

My stomach is clawing at me, complaining loudly by the time I've finished looking after the horses, making sure they're all fed, warm, and bedded down. Thick clouds have rolled in, making it seem way later in the day than it already is, but I'm about fucking over everything.

Except, nothing is ever goddamn *done* around here.

I still have to restock the firewood supply up at the house, split kindling, and get ahead with chopping more logs ready to replace what I'll use overnight.

As I slog my way through what is a very necessary and unavoidable chore up here, my body might be physically wiped out, but my mind keeps returning to last night. Maybe that's been the added layer of chafing going on inside my skull—the coarse grit underlying how pissed off I'm feeling. No wonder this entire day feels as though it's been sent to conspire against me.

With each swing of the ax and dull thunk as wood splinters beneath the metal head, events from the bar keep replaying on an incessant loop.

Fucking Raine. I'm no stranger to being left reeling and wholly shaken up by him, but our collision course at The Loaded Hog has my skin prickling. Screw him for being such a self-centered dickhead. Where does the guy get off on pulling a stunt like that? Marching over and interrupting a conversation—then acting like it was all on me that he felt like he had *no* choice but to intervene.

What kind of asshole acts like that? He looked ready to smash the dude I'd been talking to, all for lighting a cigarette next to me. I mean, yeah, of course, I wasn't going to fucking hang around with someone blowing smoke straight in my face. I'm not thickheaded. But it's not like I haven't had to spend my entire life dodging secondhand smoke anyway.

To make it worse, the bit that keeps on leaping up to grab me and demand that I pay attention, whether I want it to or not . . . is the way my body reacted to the proximity of him.

It's stupid; it's nothing. I just hate the way I keep goddamn cataloging all these details that I can't seem to outrun. The whole drive back to the ranch last night in the dark, I kept replaying the way his Adam's apple moved beneath his stubble as he talked. Kept seeing the defined veins on his hands, standing out like a map beneath the crowned skull he's got on his right hand, and the vintage-style rose on the other.

Thinking of his ink only serves to toss me back to encounters with him around Sunset Skies Ranch when I've been helping out there lately. Ridiculous habits I've developed, like noticing his forearms whenever he pushes his sleeves higher while working. The way those corded muscles flex as he grips a set of reins and runs a palm along the neck of one of the horses.

Jesus. It's bad enough having to see each other again so unexpectedly, and here I am, lying in bed, staring at my ceiling with stray thoughts fixated on him for half of the night. Even worse is the throat-tightening realization that the moment I saw him grab that girl and walk off... it was the same feeling I've had in the past if a girl I had my eye on went home with someone else instead of me.

Except in this picture, I couldn't have given a shit about that random redhead.

Why am I feeling any kind of way—let alone jealous—about seeing my stepbrother talking to pretty, available girls? Women who I should, undoubtedly, have been talking to as well. The exact kind of group who were at the Hog for a good time, the likes of which a past version of me would have been more than happy to entertain. Talking shit about rodeo antics and giving away easy smiles.

Christ, I can't seem to shake this guy off, and what's worse is that I'm getting my budding interest in the male sex all entangled with this strange animosity we've got between us.

There's no good reason for Raine to be occupying as much real estate as he's currently taking up in my mind. We're no better than strangers, having been out of each other's lives for so long.

Maybe I need to ransack Layla's veterinary supplies while I'm out here to find an equine-strength sedative, one that'll knock me on my ass so I can get some proper sleep. I'm sure lying awake all night isn't helping my cause either.

By the time I've replenished the wood stores inside and outside the house, I'm just about beat. Ransacking through the deep freeze like a raccoon looking for a midnight feast, I find something that looks like it'll feed about three people, enough to satisfy the demon currently gnawing its way through my stomach lining. No doubt it'll be some kind of stew my dad has made. Boring as shit, but it's meat and potato and serves the perfect function of feeding a rancher who has been outside in the freezing cold since early morning.

Tossing it in the microwave to defrost, I get on the radio unit briefly to check the latest weather forecast with the Sheriff's office. Still clear enough, even with the way that bitch of a wind has been whipping around my ears all day. It's not like I'm about to get stuck up here unexpectedly with an early dumping of snow.

After making sure the fire in the lounge is built back up again, I drag my ass through a brief shower. It's tempting as hell to stand under hot water and steam, to let that thaw me out for hours. But my stomach rumbles a protest loud enough to echo around the bathroom tiles, serving as a reminder that I need to eat and crawl into bed. Maybe not even in that order.

Before getting up at the ass crack of dawn to do it all again tomorrow.

Even with feeling dog tired, I'm refusing to entertain the reason my cock might be currently standing halfway to attention.

There's absolutely no need for that asshole to be perking up.

Making quick work of toweling off, before tugging on a pair of sweats and a tank, I'm hit with a mouthwatering aroma of savory goodness wafting from the kitchen.

It's more of a race to fill my belly than anything. I scoop up my bowl of dinner and some bread rolls, along with my phone, and make for the fireplace. There's a wide concrete mantel flanking the base that's perfect to sit on and be cozy without lighting your tail on fire.

As I settle in, with phone balanced on my knee, bowl cradled in one hand, and spoon poised in the other, I inhale mouthful after mouthful. My dad might have perfected the gruff asshole mountain cowboy routine, but the guy is remarkably good at just about everything. It's what his life has been, I suppose. Growing up here, living almost entirely without technology—shunning it for the most part—he's just always learned to be capable. Figure out how to get by while doing everything himself. Which includes hunting for wild meat, on top of anything he doesn't sell when it comes to the cattle he runs on the property. No surprise, he's not a half-bad cook, either.

The old man loves to keep his freezer stocked.

Using my pieces of torn-apart bread to mop up the gravy, I chuckle to myself, thinking about his expression when he gets back and realizes all that remains in there are my terribly clumsy efforts at replacing the meals he'd prepared and frozen throughout the summer.

I can already imagine him standing there, pinching the bridge of his nose with a groan.

Brushing the crumbs off my hands, I swipe through my phone to our chat. He might be halfway around the world, but nighttime for me here in Montana is the early hours of the morning for him, and if I know anything about Colton Wilder—no matter how much he might love traveling with Layla—the man doesn't sleep all that well being away from the ranch.

He agrees to go overseas with her because he loves that girl more than his own goddamn life, but it pushes him far beyond his comfort zone.

Which is why I'm hardly surprised to see him read my message straight away when I send a quick check-in.

> Your cooking sucks.
>
> Had to force down another one of those lame stews you insist on filling the deep freeze with.

THE OLD MAN:
Funny guy.

How's everything?

> Good. A few of the heifers decided to go for a wander this morning, but they didn't get far.

Fuck. Was it that same gate again?

> Yeah. Same as last time.
>
> Fixed up the post, though.

Sorry you had to deal with that on your own.

> Don't worry about it.
>
> Nothing I can't handle.

Are you sure you don't need me to get some extra help for you?

Receiving those words immediately makes my chest tighten. I don't want to let my dad down. I won't dare let him think I'm not capable, or cause him to be a whole continent away, worrying about whether I'm coping on my own. Not when he's done this single-handed year after year since he was just a teenager. He never had parents. All he had was an evil motherfucker of an abusive grandpa who he was sent to live with. The guy deserves to have something good after sacrificing himself, after punishing himself by staying isolated out here for so long.

> Nah, old man. You've got nothing to worry about.

> Well, make sure you say something if you do need an extra pair of hands to help around the place.

> Might require a day or two, but we can sort out a solution.

> What I don't need is a phone call in the middle of the night telling me you're in the hospital or some shit like that because you've tried to be a smart ass and risked your neck.

I can't help but chuckle under my breath. Considering my rodeo career, it's ironic that my dad is more concerned about me getting hurt up here on Devil's Peak by myself.

As if he can hear my thoughts, I see dots bounce as he's typing. It takes forever, like it always does with him. But I suppose the fact my technology-averse father even knows how to use a cellphone is a small miracle. The guy's only in his forties and yet has mostly lived like a hermit up this mountain. Seeing as there's no cell coverage, he just never saw the point in bothering to learn.

Until Layla came along, that is. Count that as one of the weirder moments of my life. Teaching my dad how to use a phone and social media so he could track down his girlfriend . . . my ex. Yep. That was some twilight zone type of shit right there.

> Your rodeo prep is going well? Finding enough time to get your training in?

> Yeah, Dad. I'm cool.

> Training down at Rhodes Ranch tomorrow.

> Good. The weather forecast is still looking mild.

That has me laughing out loud, the sound bouncing around the room as the fire spits loudly, seeming to crackle in time with my mirth. Of course, this prick is in Ireland, spending his free time checking on the snow updates for the ranch.

> Jesus. Take the cowboy out of Montana, but you're still a control freak in every time zone, huh?

You'll thank me if I've checked the reports before you wake up and let you know early that shit is about to turn.

> And you'll be a smug bastard about it, too.

> Thanks. I appreciate you checking in.

Let me know how you get on at training.

> Sure. Will do.

> I promise it's all good here. Chat tomorrow.

CHAPTER 10
Raine

One thing about Beau Heartford as a boss is that he takes shit seriously and acts fast. No sooner had I mentioned to Tessa about possibly needing more trail horses brought in considering the increased number of ranch visitors, he evidently made plans from afar.

Which is why I've had the instruction today to head over to Rhodes Ranch to collect a couple of new mares to introduce to the stable. It'll take them a while to get used to the place, and I'll have to see how they fit in with the pecking order of the others—not to mention how they are around new people, noises, and unfamiliar territory—before we can even start to think about putting guests in the saddle on either of them.

But if there's anything Lucas Rhodes knows, it's horses. The guy has been running his ranch and herd for decades. If he's confident these two are the perfect temperament for the job, I trust he knows what he's talking about.

Pulling up to the barn, I can see plenty of vehicles lined up near the arena—the local rodeo competitors must be training today. As my truck and trailer come to a jolting halt, I realize that means Kayce is likely to be here.

No sooner than I think it, like I've conjured his presence, I spot his now all-too-familiar dusty black truck and plates.

The guy seems to be everywhere I fucking go in this town. Considering he lives and works on top of a goddamn mountain, he bloody well has a knack for being in all the same places I end up.

My knuckles blanch around the steering wheel.

Last weekend at The Loaded Hog was a crap shoot. Having to deal with Kayce's stupid decision-making and his lack of interest in being responsible. Christ, it felt like having a sniveling little kid covered in mud, with tear-stained cheeks, and an arm in a sling sitting in my front seat all over again.

So much so, I barely made it inside with the girl before making an excuse, easily finding her another cowboy to be entertained by. She didn't seem to care all that much, either. That asshole's chest puffed out like he'd just won a fucking buckle when it became clear I was offloading her and cutting a path for home.

Getting out of my truck, I busy myself with sorting the back of the horse trailer, making sure there's nothing loose or out of place that might spook the two I'm here to collect.

As I do a walk-through and double-check everything, I hear commotion coming from the arena. Someone has just burst out of a chute for a practice ride, and they're being cheered on by the others hanging over the railing.

I readjust my hat and walk down the ramp, just as the pickup rider swings by to collect whoever had been out there. They do their job smoothly, securing the rider, who I catch sight of—a flashy grin and shaggy mess of sandy hair gives him away immediately. Chaos Hayes jumps down to the dirt and exchanges a few words with the guy still in the saddle, then lopes over to where his hat flipped off during the course of his ride.

He squares it back on his head while heading toward the railing and joins the others. A small group watches as the next rider prepares to be released.

In my chest, I feel a tightening, like a rubber band stretching to its limits. A tense withholding of breath. Because I don't have to see who is up next to know who it's going to be, and yet I can't bring myself to move from where I've stalled at the back of this trailer. My gaze turns to the chute, where all I see is a hat tipped forward, a chin tucked low. From personal experience, I know the routine. I feel the tingling in the pads of my fingers as if I'm the one sitting astride that horse, wrapping and re-wrapping my hold while absorbing the heat and breaths of the animal preparing to unseat me. Taking deep inhales so as to not go blank or lose touch with your senses and limbs once everything explodes out the gate.

The crew hanging over the back of the chute are there, heads lowered as they all wait for the signal. Each of them with a job to do. Every single person working as a team to make sure the horse and rider are safe. This might only be practice, but they'll be drilling these runs as if it's a packed arena and prize money is on the line.

Not to mention the safety of the man on the back of a bronc who is raring and ready to make his life hell for eight seconds.

From all the way over here, the intensity, the concentration is visceral. Every person holds their breath in anticipation.

That cream-color hat dips in a quick nod.

The gate is flung open, and all it takes is one perfectly timed launch by the bronc . . . they both fly out of the chute. Kayce marks out perfectly with his heels and lays back with one hand high overhead. His other is wrapped around the rope just above the horse's shoulders. In hardly the blink of an eye, they're in the middle of the arena.

To a casual onlooker, it would seem like a blur. Nothing more than hooves flying, the fringes of his chaps swinging, the rider's body being jerked around in a seemingly impossible way.

But I feel every single flicker of muscle, each heaving breath and flex of the horse as if I were out there in the middle of that arena myself.

Kayce's body holds the perfect balance of anticipating his horse's movements, and staying strong enough to withstand being bucked off. The arm he holds high looks balanced, comfortable. He's in perfect rhythm with the bronc. All that natural talent he's always had for connecting with his horse bursts to the fore with each buck and flick, but there's also a maturity present in him now, too.

At first, I can't discern what it is. The ride is over and done with—

those eight seconds are eaten up in a few rapid heartbeats. But as the pickup rider closes in, that's when the difference I've been trying to identify becomes apparent.

He's stronger. More definition to his frame than I remember him having the last time we competed against each other. It sits on his figure well and allows him to appear more in control, more relaxed, and sure of himself, like he's already got the certainty of a win locked in his bones.

When he jumps down from the back of the pickup rider's horse, he lifts a hand to run through his hair, and it shows off the shape of his back. His shirt pulls tight, revealing the way his shoulders are broader now than they used to be, with planes of lean muscle tapering down to his trim hips.

He jogs over to collect his hat from the dirt, and I get a look at his ass when he bends down. As he straightens back up, I feel it . . . something curls, hot and tight, right down low in my stomach.

Oh, fuck no.

My eyes snap away from the sight of my stepbrother's ass in a pair of jeans and chaps. The pulse thumping in the side of my neck is a motherfucking traitor because there is no goddamn way I just drifted into that kind of territory.

I was watching his form.

I was taking notes on his ride so I could give him hell about details he needed to improve upon the next time I see him.

I was watching to see if he's bothered to hone his talent, or if he's still fucking around like when he was younger.

That's all.

I shake my head and stride off toward the barn. Lucas Rhodes had better have those horses harnessed up and ready to go, because I'm very much in a mood to get the hell out of here, leaving behind a cloud of dust and fuck knows what that was taking hold of me.

"How are they looking?"

Beau's voice echoes in my ear as I do the final check on the horses for the night. It's damn late, and I'm beat, but I know he was wanting to hear how the new mares have settled.

"They're happy, eating plenty, and have been super relaxed. Even got the Duchess' approval. She gave them a good sniff through the fence and seemed perfectly fine about having new friends to get to know."

He laughs. "As long as they don't try to buddy up to her boyfriend, she'll tolerate them."

I can't help but smile to myself, leaning on the door of Pepper's stall. She comes over to cautiously inspect my jacket sleeve.

"You're not wrong there. But I'm confident they'll fit right in. I'm planning to spend a bit of extra time with them in the coming week, see if either of them have any traits we need to be mindful of, and I'll run them in the neighboring pasture until everyone gets more familiar with each other."

"Sounds good, Raine. You just keep me updated if there's anything you need."

"Will do." I give Pepper a chance to run her soft nose over my outstretched palm. She snorts, followed by a humid sigh on discovering there aren't extra treats on offer.

"I'm not gonna hold you up, just wanted to check in. But I am gonna tell you to call it a night. It's late, and I can hear those horses snorting in the background." Beau clears his throat. "Unless you want me to set Tessa on you..."

I chuckle. "Nah, I'll stay away from the wrath of a pregnant lady who would love nothing more than to tell me she knows best."

"You've learned fast."

"She's persistent."

"That, my sister absolutely is." I hear a muffled noise in the background. "Right, I gotta run. Go the fuck home to bed, man. I don't want to find out you're sleeping curled up in the stalls."

"You betcha."

We say our goodbyes and hang up, which is my cue to drag my ass out of there. Not that I have far to go. Hooking a hard right out of the main doors, the stairs up to my flat run along the side of the barn.

It's fully dark out, with only the glow of a full moon in the sky to see by, hanging plump and golden above the mountains. Over toward the main house, light spills from a handful of guest cabins, but the majority are darkened at this late hour.

It's peaceful around the place, with the faintest hint of a breeze rustling through fall leaves yet to be shed. However, the seemingly idyllic country scene doesn't do anything to soothe the tension still thrumming in my veins.

I hate that I haven't been able to kick my strange affliction from earlier today. I fucking detest this unease that lingers and lurks, unwanted.

Maybe I should have just fucked that girl from the Hog on the weekend. Obviously, all this bottled-up angst is getting to me because I'm strung tighter than ever before, and even after a full day's work on the ranch, I can't seem to settle.

My apartment is gloomy as I step inside, shades of gray and inky black, lit only with the glow of moonlight flooding in through the windows. I don't even know if I can be fucked with getting the place warm since I'll only be here to rest my head until dawn creeps over the horizon. Flipping on a couple of lights, I ditch my jacket and boots, then hang my cap at the hook by the door.

While crossing to my bedroom, I'm already stripping out of my shirt, and the bunched flannel gets tossed to the floor as I reach the shower. It's been a long-ass day of handling horses, and I'm ready to wash all the grime and restless thoughts the fuck away down the drain.

The shower takes a minute to heat, with wisps of steam slowly making themselves visible while I wait. As I unbuckle my belt and set to work on my jeans, I catch my reflection in the mirror. The black and gray scene of a wolf howling at a cold moon sits over my pec, surrounded by swirling cloud formations covering my collar bone and the front of my shoulder muscle—only I know how that ink conceals the divots embedded there from his cigarette burns.

The last ones he gave me before he realized he couldn't fuck with me like that ever again.

Stepping out of my jeans, I move under the water, and my shoulders finally drop from being up around my ears nearly all goddamn day. Warmth rushes over my skin, trickling a serene, ease-filled line down my body, wetting my hair to plaster against the back of my neck.

With both hands, I scrub my face, discovering the lengthening stubble that I'll have to trim sometime soon. Otherwise, I'll wake up one day to discover a full mountain man beard going on.

Rivulets of water track over my stomach, and in the process of reaching for the soap dispenser, I look down and curse. My goddamn dick is hardening and demanding attention. Like it knows I'm on edge and needing one hell of a release to rid myself of all this pent-up tension I've been lugging around.

Christ. I don't want to be giving into this, but at the same time, what other choice is there. I'll probably poke my own eye out by the morning if I don't take care of this situation right now.

I silently grit my teeth in disgust, refusing to give an inch of space to the acknowledgment that part of today's mental strain—in fact, the vast majority of how tightly wound I've been since arriving in Crimson Ridge—has been due to a certain blond-haired, golden-boy idiot.

As I run the soap over my chest and stomach, it's fucking inevitable that my palm is gonna keep sliding further south.

Slamming one hand against the wall, my chin drops, and right before my eyes, the length of me swells as if on cue. My cock is full and hard, jutting out before I've even taken myself in hand. And from the very moment I wrap my fist around the shaft, I feel a shudder of relief roll straight to my toes.

I squeeze roughly, tugging from root to tip, while my jaw clenches so forcibly I'm in danger of hearing a crack.

This is a fucking joke. I don't need to be popping random boners and having sudden urges to jerk off, all because of a guy I can't stand being around. It makes no sense to me why this intense frustration is giving my dick a reason to be swollen and hard as stone. Staring back at me, the world's most inconvenient erection thickens beneath my fingers.

As I stroke myself, rapid and firm, I'm not in the mood to drag this out. Whatever bullshit hornyness is afflicting me, I'm of a one track mind, needing to deal with it as fast as possible.

My eyelids grow heavy as the intense pleasure builds low in my stomach. That same heated, coiled feeling from earlier on, the sensation that hung around in that spot all day, roars to life. Wholly unwanted. Completely unbidden. With each shuttle of my fist, pressure winds tighter at the base of my spine. My stomach muscles bunch, and my balls tingle.

"*Fuck. You.*" I grunt out loud. The words hissing, spitting into the stream of water.

And it's the worst goddamn thing in the world, because I can't stop the torrent coming at me fast and hard. I can't slow my strokes. With each tug and squeeze, the image grows more vivid. Blue eyes flash, staring up at me. Flushed lips hang parted, obediently waiting. A strong hand threads through short strands of hair as my cock sinks into that hot mouth, and I fucking *groan*. It's my hand holding tight to the figure on their knees for me. It's my tattoos and my fingers that curl to yank that blond hair until I hear the soft little masculine whimper of pleasure in response to my command.

They take every inch and moan with delight when I hold them there for me to use. Hips driving in and out, I fuck that willing mouth and it's total bliss.

"*Unnghhh. Ffffuuck.*"

Cursing violently over and over, my dick erupts, shooting ribbons onto the shower wall, coating my fist in cum. The blinding force of my cock pulsing and kicking catches me by surprise. A throbbing, agonizing release that goes on longer than it has any goddamn right to.

I'm reduced to a panting mess, heart thundering against my ribcage.

And I fucking hate it.

I'm pissed as all hell at my stupid brain for getting off to *those* images, of mixing up memories of other guys with my present day reality. There are any number of past hookups I could have fixated on. Jesus, even a fistful of poker-straight red hair clenched in my grip and plush lips would've done just fine. It wouldn't require much imagination to know what that would have looked like if I'd taken her up on the offer to blow me in the back of my truck.

I don't have any interest in figuring out how or why those details invaded my thoughts. I've been with blond haired and blue eyed dudes before. Sure, at some point, I've had a guy younger than me begging me to take his mouth. Someone somewhere would've had a catalog of similar features.

A random, jumbled memory. That's all it was.

Nothing more.

CHAPTER 11

Another ten minutes and we'll be arriving at today's competition venue. This is part of our home rodeo circuit, and provides one of the best opportunities for the likes of Chaos and myself to enter and not have to spend a crap load of time or money on travel.

No one tells you when you first get into rodeo that some of your biggest lessons will come in the form of boring shit like budgeting. Learning how to manage your expenses, particularly in the early days—what gear to borrow rather than buy outright, what essentials you need to invest in owning yourself—and how to balance entering events with the goal of winning prize money while still working.

It's all well and good for those who break into the top of the top. When you're finally breathing the rarified air of arenas where life-changing cash waits on the table every time you exit the bucking chute. But the reality for cowboys like us is that we're laying everything on the line during an eight-second ride, all while doing our best to stack events back to back where possible. A simple, but effective way to avoid the inevitable red line of expenses creeping higher. That's why Chaos and I will share a vehicle, split fuel, and buddy up as much as possible. It makes doing this financially viable, whereas if you're doing it alone, you've gotta have deep pockets to line that path.

Guys like me certainly don't have that at our disposal.

That's probably one reason why it stung even deeper when I first got started and knew that Raine was in the position where we could have done this together. We were competing at the same events, entering at the same time, traveling to and from the same location.

Yet, the asshole didn't want to have anything to do with me.

My knee bounces as Chaos drums his fingers on the wheel. We know each other's routines inside out and upside down these days. Once we get close to the arena like this, our focus starts to dial in. Minute by minute, the belt cinches tighter on our thoughts and words, and even though we might have spent several hours talking shit while driving—this is where it gets serious.

We might be friends, but we also know the competition is fierce. Ultimately, one of us is going to walk away today a winner, while the other won't get so lucky.

It pushes the two of us. Professional athletes say it time and time again, that they're only as successful as their opposition drives them to be during their careers. The greats are made that way by the fires they go through in order to climb to the top. I'm thankful to have him by my side, forcing me to be *better* at every turn.

My phone vibrates in my hand, and I flip it over, expecting to see a message from Brad or the competition organizers. Instead, this particular text is the last fucking thing I need right now.

Not at this moment. Goddamn it. Could she not hold her shit together for one lousy day?

MOM:
> Kayce, I'm begging. Darling, please, just this last time.
> I've tried everything to get hold of you.

My blood runs cold as those words pop up. I should have blocked her number years ago, but if I don't pick up her messages, who the fuck will? Can I walk away from the woman who is legally my parent? My blood? Even if, at this point in life, I'm the one who always feels the pressure of bearing sole responsibility for taking care of her?

She's a teen mom who never grew up. Stuck in a time loop.

Someone who never matured past being a pregnant seventeen-year-old.

As much as it makes my jaw clench and thumb itch to delete her messages immediately, could I live with myself if I found out the worst had happened to her... again?

I raise my chin to watch the world fly by out the window, not wanting to disturb Chaos from getting into his zone for the event. He doesn't need me unloading decades of childhood misery where my mother and her addiction is concerned.

Maybe it's because everything feels so freshly reopened, like a wound that has been picked at and left bleeding freely, with all that has been going on lately, but my head starts spinning.

All the shitty decisions I've had to make, some out of desperate necessity, and some out of just being a drunk asshole which only exacerbated the problem. Either way, reality slams into me like a brutal, icy front: My mom has gotten herself into deep shit. Once more, she's relying on me to solve her problems for her.

I knew it the moment all those missed calls and messages started popping up. Deny it as I might, it had already crawled into my awareness on spindly legs. The grim truth was right there, and yet I tried to ignore it, because thinking back on the last time I bailed her out dredges up a whole shipwreck of the worst kinds of memories. Ones that I'd gladly leave trashed at the bottom of the ocean rather than have to revisit all over again.

One particular memory is so visceral, it bursts in as soon as I open the door a crack. I'm back there in a flash, hearing the asshole's voice down the phone—rough and thick with the type of menace men like him live and breathe.

"She owes us money," he drawls.

"Yeah, well, my mom has never been responsible. So why lend her anything in the first place?" I swallow heavily. How they got my number is the least of my concerns right now. I've got the kind of man who you don't want to ever be receiving a phone call from currently on the other end of the line, telling me that my mom has racked up debts she can't pay off.

"We don't care much for what folks can, or can't, afford."

Yeah, that much I already assumed without him spelling it out for me.

"How long does she have . . . how long to get the money to you?" In my head, I'm busy calculating how many days it will take me to get my ass back to the Midwest. It seemed like the best decision to move out, and keep away from her drama. Yet, here I am, with the bill for her addiction now coming due. A terse conversation that most certainly isn't a social call or friendly chit-chat.

"Put it this way, kid . . ." He sucks air through his teeth and makes a wet, smacking noise with his mouth. "Your mother is already far beyond any leniency period we might consider extending."

Fuck. I slam my eyes closed. Heart leaping into the back of my throat.

"That's a nice-looking ride you've got parked up on main," he drags out the words.

This asshole thinks he can threaten me? Presumably, with the intent of sending guys to jump me as I make my way back to my piece of shit car? He obviously wants me well aware that he knows how to get to me, just as easily as my mom. I don't care about taking a beating. My body has been through hell in rodeo, but what I can't bear is the thought of walking into her shitty apartment and finding her with a black eye, or worse. Even if it is from her own terrible choices; her constant refusal to get help.

"How much?" I grunt.

"Five large."

My stomach drops straight to my boots. There's no way in hell I can find that kind of money in the kind of timeframe he's demanding. Even with what I've got saved, and competing at the next run of events I'm due to ride in. I could take out top placing in each rodeo back-to-back, and I'd still be scraping to pull together that much cash.

"I'll have it for you. Promise. Just . . . leave her the fuck alone, man."

"You're a good boy, Kayce Wilder." He chuckles into the phone. "Don't make me eat my words." With that, the line goes dead.

Inside my chest, my heart is damn well pounding, remembering how slimy his voice was. A faceless, nameless prick. The lies I had to tell to get hold of that money overnight left me numb, doubled over, hugging the toilet bowl. Scrambling to put a loan with a finance company in my ex's name, just to get enough desperate cash at short notice will go down as one of the worst days of my life.

I went out that night and got trashed as soon as the debt had been paid off. Pretty sure I wasn't sober for weeks on end. A spiral of self-destruction that caused more damage than just being a loser to my ex-girlfriend. It cost me every sponsor. I lost my spot on the tour to boot.

As we pull into the parking lot, I would ordinarily be hyper focused. My brain *should* be dialed in, lasered in preparations for the event. All that is supposed to occupy my mind's eye are the visualizations I've spent so much time running over in the build-up to this exact moment. Everything I'm meant to be walking through to get my head on straight after our most recent training day, and a ride that felt so goddamn good I could taste the victory.

My upcoming win. Tuned the fuck into my preparations. That's how immersed and centered every cell needs to be right this second. The *feeling* I'm counting on to be staunchly set in my damn bones.

Instead, I'm drowning in harrowing memories. The yelling. Her wailing. Shouting down the phone at my mom with a half-empty bottle of vodka in one hand. Telling her to sort herself out, and that if she doesn't, I'll goddamn well inform *Colton Wilder* of everything she's done as a willfully neglectful parent to ruin my life.

Heat stings the back of my eyes, and I can hear echoes of her pathetic sobbing. *I'm sorry honey, I wasn't in my right mind. I don't remember doing that.* Followed by the denial. *You're a foul little shit, making up lies about your own momma.*

All she'd ever do was cry. Make excuses. It's like arguing with a child if I ever bother trying to talk some sense into her. She never could stay off the pills long enough to have a clear head. Never capable of making a decision that wasn't centered around getting her next fix. Most of the time, she was out of it on the very pills that doctors are happily shoving in the hands of their patients all over this goddamn country. The fucking epidemic they're enabling with people just like my mom, who are too weak to accept the help they need in order to finally say no and get clean.

Seeing her latest messages, I'm already dreading what new trouble she's gotten herself into. Who has she racked up another sky-high round of debts with? What phone call am I gonna get this time, out of the blue, that potentially derails everything I've worked so hard to achieve?

I've spent the past couple of years climbing out of that pit of shame after getting lost in the bottom of a bottle in an attempt to avoid all of this.

Now, I'm so close to making something of myself. I'm so close to actually achieving the rodeo dreams I've had my heart set on since the first pro bronc ride I ever watched.

Since the first time I saw Raine compete.

Fuck's sake.

"... wake the hell up, man." Chaos smacks my shoulder.

I jerk my head around, realizing his Bronco is parked and the engine has been cut. We're here. And I'd better get my head in the fucking game.

FINDING A QUIET SPOT, I hide out and run through my stretches. I've already been for a jog to get my blood pumping, trying to combat some of this anxiety humming and sizzling in my veins that I wouldn't usually be fighting at this late stage before heading into the arena.

My number hasn't been called yet, so I've still got time to go through my pre-ride routine. The ritual I've cultivated for myself that seems to work. We've all got our quirks and superstitions we do to settle ourselves, to lock in the mindset we need before entering the bucking chute. Some will have a smoke, some will make sure they've got their specific competition hat to wear.

Chaos disappears to hurl his guts up at the last second, without fail, every time.

As I'm quietly working on my groin, stretching out in a kneeling lunge position, my eyes lift.

Familiar black hair sticks out, wild and unruly, beneath his charcoal hat. On reflex, my chest tightens.

With all the memories of Mom and my shitty past lurking right there, my brain struggles to process what I'm seeing. Why the fuck is he here? What the hell is he doing in this section of the arena ... right where all the competitors are gathered, getting ready to be called?

Just as my stretch falters, as I lose focus on what I'm supposed to be doing, the asshole turns around.

His dark eyes drill into mine, and I'm faintly aware of the blood rushing in my ears, deadening the noise of the crowd and announcer. I push to stand up, seemingly unable to rip my attention away from Raine.

That curl to his upper lip tugs higher, and his focus dips down to take in my chaps, my boots, then back up to my shirt and vest. I'm pissed off at myself for being so easily distracted by him being right here. Right in the competitor's section.

"Why the fuck are you here?" I bite out.

He runs his tongue over his teeth. "Worried I'm gonna be in that arena and whoop your ass?"

"No." My palms feel goddamn clammy all of a sudden. "I know you're not competing."

"Sure about that?" He glances between me and the railings, the crowds.

Fuck this guy. "What the hell is your problem? Just leave me alone."

"Gladly."

"Then why are you here?" Everything I'd normally be doing right now has flown out of my brain. It's too much like being face-to-face with him when he was top dog, the rodeo king. Time after time he was the one to beat.

Just thinking about that fact, even though I logically know it isn't happening in the here and now, my body reacts as if we've just rewound the clock by years. I might as well be eighteen and staring at the guy I so desperately wanted to *be* and who looked at me like I was shit on the sole of his boots.

"It's a free country, last I checked." Raine scratches his jaw. "But since you're crying like a kicked puppy about it . . . I drove Tessa here so she could watch Oscar compete."

Swallowing down jagged rocks, I'm stuck in a place where words escape me.

"Happy now? Put your pacifier back in and suck on it while shutting the fuck up." He shakes his head. "If you put half as much effort into riding as you did to crying on my shoulder . . ." He clicks his tongue and with that, abruptly walks off. Not even bothering to finish the sentiment.

Because that's how little I matter, how insignificant I am to my own goddamn stepbrother.

How little I mean to anyone.

Instead of focusing like I know I need to, my brain is a NASCAR racetrack. Thoughts are whizzing and flying and threatening to flip in a fiery explosion as they collide with one another.

Someone calls my name. My limbs are numb as I shake them out. Every movement, each little step that I could just about do in my sleep, is done by routine, rather than conscious decision.

I'm vaguely aware that my head isn't in it. But thoughts of money, debts, thugs banging down my mother's door at three a.m. with baseball bats, all of that forms a frenzy driving me to climb onto the back of that bronc.

Being in the chute, I hardly hear the chatter going on around me. My ass settles onto the horse, with tension and anticipation rolling off the animal in powerful waves.

I've gotta do this.

I've gotta take out that top placing.

All I know is that as soon as the gate busts open . . . everything is infinitely, abhorrently wrong.

CHAPTER 12
Raine

Trudging my way up to the front door, I can already hear her shrill voice. Incessant screeching makes my ears bleed before I've even laid a hand on the doorknob.

Standing outside in the damp night air, I take a couple of deep breaths. I'm not high anymore, my head is clear. All I had was a few tokes earlier to take the edge off, and it's been hours since then. It's a shit load more responsible than any of the other almost-nineteen-year-olds I've been hanging out with this afternoon, who were on a one-way train to getting so fucked up they won't remember a thing tomorrow.

My old man isn't even here at the moment, and shit is rough. The prick won't return for another few weeks, if he bothers coming back from the oil rig at all. Knowing him, he'll hit the mainland, walk straight to the nearest bar for the twenty-odd days he gets off, and stay shacked up in some shitty motel rather than fly out here.

It's a blessing in disguise for all of us if he stays away.

Something slams inside the apartment, and I steel myself for what I'm about to find.

When I get through the door, it's dark . . . so much so, it takes a second for my eyes to adjust. Probably because she hasn't paid the electric bill again.

"So fucking help me, Kayce." His mom is going mental. Threatening the kid like she always does when she's high. "Where the fuck are they?"

Their raised voices come from the direction of the kitchen as I stride down the hall.

"I already told you. Not my fault you don't listen." *He sasses back, without any sense of self-preservation.*

Smart-mouthed little shit he is. My stepbrother is forever tempting fate where their altercations are concerned. He doesn't know what it's like to have a parent who will actually follow through on verbal threats with the physical result.

But I can handle this woman. Even with a belly full of pills, she doesn't dare try anything with me.

I round the corner only to find them both in the middle of a fucking bomb site. Every drawer and cupboard has been ransacked, with shit spilling out onto the floor. There's a wild, unhinged look in her eyes as her attention sluggishly turns my way. Yeah, she's off her head tonight.

Kayce's eyes are red. He stands there in a threadbare t-shirt and pajama pants, shuffling on bare feet against cold linoleum even though it's nearly winter. His fists are balled by his sides as she shoves a finger right in his face. Her makeup is a mess. Mascara has run everywhere, black rings surrounding her eyes, along with smudged lipstick—the rest of it smeared on the wine glass sitting on the counter beside her.

"Go to bed, Kayce." *I scowl. His blue eyes flare when he looks up at me, but fortunately for my sanity, he storms off without a fight.*

"He stole them again. A whole packet. Unopened." *His mom whines, picking up her glass and downing it so fast it dribbles over her chin.*

"For Christ's sake, Shawn. Go sleep it off. I'll clean this shit up." *Jabbing my fingers through my hair, I temporarily leave the disaster of a kitchen and stalk down the hall to Kayce's room.*

"I didn't do it." *The kid is already snarling before I set foot inside his bedroom. Pushing the door closed behind me, I glance around. It's all fucking horsey posters and shit in here. Ribbons pinned to a cork board. Trophies he's won sit lined up on the mantle. Above his bed is a poster of a rodeo bronc arching in a horseshoe shape, with all four hooves airborne, flying high above a cloud of dirt.*

Holding out my palm, I snap my fingers. "I know you fucking took them."

His red-rimmed eyes glare stubbornly in return as he sits with folded arms on the edge of his bed.

"What the hell am I supposed to do?"

"Don't swear." I snap my fingers again. Impatience grinding in my stomach. If there's one thing I can't goddamn well wait for, it's to get out of here and be a million miles away from all this mess. This hellhole of my father's world.

"She keeps buying them." His bottom lip quivers even though he tries to catch it.

"Yeah, well, you need to stop trying to deal with it yourself. Just leave it alone and let me handle it because you keep fucking it up."

"I don't need your help." Kayce screws his nose up, sniffing. "And don't swear." He mocks my voice.

This time, I've had enough, and I step forward, snapping my fingers twice with irritation, before holding my palm outstretched again. I know he'll have them hidden in here.

Kayce swallows heavily, blond hair going in about five hundred different directions, then gets up and plucks a book from a small shelf. The packet of cigarettes flops forward and he tosses it in my direction, frown firmly locked in, before he turns and slots the book back in place.

"What do you care? You're two seconds from leaving me. From leaving us."

"Damn straight." I pocket the cigarettes. Ready to drive around the block and toss them in the trash like all the others, all the times before. "So, cut the bullshit and learn to be smart. Stop making life hell for yourself . . . for everyone." I add as I reach his bedroom door.

"Dick." He gives me a middle finger.

"Snowflake." I slam the door behind me.

Drumming my fingers with one hand on the shifter, the other tightens on the steering wheel. I have no idea why that particular memory flew back in as soon as I started driving away from the arena.

Probably seeing Kayce's stupid pouty little look and bottom lip quivering.

That was one of our last interactions before I moved out. By that age, I'd begun competing as regularly as possible on the rodeo circuit, working minimum-wage jobs. I already had my escape plan.

I'd had it all straight in my head, how I was going to get myself out from under my father's fist. He was away for weeks at a time anyway, so the prick didn't know much about my life once I was in my teens. He was none the wiser that I'd steadily built myself a small nest egg, enough of a safety net that I could disappear for good.

Other than the fact he loved to hit the bottle, and then me, in turn —his bit of fun to fill his time with whenever he did get home— Ezekiel Rainer Senior had no interest in the kid who reminded him that he was a widower.

Just as I was almost at the point I could finally leave, he decided to go and screw it all up. This platinum blond woman and her kid turned up. My dad and her got married in a blink, two miserable people thinking it was a good idea to get together. The second she walked into the house with her wide-eyed son in tow, I knew she was just like all the others who had come before her.

Someone to cook his goddamn dinners and fill an empty spot in his bed. Except, rather than a rotation of strangers, this time, he decided to marry. For some stupid, unfathomable reason.

Overnight, I went from having only my own skin to look after, to make sure I survived his foul moods, to having two extra people under our roof to take care of. They didn't know what that asshole was capable of—what he is still capable of, I'm sure, if he wanted to pick on someone smaller than him.

Fortunately, I grew tall enough and filled out enough that by the time I was about to turn eighteen, I was more imposing in stature than him. The day I was able to catch his swinging fist and block his attempt to smack me across the jaw, I saw the rage in his eyes.

He knew it that day. He couldn't lay a hand on me anymore. I wasn't the little kid to beat on. But that also meant his attention was far too easily gonna turn to the two people in that house who he *could* smack around any time he pleased.

So I was stuck.

Just when I'd been so close to escaping, there was all of a sudden a deep, churning sense of guilt plaguing me anytime I stared at my packed bag.

It took me a long time to get up the courage to move on with my

SAVING THE RAIN

life. That plan I'd so carefully stitched together had to be reworked, steadily reconfigured, until the point in time I knew they would be safe if I wasn't around.

Time has flown by so quickly since then. Season after season of rodeo, of competing against the very kid I'd stuck my neck out to protect—when, make no mistake, I shouldn't have ever had to. It made me mad as hell at the time. All that searing-hot fury of a young man with a chip on his shoulder and a head full of bad memories.

The sight of Kayce at all those competitions was only ever a reminder of all the shit I had to sacrifice. All the ways I had to make sure he didn't get dragged out of his bed in the middle of the night to take a beating from the guy who loved nothing more than to do that to me when I was his age.

With his stupid big blue eyes and perfect blond hair, the kid has always been a sponsor's wet dream. A poster boy for rodeo, with that megawatt smile and ability to make friends with just about anyone everywhere he went. He's always had the looks, the natural ability. He's never had to work at this game. Riding broncs is the kind of thing that some people fall into naturally. Where Kayce Wilder is concerned, all he had to do was look at a horse, and it would just about tell him its secrets.

The rest of us were training like our lives fucking depended on it, like every single prizewinning dollar was the key to our safety.

I had to win. I had to kick his ass whenever he stepped foot in an arena at the same time as I did. Because if I didn't, without that winning paycheck, then I had no idea what else I was gonna do.

Yeah, sure, I was a dickhead to him along the way. I was the angry guy with an abusive father. *How cliché.* Of course, I hated anyone and everything that reminded me of the worst times of my life. Seeing Kayce reminds me of so much of that time of my life, even now.

It's hard to rationalize it, the way he only has to breathe in my direction to successfully make my blood heat.

I know it doesn't make any sense.

But at least I'm not sticking around to watch today. It was only a coincidence I saw him during the brief moment I was there after driving Tessa to the arena. She needed a ride, and will go home with

Oscar later this evening. There's no denying a pregnant woman when she asks for help, batting those eyelashes my way and shoving a coffee into my hands.

I've got shit to do at the ranch. I've got nothing more planned than to get my ass back to Crimson Ridge and sort out the horses for the day. To check in on the cattle. You know, to do my fucking job.

Who fucking cares what Kayce Wilder does. I certainly don't.

CHAPTER 13

Kayce

I'm jostled from the comfort of sleep by a persistent beeping. It starts off far away. Somewhere in the distance. I try to shove it from my mind.

Can't I just carry on in this cozy, dreamless place?

It's soft here. Feels nice.

Everything is usually so *hard*.

My eyes are glued shut. I'm fucking tired, man. All I want to do is sleep and sleep and then sleep some more.

But that goddamn beeping keeps on coming at me like a train, and it's only getting louder. It's more demanding. Blasting through, clawing and grabbing at my attention, so instead, I turn my head to bury my face in the pillow. No way did I set an alarm clock, definitely not one that sounds like this annoying piece of shit.

"Mr. Wilder? Can you hear me?" A gentle, male voice drifts in. Close by. Too close to make any sense because why the fuck am I hearing voices when there's only me and the horses and the dang cattle on the top of Devil's Peak?

Why is someone here?

I'm always alone.

"Mr. Wilder." That disembodied voice calls out again, and this time, I reluctantly creak one eyelid open.

It takes an extreme amount of effort just to focus. The world in front of me swims and whirls with enough sway to it the whole situation makes me kinda nauseous.

Rustling sheets accompany the scrape of starched fabric against my bare skin. I'm blinking rapidly now, my brain starting to thread together what in the fuck is going on. Grasping at memories I know are floating *right there* but can't seem to reel in.

"We're just gonna take a look at your vitals now that you're awake." That same male voice soothes me from a spot beside my bed.

Finally, I drop out of dream-space and thud into reality.

Not my bed. A hospital bed. I'm in a fucking hospital.

Although there's no pain, not that I can tell. In fact, I feel fucking *good*. Like I could get up and jog outta here, if my legs didn't feel so heavy and my head didn't feel so numb.

"How are you feeling, Mr. Wilder?"

It takes a couple of attempts to wet my mouth before speaking, which results in someone—the guy who I don't recognize, but now see has short dark hair, glasses, and blue scrubs—pressing a straw to my lips, encouraging me to sip some water.

Fuck. That's the best goddamn drink of water I've ever had in my life.

"Th—thanks," I croak.

"How is your pain?" he says, picking up a clipboard from the foot of my bed.

Pain? Pretty sure I've only got this gooey, pleasant feeling rolling around my body. Definitely no pain going on.

I run my tongue over my cracked lips.

"That's good," he hums absently, circling something on the chart.

Oh, fuck. Am I talking without knowing it? "Did I just say that out loud?"

He chuckles and pushes the glasses up the bridge of his nose. "That'll be the pain relief you're on, most likely."

"Sorry."

"No need to apologize. I'm glad to hear you're comfortable."

"What happened?" I try to rub at my forehead, but there's a tube sticking out of the back of my hand.

"We're just waiting on your emergency contact to get here. Then we can run through all the details." He walks around to look at the bag hooked up at my bedside.

"Nah, doc. Give it to me straight." Efforts to push myself higher in the bed don't really do shit. I'm stuck here lying flat on my back, and suddenly, that sense of foreboding skulks around the edges of all the pink fluffy cloud feelings I've got going on.

"Rodeo stuck through and through, aren't you?" He chuckles

"I just . . . need to know. Don't dance around it." My chest tightens.

"Well, you've suffered a concussion, and meniscus tear."

"Have I been out of it this whole time?"

"No, but that's likely to be the concussion. Your short-term memory might be compromised. It's not uncommon for a head injury to result in being unable to recall events immediately after the impact." He tucks the clipboard back in its holder and then checks his watch.

My fingers twist in the sheets bunched around my hips. As I try to focus on what he's saying, I see that I'm wearing a hospital gown, not my competition gear.

"We also want to take a look at your spine to make sure there was no damage on impact and will need to do follow-up scans once the swelling to your knee has subsided. That will be the best way to determine the extent of the injury, and you can look at options for future rehab and recovery."

Where is my stuff? Suddenly I'm wondering what the fuck just happened to all that period of time from earlier today. What do I remember? The last thing was running through my stretches and pre-ride routines.

" . . . no driving, or heavy machinery, prioritizing a need to rest." He ticks off fingers as he speaks. "There might be challenges in returning to work, so we recommend a gradual or staggered approach to any tasks that are overly physical or put stress on the injury."

Scrunching my eyes closed, those words are now hollow and tinny sounding. Drifting in from far away. I don't want to hear this. I don't want to hear any part of it. Because everything this asshole is saying makes it sound like I'm going to be in recovery for more time than it takes to slap some ice on and walk it off.

Fuck.

Fuck.

Fuck.

"Like I say, Mr. Wilder. It's a lot to take in right now, and we can go into more detail when your emergency contact arrives. Our nurse's station has let me know they're on their way here."

"There's no one," I mutter.

At this point, I'm not taking in half of what this guy is saying. That pleasant, cushy, floaty feeling has evaporated, and now I'm just feeling seasick at the prospect of what this all means.

Noise and bustle from the rest of the hospital floor drifts in, and the guy gives me a detached smile. A practiced, impartial look at a patient. One of hundreds of faces he'll deal with this week, no doubt. Before disappearing, he says something about returning soon to monitor my pain levels.

The pressure on my chest grows heavier and heavier with each passing second I lie in this tiny cot.

Letting my eyes drift closed, I search my mind for what happened out there. Do I want to remember? Do I want to recover any memories of the reason why I ended up in a hospital bed, alone?

A gruff voice cuts across my misery, causing my eyes to pop open when the bark comes from right beside me.

"I told you to lose my number years ago, dick. Why am I still your emergency contact?"

CHAPTER 14

"Why—why are you here?" My eyelashes flutter, and fog still addles my senses. I can't remember shit from today, between the knock to my head and the unknown concoction occupying my veins.

Raine's harsh glare swims into focus.

He's here.

Why the fuck is he here?

"Apparently, I'm *still* your emergency contact. Even after I told you to delete me outta your phone."

This is confusing as fuck. Why is my stepbrother—who I don't have any connection with, who I don't even goddamn well know—standing in this hospital? Our lives have been completely and utterly separate for years. Before he turned up in Crimson Ridge, I can't remember the last time I saw the guy, or had any interaction with him, that fact is telling enough.

We aren't anything to each other.

"I don't fucking know, man." The effort to talk and sit up leaves me coughing. "I'm on whatever they dish out as pain meds around here. Pretty sure that doctor just looked at me like every bone in my body was shattered. You tell me? I have no goddamn clue why they contacted you."

Raine pinches his brow and takes in the sight of me. His dark eyes narrow as he looks up and down the bed, assessing all that he finds there. Probably cataloging every single one of my failings in this spectacular example of how I'm never good enough.

"What the hell did you do to yourself?"

"Dunno." I shrug, giving up on trying to sit, and let my head sink deeper into the thin pillow instead. "Memory is fucked."

He takes a deep inhale through his nose. Then digs in his jacket pocket for his phone. "Gotta make a call." And, of course, Raine being Raine, he disappears without explaining himself.

Fuck. This is humiliating. There's not much more of a perfect punishment I could be leveled with than to have that asshole see me at my lowest. He'll be getting a real kick out of this shit, I bet anything.

My mind is whirring faster now. Still playing catch up and trying to piece together the fuzzy blanks blocking my understanding of what went on. How I ended up in the hospital in the first place. I suddenly wonder if anyone has got in touch with my dad to let him know?

Christ. He's gonna flip out. I'm supposed to be running things for him . . . and he's halfway around the world.

A new doctor arrives. This time, it's a lady with dyed silver hair pulled in a high ponytail. She's trendy, no-nonsense, with tattoos peeking out over her wrist bone on one hand.

"Hello, Mr. Wilder." She offers me a smile and checks the vitals on the monitor I'm evidently hooked up to. "How are you feeling now?"

"Have we already talked?" I furrow my brow, getting the sense that she's already done rounds past my bedside before now.

"That we have." She props her hands on her hips. "Quite a blow you took to the head."

"Are you gonna tell me I'm an idiot for riding broncs?"

She raises an eyebrow. "Sounds like you already know the answer to that question."

"Can I go home?" I hesitate to ask, but my head is murky with worry about the cattle and the horses. I'd only made plans with Storm to go up and check on them in the afternoon, and who knows what fucking time it is. Surely I can't have been out of it for that long. Raine is still wearing the same clothes I saw him in earlier.

"You can, yes. I'm happy to discharge you now that your emergency contact has arrived. But you'll need a few weeks at least for recovery. Concussion rehab isn't an exact science. It varies depending on the individual. And your meniscus tear will have to be monitored. We'll provide you with details to drop into a local clinic for a follow-up scan."

Fucking hell. This is a nightmare. As she's talking, I'm running through what that means in reality inside my head. What are my options here?

With my dad and Layla being overseas, that naturally put the care of the ranch on my shoulders, and wouldn't that just be brilliant if I'd fucked that up for the two of them. No thanks, I'm beyond uninterested in summoning those two back to Montana all because I fell off my fucking horse.

Chaos? He's competing. He's at the top of his season. I couldn't do that to my friend. Absolutely not. I'd never ask him to risk his current standing on the tour.

Storm is familiar with helping out around the ranch. Hell, the guy stayed throughout the winter before he and Briar met. But they're busy helping out at Sunset Skies Ranch for Beau. Not to mention taking care of their equine therapy horses and running Devil's Peak Farriers.

Jesus. It's never been more painfully obvious that I've messed everything up by getting hurt.

It should have been a simple task—take care of my dad's ranch for him while he's gone. Now, I've managed to go and ruin things. All because I couldn't stay on my goddamn ride for eight stupid seconds.

"Ah, I was just explaining to Mr. Wilder that he'll need support at home." She flashes a wide smile and gives Raine a handshake when he walks back in. "You're his brother?"

"*Stepbrother.*" We both grit out in unison.

"Perfect, that works well then." She doesn't bat an eyelid. "You'll need to either stay with someone who can offer support, or have assistance at home."

We're both opening and closing our mouths in protest, but the doctor carries on. She's talking about concussion recovery, about avoiding undue stresses or twisting motions on my knee until they can do a follow-up scan. She passes Raine a contact number for the local clinic where I'll need to be driven in order to assess my meniscus tear.

This can't possibly be happening.

If I can't drive—if I can't ride—that's my entire world. My day-to-day life is a charred wreckage right in front of my eyes in this stupid little hospital bed.

"Stop by the nurse's station, and they'll sort out discharge papers." She goes about removing the line from the back of my hand and inclines her head toward a bag sitting on the chair I hadn't noticed before. "The things you came in with are in there, and your brother has hopefully remembered to bring you a pair of pants. The medics had to cut your jeans off to make sure you hadn't broken your knee during the fall." Following her line of sight, I see the curtain separating me from the neighboring bed is only partially pulled. A frail older lady sleeps in the next bay, surrounded by tubes, get-well cards, and an assortment of stuffed toys propped on the window beside her bed.

"Stepbrother." My mumble comes out hoarse. He's not my brother. He's a guy who hates my guts and would probably gladly stuff a pillow over my airways the moment this doctor leaves the room.

Raine grunts something caveman-like that I can't decipher before tossing a black t-shirt and pair of pale gray sweats on the edge of my bed.

She's talking at me, and I smile and nod, but I'm not taking any of it in.

Reality is a numbing tide consuming everything inside of me. I don't know how to fix this. I've managed to screw up . . . yet again.

Fortunately for my scattered thoughts, Raine follows the woman out into the corridor. To do god knows what, but at least he's not here to laugh at my abject misery. I slowly sit up and swing my bare legs over the side of the bed. My knee is the size of a fucking grapefruit, blown up like a balloon and bruised to shit.

I wince as I struggle to hook the soft, stretchy fabric over that foot and tug until I can thread the other through the foothole. My pain isn't exactly through the roof . . . I'm sure these meds are preventing me from knowing just how goddamn sore this truly is. What I do know is that I won't be able to put any weight on that leg if I try to stand up.

If I can't even walk, I certainly can't do a fucking thing around the ranch. Hell, I'll barely be able to make it between the lounge and the kitchen.

My throat tightens, but I'm not gonna bitch out and cry about this. This is the reality of rodeo. You get injured. I've ended up in the emergency room after falling before now. It's all part of the game, and this time, I just wasn't good enough to make it to the final buzzer.

Swallowing back any trace of emotion, I go into robot mode. Shrugging out of the hospital gown, I tug the clean t-shirt on. It's soft and I can't pick what the faint smell is that lingers on it, but it feels nice against my skin.

I'm running my fingers through my hair, staring at the light reflected in the military gray flooring, when boots squeak to a halt before me. Looking up, it's Raine thrusting a set of crutches in my direction, a withering look on his face.

I don't even let him start scolding me, I just shake my head and put all my pride to the side. As of this moment, I'm fucking exhausted and more defeated than ever.

"Don't be a jerk about it, but I've got no other options. Can you stay and do the physical shit at the ranch while I rehab? I'll pay you." It's a battle to work down a swallow. The bitterness of asking for this, while knowing exactly how pathetic I must look right now is torture.

"*Please.*"

CHAPTER 15
Raine

This is horse shit.

My goddamn overly helpful boss, Beau Heartford, was the first one to suggest I take time off to go and assist Kayce. I'd hardly gotten the words out when I called him from the hospital—only because I needed to fill him in on where I was and why I wasn't back at the ranch—and the guy told me to take as much time as I needed to look after my *brother*.

We're not fucking brothers, and we're certainly not fucking family.

Yet, I've been stuck here on top of Devil's Peak running this ranch for Kayce because the guy can barely walk. He's like a one man pity party, hobbling around the house either on crutches or favoring his busted knee, trying to be a hero and pretend it's not killing him.

Storm and Briar are holding things down at Sunset Skies—where I should be. The two of them seem perfectly content to take on my job as a favor, and in the case of everyone in Crimson Ridge being one big happy circle jerk of helpfulness, they're not at all concerned that I need to be here for at least another week until the date of Kayce's follow-up scan.

It didn't take much to learn the ropes of what was needed in order to get shit done around here. Between their stable of horses and cattle, the place is already established to be run virtually single-handedly.

Colton Wilder has managed this ranch on his own for decades, so things run pretty smoothly.

The hardest part to all this . . . having to be in such close quarters with *him*.

I'm bitter as fuck that we're once again thrown together in a way that is entirely unavoidable. The fact that he's always in that house, always only a few feet away whenever I'm there. His scent and presence are forever just around the corner, along with the knowledge that he's sleeping just down the hall.

There's no avoiding the fact that I can't just switch off at night, because every bump and noise catches my awareness, pricking my hearing. Did he just fall? Has his knee given out on him? Does he need help getting from room to room? Why the hell is he out of bed at three a.m. using the microwave?

This entire situation is endlessly goddamn frustrating because I don't want to be so pinpoint aware of where he is at all times.

After a long day outside on the ranch, I'd love nothing more than to come back in, haul my ass through a shower, eat a hot meal, before collapsing into bed. All I'm searching for is to snatch a peaceful night on a comfortable mattress in the spare room. But I go through all those motions, only to end up lying there without a lick of sleep touching the corners of my awareness.

I'm constantly on edge, and it's infuriating.

We've hardly spoken since I've been here. The kid is a black cloud of misery, moping around like the world is damn well ending. Tough shit. He assed off the back of a bronc, and now he's paying the price for clearly not having his head in the game.

Other than covering the basics around what needs to be done here —going over what the horses and cattle require daily—we don't need to cross paths. At least he's made himself useful and defrosted some meals, leaving something out for me to heat up when I finally make it back to the house after dark.

Up here, things are more extreme. Weather conditions can turn easily. Mountain life is less forgiving than down where I've been working for Beau on his property. I spend about as much time plan-

SAVING THE RAIN

ning my days around the weather updates coming in via their radio system as I do actually getting work done.

I couldn't care less about shit like having no cell phone service or limited internet. None of that crap bothers me in the slightest. Colt has a solid network for communication between the radios fitted in all the vehicles and at the main house. It's simple enough to put out a call to Sheriff Hayes if need be, and they have a team gearing up for the impending winter when they'll work to keep the mountain roads passable as frequently as possible.

The very real risk at this time of year is that early snowfall could make an appearance. While down in Crimson Ridge it might not be a big deal, at this altitude it's a different prospect altogether.

In the heart of winter here the roads can get cut off for weeks at a time. Thank fuck I'm not due to be here that long, because I have no interest in playing nurse to Kayce Wilder while stranded on this mountain, unable to leave the ranch unless by foot or on horseback.

Even then, you'd be taking your life into your own hands. There's always a risk of rockfall, or trees coming down. The mountain rescue folks in this town are trained experts in what they do for a reason.

I'm just a cowboy who knows horses and cattle. One thing I certainly don't need to be doing is messing around in survivalist mode, attempting to navigate a snowstorm.

Fuck that. People die of exposure all too easily in terrain like this.

Rather than have to look at his stupid face with fathoms of hurt lingering there, muting his blue eyes, I'm keeping my head and hands busy. These horses put in a fuck load of work during summer while the ranch books guided rides, then get to enjoy a lengthy off-season through fall and winter. Mostly being spoiled rotten and pampered by Layla from the look of it.

The herd of Angus cattle here is small. Enough to run without outside help for the most part, with the occasional round-up where extra hands are brought in as necessary. Colt has already planned for all of that to happen before and after his time away from the property.

So all I gotta do is keep an eye on them, and make sure they're fed, watered, and healthy.

Of course, there's plenty of other regular ranch maintenance and chores to do. Endless jobs keep me tied-up from dawn until dusk, and that suits me down to the ground.

Sure as hell beats having to be in that house.

Tonight, I've just finished taking a shower, in the process of toweling off my hair and face while standing in front of the mirror. It's reasonably late, I spent longer splitting wood after dark than was my original intention. But the forecast is for a cold snap to come through, and I don't want to be caught without plenty of wood within easy reach of the house. Kayce is stuck in here all day, which means chewing through more logs and needing to keep the house warm.

After hanging my towel, I shrug into a t-shirt and make my way in the direction of the kitchen. The kid usually isn't around at this time of night, having disappeared off to his room, and leaves me the house to myself. It's peaceful inside, the place quiet other than the wind whipping around outside, forceful gusts swirling around the ranch.

Except tonight, I walk in, and he's there. Kayce is seated at the kitchen island, with his back to me.

I'm damn near stopped dead in my tracks.

Seeing what he's wearing pulled tight across his shoulders. The soft, heavily worn cotton clings to his muscles, highlighting the divot running down his spine.

A long line that draws focus to his narrow hips and the way his sweats sit low, showing off the slope of muscle descending below the waistband.

My eyes snap away.

Christ, what I don't need to be doing is appreciating the way he looks in *my* clothes. He's wearing my t-shirt, the one I gave him that day at the hospital, and I hate the sensation it kicks up in my stomach. I hate that my first thought that flutters in—unwanted and needing to fuck right off immediately—is that he looks *good*.

"You're up late." I cough into my fist and move into the kitchen, giving him plenty of warning that I'm here. He appears lost in his phone screen and hasn't even registered my bare feet padding through the house.

He scrubs a hand over his face and blinks at me like an owl. Kayce's brows pull together, and he seems genuinely confused for a second that I'm here. Guess he's been so used to us not crossing paths; maybe he wasn't expecting me to be still awake or some shit.

Fuck. The guy looks wrecked. His eyes are bloodshot from lack of sleep, and his stubble has grown longer than I think I've ever seen on him before.

"Waiting for the painkillers to knock me on my ass," he grunts, and looks back down at his phone screen. Scrolling mindlessly from the look of it.

As I move around to the fridge, I see the foil packet and glass of water sitting in front of him. He remains slumped over the benchtop, weight on one elbow and that hand sunk into his hair as if he's tugging it by the roots.

Keeping to myself, I go about heating up the stew waiting for me in the container. The kitchen is echoingly quiet, except for Kayce's pain, which is loud as fuck. He doesn't need to say anything, but the guy is obviously hurting on multiple levels.

The microwave whirs, and I shuffle around quietly. At first, I intend on reaching for a drink; Colt has beers and other liquor here, but then I think again. While I don't exactly know what Kayce's deal is with alcohol these days, I haven't seen him drinking since we started running into each other.

I fetch myself a soda and wave a second one in his direction. Those blue eyes are bleary and hooded when he lifts them to take in the sight of my offering, before he gives a shake of his head. His attention drops back to whatever is so goddamn interesting on that phone.

Resting my ass against the basin, I take a long sip and roll my neck out. I'm no stranger to silence and doing my own thing. Hell, there have been plenty of ranches I've worked on where I'd have given my left nut for peace and quiet like this.

But something prickles up my nape at Kayce being in the kind of headspace he's in.

Shrill beeping disrupts the quietness, and I push off the bench to open the microwave. As I move around the kitchen island, Kayce decides to leave for his room at the same time. Heaving his weight off the stool, he stands up just as I'm only a foot or so from where he's been sitting.

He stumbles immediately. The act of standing and navigating the stool tips his center of balance too heavily onto his busted leg. His frame topples against mine, our chests smash together, and I catch him before he faceplants.

"*Fffuuuck*. Fuck." Kayce winces. His features transform, going ashen and tight.

I feel his fingers dig into my elbows where I've caught him by the forearms. It takes a moment for him to collect his bearings. Everything slips into slow-motion between us as we stand there chest-to-chest, skin-to-skin, with only a few inches of breath separating us.

My pulse thumps in the side of my neck at the sight of him virtually in my arms, and neither of us seems to be able to move. I don't want him to hurt himself any more than he already has, so I just try to support his weight and let him do what he needs to do.

He smells faintly like peppermint and citrus. A bright scent, the kind that, of course, a golden boy like him would carry around. Having him this close is warm; his skin feels heated beneath my callused fingers. I'm aware that we're locked in this position—a very fucking intimately tight hold on one another—and Kayce's hands aren't on my arms anymore. His palms have slid up, pressed firmly against my chest, as he steadies himself.

But my hold doesn't ease on him. For some goddamn reason, I don't trust letting him go. I feel like if I do, he'll simply slump to the ground.

If I don't hold him up, who else is gonna?

My pulse keeps shifting up through the gears, and I don't fucking understand what on earth is happening right now. Why do I feel like my blood is singing a tune that has no right to exist? Why does the point of contact sizzle beneath his flattened hands? It's like the outline of his touch against my torso will be imprinted there, blistering through the thin fabric of my t-shirt.

I swallow heavily, my eyes tracing the length of his arms. Catching the way his muscles are highlighted by the soft overhead lighting above the kitchen island. And when I finally reach his face, there's a tic pulsing wildly in the side of his unshaven jaw.

As I drag my gaze up to find his eyes, the ones I know are weary—

filled with the rawness of pain and redness of insomnia—I hold him there for a moment. Trying to convey, wordlessly, in the only way I seem to know how to share that he's gonna get through this.

He and I have been through our own versions of hell.

He's survived shit before, and so have I.

Sensing his fingertips press a little harder over my chest, it's as if he's imploring me to back away, and in response, my grip flexes around his elbows. That's when I see it. Kayce's gaze wavers for the faintest moment; his eyes flicker down to my mouth, then back up, going wide real fucking fast.

That breaks the mesmerizing spell we'd been under.

He pushes against me, breaking us apart.

I release my hold on him, and we both clear our throats.

"Thanks." His voice is thick, raspy. And he turns slowly, carefully, moving away with the awkward gait he has had to adopt to avoid bending his knee. He might not be able to get around easily, but Kayce damn near sprints away from the spot where he'd been only a second before.

Abandoning me to linger in the kitchen, alone, feeling incredibly fucking confused by what in the hell just happened.

All the while, my pulse has ratcheted up, thudding way goddamn faster than it has any right to.

CHAPTER 16

A couple of weeks ago, all I did was eat, sleep, and breathe horses. Riding out daily here on Devil's Peak. Being around our team in the barn. Spending time training in Crimson Ridge. Leading groups on guided trail rides at Sunset Skies Ranch.

I was a bareback bronc *rider.*

My worldview came almost uniquely from a position in the saddle surrounded by the sweet, musky scent of horsehair and that lingering note of hay they carry everywhere with them. The chuffs, the snorts, and quiet rumbles. Feeling those deep, solid breaths beneath my legs and leaning forward to glide a palm over a long bowed neck, to exchange a few silent words with whichever horse I was riding.

Now? I'm nothing more than a ghost of who I was before waking up in the hospital. I haven't left the house in almost two weeks. Endlessly long days have blurred into agonizingly torturous nights without sleep. I'm on a routine of painkillers and trying to keep myself from going out of my head, surrounded by nothing but quiet on top of this mountain.

I'm caged in by self-loathing, feeling guilty as all hell that Raine has to do everything around the ranch. The guy can't stand me, and I don't blame him for using every scrap of daylight he can around here to stay as far away as possible. He's avoiding me, that much I know to be true.

Having a knee that doesn't seem to want to heal, my recovery barely moving at a snail's pace, yeah, it's utter crap. I'm crawling out of my skin at the knowledge I can't just suck it up, walk it off, fucking *cowboy* my way out of this. The grim reality is that I'm not fully fit yet, and I can't *help*.

All I'm good for is sitting around this house. Learned that the hard way when I tried to split kindling in an effort to actually do something useful with all this unwanted time on my hands. Discovered immediately that it was a shit show when swinging an ax above my head put so much pressure on my knee I was left doubled over in agony. I damn near bit my tongue in half trying not to holler with pain.

One positive, if you could call it that, is that I can shuffle around the house more easily now. At least these days all I gotta do is be careful not to twist my knee and remember to favor certain movements over others. It's very much a walk in straight lines and make no sudden movements sort of existence.

A fact that doesn't bode well for ranching, where the days are nothing but torque and pressure and brute strength for hours on end.

Underneath all of that . . . all the confronting ways that I'm unable to do anything more helpful than wash dishes, clean the refrigerator for the hundredth time, and defrost meals, are fears of what my future might hold.

I'm twenty-eight and certainly not getting any younger. It was already glaringly obvious to me that my body doesn't bounce as well as it used to in both competition and training.

Researching my current injuries at two in the morning isn't exactly helping my state of mind. I really need to stop going down rabbit holes on knee injury forums, masochistically reading up on worst-case scenarios. I gotta stop willingly doing that to myself.

Is this it? The acutely sharpened guillotine slamming down, severing me from the only good thing in my life? The moment when I have to accept my rodeo career has come to an undignified end?

Whenever those thoughts start to roll around my brain as I'm struggling to find a moment of sleep, there's a deep-seated sense of dread that rises. Blackened fingernails claw at me, tempt me, whispering promises that I can make it all go away real fucking easily. One drink would ease all this discomfort. It'd help me disappear into that place where nothing fucking matters and everything feels good, and I don't have to worry about anything or anyone.

But I'm determined not to give in.

There's enough shame in my current circumstances, and a catalog of stupid past mistakes still haunt me. Do I want to add a relapse into old habits and shitty coping mechanisms to the top of that list?

No.

I want to be *better*. I want to prove to myself that I'm not that asshole anymore.

I've also watched replays of my ride. *The ride.*

Part of our training—for anyone in the rodeo world, no matter their level—is to watch ourselves back on video. Eight seconds go by in a blink. You're tossed around, doing your utmost to put *everything* into the tiniest fragment of a second while you're on the back of a bronc. All the micro-moments and infinitesimal details that contribute to a successful ride. That's why we gotta spend a fuck load of downtime watching it back. Play-by-play. Lock that shit in. Slowing it all down to observe what we could have done better, cementing those specific points into our minds.

Seeing the way I got rag-dolled off the back of that bronc on the second buck is pretty goddamn brutal to witness. From multiple angles, in high-definition, I've seen myself hit the dirt and crumple. The side of my head colliding full force with the ground before my body goes limp.

Lights out.

Yeah, it's no surprise I didn't remember anything until much later at the hospital. The pickup riders were there within a heartbeat after I ate dirt. Medics rushed in, checked me over, got me upright and supported me to hobble out of the arena. Jesus, I even fucking waved to the crowd, which I have absolutely no memory of doing, but you can see it in the footage. My eyes were blank. Full space-cadet mode.

Apparently, I'd been awake and talking just about the whole time my knee was being assessed. I was knocked out cold at first, but had gone through all the checks with the medical team and ambulance crew. Even had Chaos offering to ride with me to the hospital. To which I laughed, telling him to fuck off and win the event since I'd let him have a free ride to the top of the scoreboard this time round.

I don't remember shit.

Chaos and the others check in as much as possible. I appreciate it, but also fucking hate it at the same time. What's left for them to say? Sorry, you couldn't hold on for eight measly seconds?

The mother hen that he is, Brad has told me I should consider coaching, depending on the outcome of my scans. Keeps reminding me that I'm apparently a natural with people and horses or some crap like that.

Which is all well and good, but honestly, I feel like I not only lost my place on tour that day but my sense of direction. The thing I'd been working toward and fighting so hard to get a second chance at, now seems to have slipped outta my fingers.

On top of all that, I lost my lucky stone. It feels like a sign.

It eats away at me, like some sort of bacteria decomposing leaves on the forest floor. Gradually wearing away the evidence that anything else was ever there, and now all that's left is the hollow reality that Kayce Wilder is nothing without rodeo.

I'M STILL WALLOWING in my misery-for-company state when I limp my way into the bathroom and start filling the tub. As I wait for the water to take its sweet time, I make my way back along the hall to the kitchen to fetch my phone off its charger.

Every time I come in here, there's a lingering imprint on my mind of that night. Unfortunately for me, I'm stuck inside this house, inside my head, and as much as I don't need to be stewing on it, I've got a goddamn giant problem. I can't stop thinking about that night. Can't avoid the imprint on my brain and my body of how it felt to be pressed against Raine. To feel his chest muscles beneath my palms when I had to steady myself against him like that. The way his big hands wrapped my forearms, supporting me, seeming content to let me linger there until I got my legs under me.

Raine didn't shove me away, and I don't know what to do with that information.

As I swipe up my phone and yank out the charger, I'm determined to keep my eyes off the spot where the midnight incident occurred. Except that doesn't do jack shit to help me because my attention drifts to the windows overlooking the yard, and fuck my life, just as I glance up, Raine is walking across the gravel, leading one of the horses.

The sight of him—jeans, boots, weatherproof jacket, and horse reins in hand—is somehow arresting, like I've never truly stopped in my tracks and appreciated the sight of a cowboy at work before. And then I see it. My eyes lock on the tiniest of details, but it's one that tips my world off its axis all the same.

He's got his cap on backward. As soon as I notice it flipped around, my stomach swoops in a dramatic swan dive. A fluttering occupies my chest, and oh my fucking god, this cannot be happening.

Fuck my miserable life; I've definitely got worse Daddy issues than I thought if seeing him wear his cap backward leaves me feeling a certain way.

Just like that night, when my fingers dug into his strong chest far longer than they should have, I turn on my heel and disappear to the other end of the house. Moving as fast as my stupid knee will allow.

By the time I've bolted to safety inside the bathroom, steam rises to coat my cheeks, burning with shame. Surely I need to pluck my eyeballs from my skull, because, hell no, I did *not* just look at him and feel butterflies.

Wrestling out of my t-shirt and sweats, tossing them into the hamper, I'm both pissed off and weirdly, confusingly horny.

I've taken to having baths in my sorry state. Lowering myself into the water feels nothing like being a rough stock riding rodeo stud, and a whole lot like a Victorian Lordling suffering from some unknown malady.

Basically, I hate it.

I hate that I can't rely on myself to do normal shit like stand in a wet, tiled shower. My body isn't trustworthy, and that makes my blood curdle with distaste for my own uselessness. It's a special kind of embarrassment to endure, and it's all thanks to my mistake.

What the fuck was I thinking? I know better than to get on a bronc when my head isn't in the right place.

Even worse than all that, is the fact I'm reclining in this stupid oversized bathtub, floating like a fish in a tank, and my cock is heavy and semi-erect on my lower stomach.

It sits there, defying my grumbling protests to stand the fuck down.

And the longer I stay like this, with the swollen crown sticking out, and my length flinching and twitching as it fills, the more ashamed I feel.

Not for the impending situation—the guarantee that a soak in this bath is gonna end up in me jerking off—but for the deeply depraved core of a thought, the root of this horribly erect problem. A moment's weakness, a shadow which has managed to slip past the barricade inside my mind. Now, here I am, with a rapidly thickening cock, and the reason that motherfucker is demanding attention is because of my stepbrother.

What in the actual fuck is wrong with me?

Is it the meds? The concussion? Did I smack my head so hard my wires have fractured apart and then fused together in a messed up, deeply troubling arrangement—one where I'm left fighting the urge to relieve this insanity?

There is no way in hell I should be fixating on *Zeke Rainer*, or his obsidian gaze, or how his rough touch might feel cupping my jaw. None whatsoever.

This is some prime-time, trash TV, reality show level of bullshit.

I let my head thud back against the lip of the bath as a groan bubbles up.

With fists curled at my sides, I'm clinging tooth and nail to the moral high ground of not touching myself . . . not yet, not so enthusiastically. Except it's pathetic and futile because my dick is right there, only inches from my palm, and as much as I wince at the reality of my dick-compass pointing in the wrong direction, I'm not gonna be able to retreat to my bedroom looking like a wounded creature with a cock bobbing and slapping against my abs while determinedly at full-mast.

This is so many levels of wrong. I'm the worst newly fledged gay man—or whatever it is that I am—because I clearly can't be trusted with these sorts of *feelings*. I'm sorry, everyone; I let the team down in spectacular fashion from the second I burst out the chute, because my attention is fixated on the wrongest of wrong men to be lodged inside my horny brain.

Why can't I be getting hard to memories of the guy I kissed? Why isn't *that* the secretive, passionate moment making my dick ache and my balls feel heavy with need?

Why do I want to know the textured glide of Raine's fingertips mapping my muscles . . . his mouth going places on my body I've only ever explored with fumbling, awkward prods of my fingertips?

Jesus.

My dick jerks, a heavy thump landing in my balls as soon as that idea crosses my mind.

I'm weak, and I give in. Spitting in my palm, I wrap my hand around the wet length of me straining for relief. The moment my fingers curl around the hot, smooth skin, I shudder and fight against the noise that threatens to escape.

Casting a furtive glance at the door to make sure I did, in fact, close it behind me—my eyes slam shut. This feels way too fucking good, too fast. Heat is already surging through my groin from the first second my hand starts to move. Yet, as awesome as it feels to be stroking myself with this added slickness, I can't bear to watch. Thanks to the source of this throbbing situation in my fist, it's clear as day . . . I'm deeply messed up.

It gets worse the faster my hand glides from root to tip, and my heart rate kicks up several notches. I'm not lost to the allure of a slick pussy to sink into, nor am I turned on by imagining a feminine mouth sucking me down.

No. The scene my brain has settled on is *so wrong*. I'm back in that kitchen, late at night, with my palms flattened over his chest. The scents of him wash over me, masculine and tinged with soap as his dark hair hangs slightly wet and tousled over his forehead. That short-cut beard coats his strong jaw, and hooded, dark eyes capture my own.

I work myself harder, pressure building along my spine, with the need, oh god, the feverish urgency for what comes next. I feel it racing forward, the dryness in my mouth heralding a nervous anticipation. There's no pain as I sink to my knees, and he lets my hands slide down his stomach. He's not stopping this. My touch is fucking ravenous, tracing every firm, solid inch of his torso beneath that thin fabric.

If my blood could scorch to flames right now, it would. I'm chasing the stroke of my fist, subtly shifting my hips beneath the water.

God, he's so imposing and silent, looking down on me as I settle between his feet. Raine watches my face with darkened eyes, and I swallow thickly beneath that quiet judgment. His cock presses against the front of his sweats, forming an impressive outline. As hard as my heart is hammering right now, as nervous as I feel, I want this so badly.

Jesus Christ. A choked noise echoes around the silent bathroom, the only other sound comes from water sloshing gently against the tub, because this is dizzying to let myself think about. I'm tugging rougher, faster, more urgent now as I allow myself to fully fantasize about a *guy* for the very first time.

I've never done this before, never jerked off while putting myself in the position of being with a man, and oh my fucking god, it's my stepbrother I'm imagining being on my knees for. It's the biggest asshole I know who I'm imagining reaching out to cup my face.

He flicks his eyes in silent command, and I hastily drag his sweats down. The massive goddamn length of him bobs in my face, and I'm so eager, it should be embarrassing. I lean forward, wrapping my mouth around him, and suck down.

It's blurry, a fragment of my imagination pulling on memories of having my own dick sucked and how good that felt and transferring that to what it would be like to be the one lapping and running my tongue along his length.

My fist tightens, my hips lift, and I'm so close. The tingling sensation extends from my groin down to my balls, and a flash like lightning zaps to the base of my spine.

SAVING THE RAIN

In my dirty little forbidden fantasy, Raine strokes my hair, and I don't exactly know what he's saying, but it doesn't matter. Sparks burst behind my squeezed-shut eyelids, blood thunders in my ears, and my fist pumps my cock, desperately seeking a release.

Is he gonna spill down my throat? I think he is. My teeth dig into my bottom lip as I imagine what he might taste like, how he might let out a satisfied groan as he comes.

That's the thought—of how pleased he might sound when he unravels—that shoves me over the edge. My balls draw tight, and my chest damn near explodes at the same time as my cock does. Gasping, panting breaths leave my lungs as cum shoots forward. Thick, hot ropes land on my stomach, splashing up my chest, coating my fist, and I swear I'm gonna float right out of this bathtub.

Heady, overwhelming relief floods my veins as my strokes slow.

It takes a moment to focus. Peeling open my eyes, I gradually find my bearings.

Holy fuck.

Rejoining reality, I'm met with the evidence of my illicit trance I'd fallen prey to. Cum streaked over my damp skin, my hand still wrapped around my length, also slick with my release.

It leaves me momentarily struck by how much I enjoyed that sordid daydream. Followed by an even deeper dread that this is incredibly dangerous territory to be entertaining thoughts of.

In no world should I be shooting cum like a fucking rocket while fantasizing about my stepbrother's dick. Certainly not at all, and definitely not because it felt good to imagine how the weight of him might fill my mouth.

I've got to get my shit together.

And no matter how upended I am sexually, I've got to find myself something, someone—anyone else—to fixate on.

Because this can never happen again.

CHAPTER 17
Raine

"You checked the forecast?" My eyes meet Kayce's muted blues as he walks out of the small office where his father keeps the necessities for running the business side of the ranch. Bookwork. Computer. Radio unit for communications.

I toss back the remnants of my coffee, before rinsing the mug.

"'Course I did," he snips.

"And?" My eyebrow lifts as I wipe the wetness off my palms against my jeans. There haven't been many words exchanged between us since I arrived here, we've kept to ourselves, but today calls for a trip down to Crimson Ridge. *Together.*

Which means checking in with the Sheriff's office before leaving the ranch. No one does anything on Devil's Peak without getting the latest update on the conditions first.

While the leaves might be fluttering pretty shades of gold and bronze at every turn, there's always the chance of early snowfall. Setting off unprepared at this time of year puts us at risk of leaving the mountain while skies are blue overhead, only to have our return blocked later this evening if a front rolls in unexpectedly.

"Everything is clear," Kayce mutters and shuffles off toward the front door. As he passes, I catch a drift of scent, the faint mix of soap and laundry powder hanging off him. His hair is still mussed and damp, but at least he's taken the time to shave after rolling around looking like a stray dog for the past couple of weeks.

I bite my tongue rather than giving in to the urge to lash him verbally for being an asshole about this. While I'm the one running around doing the kid goddamn favors left, right, and center, he certainly ain't acting like it. But I've got enough of that bronc rider blood left in my veins to know his mind is firmly elsewhere.

I'd bet anything he's already sitting in that waiting room, with a restless knee, and clammy palms. Waiting. Waiting. Waiting.

There's nothing worse than knowing you can't do anything but accept whatever news gets delivered after a scan like he's about to have.

Kayce has so much riding on this appointment, and neither of us needs to say a word to know that there are potentially far bigger things at stake than just the health of his knee. His rodeo career dangles in the balance, and it's not a scenario anyone wants to face, no matter their age.

So, I clamp my jaw shut and fist the keys. Following him outside, I let my attention fall to his movements as he walks ahead of me. That limp of his isn't as exaggerated as it was; he appears to be moving smoother. I've already got the crutches in the back of the truck on the off chance he might need them. I honestly have no idea how much of this is just for show—how much he's biting back agonizing pain while staring down inevitable defeat, knowing his knee is about to buckle under him with one single misstep.

"Got everything you need?" I grunt across the top of the truck.

All I get is a thinly veiled eye roll in return as he slides in the passenger side, before he mumbles something in the affirmative.

Christ. It's gonna take every shred of patience I can muster to get through today. The two of us are oil and goddamn water at the best of times. Throw in pain and an anxious mess of overthinking on Kayce's part, and, well, it leaves the air ready to combust. Tension thick enough to almost rock me back on my heels. I just about need a machete to hack my way through a heavy, weighted wall of agitation rolling off his shoulders as I get behind the wheel.

The drive down the mountain follows much the same pattern.

Kayce stays locked inside his head. Stewing in silence and gnawing on his damn lip until I'm sure the thing is going to be bloodied and raw by the time we reach our destination. I just keep my focus on the road.

As we wind our way out of the sleepy little dot amongst the mountains and make the trip to the next town over where the medical center is located, I can tell he's damn near crawling out of his skin.

I turn the radio up, just to give us something to focus on, other than how palpable his discomfort is. This isn't my shit to get involved with. All I gotta do is drop him off and pick him up since he hasn't been given the go-ahead to drive, or do anything using that knee . . . yet.

After we've been driving for what feels like hours, even though it hasn't been that long in reality, Kayce shifts in his seat and pulls out his phone. From the corner of my eye, I catch him staring at the screen, swiping a raft of notifications away, before threading his hand back through his hair. His fingers stay shoved in the longer strands on top as he stares blankly out the window again.

My throat tightens, and my fingers do the same on the wheel.

It's none of my business. We're nothing to each other. As soon as he's fit, as soon as he's been given the green light by a doctor to get back to work, I'll carry on with my life.

A version of events that *doesn't* include Kayce Wilder.

PULLING into the medical center lot, I park as close to the entrance bay as possible, leaving the engine running.

"I'll get that list of supplies from town." There's rust in my throat as I speak for the first time since leaving the ranch. "Anything you've forgotten to tell me that we need to stock up on?"

His blue eyes flare. Glints of mercury thread through his irises when his head snaps up.

"Yeah, sure. It would be because I've *forgotten* to tell you. Way to always make it my fault, jerk."

Running my tongue along my teeth for a pause, I narrow my gaze across the space between us on the bench seat. "Well? Is there anything else?" I do my best to keep my voice level and not get down there to wrestle in the dirt with him like he's fixing for with that kind of shitty attitude.

"No," he huffs and shoves at the door, taking a few attempts to get it open.

I've already started moving, unbuckling myself before he's even managed to swing his damaged knee around. I'm in the kind of mood that I should tear strips off him for being such a prick. The younger, angrier me would have rounded on him, but I swallow back the retorts that aren't going to do anything productive right now.

It's extremely fucking hard to erase all the ways you were taught to react. To fight back the instinct to lash out, because that's all I knew for so goddamn long. And being with Kayce like this only serves as a reminder of a time in my life I'd rather forget for good.

As I open my door, I hear his hiss of a curse.

"Don't," he barks at me.

"You got some sixth sense going on over there, kid?" I let out a wry, cold laugh. "Like you know what I'm gonna do, or what?"

Kayce writhes around in his seat, getting himself out of the vehicle a little awkwardly. "Don't go inconveniencing yourself." His upper lip curls.

"Trust me. The only thing inconvenient here is how goddamn long you're taking to get your ass out of my truck."

As I say the words, his nostrils flare. He doesn't look me in the eye, but grips hold of the door so tight I can make out the pale ridges of his knuckles.

"Of course. Of course, you're gonna be an asshole about this. Why did I expect anything different?" Kayce shakes his head.

"Seeing as you're such a ray of goddamn sunshine over there, can you blame me?" I make the move to fetch his crutches from the backseat. Even though we're close to the front entrance, I don't know how far he's gonna have to walk once he's through those doors and on his own.

"I'm not some little kid you can't wait to get rid of anymore." It's almost like he says it to himself rather than me.

I'm about done with this performance. I've got places to be and jobs to get done while he's with the medical staff. There aren't enough hours in the day as it is, and we're wasting daylight and breath having a pointless argument in a parking lot.

Yanking the rear door open, I grab the crutches, and round the back of the truck to meet him on the other side—all before he's even gotten himself out of the seat. Kayce is only just straightening to stand upright as I move forward, standing virtually eye to eye. His shadowed brow hangs heavy, creases form around his mouth, and there's no disguising the flinch as his foot hits the asphalt.

"Here." I shove the crutches in his general direction, nudging his shoulder. "I'll be back in an hour."

Kayce's attention flicks from my hand wrapped around the aluminum, then toward the front doors, and swallows thickly.

Stubborn little shit.

I can already see it in his expression, his features hardening, blue eyes gathering a steely edge to them. Hard-headed 'til the final buzzer, as always.

"Don't touch me." Those words of his snarl out with snapping jaws. "I don't need the fucking crutches. And I don't need your help."

With that, he charges past me and disappears inside without looking back.

CHAPTER 18
FOURTEEN YEARS AGO

I'm shivering.

It's not even that cold, but my body has been wracked with non-stop chills the whole time I've sat here in the dirt. My tattered school bag sags beside my boots, the strap on one side held together with a safety pin, and as I pick at the frayed canvas threads, my eyes sting from the effort not to let tears roll down my cheeks.

There's no way I'd be caught dead crying.

It was my own fault. I'm the one who fell.

My horse wasn't the problem, or the bad guy; I just read everything wrong.

For some dumb reason I couldn't get my grip right, and my head has been aching all day. Mr. Jones barked at me so many times in math class earlier, I thought he'd throw my ass in detention. Making it to the final bell was like swimming through thick soup to concentrate.

Last night sucked. I hate when Mom gets like that. The nights when she's had too much to drink and yells and yells and yells. It's not like I try to piss her off or anything. But I don't have any choice. I gotta steal them from her so she doesn't fill our house with cigarette smoke until I can't breathe.

She wasn't awake by the time I left for school this morning. Nothing new there. Then, this afternoon, I walked to the place where I train for rodeo, like I always do. The problem is that by the time we're done, it's late, and buses don't run all the way out here after dark.

Now I'm sitting in the dust. Not knowing if she'll remember the time, or that today's the day I need to be picked up from the arena. So I'm stuck here long after everyone else has gone home. *Waiting*.

I sniff and gulp back the agony climbing up my throat. My arm throbs so hard I tuck it tighter against my stomach on instinct. A stupid, pathetic little noise comes out of me when I hold it with my other hand. There's no point being a crybaby when it's my fault I fell. Now I just gotta toughen the hell up.

What I wouldn't give right now to have my own car. To be old enough to get around by myself . . . to have that *freedom*. I'm stuck sitting on the ground like a stray pup with dirt on my face, all because I can't get up and start walking. Tried that once and found out the hard way to never bother again. Mom tore my head off when she eventually pulled up to the curb beside me, cussing me out for wasting her time on needing to drive around searching for my ass—all because I got tired and hungry and decided to start walking when it was obvious she'd forgotten to come get me in the first place.

It's not my problem that she can't ever afford to keep her cell phone on.

From somewhere down the far end of the block, I hear it; the muffled thump of music and whine of his engine. My chest tightens at the same moment as I register the all too familiar sounds, and anticipation of the crushing embarrassment I'm about to endure burns hot and bright in my cheeks. It sets my gut twisting that he's the one who has gotta come pick me up.

He hates me. I see it in his eyes whenever he looks my way. They go from smoldering to deadened lumps of coal in an instant, like a bonfire that's had ice water tossed over it.

As the beat-up car rolls into the parking lot, wheels skid to a halt in the gravel. My mouth is bone-dry when I swallow hastily, before I climb to my feet as carefully as possible. Quickly dusting the dirt off the seat of my jeans using one hand, I pick up my bag, slinging it over my good shoulder. The one that doesn't feel like it's on fire.

Approaching the passenger door always feels like walking toward a viper. Not knowing if lifting that handle will be yet another opportunity for him to chew me out and blame me—to curse me for merely existing—like I'm the idiot responsible for our lives being such hell.

I try to make myself as small as possible, sliding into the front seat and clicking the door shut behind me. The scent of him immediately wraps me up, forceful and so weighty it hits my lungs with a potency I'm sure I'll struggle to forget. No matter how far into the future, I think I'll always associate these scents with him. Engine oil and worn leather seats. The faintest hint of something kinda herbal, sharp, but there's a pungent earthy undertone to it all. *Weed.*

My heart speeds up as soon as I lean back, not daring to fully lift my eyes his way. He's so big. So imposing. One hand drapes over the steering wheel and the other rests on the shifter.

I don't need him to say a word to know his thoughts.

This shit again? Running around after a stupid little kid after dark, like a babysitter.

Reaching across my body, I tug on the seatbelt, and as soon as I pull it tight to click the buckle, pain sears through me. It sizzles just like all the times I've seen cattle get jabbed with a red-hot brand. Except there's no billowing smoke or gross smell of burning fur to make you gag. Only a cry that punches the back of my throat as it tries to tear its way out the roof of my mouth.

I catch that son of a bitch before it can escape, but I don't manage to stop the wince from flashing across my face. Even though I keep my chin tucked against my chest, it happens before I can do anything about it.

"What the hell is wrong with you?" Raine's voice is low, rough-edged, and dangerous. He sounds like he's been sleeping.

"It's nothing."

"Kayce." My stomach always does this stupid thing when he says my name. It's so rare he does, that when it actually happens, the sound of those letters dragging over his tongue is unsettling. "I've had to leave a hot piece of ass drooling for my cock to come and deal with this horseshit. So tell me what the problem is."

His fingers flex around the top of the shifter.

"I fell." It tastes like broken glass to say those two words.

Raine never falls. He never messes up. Every ride, he's strong and sure of himself, and makes it look easy.

"Christ." Pinching his brow, he tips his head back, and from the corner of my eye, I see the slope of his throat. It's stubbled with a two-day-old shadow of dark hair, and his Adam's apple protrudes forward. Like everything else about him, it's perfectly proportioned to his neck and jawline. My pulse flutters low in my belly, and I quickly drop my eyes to look at the faded strap of my bag nestled between my knees.

With a loud rev of the engine, we start moving, and I stay braced in that position. Not daring to flinch or allow my attention to wander to the side. Refusing to look or breathe in his direction, because my eyes *always* want to drift to him. The last thing I need right now is to have my lights punched out by my stepbrother. He'll probably think I'm gay or something if he catches me sneaking a glance.

I don't understand it, but I can't ever seem to stop myself from watching him. There's a certain energy he has that feels so damn frightening, but not in a terrifying way. Not in the way his dad scares the shit out of me—to the point I never want to find myself left alone with that man, always locking my bedroom door if he's in the house.

When I'm with Raine . . . he feels like the idea of getting on a roller coaster for the first time.

Like there's a hidden part of me who wants to enjoy the thrill, but my rational mind keeps yelling *can't you see the danger?* A default sense of self-preservation tugging on my limbs. Warning me that I should run in the opposite direction from this hypnotic, uncertain sensation.

Of course, my stepbrother would happily bust my nose 'til blood soaks my shirt and watch me slam into the dirt a hundred times, just for fun. So I listen to the part of my brain that hauls me to safety. I keep my chin lowered and struggle to ignore how much my arm hurts.

The car jerks to the side of the road, and we turn off unexpectedly. Even though I haven't paid attention to anything under the streetlights whizzing by outside this vehicle, I do know the route back to our apartment—it's imprinted on my awareness like an invisible roadmap. Wait at this set of lights. Take the third right. Slow down for the cops parked on the corner of Smith and Easton.

This isn't the way home.

What greets me when I lift my head is a big sign, all lit up in red and white. Rows of lights glow outside a maze of buildings. Cars half-fill the lot. An ambulance is parked in the covered bay, waiting for its next assignment.

"Hurry up." He slams out the door; impatience colors his voice to an even colder tone than normal.

The next parts all go by in a blur. Nurses and waiting and more nurses followed by more waiting. Unforgiving seats and harsh lighting. Disinfectant smells and hushed conversations. My stomach knots itself, and a creature gnaws away on the inside with hunger throughout all the examinations and X-rays. I'm pretty sure I fall asleep in my seat at one point. It's only when Raine shoves my knee and grunts at me to follow the doctor that I lurch to my feet and stumble after her, rubbing at my itchy eyes.

She's got a nice energy. Kindly. Wears a soft smile as she puts the plaster on my wrist and forearm to immobilize the fracture and tells me about her three cats.

By the time we get back to the car, I have no idea what time it is, and my stomach lets out a long rumble of protest. My cheeks grow hot as I feel those dark eyes drill into me from across the flaking paintwork on the roof.

"Sorry." I'm not even sure what I'm apologizing for. All of it? This whole night? For being born in the first place and just being a giant goddamn burden on everyone's lives?

"Just get in." He's already sliding into the driver's side before the words are past his lips. Wrenching the door shut and starting the motor in quick succession.

I curl into my seat and don't know what to say. I'm gonna be unable to ride for a while, not until I get this cast off. And it sucks so bad. Why did I have to go messing up the one positive thing I've got going on? My grades suck. I'm useless at school. Rodeo is the only thing I feel like I'm any good at. The bright spot at the end of my day when I can forget about everything at home.

Hopefully, I can still hang out at the arena and offer to groom the horses for free. The stables next door give me a bit of cash, but I'll do it without pay just so I can go there rather than straight home after school. At least that's a job I can do with only one hand, surely?

We continue a few blocks before turning off again. This time, we pull into a drive-through, and Raine doesn't bother asking me what I want. Just orders for us both, two identical sets of burgers, fries, and drinks, before we park up to eat.

The smell is so fucking good; my mouth is watering before I've even peeled back the greaseproof paper. We sit there in a weird sort of mutually famished silence, a temporary truce brought about by our hungry stomachs. The two of us chomp down our takeout with a dull thudding baseline to accompany the moment. Some sort of eighties hair-band rock vibrates through the speakers as a backing track to our meal.

"You done?" Raine bunches up the wrapper and used napkins, tossing them in the bag, before holding it open for me to do the same.

"Th—thanks." I hurriedly swallow the last mouthful of fries and shove my trash in the offered bag.

Of course, my stepbrother has much better things to do and more important places to be than in this car with me any longer than necessary. He makes quick work of jumping out to toss our trash before getting back in his seat. We're on the move before he's even put his belt back on.

As we pull onto the main road, Raine scrubs a hand over his mouth. "Just . . . take it from me . . ." He pauses, leaving me hanging on those words with too much anticipation for my own good. "The swelling will go down in a day or two. You'll have to get the cast refitted, or else it'll be loose." His words are curt. I notice him roll his wrist absently as he speaks. I don't know if he realizes he's even doing it.

"You've broken your arm before?" I peek a longer look at him. With a hot meal now taking away that stabbing, empty feeling in my stomach, I feel bold enough to dare a proper glance across to take in his side profile. It's stupid and foolish, but I do it anyway.

"Yep." His tongue pokes against the side of his cheek.

"How did it happen?" God. I need to shut up. Why am I still talking?

"You don't wanna know."

My throat tightens, and that snarl of finality on Raine's lip tells me everything. It's all he's willing to give me. Of course, if I push my luck any further, I'll get my head bitten off in return.

For the rest of the time it takes us to drive across town, I remain quiet. It's easier to keep my mouth shut and try to disappear while staring out the window.

We slow to a stop, and Raine stays exactly where he is. Engine still humming quietly. He doesn't even apply the handbrake. We're just idling by the curb, and I'm totally confused.

"Are you not—" *He's not coming in?*

"Nope." He runs one hand up over his hair, tousling the dark strands into an even wilder mess.

"Where are you going?" The clock on his dash is cracked, so I don't know what time it is, but I know we were at the hospital for hours.

He coughs out a dark laugh. "Jesus. Good thing I'm leaving, so I don't have to deal with this fuckery anymore."

The way he snarls it leaves my stomach flipping upside down. What is he saying?

"You're not gonna . . . you're not staying here anymore?" The words feel sluggish, numb on my tongue.

"Hell no." He shifts his weight and cracks both sets of knuckles, one after the other. "I'm out."

Why are those two words so brutal to hear? The second he utters them, I feel my chest cave in on itself. I'm not upset. *I'm not.* No way. I'm just mad as hell with this guy, because he should have been my brother. If your mom marries someone who already has a son, then surely you're supposed to all get on. Right? You're supposed to become this bonded family unit who can rely on each other and trust one another.

Or, at the very least, to just stick around.

"Have a nice life."

The world collapses around my ears. Those four words cut all the knots and ropes holding me together, and the fear I've been keeping locked away breaks free. It's the shock of how suddenly it's thrown in my face that makes me say the dumbest thing possible.

"Can I come with you?" My voice is so small. It's so embarrassing that it slips out, and I can't take it back. All I want is to swallow those feeble words down the moment I hear myself say them out loud. Prickles sting behind my eyes and I bite down on the inside of my cheek to hold the tide of emotion threatening to flood through.

Raine simply laughs in my face.

He laughs.

"Aw, little rodeo princess. You crying?" Those words are cruel and horrible, and I goddamn hate him. I want to scream, and at the same time, I want to beg him not to leave, and it locks me up inside my own skin as if I'm in a cage. Unable to think or breathe or damn well move.

"Toughen up, snowflake. Stop being a little bitch." He snorts. "That's my advice."

"Go to hell." I gasp the words out, awkwardly undoing my seatbelt with my good hand, before fisting my backpack. It bashes against my knees and the door, and I have to throw it on the ground just so I can haul myself out of the seat. "Screw you."

Behind me, there's another mocking laugh and a snarl that I'll replay for hour upon hour while lying in bed with tears streaming down my cheeks.

"Get outta my car, and get the hell out of my life."

CHAPTER 19
Raine

Kayce hasn't said a word since I picked him up from the medical center.

Sitting there like a statue, he listlessly watches out the window, and I honestly don't know if anything will make this better for him.

When I pulled up, he was already waiting out in the cold. Sat on the wooden bench beside the automatic doors with his head resting on one hand, phone in the other. I didn't need to hear the words because there's a universal language across rodeo. Slumped shoulders and a faraway look in his eyes when he blinked a couple of times at the sight of my arrival—like he was trying to figure out what planet he was even on—the standard symbol for *bad fucking news*.

I don't want to push it. If he talks, he talks. If he wants to self-destruct, then who am I to stop him?

He's got friends. He's got his dad. They can be there for him.

Clearing my throat, I jerk my chin in the direction of a burger joint with a drive-through. "I'm gonna grab a bite before we hit the road."

"Sure."

"Need something to eat?" I hit the blinker and we bump over the curb.

Kayce exhales heavily, both hands dragging over his face. "I don't fucking know. Might just end up hurling it all back up," he croaks into his palms.

"Some food will help." I wind the window down and rattle off an order for both of us into the speaker.

I don't bother pulling over to stop and eat. There's too much shit I'll need to do when we get back to the ranch, and I'm hoping we can make good time to arrive before dark. As much as I don't care about needing to be out in all weather, I'd prefer not to be checking on cattle by flashlight while freezing my nuts off if I don't have to.

We eat as I drive, and music from the radio fills the front of my truck. Kayce picks at his fries and takes a few reluctant bites. Eventually, he starts eating properly. I've already polished off everything of mine before he's made it halfway through his burger. Who fucking knows when he last ate a decent meal. As I shoot a glance to see if he's finished his food, I get a good look at the hollowing of his cheeks. They're more sunken than a few weeks ago.

Christ. If there's one thing to guarantee about Kayce Wilder is that he fucking excels at not looking after himself.

His phone buzzes several times and I can't help but notice that he doesn't bother checking or replying to anything coming through. For someone who is such a goddamn social butterfly, seeing him act that way makes my jaw tighten. So I turn my attention to the road and just keep my goal focused on getting us back to Devil's Peak.

Who knows what's going on for him, but eventually he's gonna have to open up about it. I've got an actual job I need to get back to. Beau has told me to take as long as I need, but that generosity will only go so far. I can probably offer a couple more days to help Kayce out, and that's gonna be the limit. This sorry little routine of silence and ignoring reality he's got going on? Yeah, that ain't gonna cut it.

By the time I've finished up with the horses and cattle tonight, my stepbrother had better damn well have loosened his tongue and be ready to *talk*.

FORTUNATELY, I didn't have to resort to needing a headlamp while out with the cattle, but by the time I handle the horses and leave the barn, it's the time of night when everything is pitch black.

No moonlight. No stars. Just an endless inky void overhead.

When I move further inside the house, I'm already on high alert—my hearing attuned to where Kayce might be. As much as I don't want to have to go beat down his door like we're back to being teenagers, I'm not gonna let him avoid this conversation.

Though I don't have to worry about any of that, because the sound of his voice floats my way. I can't make out what he's saying, but the familiar crackle and tinny sound of the radio intersperses his words.

Pausing in the kitchen, I take a moment to rest my ass against the counter and briefly check my phone for any emails from Beau or Tessa. As I linger here, I can make out Kayce's conversation with more clarity. He's discussing the long-range weather report, confirming the supplies and medical gear we've got on hand here at the ranch. It's not a social call, but he chats to the male voice on the other end with familiarity and, well, just the usual dose of *Kayce* that warms people to him immediately.

I exhale through my nose, steeling myself for what comes next, because this spot right here is where he's gonna damn well stay until he's explained every detail from earlier.

When Kayce finally emerges from the office, one hand is wrapped around the back of his neck, his attention on the phone in his other palm. He doesn't notice me for a moment, and I can't seem to take my focus off him.

He's in sweats and a white tank. With one arm raised high to run over his nape it shows off his well-defined bicep, flexing the underside of his muscles and outlines of the slope between his shoulder and neck. I have to swallow back a whole lot of inappropriate goddamn thoughts when my eyes track down, noticing the way his top has lifted with the movement. The soft fabric has hitched up to reveal one side of his stomach. A defined line extends below his abs, a v pointing directly to that low-slung waistband and the hint of what lies below the fabric. He's much fairer-skinned than me, but has that golden glow about him even as we're approaching winter—even after being stuck inside recovering for these past weeks.

Screw him and all his goddamn pretty boy looks.

Kayce being in such a vulnerable sort of state makes me want to rush straight over there. I hate seeing him like this—I'm so goddamn sick of always feeling like I gotta scoop him up and that he's about two seconds from crumbling beneath the weight of his own nonsense.

There's no turning it off, it's been there right from day one. A deep-rooted sense that he is somehow my responsibility, and none of it makes any fucking sense because he's not *mine*. He's my stepbrother. The kid who I was forced to protect and put my ass on the line to safeguard time and time again. The idiot who I had to beat in the arena. We've always been at odds, forever clashing on so many levels.

So why the fuck does my body feel drawn to march over there? All I wanna do right now is snarl in his pretty face. To tell him to pull himself together, because rodeo was never going to be promised to him forever. None of us get to carry on for an eternity. It's a young man's game, and Kayce, whether he likes it or not, is on the wrong side of that equation.

My weight shifts, and I clear my throat. Finally, that attracts his attention, and Kayce's head jerks up. Those blue orbs grow wide for a split second when he catches sight of me. There's such a glimpse of innocence there sometimes. On the outside he's got this shell, an armor that's been carefully put together so that everyone sees him as one thing. The persona he allows them to see.

But I've had the insight to what's underneath all of it. If there's one thing about Kayce, it's that he hides the truth . . . it's all for show.

And he knows that I know.

"Everything good?" I ask, setting my phone aside and crossing my arms.

"Yeah." Puffing out his cheeks, Kayce looks to be about two seconds from turning on his heel and bolting. He hovers, weighing up his decision, and I let him make it for himself. Either way, we're gonna do this, even if I have to chase him down and order him to spit it out. But I'd much rather he chooses to enter into this moment voluntarily.

To his obvious discomfort, he steps forward. Yeah, the knee is still a problem, but the tautness in his features is less about the injury and more about facing down his torment without those shields in place. The details he's gonna have to vocalize as soon as he steps across that invisible threshold—when he joins me under the warm glow of the kitchen lights.

Tension rolls my way in thick waves as he approaches, but I keep my ass firmly rested against the countertop.

"I'm out for the rest of the season." He weighs each word. It's as if he's practiced the phrase over and over to himself, remembering it by rote. There's a listless detachment to what he's saying, kinda like he's still not believing what he's uttering out loud, but knows he has to.

Something tightens like a fist inside my chest. But I stay unmoved, allowing him to get close enough that he pauses on the opposite side of the table.

"I won't be competing." His Adam's apple dips, and his eyes are lowered, unfocused, hovering somewhere on the wooden surface. "Probably ever again."

Those last words bounce around and around, forming a desolate echo. The only other sounds filling this kitchen are the distant crackle of the fireplace drifting through from the lounge and a clock ticking.

"Did the doc tell you that?" I clear my throat.

Kayce shakes his head. "Not in so many words. But it was in their eyes." He pinches the inside of his cheek with his teeth. "I gotta go back for another scan to make certain . . . but the writing is on the wall."

"So you're giving up already?" My eyes sharpen on him.

That brings his gaze up to mine. Finally.

"See, this is why I didn't want to talk to you about any of it." The spot high on his cheekbones darkens a shade. "You're just gonna be a fucking douchebag about it. Like always."

"Age isn't on your side in pro rodeo." I tilt my head. "In case you've overlooked that detail."

He lets out an exasperated noise and looks around the room. "Jesus. You never change, do you? Always ready to kick me when I'm down."

There it is. The frightened little kid who wants to blame everyone else.

I let my tongue run a slow line across my bottom lip, and study him through the silence. He's not running away, yet, but I can see the way he's fighting the urge to flee tooth and nail.

And that's when his eyes snag on my face. They lock there, watching my mouth, like he's a kitten suddenly been scruffed by the back of his neck and he's unable to do anything but follow the motion—standing there staring at the place where my lips are wetted.

Fuck, I have no idea why that does something to my insides, but it feels powerful. That magnetic sensation from earlier, the one insistently drawing me into him, starts to thump harder. It grows more demanding with each passing second and I'm not sure that it's a good idea for me to dare shift my weight.

I'm pretty sure if I push off this bench, I'm not gonna be able to hold myself responsible for what I say, or do.

"See, that's your problem, Kayce." My voice is low. "You're always looking for someone else to blame. I'm asking you a simple question, and you're avoiding it."

"What fucking question, Raine?" he snaps and waves a dismissive hand in my general direction. "It's written all over your face. You love nothing more than to see me lose."

"I'm asking if you've given up."

He just about chokes with incredulity. "Of course not."

"Then quit acting like you have, snowflake."

He huffs and rolls his eyes. No better than the teenage version of himself. The frightened kid who wanted to fight me at every opportunity. "Fuck you, I'm going to bed." Kayce turns and starts to walk away, before pausing. He whirls around to face me again. "Oh, and you'll be pleased to know I've been cleared to drive, to go back to work. So you can take your ass back down to Crimson Ridge. Don't gotta endure being here any longer on my account."

I scrunch my eyes. Heart thudding faster, and pulse rushing in my ears. There's no good reason for me to chase after him, not since he's laid it all out now.

And yet, my feet are moving.

Within a few paces, I've caught up to him, and Kayce spins in the hallway when he feels my presence nipping at his heels. I'm met with eyes flaring that deeper shade of turquoise in the dim light as he whirls to face me.

"What do you want?" His lips are flushed, hanging parted on the shallow breaths he's sucking down. "Wanna be the big bully older brother and spit in my face some more?"

My bulk crowds him, and Kayce stumbles back a step. His shoulders connect with the wall straight away.

"Quit running away," I grit out. "You've already given up, so don't pretend like I'm the bad guy here. That whine you've got going on ain't fooling anyone."

A muscle flickers in his jaw, and his chest rises and falls a little faster now that our bodies are almost flush.

"God, you're such an asshole." His eyes are locked on mine, but I see the fight going on behind them . . . they want to stray.

Blood whooshes in my ears as his scent starts to curl around me. That now all too familiar citrus tinge mingled with a woodsy scent hits my awareness.

"So you keep telling me. The same old tune you keep crying is getting old now."

His mouth drops open a little more, and I hate that I'm taking note of the way his bottom lip has a plump swell to it. I can't seem to stop pushing him like this, needing to crack open something that has been sitting there. A volatile pressure building and building the longer we've both been under this roof.

"Does it get you off, huh?" He breathes, voice going a little rougher. "Always ready to lay into me? Well, newsflash, prick. I'm not your punching bag anymore."

Hearing him say that triggers my boiling point. Memories and past hurts, long shoved down and sealed inside a box, are unshackled in an instant. Those words falling from his mouth sever any thread of patience I have remaining.

My arm shoots out to slap a palm against the wall, and our chests brush up against each other as I get right in his fucking face. Just like he's been asking for this whole time.

"You have no goddamn idea what you're talking about." My jaw tightens as I breathe harder through my nose. "No. Goddamn. Idea."

"Wanna take a swing at me? Bet you do." This time, Kayce's focus starts to wander. His upper lip curls, and he lets his eyes drift back and forth between my own. "I bet you've *always* wanted to."

"Don't you fucking dare compare me to him," I hiss. "I did everything I could, and you don't even know the half of it. So I'd shut the fuck up if I were you."

Kayce's hands are balled into fists, and this time, they fly up to shove at me.

It's half-hearted. A soft pressure digging into my stomach. Nowhere near enough assertion to move the weight of me.

"Get out of my face," he mumbles, and I see it. This time, he loses the battle. His blue eyes flicker down to land on my mouth, and he gulps a heavy swallow. "Get away from me."

What the fuck is this? What the fuck are we doing here?

I don't understand why I can't move off him. My hand feels like it's cemented in place beside his head, and my pulse kicks harder in the side of my throat.

"That sounds like another lie." There's a ragged edge to my voice. "Time to start telling the truth for once."

Our breaths fan across one another, tension rolling and billowing to fill the space around us, there's hardly an inch separating our torsos.

Kayce is damn near panting, his chest rising and falling in time with his quickening breaths. And goddamn it, but something awakens inside me at having him timid and trembling like a leaf beneath me.

He wets his lips, then squeezes his eyes shut for a moment. Defeat and acceptance and a whole lot of hidden emotions we should never be daring to allow are right there bubbling to the surface when he opens his eyes again. Long lashes flutter heavily as his throat works.

"I fucking idolized you." Those wide eyes still trace back and forth over my mouth as he gives me his soft admission. "I hated losing to you... but I loved seeing you win."

Raging heat floods my body, hearing him finally say those words out loud.

"It's so fucked up." Kayce wets his lips, and I feel like we've plummeted out of space and time. "All I ever wanted was for you to succeed. Even if it came at my own goddamn cost."

His fists tighten, and he presses harder against my front. Still not trying to shove me or move me off him. Instead, it's as if he's trying to reach out for me, yet, is unable to bring himself to actually uncurl his fingers and do it. "And I can't stand that smug asshole look. I hated the way you would look at me, just like you are right now."

I swallow. Hard. "What way is that exactly?" I know. I know what he's saying, even if I never necessarily admitted it to myself either, but the sick and twisted part of me wants to hear him say it . . . just one time.

Our bodies line up as he sinks back against the wall. I've only got a slight advantage over him in height, but the biggest difference between us is how much broader my chest and shoulders are compared to his. He fits beneath me in a way that I shouldn't even be goddamn acknowledging right now.

There's no way I should still be here, not pressed up against my *stepbrother*. It's so fucking wrong that we're tangled together like this.

Kayce makes a soft noise in the back of his throat. "It's fucked up. I'm so messed up for thinking it, and I bet you'll hold it over me forever . . ." As he speaks, his voice cracks on the final words. "You looked at me like you knew. You knew that I wanted you to win . . . I wanted you to have it all."

CHAPTER 20

Kayce

I want him to have it all.

I want Raine to take away this feeling—this out of my head desperation to escape the hell I've found myself in.

All I can think is that I want out. To run from the gut-churning sensation of fear and agony, the endless uncertainty about anything. Feelings that I don't know how to handle without the drink, without something to lose myself in. There's no way I can stand being inside my own skin anymore, and I'm falling apart.

He's so strong. He's like a goddamn mountain standing over me in this hallway, and I need him to be the one to fix this.

Raine takes in the sight of me with a fierceness smoldering from the depths within his eyes. A piercing arrow shoots straight through my soul and pins me to this wall in a way that I don't think I could evade, even if I wanted to. And the truth that whispers relentlessly with each wild, panicked flutter of my pulse in my throat is that I don't want to escape him.

I hate him, and I don't, all in the same breath. Because I think the thing I hate the most about him is that he won't allow me in. He's always swept me aside, always blocked me from getting close, always sneered at me if I attempted to be in his orbit.

Now? Now, he's got me shoved against the wall, and I'm so lightheaded I feel like I'm about to pass out, to slide helplessly to the ground at any second.

"Please don't be cruel about this." My heart is beating so fast it's like I've got hummingbird wings inside my chest instead of muscle. "I just . . . I just need . . . " I can't even say the words. I can't get them out because I'm terrified that he's gonna drive his fist into my jaw.

He's the one pushing me to admit things, the kind of secrets I haven't ever dared say out loud. I don't know what kind of fucking spell he's put on me, but I keep finding my thoughts drifting on a string to obey his command.

The longer he stays so close, the more this heat and urgency keep threading needles through my veins. Like I'm sizzling from the inside out with every pricking, keen-edged point. And my dick is *throbbing* with the way he's so near.

We're chest to chest. Our groins are almost touching. And that's the breathless moment when Raine drops his eyes down from my face. His gaze lowers to the space between us, and he sees it.

A dark noise rumbles out of him, and I think I'm gonna die. This is it. This is the moment I self-destruct and combust into a fireball of shame and embarrassment because my dick is straining, outlined against the front of my sweats. Eager and naive and leaping forward even though it's because of the person who despises me most in this entire world.

"Go on," he grunts, flicking his eyes back up to mine. They're so dark, hauntingly so, with shadows carving deep and dangerous lines across his face. "What is it you need, *hmm*?"

As he lets that noise vibrate out of his chest and straight into mine, he shifts his weight and lets his bulk sink against me. Flattening my body against the wall, he forces our hips together.

I whimper.

I fucking whimper.

The overpowering closeness and, oh my fucking god, the pressure of his body weighing down on my thickening cock is like nothing I've ever felt before. Even when I kissed that guy, it wasn't like this; we didn't crowd against each other so intimately. This is completely new, and it sends a spiraling trail of fireworks in motion from the head of my dick all the way through my lower stomach.

My fingers claw at his shirt as I suck in a shaky breath. Until now, I haven't dared unclench my fists, refused for one second to allow myself to touch him. Right now, I don't know whether to defend myself, or perish beneath his imposing size.

As he hovers over me, pressing me into the wall so hard that I'm sure I'll melt at every single delicious point of contact, I recognize what I'm feeling. It's enough to make my heart stutter, because he's hard, too.

Holy shit, he's hard as stone.

The outline of his cock presses through his jeans, and I'm struggling to stay in my body. I don't know what the fuck to do right now. Is he angry at me for causing this? Is he pissed off that all this tension and fight we've had going on—so much so that we're messed up beyond reason—has brought us to the point when our dicks don't know how to react appropriately?

My stepbrother's erection is ever so slightly rubbing against mine, and I've never felt more alive.

"Use your words, Kayce." He issues me a warning. The deep, weighty pronunciation of my name makes my cock jerk in response.

"I need—need to get outta my head," I gasp. It feels like all the blood in my body is surging into my groin, and I'm painfully erect now. The sticky, smeared evidence drags along my thigh, proving just how desperate my dick is for this agonizingly small amount of friction. I'm probably gonna have a wet spot on the front of my sweats. One more thing for Raine to mock me over.

Leaking precum like a horny, panting teenager.

"That's not an answer." Grinding into me harder, he scolds me through a clenched jaw. Coating me with harsh words in a way that makes my skin flush red-hot. And this time, I straight up moan at the way that feels so good, but it's not enough. It's nowhere near enough.

That gritty, commanding voice of his does me in. I fall into his trap, tumbling straight into those razor-sharp jaws, and my fingers bunch into the soft flannel of his shirt with a desperate plea, a barely-there whisper feathering across my lips.

"I need your help. *Please.*"

Take control. Take hold of all this misery. Rope it and wrestle it to the ground, and let me feel anything other than this sense of dread.

"Are you sure this is what you want?" Raine is making me take every step in this. Controlling asshole that he is, he won't give me an easy way out. He's not letting me be used or unconsciously let go, even though that's what I crave. It cries out in the depths of my bones so bad. Let me dissolve and not have to *think* about anything.

I nod. "Don't make me beg." That's a lie. I'm not above begging. Not when the head of my dick is slicking a smear of wetness against my skin while absolutely aching for relief.

"Maybe I like that," he hums, the kind of dark and wicked noise that absolutely shouldn't turn my insides molten, but hearing him say that out loud is something I never knew I needed before now. "Maybe I'm an asshole who likes it when you're timid and shaking."

"*Raine.*" I breathe his name, as my hips now move of their own accord, grinding against him. Goosebumps flurry down my arms at the added pressure rubbing through the soft cotton. "We can't." This is so wrong. So very, very wrong.

I'm fucking everything up. Another way that I'm at fault.

"Want to stop?" The evil tormentor he is, his hips thrust a little in return.

"N—no." Oh, my god, it feels incredible, and more goosebumps pop up as I struggle to form words.

He does it again. A slow, rolling motion that rubs fabric against fabric. There are still multiple layers between us, but he's successfully disarmed me, crumbling me into a mess. "Want me to walk away?" The hint is there, the power dynamic between us. He's forcing me to *ask* for what I need.

The worst thing in all of this, is how composed he remains. My stepbrother stands over me as if he could easily push away from this wall and walk off at any second. Like he'd gladly leave me slumped here, with a rock-hard cock, and longing for something I've never sampled a glimpse of, but want *so fucking badly,* I can't even begin to put it into words. And that thought, that realization, sends a thud of desperation right to my balls.

Apparently, that little tinge of humiliation does something for me.

I don't think I want to examine that new piece of information about myself right now.

"No. Pl—please." Rushing blood drums in my ears, damn near deafening me as I keep stumbling over simple words. All I can focus on is how good it feels to have that heaviness and searing heat of his body up against mine. I don't want him to keep that from me.

"Take me out," he utters the rough demand, reducing me to a shivering, trembling wreck as I slowly unwind my fingers from his shirt. Mustering as much false confidence as possible, I slide my fingertips down his stomach, gravitating to the way his thick torso rises and falls as my touch descends toward his waistband.

As I hit the top of his belt, my fingers curl, and I suck in a sharp breath. It makes me pause, hesitate for a second, all thoughts flying out of my head except for one. *This is happening, and I have no clue what I'm doing.*

Will I be terrible at this? Will I mess it up somehow? Will this forevermore be something he looks at me and sneers in derision about—even more so than he already does whenever he looks my way?

With shaky fingers, I trace my way to his belt buckle, and there's a wild-eyed racehorse with thundering hooves occupying the spot where my pulse should be.

Raine's other palm comes up to brace against the wall. The motion leans our foreheads so close together they're lightly touching. At that point of contact, we both look down to where my frightfully unsteady hands linger between us. I can't help but hitch in a breath, the forbiddenness of this is enough to choke my lungs. We're stepbrothers. We're strangers. Although, at the end of the day, we're still *connected* and that means something like this should never even be a whisper of an idea. Let alone for us to be rocking against one another—for me to know the feeling of his bulge dragging over mine—while all alone in this house.

"I . . . I've never done this." My mouth is bone-dry. I'm stammering, quaking at the way he's so imposing. And yet, there isn't a single force in this universe that could drag me away from where I'm standing right now.

Raine arches a superior eyebrow at my hesitation. "What? You never seen a dick before or something?"

My eyes connect with his, and I see his pupils have blown out completely. It's that tiny glimpse of a reaction, the first hint that maybe he's just as caught off-guard by this strange yearning as I am, that gives me a fraction more confidence.

I make quick, fumbling work of undoing his belt and jeans. Each noise, each spine-tingling rasp as fabric eases and his zipper descends, it all leaves my blood singing. I'm somehow not here and also so unbelievably present in this moment it aches. Watching myself do something for the first time as if I'm an onlooker staring in rapt fascination, while also being completely intoxicated and sucked under by these wickedly vivid details beneath my fingertips.

My knuckles graze the bare skin and trail of dark hair just above the waistband of his briefs, and I shudder. At the same time, Raine's stomach caves at the first skin-on-skin contact, and he makes a sinful, rumbling noise.

"What a pretty thing you are when you blush for me," he murmurs, and I nearly combust on the spot at the way that turns me inexplicably and confusingly to absolute stone.

I was hard before, but now that hint of desire and rasp in his voice has made my dick pulse to the point of agony.

"No one can know this happened." The words rush out, even as I push the material over the sizable bulge behind the black cotton of his underwear.

His dick bobs up, long and thick and veined, and holy fuck. *Holy fuck.* I'm staring at his cock with its swollen head, the glistening evidence of precum already waiting there. My heart kicks into overdrive.

"You gonna stare all night, or do something about it?" Raine grits his teeth. "Get your dick out and stroke us both."

His harsh command shakes me out of my momentary freeze. I can't believe this is happening, and I don't pause this time. Shoving my sweats down to free my cock, it springs forward with all the eagerness I've been attempting to will away to no avail before tonight. My crown is reddened, so very obviously desperate for any fragment of attention he might give me. If I wasn't running on pure lust and adrenaline right now, I might be embarrassed at how painfully evident it is that I've been impatient and leaking... all for him.

My throat works a heavy swallow as I take in the sight, our cocks jutting out and only a fraction away from touching—from sliding together, feeling that brush of sensitive flesh in the most forbidden of ways—for the first time.

We're similar in length, but Raine's fat cock is thicker, heavier, and that thought, that obvious size to him, sends a coil of longing winding tight and low in my belly. I'm suddenly seeing replays in my mind's eye of the night I succumbed to my forbidden little delusions in the bath. My mouth begins watering immediately.

I want to feel the weight of him on my tongue.

Raine clears his throat. "Hold out your hand."

Of course, I do as he says without a second thought. Which seems to please him, because there's a glittering darkness right there in his eyes, his nostrils flare, and he lets a long line of spit fall into my waiting palm.

Jesus. That has no right to make my stomach clench.

"Well? You wanted this, didn't you... or was all your pleading just an act?"

I drop my hand, and there's absolutely no way to explain the feeling that comes next. Wrapping my fingers tentatively around both of us, the second our swollen, sensitive heads touch, it's game over. Electricity zaps around my body, lighting my veins and blazing a trail through every cell. The velvety smooth feel of him, the slickness of his saliva—as I readjust my grip to take both of us in hand, it's as if my entire DNA gets recalibrated at that moment.

I've never felt anything like this. Pleasure rockets through me and floods to crowd out any uncertainty about who I might be. All I can think and feel and goddamn breathe is him. The muskiness of his scent, that masculinity, and the lingering pine and spice clinging to his shirt, winds up to snare me.

Have I ever felt so intensely consumed by someone, all from a few slow strokes and furtive presses of my fingertips?

"Harder." The gruffness in Raine's voice is so close to my mouth. I feel his breath fan across my skin, but I know this isn't a moment for anything other than this. He's not opening an invitation to more than just this physical release, and to be honest, right now, I don't even care.

It feels so goddamn amazing as my grip tightens, squeezing us together with a firmer hold, that I deliver another one of those stupid little whimpering noises. I serve it up on a platter just for him and can't help myself. He can have it. He can mock me forever, hold it over my head until the end of our days.

Right now, all that matters is that I'm stroking our cocks, rubbing our lengths together, and it's the most incredible feeling. It's so wrong that we're doing this, but I haven't got a single brain cell left. Certainly not one that is able to stop where this is heading.

As I switch hands, shifting up and down, working us harder, our breathing grows more labored in the barely there distance between our mouths. We're both watching on, transfixed by the sights of our cocks. Raine makes a hissing noise of pleasure when my calloused palm slides over the tips to squeeze them both tight together. So I do it again. And again.

God, I love hearing that smallest indication that he's enjoying this. My balls tingle, drawing up tight. Another gasping noise, a heady moan, a breathless realization escapes me.

"Look at the mess you're making." As his hips shift a little, he grunts and thrusts ever so slightly with the rhythm of my strokes. "The little Crimson Ridge golden boy, stammering and blushing for me. Not so cocky now, huh?"

My teeth sink into my bottom lip in an effort to avoid revealing the desperate noises I'm so very close to making.

"We can never... never fucking talk about this." I hitch in a breath as that familiar pressure starts to load at the base of my spine.

"Just get it done." Through a clenched jaw, he hisses at me.

"No one can know." My words drop into a whine, because I can't stop it rushing toward me. The shuttle of my fist works us harder and harder and I get lost in the seductive need to fucking erupt.

"Raine... no one..." I swallow back the riot of needy sounds. My eyes grow hooded, watching the way my dick fits right alongside his beneath my fingers. Christ. My balls are primed. Ready to unload. White-hot sparks fly through my blood. I'm so close.

My movements grow jerky, rougher, tugging a little more frantically now—giving the world's worst hand job, I'm sure of it, but I don't fucking care because this is mind-blowing in the extreme.

"Stop talking." The groan affecting his voice does me in. I feel him throb, hot and hard beneath my palm, and it goes straight to the base of my dick.

"*Fffffuck*. Oh fuck. Oh fuck." My climax cascades through my groin. Leaving me gasping incoherent curses and words as everything goes blank. Beneath my tight grip, my cock pulses and spurts thick ropes of cum to coat my fist.

I'm thrusting into my hand, chasing the slippery sensation and the agony of pleasure as it pours through me. And that's when it happens; Raine's release spurts to join mine, and I swear to god it drags even more out of me just seeing him fall apart.

He lets out a deep gasp, a captivating vibration bursts from somewhere inside his broad chest. I can't believe this is actually happening. More cum, *his cum*, pumps forward to mix with my own, covering my hand in a slickness that is both of us and impossible to tell apart. The stupid fluttering thing inside my chest likes that, wants more of that, enjoys the fact we fit together so easily in this way. As my fist keeps stroking, it's goddamn everywhere—a wickedly, oh so very filthy, trail of evidence coats both our lengths.

It's unbelievably hot. The sexiest fucking sight I've ever witnessed, and yet at the same time, I have no idea what to do in the come-down beyond this moment.

What becomes evident, immediately, is that Raine isn't keen to stick around.

When our dicks have stopped pulsing, and we both manage to catch our breath, he swallows and pushes off the wall. His broad frame moves away, leaving me feeling the immediate sense of loss without his body blanketing mine anymore. A sharp pang at the realization hits... he didn't touch me at all.

His cock slips out from my hold, and I'm standing there quite literally with my dick in my hand, watching him tuck himself away.

Scrubbing a hand over his mouth, he looks me up and down from beneath hooded eyes. I can't tell what he's fucking thinking. Fumbling to follow his lead, I drag my sweats up over my cum-covered dick. Stuffing my cock out of sight, the drying evidence is *right there* that I'm smeared with *his* cum, too. And in that moment, our eyes connect.

Raine's jaw works, as if he's going to say something, but then thinks better of it.

What is there to say anyway?

Giving a slight shake of his head, he turns and does what he does oh so very well. He walks away. Leaving me standing in shock and timid awe, with a swirling, strange feeling occupying my limbs. Because he just gave me what I asked for, didn't he? I wanted help to get out of my head, to find a way to relieve that awful feeling of being out of control, and he did exactly as I asked.

But I'm the one who couldn't shut my mouth, who insisted on *never talking about it* and *no one knowing*.

Those were my words.

So I guess now we just forget. And we move on.

CHAPTER 21

CHAOS:

So, sweet cheeks . . .

Do I need to haul ass up to your hillbilly mountain shack, or what?

You've got one hour to stop leaving me on read, or I'm gonna turn up and haunt your sorry self.

Consider this your final warning.

Put some pants on and get your dick outta your hand for five minutes. I don't need to walk in only to find you jerking off until you go blind.

I shake my head at the sight of my Instagram inbox blowing up thanks to Chaos. As I slurp my coffee and at least make a half-hearted effort to finish breakfast, I'm tempted to avoid the conversation altogether. But then again, if things were the other way around, I'd be the same way. So I decide to suck in a deep breath and reply, even if I'm not prepared to tell him the whole truth at the moment.

Jesus. You're a total pain in the neck, you know?

Dots flurry as he types a reply straight away.

> Ahh. He's alive, folks.
>
> Kayce Wilder hasn't gone mad, stuck on top of Devil's Peak with nothing better to do than beat his dick.

> Starting to think you have an unhealthy obsession with my junk, Chaos.

> Maybe. Maybe, not.
>
> So what's the deal? You had your scan yesterday, right?
>
> Way to leave me hanging.

The deluge of nausea and worry is right there, threatening to spill over. I don't want to accept the reality, and I don't want to lie to my friend. So, I settle for a dumb half-truth, one that I can at least stomach right at this point in time.

As much as I don't want to admit it, Raine's words are still ringing in my ears from last night. *You're giving up already.* If I type it out in little black letters on the screen, then maybe I've taken the loss. So I bite down on the anxiety and stick to the simple explanation that Chaos needs to hear. Facts. That's all I have to face in the here and now.

> I'm out for the season.
>
> You're gonna have to find someone else to put up with your snoring and farting in your sleep while on the road.

> Man . . . that's shitty news. Sorry to hear it.
>
> I'm gutted for you.

> It is what it is. Nothing to be done.
>
> Got a follow-up scan booked in.

> How long 'til you're back on tour?

I laugh to myself out loud in this empty kitchen. How about probably never? It's impossible not to stare at my phone screen and see the sympathy in my doctor's eyes instead of a message thread. Easily recalling the downward tilt at the corners of their mouth that left me spinning. I'm not an idiot; that look was more than just a *commiserations for losing out on the rest of your season*.

It was an unspoken moment that said *have you thought about what your future might hold?*

> Shouldn't be long.
>
> I'll be back to kick your ass in no time.

That's about the limit of what I'm prepared to divulge. So, I leave my phone in the kitchen and make my way out to the barn. There's still one more scan I have to go through to fully confirm my prognosis for recovery. But considering the standard process from here on out for the kind of meniscus tear I've suffered includes surgery—well, my chest is already so tight I'm struggling to fully inhale the damp air. The skies hang heavy with the promise of rain, and as I make my way across the yard, all my thoughts are a mess of medical information and details I was given yesterday.

Christ, has it only been one day?

There's no guarantee going under the knife will even do anything. Between the wait time to be seen, the recovery after the fact, not to mention the goddamn cost . . . what use is it gonna be? I've already got one eye-watering bill to cover from my brief stint in the hospital. That alone is enough of a reason to toss the idea of surgery in the trash.

As I approach the barn, my hands stay tucked into the front pocket of my hoodie. I'm still rocking sweats like it's my only job. Putting on jeans feels too uncomfortable, too restrictive on my movements. At least soft, stretchy fabric accommodates my knee, and I've been relieved to note the swelling hasn't been anywhere near as bad by the end of the day lately. I'm in a weird state of limbo, where I need to build my range of motion back up, to regain strength and stability, while also being *careful* all the goddamn time. Ultimately, I'm having to face a future where my knee will always potentially have a nagging dose of low level pain going on.

If there's one place I want to be right now, it's out here with the horses. I can't survive another day being stuck inside that house, and now that I've been given the green light to be back at work—even if not actually getting in the saddle—I can drive a vehicle, which means I'm able to do what I gotta do up here. A truck and a tractor are better than nothing. It just means I won't be able to do any of the other trail guiding work or rounding up cattle on horseback.

I'm not sure what I'm gonna find when I set foot inside the barn and get amongst the stalls. Is he here? Raine has successfully avoided me since our *moment* last night.

Even just briefly revisiting thoughts of him and us and what in the hell happened . . . well, my heart does a kick. My stomach swoops, and I'm thrust right back in midst of that sensation, frozen in that hallway, trembling out of my skin with desire.

Yeah, if there was ever a doubt in my mind about enjoying being with men, I've certainly answered that question with an enthusiastic explosion of my cock. The kind of toe-curling, life-altering orgasm I've never experienced before.

Why the hell did it have to come as a result of pumping my length against my stepbrother's? What the actual fuck was I thinking, begging and pleading with him like that?

And the worst part to all of it is that I don't think I've managed to go more than five minutes without going back over everything since he walked away. I've been stuck replaying loops of all the details. Fixating on what it felt like to have that with him last night. I've got to somehow rewire my brain to not keep fantasizing about his cock, to not keep running through memories of smooth, warm skin pressed tight against mine. Slickness coating us in the temptation of wanting more. God, it was so good—too good.

What I need is to keep myself busy. To be occupied in a way that can hopefully take my mind off the overwhelm and onslaught of inappropriate thoughts and feelings where Raine is concerned.

His truck is parked outside, so he's still here. The guy is *somewhere* on the ranch, but fuck if I know what he's doing today. It's not like we've talked much at all since he brought me up here after the accident, and well, he clearly hasn't changed that tune since I fisted his dick and whimpered.

What a pretty thing you are when you blush for me.

Holy fuck. Those words hit me square in the chest, leaving me damn near staggering at the memory. I'm a bareback bronc rider. I've never had any interest in being considered *pretty*. That's the type of thing you say to someone who is soft and feminine, right? But apparently, my cock is untrustworthy as all hell because that one word tipped my world on its axis. It's been a struggle not to find myself bricked up for hours on end just thinking about how it felt to have his wicked words dancing in such close proximity to my mouth.

A quick glance around the barn confirms he's not here, and Winnie's stall is empty. The sort of detail that should be a relief, and yet I realize while strolling further inside that maybe I was kinda sorta hoping to catch sight of his dark, scruffy hair. At least having time to myself should give me time to disappear into work. Grooming. Mucking stalls. Water. Bedding. God knows there's plenty that needs to be done, and while it feels a little awkward at first, after being so lethargic for a while, I'm quickly absorbed by mundane tasks that somehow feel... amazing.

Routine and muscle memory and lungfuls of chilled air. Running through the motions eases something that has been left hanging, teetering on edge and awkwardly untethered within my chest since I woke up in the hospital ward.

Working soothes my frayed nerves, and pretty soon, I've spent an hour or so making my way through the stalls. Being around the horses reminds me just how much I've missed their odd little quirks and personality traits. Stamps and snorts and whinnies give me a soundtrack while I dote on them. Being cooped up in that house and unable to come out here each day like I'd usually do took more of a toll on me than I necessarily realized.

What raises a little glimmer of something warm and comforting inside my chest is that the longer I work, the more my knee holds up to everything without too much irritation. Yeah, I can't exactly do a fucking ballerina pirouette, and I'm not gonna be dropping to crank out a set of burpees in the middle of the barn, but I can lift saddles and bend down to sort out horse feed. I don't know how I would have coped if this had felt too challenging or painful. For now, there's a sliver of something that feels a little bit bright, and a lot like I can hang onto that feeling.

Maybe it'll be ok after all.

I'm in the middle of grooming Peaches when I hear hooves clipping and boots scuffing from the other end of the barn. The sound makes me freeze mid-brush-stroke, because I don't goddamn know how this is gonna go.

How is Raine likely to react after what went down?

Will this unexpected meeting, this bumping into each other without warning, be the moment he loses his shit at me?

The guy couldn't scramble away fast enough last night. While I don't exactly blame him—I mean, I was left damn well reeling with the aftershock myself—he's a volatile sort of creature. The cold light of day might bring about a different perspective on things, rather than the quiet assessment he leveled me with while scrubbing one hand over his stubbled jaw. The kind of shift in thinking where now he's angry as all hell and lets me know exactly how much of a fucked up piece of shit I am for landing us in this mess.

My eyes squeeze shut, and I drop my forehead against Peaches' soft neck. Hanging out, as if this horse will hold the answers to my misguided dick and ridiculous, absolutely *no-go-territory* interest in my stepbrother.

Winnie's stall is down the far end of the barn, by the outer doors, but they come closer to the tack room at this end. With each step they draw nearer, I feel like my heart is trying to scale the back of my throat, like a prisoner attempting to escape my mouth. Should I make a noise, cough, talk to the horse . . . anything just to alert him to the fact I'm here?

Raine might be good at maintaining a cool exterior now, but the guy used to fight all the time when we were younger. He had a temper. I still remember all the black eyes and purpled, swollen cheekbones. The split lips and blood-stained t-shirts.

I'm struggling to get a handle on this, because if there's one thing I have no idea how to be, it's a man who apparently really likes the feel of another man's cock and definitely wants *more*. It's a terrifying prospect that he's the person who has unlocked that particular, startling insight into myself, while also being someone who probably wishes I was never born.

Jesus. I really am such a screw-up.

I hear him moving around with Winnie as he removes her saddle, and his voice rumbles low as he shares words with her that I can't quite decipher, yet my ears strain to catch what he might be saying.

Help me, I'm so pathetic. This crush—or whatever the fuck you call developing an unhealthy fascination with seeing your stepbrother's cock erupt cum all over your fist—is surely a one-way ticket to a shattered nose.

I'm so goddamn awkward, creeping out from Peaches' stall with the grooming bucket, and end up clearing my throat loud enough that probably the entire mountain can hear me. After setting everything down, I jab my fingers through my hair until the strands are on end.

Raine's dark eyes flick to mine from across the other side of Winnie's back. I see his tattooed hand run the length of her spine to rub over the spot where the saddle rug had been only moments before.

"Hey." I shuffle my weight. He makes me tongue-tied and so uncertain how to act; there's absolutely no hope in hell of me knowing what to say.

"Is your knee feeling all right?" He turns back to Winnie, letting his gaze drift away. I'm not sure if it's a good thing or a bad thing. Do I want his attention transfixed on me, or not?

"It's been good so far." Lifting my shoulders inside my hoodie, I catch a waft of sweetness in the air. Rainfall starts to shower down in a soft thrum on the roof, and the freshness mixed with damp earth drifts in from the open doors.

He dips his chin and makes a noise that I guess can be interpreted as an acknowledgment. As much as I scolded myself throughout the process of cleaning up last night, tossing and turning in my bed, and taking a shower this morning, there's no avoiding the reality. I can't stop recalling what it was like with Raine, and seeing him in the here and now only amplifies all of that.

My only intention was to come to the barn to spend some time with the horses, to get my legs back under me—in the most literal sense—now that I'm approved for ranch work.

But here Raine is, turning up in his goddamn backward cap and well-worn jacket, looking so rugged and at ease around our barn. He moves like he's been here for years, not a couple of weeks, and the thundering feeling inside my chest says it all. A loud and unrestrained holler, pointing out just how *fine* he looks.

If I was ever in any doubt as to how fucked up I am, it's been confirmed by a flood of warmth making its way up the back of my neck and palms going clammy at just one glance.

There's no moving on from what happened last night.

Not for me, at least.

My body leaps to attention, every single thought swirls into his vortex, trying to make themselves at home beneath those thoughtful, gentle pats he gives to the horse. Raine didn't lay a hand on me last night, and I'm watching with hungry eyes as his heavy palm smooths across Winnie's glossy coat.

I'm officially pissed off that a horse knows what it feels like to have his fingertips offer a gliding touch like that, and I don't.

"Finished fixing the fence out on the southern boundary." His voice is steady, matter of fact. No obvious sign of anything *deeper* affecting him.

"Raine . . ." I lose the internal battle and step across the aisle to come around the same side of the horse where he's standing. I gotta know what he's thinking, or I'm pretty sure my stomach is going to knot itself irreparably.

"The cattle have been fed. You'll only need to look in on them tomorrow," Raine continues, this time fisting Winnie's halter and walking her back in the direction of her stall.

He doesn't even look at me while passing by.

"*Raine.*" Swallowing heavily, I repeat his name, because I don't like the sound of this. It's like he's handing over instructions, turning off the lights, and locking up at the end of the day. There's a hint of finality in his tone, the kind that makes my blood pump harder.

"Forecast seems to be mild for the next week at least." He settles

Winnie inside her stall, then closes the door. As he does so, his head tilts to one side to take in the sight of me. I'm standing there, consumed by this maddening unease as he reaches out to hand me the halter and dips his chin.

I immediately toss it to the ground and take another step closer. A goddamn band tightens around my chest with each passing second, and I don't know how to do or say anything that might successfully stop what's happening.

Raine readjusts his cap and flicks his eyes over the barn, landing on me for the briefest second, then he coughs into his fist and starts to walk outside.

"Wait. What the hell?" I'm back to tripping over my words in an effort to get him to damn well slow down, or to at least talk to me. I know that's not his style. I know he doesn't communicate easily. But at least for the sake of everything we've just been through, we need to clear the air . . . surely?

"I'm leaving, Kayce." He keeps walking but turns his head to toss the words over his shoulder. "You said it yourself. You wanted me to go, to leave you to it, so I'm out."

My head spins. I feel like a jerk, because I only said that when I was frustrated and bitter about everything falling apart in my life. And as much as I know he can't stay, it feels wrong that this is how things are gonna abruptly end between us. Except there isn't any *us*, and shit, I don't know what the hell is going on inside my head.

Those faintly drifting showers from earlier are now heavy droplets falling steadily, and Raine keeps on striding away in the direction of his truck.

All I can do is chase after him. Stuttering and damn well stammering in his wake.

"You can't just leave."

He shakes his head to himself. "What do you want from me, Kayce?" His voice is heavy and filled with resigned irritation. "You said you didn't want to talk about it. That you never wanted to speak about this."

I skid to a halt right behind him as he reaches the door. Through the truck's window, I see that he's already packed and ready to leave—his bag sits on the far end of the bench seat.

"I didn't mean—"

Raine's cold laugh cuts me short. "You did. So, just keep on living a lie. Go throw yourself at some hot little cunt and pretend and continue to hide who you are. Because that's what you do best, right?"

Wetness seeps through the shoulders of my hoodie. My hair starts to cling to my forehead the longer I'm out here pleading with him for god knows what reason.

"I don't want to hide." My fists clench, and I'm outright staring at the water droplets clinging to his close-cut beard and stubbled mouth.

"Yeah . . . yeah, you do." His tone is just about as icy as the wind that rips through this mountain for half of the year. God, why did I ever think he'd be willing to *talk* or anything approaching some sort of chance to get our heads around last night?

"You're such a dick."

That makes his upper lip twitch. A sneer or a snarl, I don't know, but it's a derisive look he coats me with. One long assessment dragging down my body from head to toe. "Have you told all your little friends about your knee?"

My face falls.

"No? Didn't think so." Lifting his cap, he rakes through his now damp hair before shoving the hat back down.

"I'm sorry, ok?" I blurt out. "I just . . . I don't know how to do any of this. I don't know how to get anything right."

"Well, excuse me for not being available to gather up the pieces of your life for you." He turns, one hand already on the door handle, and I'm moving without thinking a goddamn thing through.

An unfamiliar, illogical urgency propels me to stop him. All I can think is that I don't want him to leave, and I have no goddamn idea why it seizes me with an impulse I can't deny or turn away from.

"Raine . . . just, please, wait . . ."

Reaching out to catch his arm, I try to prevent him from opening the truck door. My fingers catch the elbow of his jacket, and that's when my world flips. One moment, I'm standing there, hand extended out to grab hold of him; the next, I'm being manhandled with a punishing grip and shoved away.

My spine collides with the wooden railing running along the perimeter of the yard. Except I'm not being shunted aside or thrown off balance. With a yelp, I'm pinned in place by a vise grip powerful enough to leave the air rushing from my lungs.

When I blink through rain-soaked lashes, blazing, dark eyes hover only inches from my own.

CHAPTER 22
Raine

"Stop touching me." Through a clenched jaw, my words seethe out. "Stop. Goddamn. Touching. Me."

My stepbrother just keeps on being an unmitigated headache in my life, and I was all of two minutes from disappearing down the mountain. Ready to leave Devil's Peak and be rid of this place.

I should have gone earlier today. This morning would have been the time to leave if I'd been in my right mind.

I shouldn't have stayed as long as I did.

Now . . . this is exactly what I didn't want to happen.

One of my fists is locked tight on the front of Kayce's hoodie, the fabric partially sodden from how hard it's raining. The other has him gripped by the collar, the fold of worn cotton on the side of his hood. And as I glare down at him, I realize we're in almost exactly the same position as last night.

This time, however, there's something intensely different hanging between us. Last night felt as if I still had a tenuous thread of my control left. I gave him what he was searching for; I took charge in the way he needed me to.

In the here and now, with Kayce shoved against a wooden railing, his cheeks flushed, I'm entirely out of bounds.

"You should have left me the fuck alone today." I bite out, and his stupidly blue eyes grow wider.

His throat dips, and words drop as a whisper. A confession flying over shivering, wet lips into the mountain air. "I can't."

My grip tightens on the fabric, and I let out a groan of frustration. "Fuck this. Fuck you, Kayce." I've been crawling out of my skin since last night. The way he touched me, so hesitant and uncertain, felt like nothing I've ever experienced before, and I damn well hate that it's *him*. Because none of this makes sense. This is monumentally fucked up, and surely I should be pushing him away. I'm supposed to be halfway back to Crimson Ridge, and yet I can't seem to unclench my fingers from his fucking hoodie.

His little noise, the flutter of a gasp that comes out when he feels our bodies press harder together... when my weight pins him against the railing at his back, it does something to my brain. I'm dumped upside down into a place where I can't seem to focus on anything but his pouty lips and desperate looks.

"I'm sorry..." He gives me *that* expression. The wide-eyed stare of someone who has absolutely no idea how to navigate any of this and goddamn begs me with those bright blues of his.

"You should be staying the fuck away from me." A dark noise vibrates from somewhere deep in my chest, and I lose it. I finally lose any sense of control.

I dive against his lips.

Keeping my hold twisted in the front of his top, I angle our mouths together, and it's the sort of kiss that goes from zero to a hundred the instant we connect.

Kayce makes a sobbing little moan straight into my mouth, and that noise—that intoxicating sound, like a purr of relief—twists me and drives me to go harder, deeper, and goddamn own him. I'm demanding entrance, pressing my tongue against his... and he's so fucking soft. That pillowy bottom lip fits perfectly beneath my teeth as I pull back and nip at his flesh, before sinking forward again.

My fingers leave the side of his collar and slide up to hold his jaw. Securing him in place so I can command him and drink down all those tiny noises he keeps making. It's like he can't stop them from bubbling up one after the other. I'm certain he's never been kissed properly before now, and each slide of my tongue owning his mouth, my stubble rasping against his skin, it sounds like it's too much for him to comprehend.

He tastes like the faintest hint of coffee, something sugary sweet, and the freshness of rainwater coating his lips and corners of his mouth.

I've officially lost my entire mind.

I can't stop kissing him.

His whimpers are addictive. Something deep inside my awareness is already on high alert, trying to warn me that this is a terrible idea to let myself continue what we're doing. But he damn well started it. He begged me to cross a line with him, and now all I can think is that I need to see him fall apart for me again.

Last night wasn't enough to satisfy the part of me that enjoyed his shaking, blushing innocence.

"We should probably stop," I growl against his lips as our mouths keep moving. I realize at that moment, when I pause long enough to speak, that Kayce is kissing me back.

Moving his mouth hesitantly, he chases after me with all the timidness that mirrors the way he chased after me just now.

"We should . . ." *Kiss.* "Probably . . ." *Lick.* "Oh, god . . ." He can't finish that statement. Instead, Kayce straight-up moans for me when I squeeze a little tighter, collaring him just below his jaw. Beneath my fingers, his pulse is absolutely hammering in the side of his throat.

That noise . . . that fucking noise. He has no idea what it does to me.

Both of us are damn near soaked, water droplets running off the strands of Kayce's hair and down the bridge of my nose. The way we're kissing is kind of messy and sloppy anyway, with how fiercely I'm sucking on his tongue and trying to drag more of those pathetic little noises from him. Now mixed with the rain, our mouths are even more slippery, roaming freely, slanted over one another.

My dick is a steel bar in my jeans. Every inch of Kayce juts against me, hard as stone through the front of his sweats. Jesus, I couldn't stop picturing his cock last night. About how good we looked together. No matter how hard I tried to shove it from my mind, I couldn't deny that it might have been insanity to let things get that far, but goddamn, if it didn't *feel* so fucking incredible.

I tug him toward me, and he comes easily. Kayce is almost boneless underneath my hold. He's gone from being the feisty, smart-mouthed rodeo star to a pliant little thing, following my every command without question.

Something I find myself liking far too much.

Goddamn it.

Walking him backward, while pinching his bottom lip between my teeth, he hangs onto my forearms in an effort to keep himself upright. But it's a shaky hold at best. Last night, he only touched me when I told him what to do and how to do it. Right now, it's as if he still doesn't know where to put his hands. All he seems to be able to do is white-knuckle the fabric of my jacket.

As we reach my truck, I let him slump against the side—releasing my grip just long enough to yank the door open—before swiping my bag into the footwell and shoving him by the chest so that he tumbles onto the bench seat.

He falls on his back, elbows propping his weight up to stare at me where I stand, filling the doorway. Everything about this is wrong, so immensely wrong, and under no circumstances can it be happening, but I can't deny that something too powerful to ignore is drawing us together over and over.

Maybe we'll both regret this tomorrow. Maybe we're making the most reckless decision possible, but I'm too far gone, entirely swallowed up by this, and unable to put a stop to it now.

Kayce's mouth hangs open, lips swollen and reddened from my stubble and the force of how hard I took his mouth. Has he ever kissed a guy before? From the stars in his eyes and out of his head expression —sheer surprise and something like awe written across his features— I'm not so sure.

With one hand, I cup his erection through his sweats and squeeze. Kayce's face contorts with pleasure, and his palms slap against the seat.

"*Umphhhfff...ffffuckk...ohmygod.*" He lets out the sluttiest whimper. Head dropping back to expose the line of his throat. Pleading flashes in his eyes as he hits me with a hooded gaze, and the length of him throbs beneath my hold.

"All shy now, *hmm?*" I scold him. "Haven't got anything to say for yourself?"

Kayce's hips lift, chasing the weight of my hand rubbing him through the fabric.

"*Please.*" His eyes fight to stay open when I curl my fingers and push between his thighs to part them. Trembles roll through his limbs as he stays there, laid out for me. Those perfect cheekbones are dusted pink, and he's so goddamn pretty like this. As I cup his cock trapped beneath his briefs, I keep massaging and explore lower with my fingers to seek out his balls.

He nearly levitates off the seat, a desperate noise bursting out of him. "Oh my god. Raine. *Please.* Jesus." That slope of his throat is so tempting, I want to crawl over him and bite down on it. His Adam's apple dips and works as he gulps for air.

"You don't even know what you're begging for." Clicking my tongue, I let the weight of my gaze drift over him.

"Y—you," he stammers. "You make it feel good."

That draws a chuckle from me at his nervous little routine. "Writhing in my truck, staring at my dick." Running my tongue over my lips, I watch the flush on his cheeks deepen a shade. "Staring at your *stepbrother's* dick, like a little slut." My words are harsh, taunting, and I feel him kick under my palm in response.

Smug satisfaction has no right to be there glowing so brightly inside my chest, but here we are.

"Is that what you are, snowflake?" I murmur, watching his eyes turn a deeper shade of turquoise as his pupils keep dilating. "A pathetic little thing who wants to be fucked?"

Kayce squirms and sinks his teeth into his abused bottom lip. But it does nothing to hide the pornstar-worthy moan he lets out.

My bag is right there beside my knee, and I rummage around quickly until I find what I need. Those blue eyes grow round as he sees the lube in my hands, like he's never fucking seen the stuff before, and his gaze flickers between what I'm holding and my eyes.

"You want to be a brat? Or do you want to be a good boy for me?"

His panting intensifies. "I—I want to . . ."

"*Hmm?*" I arch an eyebrow at him, flicking the cap open. That click rockets around my truck like a gunshot and makes him shiver.

"Blushing and being all shy again?"

Kayce's fingers claw the seat, and there's a darker spot on the front of his sweats where the head of his dick strains against the damp fabric. I don't fucking care that I'm standing here with the rain still falling down on my cap and hitting my jacket. I could climb in there and do this differently, but the sight of him spread out wantonly, looking up at me like this, is far too inviting.

Besides, I really, really do not think it's a good idea for me to seal myself in that front seat with my stepbrother. We're already pushing boundaries to a breaking point and obliterating an unconscionable number of lines, all of which are supposed to separate two cowboys like us. There's every possibility I'm gonna end up doing something we'd both regret if I get any closer.

Especially if he's a virgin when it comes to guys, like I suspect.

"I want . . ." Kayce braces his weight on one arm, and then quickly shoves his waistband down, until his cock leaps free. "I want to be good. *For you.*" He rushes out the last part, shuddering as he breathes life into those words.

Jesus. That damn near makes me feral. My dick pulses and demands to get involved, but that's out of the question. He's not ready for that, and I'm not sure either of us is in the headspace to make decisions of that nature right now.

Probably everything we've done to this point should fall under that category, too, if I'm being honest with myself.

But here Kayce is, offering himself up for anything I'm willing to give, and goddamn if I don't love the look of him so responsive and straining, ready to be tormented.

With one hand, I reach out to wrap my palm around his rock-hard shaft, and tug him in a long glide from root to tip.

Kayce lets out a gritty, tortured groan and nearly melts into a puddle on the seat. His expression tightens into a ball as he gets lost in the glide of my strokes. Fucking hell, he's so hot and smooth beneath my touch. While he felt incredible last night, getting to run my fist up and down his velvety length like this feels exhilarating. This whole scenario is totally wild and so surreal, but it doesn't feel as forbidden as it, without a doubt, should. I can't explain it, but touching him at this moment—while we're both wet with raindrops and the windows of my truck are fogging up from how hard we're both breathing—only feels completely natural.

I give him a few more strokes, then drizzle lube into my palm. His gaze tracks my actions, mouth hanging parted, watching transfixed as I reach down to take his cock back in my hold.

"Raine—oh—fuck—god." His lips and body shiver. Words mumble out as his fingers clutch at the leather. The sensations he's undoubtedly feeling have him completely at my mercy.

"How badly do you want me to fuck you, my pretty thing?" My breathing intensifies as I watch his shaft pulse and twitch beneath my palm. He's leaking harder now; drops of precum mix with the lube, and his veins stick out prominently along his length. Of course, he's got a gorgeous dick to match his golden boy good looks.

He's chewing on that puffy bottom lip, unable to answer. Suspended somewhere in an out of body state where all he can do is keep bouncing his gaze. His stare flickers between my hand, squeezing and twisting as I run up and down his shaft, returning to meet my eyes, then back down again.

I like seeing him just like this.

Far too much.

I shouldn't be saying any of this kind of shit out loud. They're just words, but goddamn does it feel right to push him and shove at him to see how far he wants this to go. Getting Kayce to reveal what is actually going on inside his head is like my own secret little game. It feels like winning to be the only one he admits things to.

"Looks like you're a desperate little slut for someone to come along and fuck that tight ass of yours." I let go of his dick and load up some more lube before slipping my hand beneath him. With the other, I shoot out a palm to steady myself against the doorway of my truck and brace my weight while letting my slick fingers explore.

Kayce turns into a shuddering, trembling mess. Eyes completely lust-blown now. Angling his hips, he tries to spread his knees wider, but his sweats get in the way. I kind of like that he's trapped, because it makes it more apparent he's trying his hardest to give me better access.

"Holy fuck." A raw, needy whine of surprise escapes his throat in response to my touch. Circling over his rim, I press and rub slowly, easing him into the sensation.

My body is white-hot. I wouldn't even know it was raining outside, scorching sun might as well be beating down on my neck. It could be midsummer for all I know because my skin feels undeniably overheated.

He's so damn tight, and yet so ready and willing. The more I keep working him, the more he blooms for me. All while feeding me those choppy, breathy groans and whimpers that drive me absolutely insane.

"Jesus. Look how much of a mess you're already making. All from the thought of me slipping into your tight little hole." At the sound of my voice, his dick keeps leaking and kicks, bobbing against his stomach.

"Fuck. *Fffffuck*. That's . . ." His face contorts with pleasure, words dying on his lips as I press a finger inside and gently start to work him.

"Don't even fucking think about it," I growl, as his hands start to inch toward his pulsing cock. He's so hard and swollen, it's a dizzying sight to appreciate, but I'm too much of an asshole to let him lie there and relieve himself. Right now, I'm selfish enough to want to watch him absolutely lose his goddamn mind.

I didn't get to touch him last night—didn't dare allow myself to—so it feels only right if we're gonna rampage across all these lines and plunge into the forbiddenness of this moment, he'll lie there and take everything.

"Good boys swallow my fingers. This ass has never had a fat cock in it before, has it?" I study his face, as his breathing shallows more and more. "No . . . the way you just clenched around me, snowflake, I know you haven't. But you've been dreaming about it, haven't you?"

Kayce nods without hesitation. "*Please*."

"So sweet when you want to be." I hum and keep stroking inside him. Sinking deeper, until I feel him quake and let out a sultry little noise, a gasp of unrestrained pleasure.

"*Mmmmfuck.Ohgod.There.*" His mouth moves, panting breaths hitching higher in rapid succession. All these desperate little whining sounds pour out. He responds beautifully as I graze his prostate again and again.

"You're so tight." I can't help but groan as I keep working that spot, and he starts to fall apart. It takes no time at all, and he's wild-eyed, staring at me like I've just tossed him off a cliff edge, as his body shudders with the intensity of his climax about to claim its hold. "That's it. Just like that," I rasp out the words, transfixed by his expression and then the sight of his dick, the glistening crown right fucking there. Enticing me to lean forward and wrap my lips around him, to blow his entire goddamn mind.

A temptation, a feral need to taste him, that I willfully ignore.

"Jesus. What . . . what is . . . oh god. *Ffffuck.*" Kayce's palms slap against the faded leather seat, and his ass grips my finger tighter.

His cock swells, throbs, and fucking unloads with a gasping rush of curses flying from his mouth. Cum spurts out in thick ropes as he bursts from merely having a finger tease his ass. It's hypnotic watching him throb and quiver, without a single stroke of his length. And my own pulse is racing harder than ever at the knowledge that he just unloaded cum all over himself, and it was under my touch.

In my front seat.

Splayed out and moaning for me.

CHAPTER 23

My eyes blink open, attempting to focus. Trying to reach for the thread tethering me to this new plane of existence I now call home.

A world where I can apparently spill cum everywhere just from having a thick finger wedged inside my ass for all of a few minutes.

One graze over that spot inside that I've never been able to reach myself, and my body lit up like the Fourth of July.

Digging the heels of my palms into my eye sockets, I groan out loud. My voice echoes around this empty bed, this empty room.

I'm so undeniably screwed.

Raine is gone. He had to leave. His job isn't here and he certainly wasn't going to stick around after the enormity of what transpired yesterday.

Well, shit. If there was any question mark still lingering over my sexual wants or preferences, I think I've formally stepped into my identity as a gay man. I might still appreciate women, but my dick has never once responded that way when presented with pussy.

And if I even try to think about sex—the kind that involves a warm, silky wet cunt—it's like my body knows. It knows for absolute certainty now that I'm not pursuing that direction anymore.

I'm wholly consumed by thoughts of Raine, and how it felt to be stroked by him, to have his rough, calloused palm tugging on me until my eyes rolled back in my head, and then to fall apart thanks to one wickedly skilled finger.

I'm not even interested in what it might be like to hook up with another guy. This isn't a case of being awakened to cock and now wanting to go fool around elsewhere. No ... I can't help but remember Brad's words that day about feeling close to someone, trusting them, and all that other crap he was saying.

Needing a deeper connection.

I've unfortunately slipped under some sort of Raine-spell and I'm not sure I have any intention of seeking out an antidote.

I puff out a heavy breath and slither toward the edge of my bed, hauling my sorry self into motion because, as of today, I'm back to *work*. Returning to business as usual on this ranch and doing my best to keep everything operating smoothly.

My dad checks in regularly. I've given him the bare minimum of details. Enough to not freak him out and have him turning up here to roll up his sleeves, and yet, as much as I've been in touch with him, I have neatly side-stepped the whole issue of my rodeo future. Much like I've done with Chaos and Brad, in our brief exchanges also.

Raine might as well still be here with me; the gorgeous asshole occupies just about every single brain cell as I set about my day. I remember exactly how hard he studied me through my comedown from such an explosive release. As he slipped his hand out from my ass, I wasn't sure if that meant he'd turn his attention to his own needs. Would he then take his cock in hand? Lying there with shaking limbs and a thundering pulse, I felt a dashing, enthralling sense of hopefulness ... was there going to be *more*?

Of course, it wasn't to be. Instead, he shifted into a different energy.

He helped me get cleaned up, in a sort of stupefied silence. My stepbrother towered over me as I awkwardly wiped cum off my skin with clumsy hands and noticed the damning streaks painting my hoodie. Then, I had to tuck myself away while he hovered and cleared his throat.

"Thanks for . . ." I stumble over what to say. Unable to look him in the eye.

"Yeah." From the periphery of my vision, I see his chin dip. He gives me a brief nod.

Then it was all over. Taillights disappeared beyond the threshold of the ranch. The hum of his truck's engine faded away into the thick cover of pine trees. Leaving me standing in the downpour, with veins damn near vibrating, blood racing, and a churned-up sea frothing inside my chest.

It wasn't like there was anything to be said. What happened should never have happened. I'd already pushed him away the night before, with all my stupid whining about *no one knowing* and *never talking about it.*

So, of course, what else was there to expect than for my stepbrother to leave, just as he had planned to do before I went and chased him down.

It's for the best, a good idea, all things considered. This way, I can focus on what I gotta do around here. I'll keep getting the ranch prepared for winter, and stay on track to figure out what the future is gonna hold where my knee is concerned.

So now it feels like all that is left for me to do is wander around this property, going through the motions, once again hanging in motherfucking *no man's land* until someone with a fancy stack of degrees and a clipboard declares the fate of my days on horseback.

It's a good thing Raine has gone. He doesn't need to put up with any more of my shit, and other than depositing the final payment for his time working here, that could be our last goddamn interaction, for all I know.

His finger stuffed inside my ass, milking my cock . . . hands-free.

What a fucking trip.

I mean, theoretically, I knew that was a thing. But did I ever think I'd be the guy shaking with ecstasy while blowing my load all over myself—not a single stroke, or grip wrapped around my length, required? That's a true *holy fuck, I don't even know what just happened* moment right there.

It leaves me squirming at just the thought of how I must have looked, because I know for sure my eyes rolled in the back of my head, and I have no goddamn clue what came out of my mouth as it all unfolded. There's every chance I gasped and cursed things I did *not* need my stepbrother hearing, and I can only hope to all hell the constant drumming of rain on the roof of his truck drowned the fuck out of my pathetic mewling.

Apparently, I'm in a whole lot of trouble where my stepbrother is concerned. He already had the upper hand on me—physically and mentally, he's always been further up the scoreboard—and now I've handed him the goddamn keys to the castle, haven't I?

Telling him shit like I always wanted him to have it all. *Christ.*

As I get in my truck and start the motor, it gives a brief protest at being left unused for weeks before coughing to life. At least for the moment, the path down to the cattle is passable by vehicle. Once the snow hits, we do most of the work we gotta do on horseback, but for now, I can bump my way over the rutted dirt track.

As I ease down on the gas pedal, taking it slow and steady, my knee gives a twinge. It's just enough to remind me that I haven't done this sort of movement—haven't used this combination of tendons and muscles and ligaments since the accident. However, my shoulders drop with a grateful sigh when I realize it's only a brief taste of sensation. Like a waft of a candle flame, it licks over my knee and then vanishes.

This, at least, I can do.

With one hand on the wheel, I readjust the brim of my cap. Feeling the material beneath my fingers only reminds me of how Raine looked wearing his. Of course, it would be all of a few seconds before I found some other excuse to drift back to thoughts of him. Obsessed much? The peak of my cap reminds me of what it was like to get up close to his own flipped backward. How it grazed the damp skin on my forehead when he pushed me against the railing.

And then everything that followed.

He kissed me.

Even though it should be a line marked in bright red, guarded by hazard tape, and banned from ever being crossed . . . the truth is, I don't hate the feel of his lips on mine.

In fact, I enjoyed it. I liked the way Raine confidently took my mouth, as if he knew that kiss was rightfully his, and didn't even hesitate. There was only the heat and scent of him, overwhelming me in the best possible way. His hold on my body was so goddamn fierce, I still feel the outline of his strong fingers circling the front of my neck.

Right on cue, I swallow, and the ghost of his touch is as much of an imprint on the slope of my throat as that part of my psyche. Along with the scrape of his stubble against my lips. God, I've spent years exchanging kisses with women—only ever experiencing the sensation of softness, smooth skin, and sweet little feminine licks and whimpers.

Now, I can say with full certainty, I've never been kissed like it felt to have Raine's mouth owning mine. Like I could melt into him, and he'd safeguard me, keeping me upright through every second our mouths collided. To have him rough and commanding, taking charge of the moment, was enough to steal my every shred of sanity.

Why did it feel so right with him? Why does it have to *be* him? The whirlwind inside me is at peak levels of destruction, spinning and thundering a path through everything I used to know. Laying waste to an old version of me who has been completely decimated, overpowered; now nothing more than rubble and dust and scraps of a man.

He branded my mouth and my body in a way that I didn't know to ask for . . . didn't even know I wanted. And now I'm alone here, surrounded by the wide-open skies, pine trees, and endless emptiness of the ranch.

So it's definitely, absolutely a good thing that he left.

What was I gonna do? Ask him to stay? I'm not an idiot; that's a laughable idea. This kind of thing we've just stumbled into isn't some kind of budding romance to get excited about. Not some sweetly hopeful chemistry between two people who start dreaming of a future together.

It's the kind of thunderclap that leaves you shell-shocked, with ringing in your ears, and your life dramatically and irrevocably altered.

Life has to go back to normal . . . or at least, something approaching what the *new normal* looks like for Kayce Wilder from here on out.

CHAPTER 24
Raine

"Mr. Rainer?"

"Just call me Raine." I pull my face away from my hands, muttering my reply. The nurse who called my name peers at me over thick-rimmed glasses. Tonight has dragged on for what feels like forever. I'm itching to get the fuck away from the glare of these fluorescent lights and cloying scent of disinfectant.

All it does is remind me. Digs up too much dirt from my past.

She beckons me to the desk with a wave of a file clutched in her hand. Hopefully, it's Kayce's goddamn discharge paperwork. His fractured wrist is currently being set in plaster while I wait out here amongst the rows of plastic chairs.

When I reach the counter and hover, keeping my hands shoved in my pockets, she taps away on her computer, then lifts one eyebrow at me. How the woman can type so fast without looking at those letters on the keyboard, I have no idea.

"Do you need me to sign something for Kayce?" I ask. Hoping to hell she's not gonna push those Coke bottle glasses up her nose and tell me there's some extra horrific surcharge we have to pay. More dollars heaped on top of how much this is already gonna cost.

"Are you his next of kin?" She stops typing and glances at the computer screen for a moment, before turning back my way.

"No." My head aches. I'm fucking starved. Let us just get the hell outta here, please, and thank you.

She narrows an unreadable gaze on me, clicking a couple of things with her mouse, while a phone rings in the background. I'm not quite sure what this is about, but she clicks again and then turns to fully face me. This time, she takes her glasses off and gives them a quick polish with the hem of her scrubs.

"The home address listed on Kayce's file . . ." She pops the frames back on her face and studies me through the lenses. "There has been a history of similar injuries—of a young man sustaining repeated broken bones while living at the same address." Her voice is soft to match her brown eyes.

My jaw tightens, and inside my pocket, I let my fingertips run over the ridged metal of my keys for a moment. I push the pad of my index finger down against the pointed end.

What she's insinuating might be uttered in hushed tones in a bustling hospital emergency room, but it might as well be a foghorn sounding right beside my face with enough impact to burst my eardrum. The message is delivered loud and goddamn clear.

I shake my head and clear my throat. "The kid does rodeo. He fell off a horse."

The nurse adjusts her weight, continuing to assess me with a long look and I stare right back. I don't recognize her, and I'm pretty sure she doesn't know my face either. But my name is on that computer. My files are there. All my patient history from the times it was bad enough to demand medical attention.

Eventually, she exhales and reaches for the paperwork that had been waved my way before. Pushing it across the counter toward me, she picks up a pen and uses it to tap a location on the page. It's a full A4 sheet. A chaotic cluster of fine print. Kayce's details, and endless jargon. The sort of form I always struggle to fill out because the letters all jump around and jumble themselves out of order in front of my eyes.

"He doesn't have a valid emergency contact. The phone number listed goes dead." She tilts her head to one side, flicking her gaze up to my hair that hangs in front of my eyes and down to my faded t-shirt.

"Fine. Put mine down." I fist the ballpoint and write my cell number.

Filling in the tiny, blank box his mom has abandoned responsibility for with my details instead.

"Raine?" Tessa's voice jerks me out of the memory I'd been lost in. The sound of her calling out makes my head fly up, focusing away from the point on the saddle in front of me. A spot that I'd let my eyes drift to while my mind wandered to another place and time so many years ago.

Mist knows the way back to the barn and hardly needs any guidance to know where to go around this ranch. When I saddled him up earlier, he looked at me with equal parts distaste that he's been cooped up, unable to get out as often as he'd like during the time I've been away, and sheer joy to be heading out for a proper ride at last.

I swing out of the saddle and lead him over to where Tessa waits outside her office. She's all wide grins and a rounded belly that seems to have grown rapidly since I last saw her.

"We missed your bright smile."

That earns her a scowl, and my eyebrows furrow together.

"Yep, that's the one, right there." She props her hands against the middle of her back and stretches a little. "You're looking radiant as always, my favorite grump. Staying atop a mountain with your brother has obviously done you a world of good."

"*Stepbrother*," I mutter. An immediate prickling feeling races up the back of my neck. A flutter of worry makes itself known. Does she know something? Have suspicions? Small towns are magnets for gossip and rumor, the kind that spread like wildfire.

As Mist's hooves clop in rhythm at my side, I have to fucking shake myself internally. There's no possible way she could know shit, so what the hell am I even concerned about?

"How is Kayce? I miss seeing his pretty blue eyes." Tessa coos at the horse and strokes his nose when we stop in front of her.

"As good as can be expected." Goddamn. I really, really do not want to be talking about *Kayce Wilder* or his *eyes* right now. I unwrap the reins from my fist and then wrap them again. "He bounced back well enough that he's able to work again. So here I am."

Jesus, even just saying the words out loud brings on a rush of memories from the past few days. Everything pops up, so vivid and fresh, sitting right there, ready to remind me of the most reckless thing we could possibly have done. We should *never* have crashed across those lines. Yet, all I can think of is how soft his lips were and the desperation in his little noises . . . the way he responded to everything in just the way I like.

And I can't keep fucking dwelling on that fact.

"Anytime you need to go help him, just shout." Tessa's fingers glide along Mist's neck, and I'm struggling to stop from shifting uncomfortably. Fighting an inner battle not to give her any indication that I know what it looks like when my stepbrother climaxes from simply grazing his prostate.

"Won't be necessary." My words are like chalk in my mouth.

"Well, our sweet city girl, Briar, had her bottom lip dragging along the floor yesterday when she realized you were due back. She and Storm would return tomorrow if you asked."

"I can't keep walking off the job, Tessa."

She gives a little tinkling laugh. "Look . . . I know you've been doing your lone wolf routine forever and a day, but here's the thing about Beau; my brother is all about taking care of what needs to be taken care of." Her inquisitive eyes drift over me while I study the patch of dirt my boot heel is grinding down on. "He's gonna be the first one to tell you to get your ass back up the top of that mountain if Kayce so much as develops a sniffle."

Why that makes my chest tighten—why the prospect of going back up there and seeing him again leaves me with a strange swirling in my gut—I don't want to examine. This is madness, and what we did was obviously the result of being out of our minds. Wherever all those heightened emotions and pure, carnal need to experience something on Kayce's end came from . . . I can't pause to examine.

It's too dangerous to let that particular spark catch light.

"That's very generous of him, but what about the guests . . . the trail rides." This conversation needs to be over, and I just need to get my ass back to the barn so I don't have to continue *talking* about anything.

"Chaos is all over it." She stifles a yawn and gives the horse a final pat. "That man could charm angels into handing over their wings. Probably their little angelic panties, too."

"Right, well . . . I'm gonna go figure out what needs to be done since I'm sure Prince Charming hasn't been doing my damn bookwork for me, has he?" With a grunt and dip of my chin, I leave Tessa chuckling, confirming my exact suspicions as she makes her way back inside.

The rest of the day goes past in a blur. A kind of rhythm and routine that I've come to feel in my bones. And the entire time, my mind keeps straying back to the top of that goddamn mountain. Physically, I might be here, handling saddles, filling water buckets, and checking on the new horses to see how they're acclimatizing to the stables. Mentally, I'm somewhere else entirely.

Devil's Peak Ranch.

My teeth grind at the unpleasant realization that Kayce has managed to embed himself in my awareness once again. It took me years to fully shake off thoughts of him after leaving. No matter how far I traveled, or the remoteness of the wilderness I found myself on horseback rounding up cattle in . . . he followed me around. In those early years, he'd managed to worm his way into my thoughts unbidden.

Eventually, I was able to move the fuck on with my life and stop having any shred of care or concern for *Kayce Wilder.*

So this unexpected collision course we've found ourselves on . . . yeah, that shit is done. I can dust my palms off and move on. I'm leaving Crimson Ridge soon. This was only ever a temporary gig, and I certainly don't need to hold his hand while he figures his life out.

That look in his eyes was so adamant—the utter terror when he stammered and gasped, pink-cheeked and flushed-lipped—it left no doubt he believed what we were doing was something to be ashamed of.

He got the message across loud and clear that night. We should never talk about it. No one can ever know.

Ain't that the fucking truth.

I've had to protect Kayce for too long. I've had to physically put myself in the way and take punches that my father would have dealt to him, or his mom, if I hadn't stepped in his path first. If I didn't purposely start shit to keep his focus off them, then who knows what damage he might have caused.

I'd been there and seen it all. He couldn't hurt me any worse than he'd already done when I was growing up. All alone in that house with just a sick bastard who couldn't handle the fact my mom had been ripped away in a car accident.

Life doesn't treat you kind, and the fact they walked into our lives that day—the fact Kayce's mom unknowingly married a sadistic prick—meant that I had to carry the weight of saving them from their own stupid decision.

They should have stayed away.

At least now, Kayce is back on his feet. He's capable and certainly goddamn big enough to look after himself. Even though it feels like I always have to be there to take the hits, wear the black eyes, and suffer the body blows to shield him from the worst of the worst... that time is over.

He's gotta figure out things, and clearly nothing we did meant anything.

It's just a moment in time.

One that I'm moving the fuck on from.

CHAPTER 25

Today can go fuck itself.

Doctors and medical clinics and sitting around waiting for news that I don't even know if I want to hear. Yeah, I'm struggling to sit still or focus on anything other than the pressure ratcheting up inside my lungs. My heart wants to burst out the front of my chest, to splatter a sweep of red across this waiting room as if it were a paintball gun going off.

They're running late—of course the team here is behind. So I've had to sit here for an eternity, and my foot is about to wear a divot in the floor, seeing as I can't stop my good leg from bouncing uncontrollably. Meanwhile, I've damn near chewed a hole in the side of my cheek, gnawing away at the frustration and stress of awaiting this scan result.

I've spent the better part of the afternoon in this room, and there's no chance of being back to the ranch before late tonight. That much I knew long before leaving earlier. The horses and cattle just gotta put up and shut up with a change to their routine today, even if they all looked at me like I had three heads when I was rushing around to get everything done before midday.

My phone vibrates in my pocket, making my gut clench.

I hate that my first tiny balloon of hope is that it might be *his* name. I'm sick in the head for having even the tiniest hint of butterfly wings kicking up inside me, hoping that Raine's contact will be there on the screen when I check the notification. He's my stepbrother, for fuck's sake, and loathes me. I've had enough years of his disgust and disinterest to know that's never gonna happen. Unless we run into each other on the main street of Crimson Ridge, the odds are I won't see him again.

I don't want to acknowledge how itchy my skin feels at the prospect of never having a reason to cross paths in the future.

A lump forms in the back of my throat. I wish I could go back and fix my stupid, fumbling words. I wish I could've been more eloquent. More confident. To explain myself properly. To express things in a way that didn't make it sound like I was a giant jerk—like I was ashamed of being gay, or bi, or demi, or what in the heck I am.

I've spent an awful lot of time living on the internet while wide awake in the middle of the night. Fortunately for my sake, there are hundreds of thousands of places where guys just like me have been willing to open up and share. Forums where people have generously talked about their moment of realizing everything they once thought about themselves was muddled. It helped make me feel like less of a screw-up, and not so alone.

Thinking back on my words—my clunky, god-awful fumbling over myself—I regret not being able to properly say what I meant to say.

But then, what did I mean? Was I supposed to leap into my stepbrother's arms, giddy on the high of accepting I'm attracted to men? To ask him if he'd like to become more than just heated rivals in the arena and two guys who made it their business to get on each other's nerves?

Jesus. I drag my fingers through my hair and swipe open my phone.

What awaits me is the worst possible outcome. A name, and slew of texts that immediately set my nerves on edge.

> MOM:
>
> Please, Kayce. Honey, if you can just help. This is the last time I'll ask.
>
> I promise I won't do it again.

"Mr. Wilder, sorry to keep you waiting. If you could come this way."

There's numb hopelessness in the place where my blood should be. Instead of replying to the rest of my mother's illogical demands, I stuff my phone back in my hoodie. With a heavy sigh, I follow the guy carrying my fate. My future tucked in one of those folders amongst a stack of other files and papers he's carrying.

He ushers me to take a seat once we reach a tiny room at the end of the hallway, and closes the door.

Everything from that point is just static. White noise. A chainsaw buzzing. Whirring that slices through my brain. Medical terms and complex phrases rocket around the room, bouncing off every surface in a pinball effect.

The secondary scan results are presented to me as if they're something I'm interested in hearing or seeing. My ass might be sitting in a chair, but it feels like being locked inside some sort of strobe lighting effect. A hallucination. Things move so rapidly, I only connect vague points, brief flashes in between blinks.

High-grade tear. *Blink.* Surgery. *Blink.* Occupational therapy.

The specialist chatters on, but I'm struggling to comprehend anything over the ringing in my ears.

Limited mobility. Loss of functionality.

The torturous throb settled in behind my eyes only intensifies, and it's not until I find myself seated on the driver's side of my truck, knuckles clenched around the steering wheel, that I feel it settle into my bones.

I'm never going to compete in rodeo again.

Sure, I'll be able to get on a horse—all indications point to being able to live the life of a rancher without too much difficulty. But I can kiss my dreams of a championship, or to climb on the back of a bronc under spotlights, goodbye. There won't be any more chances to go after a winning buckle in my lifetime.

Bile races up the back of my throat.

On top of that, I've got a mother who is in deep shit and begging for me to bail her out of another round of feeding her addiction.

It's too much. The blackness weaves a course through my veins, whispering at me to feed it, give in, let it sip from the bottle, and allow all of this to vanish, to be washed down with every hasty gulp.

I feel like I'm going to hurl.

The band wrapped around my lungs tightens, winding the devastation higher and higher until I feel like every bone is on the verge of shattering.

What am I supposed to fucking do now?

My fingers flex, and I thump down on the steering wheel with a heavy palm. Violent curses fly out of me, flecks of spit burst out. I have to ball my fists, stuffing them into my eye sockets.

This is a waking nightmare, a haunted theme park where every step is threatening to cut me to pieces. I'm already bruised and broken; this only wants to add to that and see me bleed.

Snarling in deep, agonized frustration, I start my truck and fly out of the parking lot, tires screeching. I don't fucking care. Get me a million miles from that place, and those godforsaken scan results confirming the worst.

All the nagging fears I'd been attempting to keep at bay have lined up and taken over. A conquering army come in to lay waste to my life as I knew it. Everything I'd worked so hard to do, to turn my life around, to get my shit together . . . what was it all for? I might as well have just stayed in my loser, waster state. That's clearly all I'm good for.

My head is a snake pit. All I can think about is what it would be like to take the edge off, to escape for a while, and I'm just blindly freewheeling. I could be driving to Crimson Ridge, or halfway across the country.

I don't know how to do this—how to pull my life back together again after having to do it once already. This is just another glaring example of how fucking useless I really am.

A waste of space. A mistake. *You should have never been born.*

My mom's favorite insults. She used to love hurling them my way when she was off her face and mad as hell with me for some unknown reason. They're all carved into my psyche, like scratches grooved into wood. I've tried to erase them, tried to scrub at those invisible scars until the surface is returned to a smooth, unblemished, untarnished canvas. But the stained evidence is still there. There's no obliterating the memories. The only time I truly have ever felt like I could *forget* was when I was buzzed, veins brimming with liquor.

With my foot on the gas, I end up driving, driving, driving. The whole time I'm fighting against every strangling urge to say screw it all. To pull over in one of these shitty little service stations and drown in a bottle of something with the highest proof on the label. I don't care. It only needs to do one job, and that's to knock me on my ass, to wipe my brain from functioning.

My phone lights up on the passenger seat with a text coming through. It's from Chaos, and while I can't make out everything, he's telling me to hurry up and join them at the Hog.

He knows I was due to have my follow-up scan today.

If there's anyone I can't handle being around right now, it's the rodeo crowd. I can't fucking deal with the pitying looks they'll have in their eyes. The pats on the shoulder telling me how *sorry* they are.

Just thinking about it turns my stomach sour.

Another ping comes through right on the heels of Chaos' attempt to reach out, and it's the final straw. I flip my phone into the backseat. I don't want to see another fucking message. Not one from my mom meant to harass me. Not another pity text from a friend.

All I want to do is escape everything.

CHAPTER 26
Raine

A heavy chill hangs around my shoulders as Mist and I make our way down from checking on the cattle in the hills. The mountains are blanketed by low-hanging clouds, sweeps of gray float about, curling along valleys and weaving through trees to create an eerie sight.

Darkness nips at our heels on the ride back to the barn. Much like the thick fog dampening everything it touches, there's no evading it. Nightfall sneaks up faster and faster at this time of year, and a whispered foreshadowing hangs in the cool of the evening. Winter isn't too far away, and she doesn't halt her pending arrival for anyone.

A snow-laden reality that means I'll be moving on. Not that I know where that destination will be just yet. But I've got plenty of other ranches I've worked on before, and all of them have told me that they'll have me back in a heartbeat. It's only my own damn restlessness that keeps me moving, the sense of knowing if I stay somewhere too long, I'm inviting trouble to follow behind. I feel like I owe it to the good, kind, generous people I've worked for over the years that I don't bring any danger to their front door.

I tuck my chin into the collar of my jacket, feeling the chill starting to seep up from my fingertips. Mist is like a giant goddamn heater beneath me, but even so, riding at this late hour, the bite of cold flowing off the mountains is enough to have me ready for a hot meal and a shower. To fall into bed and stave off thoughts that want to stray elsewhere.

I've always enjoyed being alone; it feels like peace to me. There's a comfort in the quietness that comes with being a man alone on a horse. To be surrounded by the kind of landscape all these tourists pay good money to seek a temporary escape to. While I can't comprehend their need to rush back to cities and crowds—days spent in front of computer screens and under harsh lighting—I do understand the reason they come to a place like this.

There's no denying that mountains, with their thinner air and horizons that seem to stretch on forever into the distance, find a way to burrow into your soul. For me, I couldn't fathom living any other way.

Yet, there's a lingering notion, that maybe a part of me enjoyed having someone around. We didn't talk, we hardly spent any time in each other's company, and yet invisible cords continue to bind us together. Even more so now since we crossed far too many illicit fucking lines.

So, I've either got to suck it up and move on this winter, to do what I've always done . . . or maybe this season will be the one I entertain the idea that letting someone in, letting the right person get close, might be a challenge I could pause to consider?

While the horse beneath me sways with a gentle pace, the notion floats there in my mind's eye. As soon as I let the idea breach the surface, my upper lip curls. The idea of trusting anyone is a goddamn joke.

Yeah, I can already predict how that would go. No thanks. I'll stick to my one-night stands and hookups. The kind of brief connections that make it real easy to walk away. Chasing after a need. Satisfying the drive for a release. That's all.

By the time I've returned to the barn, settled Mist in his stall, and made sure the other horses are attended to, my head is more than a little murky. Beau's almost daily reminders ring in my ears not to slump against the wall and end up falling asleep down here amongst the horses.

SAVING THE RAIN

Lethargy hits hard as I'm doing a last tidy-up in the tack room after the group who were out on a trail ride earlier. Hayes has done a half-decent job of handling things, I'll give him that. It doesn't escape my notice that he's instinctively picked up more of the day-to-day jobs around the stables. The guy has got ranching in his blood and knows there's always something to be done rather than idling about. But even with his quiet help, there's still always extra work after so many of the horses have been in action at once.

Either way, once I'm walking out of the barn, just how goddamn heavy my boots feel finally registers as I take that first step to climb the stairs. My strides hit each plank, and I dig my phone out, checking if there are any last instructions from Beau I might've overlooked.

It's only when I reach the top that movement registers. I freeze in place, realizing there's a shadow in front of my door.

A figure huddled in the darkness that I can't make out at first. My eyes sharpen their focus, immediately thinking it must be some sort of animal.

But that's when the hidden figure moves, and the glow from my phone lights the space enough for my eyesight to adjust. Sitting on the floor, he's slumped against the outside of my room, head in his hands. His blond hair sticks haphazardly on end, slightly wet from the drizzle setting in.

I flip on the flashlight from my phone as I step closer, illuminating the narrow landing where Kayce sits. As I close the short distance, his chin tilts to look up at me, and those blue eyes of his are fully bloodshot.

He drags a hand down his face, looking shattered and defeated, as his words hang broken on the night air.

"I had nowhere else to go."

CHAPTER 27

My throat tries to work down a swallow. A vain attempt to digest the intense vulnerability of this moment.

Raine stands over me, shining a pool of warm light just in front of my boots.

I truly don't know how I ended up here. It wasn't so much a conscious choice as one borne out of desperation. A weak, pathetic part of me who couldn't think of any other course of action.

He wasn't at the barn when I arrived, and I didn't even know what I was going to say if I came across him amongst the stalls and the horses, but I found myself climbing these stairs, and this spot is where I crash-landed. Crumpling into the morose heap he's discovered me in. Stuck somewhere between self-loathing and the aching need to escape the voices in my head. The clawing melancholy encouraging me to slip back into old habits.

Now, I'm half-expecting him to kick me out. To toss me back onto the trash heap I came from. The guy who, for so long, has taken any and every opportunity to see me lose. Well, won't he be thrilled that right now, I'm back in the dirt. Once again, I'm on my ass, and he gets to witness the crumbling mess of my life firsthand.

Raine's silence is so oppressively loud. He remains stock-still, the tiny beam of light hovering over the few feet extending between us.

Blowing out a long breath, I run my hand through my hair, down the back of my neck. Everything feels tipped off center, and I don't know how to straighten myself in the saddle again.

"I'll just . . . I'll go." I croak. My voice hoarse and downright pathetic sounding, even to my own ears.

He's gonna laugh in my face, if not spit in it. So, I should probably take the opportunity to leave with my tail between my legs before this gets any worse. Before I make an even bigger mess of things.

Raine doesn't want to see me. What the fuck was I thinking?

A boot thuds beside me, and he nudges at my shoulder. At first, I think he's truly going all out on treating me like the unwanted stray I currently resemble, about to chase me off his doormat with a broom handle, but then I realize he's pushing me to sit upright so that he can open the door.

"Get your ass out of the cold," he mutters, and walks past, flicking on lights as he does so. My heart kicks into overdrive when he leaves the entrance wide open for me to follow behind.

Scrambling to my feet, I'm more than a little unsteady and stiff-limbed after being huddled in the chill and damp for so long. I'm also thoroughly unsure how Raine is going to react to me turning up here—especially when our last interaction was nothing less than a short-circuiting of my hard drive.

He's already crouched in front of the firebox to one side of the kitchen by the time I creep in after him. Now free of his ranching work wear, that leaves him in his jeans and one of those faded flannel shirts he always favors. The sight of him is more arresting than it has any right to be. My eyes snag on the details I shouldn't be taking in so eagerly. Powerful thighs and corded forearms. His strong jaw covered in that short cut beard. Stray curls falling forward across his eyes. I'm consumed by an all too familiar sensation of being sucked under when I see him like this, looking so strong and steady it steals all the air from my lungs.

"Boots off inside." He doesn't look my way as I let the door click softly behind me, instead focusing on continuing to feed kindling into the low flames. It's a small, freestanding firebox, barely an ant compared to the giant thing we have up at Devil's Peak Ranch roaring fiercely day and night. It's a practical detail for a place so small, designed to keep a loft of this size comfortable and warm since it's virtually one big room up here. The entire thing is probably four hundred square feet at the most.

It's sized perfectly for one person to stay in, fitted with the basics. And that thought immediately sends a bolt of heat to a place low in my stomach. I'm suddenly very, very aware of how intimate this space is. I've pretty much invaded Raine's quarters without warning. My attention snaps straight to where his bed sits, with rumpled sheets and bed covers, in the corner.

Goddamn it, seeing the obvious location where he lays his head at night sends a giddy pulse racing in the side of my throat.

I'm immediately flustered, wondering who he's had in that bed since he's been working here at Sunset Skies. Did he bring that redhead home from the bar that night? What about Jessie, since she was hanging off his every word at the bonfire? Was there someone here waiting for him the moment he left me behind on Devil's Peak?

Jesus. Another shot of something heated drives a barb, a jagged gut punch, straight to my core when I picture him tangled in those sheets... only this time, with another guy.

My mouth goes dry, fingers all tingly as I take my boots off as he instructed. While bending down, I realize my hoodie is damp, and yank it off to hopefully let it dry in front of the fire for a while.

God, I'm suspended in the middle of something I don't understand, fluttering around on the spot beside the door. Right now, I'm torn between bolting into the night without another look back, or staying.

But then, Raine's movement catches my eye. He stands up and takes a last glance at the fire, giving it one of those familiar penetrating assessments. The kind that is oh so very good at stripping me down to my very bones whenever one of those looks lands my way.

I used to detest that look. Now, I feel like I'd do just about anything to be on the receiving end of it again.

He drags a forearm across his brow, then crosses the room to the small kitchenette. On the outside, his demeanor is impossible to interpret. Guarded body language I've always struggled to understand; he's just so damn wary at all times. While I've always had the inclination to make myself likable, and mold to any crowd I'm in, Raine has always been closed off.

Something about that, about knowing that he's even invited me to step through that doorway—that he didn't shove a shotgun between my teeth and order me to leave his doorstep—has me shifting my weight from foot to foot. It's nothing to do with my busted leg, either. In fact, right now, I'm not even sure my brain registers my knee at all.

I'm snared in his silence. Waiting for the tiniest flicker of something to make its presence known. With heart pattering away inside my chest, I'm terrified of what he might be thinking.

"You want a soda or something?" Wrapping one fist around the handle of the small fridge, he grunts in my direction. With his other big paw, he threads fingers through his curls, dusting them back off his forehead in a way I feel like I've watched him do a thousand times, yet never truly appreciated what that movement does to his figure.

Reaching up with one arm puts his broadness on full display. A heady showcase of his back, the thickness of his torso, and the solidity of that bicep. All of him is perfectly highlighted as soft fabric cinches and folds to encase his body.

"*Uhh.* No. I'm ok." Quickly averting my eyes, I drop them from the spot where his dark hair brushes against the collar of his shirt. Which is a mistake, because that only makes me stall at the sight of his ass, and so help me in my newfound identity, but my body flushes from head to toe.

This is so wrong. We've kissed, he's made me blow my load all over myself twice now, and yet somehow, this feels like I'm stepping into even more dangerous territory. Because those other times were sudden, desperate moments. Rash decisions made while swept up by a compulsion neither of us could walk away from. And here, now, I'm seeking something entirely different from that.

Or maybe it's what I'm here to search for, yet again.

He's become my sun, and without him, I don't know which way to turn. I've wilted even in the space of a single day without him nearby, and it's frightening to acknowledge that I'm more strung out by this man than I dare admit.

Raine scrubs a hand over his jaw, then closes the fridge. Instead of pulling anything out to drink himself, he turns and leans his ass up against the counter next to the small sink.

"Your knee." He folds his arms, glittering dark eyes boring into my soul.

He's breathtaking, and I don't know if this is a realization that has come about as a new piece of information, or I've known it all along and just shoved any of those feelings so far down I forgot they existed.

"Fucked." My throat is tight.

Raine's expression stays harsh, no secrets unwittingly revealed. That strong jaw remains tense, and his gaze drops to the knee in question before dragging up my body and fuck my entire life, I feel like I come alive. A trembling sort of terror takes hold at the prospect of having him look my way so openly.

"You can work? Ride?"

Dipping my chin, I stand there without a clue what to do with my hands. In fact, I don't know what to do at all; maybe just melting into a puddle on these floorboards might be my best course of action.

"At the ranch, yes . . . but . . . rodeo is done for me." It's a struggle to get the last part out without succumbing to the thick layers of emotion that drag up the back of my throat, clinging onto those words.

The fireplace cracks and sparks as the weight of my confession lingers. I take in a deep breath through my nose, before letting it out. Fuck this. Fuck everything. I'm just so goddamn tired.

Rubbing a palm over my nape, I can't face him anymore. My eyes fall to the side, feeling the shame flood in for coming here. For not being strong enough to handle this on my own when that's what he would do. My stepbrother deals with everything in his life alone, without needing to go running to others for help.

As I try to wrangle the way my body is reacting to being here with him, amid the uncertainty of what my future is gonna be now that I can't do the thing I'd been so goddamn heart-set on achieving, I feel him step in front of me.

Raine fills my vision, and tilts my chin up to look at him. When I follow that feather-light touch, I'm met with his deeply furrowed brow and angular cheekbones highlighted by the fire's glow.

"You said you didn't want to talk about it. That no one could know." A muscle tics in his jaw. "And yet, here you are."

Those words have an edge to them. Something dangerous, considering the state I'm in.

"I'm sorry." My eyes bounce between his, searching for any clue as to what he's thinking. "I just don't even understand what is going on for me." It comes out as hardly a whisper.

"Why are you *here*, Kayce?"

I remain as quiet as a mouse, but surely he can hear my heart hammering away inside my chest now that he's standing so close. There's no possible way to respond to that. Or at least, not anything I should dare breathe life to.

"What I think is . . . there's an answer to that question you don't want to admit out loud." Raine knows how to read me like a goddamn book, and I don't understand the thrilling, weightless sensation that knowledge brings. He sees me, the worst parts of me, but it's me all the same.

"Doesn't it scare you?" I wet my lips, and that's the moment we drop from altitude. It's like my ears pop, and my stomach fills with fluttering wings.

His onyx gaze descends to the swipe of my tongue with ferocity. *With desire.*

"Not in the way it obviously scares you."

"I've never . . ." God, I feel like I'm tongue-tied. "Nothing has ever been like this for me."

Raine grunts, and one of his strong fists reaches for the front of my t-shirt. "Are you trying to hide away, Kayce? Trying to sneak around in the dark so you don't have to confront who you are?" He holds me tight, but the reality is, he could pin me to the spot using nothing but a whisper. I cannot and do not want to move away from him.

"No. No, that's not it at all." Shaking my head, I make no attempt to break away from his gaze. "I just don't know why it's you . . . you're always there. Burrowed in my brain. I'm constantly searching for hints of you. It's so fucked up because I know you can't stand me—"

"What?" His eyes narrow on me. That word whips between us to interrupt my blabbering.

"I know you hate me." With a hasty swallow, I wonder if he can feel me quaking. Does he judge me for being such a disaster? Surely, he does. "So, I'm sorry to barge in like this. I bet I'm the last person on earth you want to see right now . . . I just . . . I didn't know where else to go and not feel like I'm losing my mind about everything."

A loud pop from the fire cannons across the room, and my heart lurches. His fingers tighten in my shirt, and I watch Raine's eyes slide over my face. I'm transfixed as he tracks down to my lips, and every part of my skin tingles when exposed to the high beam sweep of his gaze.

"I don't hate you," he grunts, focus locked on my mouth, and I'm unable to wrench my own attention off his.

"Could've fooled me." I'm not sure what Raine's expression is right now, but as he watches me breathe those words into the fraction of a gap between us, I feel a rumble of something inside his chest. A dark noise of warning. A look that says he's just as confused by this magnetic pull going on between us, yet he's still undecided whether he wants to kill me, or kiss me.

"You frustrate me. You confuse the shit outta me. You downright piss me off."

Raine drags me into him. So much so, it causes my back to bow. Yanking me by the front of my shirt, our bodies are flush and we're so close the heat radiates off his massive chest in waves. Tension pulsates and writhes between us as I have to grip hold of his forearms just to steady myself.

"But I could never . . ." He lets his lips hover over mine, and I'm *trembling* beneath his hold. Every part of me screams to know another of his kisses. To have him give me another hit of the wicked rasp and scrape and taste of him.

The sexiest, rumbly noise bursts forth as he dusts those lips that I so desperately ache for over mine. Relief and a pure lust-fueled appetite coil through me as Raine speaks against my mouth, and I damn near feel like I'm about to fly off into the night sky.

"I could never hate you, snowflake."

CHAPTER 28
Raine

The soft little noise Kayce makes beneath my mouth sends a searing, feverish burst of desire straight down to my toes. I didn't expect to find him waiting for me, and I certainly had no idea it would be with that tormented look dulling his blue gaze.

And now, here I am, sealing our lips together, losing myself to this undeniable, insatiable hunger for *him*.

I don't know what Kayce wants from this, or why it's me he's seeking out, but I don't really fucking care right now. That continual struggle I've been left with—of feeling so inexplicably drawn together—turns into a white-hot blaze roaring through my bloodstream.

My tongue presses past the seam of his mouth, demanding entry, and even though we absolutely should not be kissing, I can't stop this. To add fuel to the flames, there's no hesitation in him tonight. He clings onto my forearms, still unsure what to do, but his lips move against mine right from the outset.

He's as sweet as I remember, and the lingering scent of pine and the dewiness of the mist outside fills my awareness. And the noises—all those fucking noises. He lets out another soft whimper as I take his mouth, letting my kisses turn more forceful. I can't stop chasing after new ways to have him feeding me those breathy little gasps, to devour the first hint of a moan climbing up his throat.

Everything crackles to life, a bonfire bursting and soaring, and I'm hanging onto decency by a tether. Because right now, all I want is to feel his body writhing beneath mine, to see him fall apart time and again, for me.

I pull back a little, pinching his bottom lip between my teeth, and tug on that soft swell that's always so damn tempting. He stares back, all wide-eyed and slightly ruffled. Taking in the sight of him like this, it quickly becomes my favorite version of Kayce Wilder. His golden boy look so easily upended with something as innocent as a kiss.

There's no way that should make my dick jerk in appreciation, but the time for trying to pause and figure out this strange attraction between us is a ship that has long since sailed.

"Tell me why you're here, Kayce." My words are low, gritty with craving him. At the pace this is galloping forward, I need to hear it from his lips. Because otherwise, my stepbrother might wake up tomorrow with a head full of regrets and I've certainly got zero interest in being any part of that. "Walk out that door right now if you aren't sure about this." I let my mouth roam along his shaved jaw, tracing the faintest hint of stubble there.

He swallows and makes a tiny humming sound. Those hesitant fingertips curl tighter against the sleeves of my shirt.

"I don't know why I'm here." His words dissolve into the sluttiest little noise when I start kissing the side of his throat. Goddamn, the way that turns me feral. It's like every part of him I touch, every patch of bare skin I come into contact with, has him reacting like no one has ever explored that part of him before. And fuck my life, that drives me wild in a way it has absolutely no business doing.

"Then I think you should leave," I murmur against his pulse point, nipping the delicate skin. That sting—the pressure of my teeth marked into his flesh—leaves him shuddering and arching his neck. Offering up that sensitive part of his body for more attention. Kayce might be saying he doesn't know what he wants, or why he turned up on my doorstep after dark, but his body sure as hell does.

He gasps when I do it again, a little harder this time, then suck down to ease the sting.

"I—I don't want to leave."

Beneath my lips, I feel his throat work another swallow. Roaming hot, wet tracks over his fluttering pulse with my tongue, I can't help myself. Pure need is in the driver's seat. And I want to push him to distraction as much as I know I really, really, *really* should be slowing down. If I were a better person, I would be pausing until he can think straight, or something approaching that at the very least.

Letting go of the front of his shirt is the hardest thing to do, but it seems to be the secret to unlocking the restraint holding Kayce back up until now. He clings tighter in response, presses our bodies closer, and wets his lips. Hints of turquoise streak his gaze as he searches my face, flitting his attention between my mouth, my jaw, and back up to reconnect with my quiet stare.

"I feel safe with you."

It's a hushed admission, an unexpected gift, lined with a faint hint of pleading. There's so much disguised within those simple words. A whole lifetime of unexplored parts of himself wrapped up in one soft statement of need.

Please. Make it good for me. Help me navigate this thing I don't understand.

Who am I to turn him away? I'm already so far gone with this, I've been unable to keep my mouth off him, and barely fought the driving urge to drag him into my arms the moment I saw him slumped outside my door. So what kind of asshole would I be to abruptly end this?

Truth be told, I'm attracted to him in a way I didn't think could ever be possible or certainly in a way that I didn't *allow* myself to consider. It's not like we're actually related. It's not even as if we truly know each other. This craving burning hot and bright between us while here in Crimson Ridge has been as near-strangers more than anything. A palpable tension that, in all of a moment, transformed without warning.

My feelings for Kayce have shifted, grown, evolved. No matter what label you might attach to it . . . there are two distinctly different versions of how it feels to be around him. Years and years ago, it centered around obligation and a deep sense of hatred for our circumstances. But here and now, he's a guy I can't wipe from my mind. When I'm with him like this, it feels like the most natural thing in the world to let my tongue run across the column of his throat, tasting the hint of salt and night air coating the warmth of his skin.

"That doesn't answer my fucking question." I fist the back of his head and drag a biting kiss over his Adam's apple. Licking a long line up his neck, I stop once I reach his mouth, letting my eyes settle on his because I need to see what lies there waiting for me.

His stare is wider than ever. Big blue orbs with pupils almost fully blown out.

Kayce looks like my next fucking meal.

"This little naive cowboy routine is endearing and tempting and all, but a few stolen kisses after dark is one thing..." I give in to the urge to tug on his bottom lip again, drawing out another moan of pleasure, before pulling back. "Asking me to take care of your needs is another demand entirely... and you know it."

Kayce's palms drift from where they've lingered at my elbows and forearms, and he finally puts his hands on me. Properly this time. It's still unsteady, but he catches hold of my shirt, and then gingerly slides both palms around my back.

My eyelids grow a little heavy at how good that feels, to have Kayce touch me in a way that seems as though he genuinely wants to trace my muscles and explore the planes of my body. There's a curiosity there, a cautious mapping with his fingertips, and it leaves my heart rate doubling to have him wrapped up in me like this.

"Please." He ushers that word, with just enough certainty that I'm already starting to walk him backward before he gets to the next part. "I want this... with you."

"Jesus. You don't know what the fuck you're getting us into." A groan escapes me as I seal our mouths back together. This time, the brakes fail. I'm tearing at his t-shirt, dragging it up his stomach—only pausing my next kiss for the brief second necessary to peel it up over his head before tossing it aside and stealing his lips once more.

His fingers fumble blindly with the buttons on my shirt, managing to unfasten a couple over my chest as I cup his face in both hands. Guiding us toward the bathroom, my tongue thrusts against his, urgency thrumming through every part of me. My cock is fully hard against my jeans, and Kayce has a bulge in the front of his sweats to match my own.

I shove him through the doorway, and he's damn well panting. He looks at me and swallows hard, bare chest heaving. With the two of us in this cramped space, there's not a lot of room to get undressed. Using my bulk, I crowd him against the vanity until he has to brace himself on both hands against the edge of the counter. Kayce's eyes bounce everywhere as I forgo the effort of undoing any more buttons, reaching behind my neck to shuck the shirt over my head. It makes something inside me sit up and enjoy that tiny fragment of attention. When I lean across to turn the water on, and then start working my belt, he's unable to stop staring at me open-mouthed the entire time.

Arching an eyebrow his way in silent question, I step out of my jeans and briefs.

Pink floods Kayce's cheeks as his eyes drop straight to my groin. With one hand, I take myself in my fist and stroke, watching the blush darken as he can't rip his focus away from the sight of me naked.

Why that feels so good, oh so right, is a concern for another day.

His tongue pokes out to wet his lips, and I see his fingers unclench from where he's been gripping onto the edge of the vanity like it's a goddamn life raft. I don't wait for him to figure out how to do this next part, he's gotta take this step for himself.

I'm uninterested in forcing anyone into anything they're not fully sure of.

So, I keep stroking my cock and stand under the warm jet of water, letting it flow over my hair and face in a cascade. My dick is absolutely aching, pulsating under my palm, and the sensation of the shower spray flowing over my hand is only amplifying that scorching feeling. From the corner of my eye, I see Kayce finally start to move.

Turning to let my back rest against the wall, I pump a handful of soap and lather up quickly as I watch him through the running water. Christ, he's fucking hot, with his body all toned and lithe from rodeo. He drops his sweats and briefs, kicking out of them, and his erection bobs up, slapping against his stomach. I see the moment his blue irises flicker to the sight of himself, hard and needy, before drifting over to me. Taking everything in for a second, his Adam's apple dips, and he hovers in place for a long pause, transfixed by the sight of my hands moving over my torso and arms.

It's nothing done for show, a functional act to wash off the day after being in the saddle and working with the horses, but he appears to like what he sees.

With both of us naked like this, the differences between us are more noticeable. His muscles are leaner and more defined, whereas my chest is thicker. I've always been bigger than him, but now, with age and not competing, I'm not sporting any abs like he's got going on. His dick swells more the longer he takes in the sight of my nakedness, and a shining bead of precum gathers at his tip.

He's not turning tail and fleeing, but there's obviously a moment he's needing to take, to mentally build up enough courage to get over here. Even if the yearning burns bright in his eyes. Tilting my head to one side, I watch him closely as those lips part—all kiss-bitten and flushed after being claimed by my mouth—and goddamn if he doesn't look gorgeous when he's staring straight at my dick like he wants to drop to his knees right this second.

"Well, what are you waiting for? Gonna just stand there, or are you gonna be a good boy for me?" I cup the stream of water to scrub over my face, watching him through my fingers. As rivulets run down my throat and lingering droplets cling to my mouth and beard, I bring both hands up to drag through my hair.

There's barely enough room for two guys in here, but that works in my favor. Kayce has nowhere to hide once he joins me under the shower spray. His long lashes flutter closed as he tilts his face up to the water, and fucking hell, my erection kicks, seeing the exposed slope of his throat up close. I just want to bury my face there and keep sucking on that sensitive point hard enough to mark him the fuck up. A twisted part of me wants to see if the cowboy with all the charm and charisma will turn into a writhing mess from that alone. How far can I push to see if he'd blow all over himself again just from the pleasure of a man's mouth teasing his body, his nipples, his ass for the first time?

Reaching for more soap, I nudge him to spin and swap places. Now, it's his turn to be backed up against the wall, and I start running my lathered-up palms over his chest. Experiencing my touch for the first time, he shudders and lets out a noise that almost sounds like a whine of protest, except he catches it. Slamming his mouth shut and biting down on his bottom lip instead.

I keep studying his face as I slowly wash him. Moving from his chest, along each arm, tracing those veins and muscles, then gliding down his torso. By the time I make it to the trail of darker golden hair at that v pointing to his rock-hard cock, his stomach caves, and goosebumps fly across his arms.

Kayce's palms flatten against the wall, permitting me to continue. I don't miss the way his narrow hips lift, his dick straining and veins popping, as I stoop to run soap over his thighs and down his legs. Crouching down in the small space, I bite back a wicked sense of satisfaction at the desperate way the indents on the side of his ass clench. Having me only an inch away, but not making contact with his length jutting out, he's quick to become a slutty little thing, silently begging for my mouth.

That can come later. First, he damn well needs to get used to being touched because right now, his skin is still quivering and flinching. Mostly with pleasure, but I know one thing's for certain . . . he's never had rough, calloused caresses over his body. Kayce has never experienced hands like mine, roughened and worn after years working horses and cattle.

I like that I'm the first to give him this more than I'm ready to admit right now.

"Turn around." My voice is quiet, almost drowned out by the rushing water and my own heartbeat, thudding away at the prospect of what is going to come next.

"Please . . ." Kayce says resolutely, dipping his chin as he dutifully shifts and rests both palms against the wall. "You don't need to treat me like I'm fragile."

That makes me chuckle. Midway through soaping up his shoulders, I indulge in letting the backs of my fingers glide a slow track down the curve of his spine. Heading lower, until I reach his ass. The pathetic little mewl he lets out when I grab hold and squeeze both cheeks is enough to drive me insane. Kayce immediately pushes back against me, and I tut out loud, bringing my mouth to hover close at his ear.

My cock nestles right there, and he sucks in a sharp breath feeling the weight of me pressed up against him, thick and heavy with need.

"I don't like to break my toys." I nip at his earlobe, then suck down until he's moaning out loud. Yeah, he might be the rodeo star on the outside, but he melts every time my mouth connects with those soft little parts of him. I get a kick out of finding those tiny places he obviously doesn't want to admit he enjoys, yet surrenders to immediately, tilting his head on reflex.

"*Raine*." My name is a mumble, shivering over his lips. While exhaling shakily, his long fingers press against the wet tiles.

"Keep your hands on the wall." My teeth graze his shoulder, before I pull back and spit into my palm. "You like saying my name all sweet and innocent now, don't you? When you want something from me."

Kayce shudders and lets out a guttural noise as my hand starts stroking and spreading his ass, letting the saliva coat over him.

"Or are you still fighting me, *hmm*?" I press and rub a little harder over his hole, and each time I do, his breathing hitches. "Are you actually wanting this, or do you want me to leave you in this shower, and you can get yourself off?"

His back arches, rubbing his ass against my dick and lets out a whimper. "You . . . I need . . . I want you to touch me." Kayce's words are garbled as he lets his forehead drop against the wall.

A groan vibrates deep inside my chest hearing him say it out loud. "Relax for me." Coaxing him with a deep hum, I gradually work up to ease one finger past that tight ring of muscle. "*Shhh*. That's it. Just relax." He's so goddamn tight, clenching as I rock my hand slowly back and forth. My dick is a leaking mess at the thought of what it's going to be like to actually try and fit inside him.

Reaching around, I hold out my other palm. "Be a good boy and spit." That earns me another delicious shiver, and Kayce whimpers. It's a soft, sensual little noise amongst the flowing water, and he lets a long track of saliva drop into my palm.

"Why do I like you calling me that?" His whine is almost more to himself than anything.

"Always so eager to please everyone." I let my hand drop and wrap his length firmly.

"*Ummpphhf.* Oh, god," he gasps and immediately rocks into my hold.

"No, snowflake. There's no one here but me giving you this. I'm the one fingering your ass, with your dick weeping, all for *my* hands." I bite the back of his neck, and Kayce absolutely fucking melts.

As I stroke him from root to tip, he throbs in my palm, and I swear to god, with how swollen his cock is, it feels like he's going to fall apart any second now.

"Oh my . . . *fffffuck.*" He claws at the tiles and starts shifting his hips, chasing my touch on both ends. "Raine. Holy shit." The way he says my name, the way those letters shiver across his lips, it's goddamn heady to see him so undone already. As he bucks and slides through my grip, his precum mixes with the slipperiness of his spit.

His muscles relax more as I add more spit and work another finger inside him, gradually scissoring to encourage him to open for me. Just as his whimpers start reaching a higher pitch, I ease off stroking his cock, and he curses.

"Please. Please don't stop."

"Do you want more? Are you a needy little thing that needs to be stuffed full with more than just my fingers?" I grunt against his ear. The way his ass is the fucking hottest and tightest thing, clenching around the digits I've worked into him, leaves me growing more wild.

He nods frantically. "Yes. Yes . . . I need . . ." Those words die when I tug on him, squeezing his cock harder at the same time as pushing further to sink into his back entrance.

"Look at you. Desperate for two fingers and a hand job." I scold him in a low voice. "I should leave you to do it for yourself if you can't ask properly."

"*Fffffuck. Unnghhh.* Raine. Fuck." Kayce's words tumble out as his body clenches, and I keep working him harder.

"Say it." My fist tightens around his dick, and he's thrusting into my palm, then back against my hand wantonly. Frantic noises burst past his lips as he flies towards that edge.

"Fuck me, Raine. Fuck me. *Fuck me, please.*" The sound of his begging morphs into a deep groan as his cock swells and pulses. He jerks and shoots cum everywhere, in thick ropes, as he dissolves into a gasping orgasm in my arms. The feel of him tumbling over the edge is the most incredible thing, leaving me light-headed while witnessing him absolutely fucking melt for me.

I keep stroking him, letting the water wash away the cum covering his shaft and my fist, as I ease out of his ass.

Turning him around, my weight presses him against the wall. I let my erection dig into his stomach, and holy fuck. Just the feel of having the sensitive tip shoved tight between our bodies is heaven.

Kayce is the one to kiss me this time. His hands fly up to my neck, threading into my hair, and he clings to me. Still breathing hard, he slams our mouths together and feeds me a low moan.

Blindly fumbling around, I flip the water off. The silence that ensues is nowhere near as echoing as it would be if it weren't for the racing of our heartbeats consuming everything.

"Wait—Don't—" Whining against my lips, he tightens his hold on my wet hair. As if he thinks this is all over. As if that's all it'll be, and I'm about to send him on his way.

Little does he fucking know.

Drawing back enough to nip his bottom lip, then to bite along his jaw, I stop when I reach the shell of his ear and let my stubble brush against his damp skin.

"*Shh*. Go and get on the bed for me."

CHAPTER 29
Kayce

"Hang your head over the edge."

Oh my fucking god. I swear I'm floating somewhere out of my body, infinitely high on this man. My stepbrother, who just turned my entire life inside out with a few strokes and touches and dirty words in my ear.

Raine stalks behind me, completely naked, while roughly dragging a towel over his hair. Fuck, I've never seen him like this before—I think he erased every last brain cell when I was first treated to the sight of him undressing and getting into the shower.

Of course, I've seen plenty of dudes naked. Between locker rooms and training, being on the road for rodeo, it's not like I haven't encountered other men fully undressed.

But this? Raine? To see his body without a stitch of clothing . . . those rioting wings in my stomach are going to beat so fast I might spontaneously lift off the ground and drift somewhere high into the darkened sky.

He's thick through his middle, in a way that holds so much potent strength. Muscle definition runs down the sides of his torso, ending in a prominent ridge of his adonis belt dusted with dark hair. His tattoos extend from his arms across his chest on one side, too. It seems fitting that the man with hungry, ruthless eyes has a wolf inked there.

And Jesus Christ, his cock is thick and hard, and I'm right back in that place where I feel like I'd do anything to know his taste. Even just that sensation of him pressed hot against me left my insides doing backflips.

Does he have any idea how gorgeous he is? I know he's confident, having always worn that winning attitude like a second skin. So right now, right here, staring at the sight of his bed, I'm struck wondering why he's even interested in me.

I'm a fumbling, naive idiot in comparison. Someone who keeps fucking up over and over, and yet he's prepared to give me this. To step over a line that I'm still reeling from the intensity of my own obsession to cross.

None of it makes sense, yet when Raine's steadfast hands are on my body, I feel more alive and secure than I think I ever have in my life.

"You're taking a long time thinking about this." Raine comes up behind me and does that thing where he yanks my hair, tilting my head back so that he can assault the side of my throat again. The fool I am for him, I'm fucking obsessed with how good it feels. As much as I'm both dying for this and insanely nervous, I gladly melt against his torso while he drags his mouth and scrapes his beard over that patch of skin that leaves me feeling all gooey from head to toe. "I'm clear. I've been tested. Anything else you wanna know?"

Shaking my head, I just want to drag him on top of me and demand that he pins me to the mattress.

"Tell me where you want me." I hum. This is too good and too much, and I'm lost to all the ways my body comes alive under his command.

He makes a satisfied noise, running his tongue up the side of my neck. A move that he probably already knows by now will have me obeying anything he says. "Lie on your back, head off the edge just there." With a final nip of my ear, he directs me where to climb onto the bed.

My heart is trying its best to drum a path straight out of my mouth.

I'm nervous as hell. So far, all I've done is pump cum all over myself just about every time he looks my way. I've done nothing more than stare at his dick and stroke us together. This is the immense power Raine has over me, it would seem.

The world spins on its axis once more as I settle into the position he told me to. Lying back, I stare at him from upside down with my head hanging a little over the edge, surrounded by soft sheets that smell of him. With his giant cock right there in his fist, he's my entire world right now. There's nothing else except pleasing him and being swept up in him.

And maybe that's why I'm here. Perhaps that's all this is for tonight . . . an escape. I don't fucking know, but I also feel like something deep down inside is blooming to life. That tangled web of me and him and our circumstances is way too confusing right now to try and separate or comprehend.

The simple answer to this equation is that I want this, with him, and I'm drawn to him in a way that defies logic. Being tugged into Raine's orbit feels predestined, like how I felt the first time I walked up to a horse and felt as if I could hear its thoughts. There's something in our connection I can't put words to.

What I do know for certain is that I might die if he doesn't slide his cock past my parted lips and let me know what it feels like to suck him down.

"*Mmm.* Such a pretty mouth for a pretty golden boy." Dragging his thumb over the slit at his tip where a glistening drop of precum waits, he uses that hand to swipe over my lips. They feel puffy after kissing him. Scratched up in the best fucking way by his beard. As he gives me that first hint, oh god . . . the tanginess . . . the muskiness . . . the salty kick . . . all of it roars through my senses. "Open for me. Keep your throat nice and relaxed." His voice stays low and measured as those dark eyes glimmer under soft lights.

I swallow hastily, licking my lips to catch another glimpse, a little preview of what it's going to be like to take all of him.

"Tap my thigh if it's too much, ok?" Raine hovers, stroking himself leisurely, but I can see those veins and feel the radiating warmth of his body. I really want to make this as good for him as he's already made it for me tonight.

"I can take it." Gritty determination comes out of me, borne from all the foolhardy stubbornness that led me to riding broncs in the first place. I'm rewarded with the Raine equivalent of a smile. His lips twitch, and he slides two fingers onto my tongue.

If I thought my climax was over and done, suddenly, a flash of white-hot sparks rocket straight to my groin at the feel of him pushing into my mouth and forcing my jaw wider. After a few more presses, encouraging me to relax and let my head hang for him just the way he prefers, that tattooed hand vanishes.

Then his cock is right there. *Right. There.*

Fuck me. The glistening crown of him slides over my lips, as he paints my mouth with a smear of precum, a hint of what I'm in for, giving me a moment to acclimatize to this dizzying altitude before he eases forward.

He's so velvety smooth, weighty, and feels impossibly large. At first I have no idea how this is going to work. I mean, I know what it's like to have a set of lips wrapped around my own dick, but this is completely new, and holy fuck, the vulnerability of it does something inside me. Sparks shoot in every direction as he lets me get used to the size of him, with small pulses of his hips, feeding me just the tip and fitting the head of his length inside my mouth. My tongue flicks against his shaft on instinct, and I find myself rapidly drifting to a place where this turns me on. More than I ever could've imagined.

I kind of like the fact that he's standing over me. I relish the feeling of him taking charge. And I really, really enjoy the feeling of having him swell and pulse inside my mouth.

Like I'm pleasing him, just by being a hole to sink into.

Christ. The moment that thought bubbles up, my dick surges. Pleasure and warmth spread through me as the tanginess of him coats my tongue, and he shifts his hips to push a little deeper.

At this angle, it feels like the most natural thing.

I have no idea if I'm managing to take more than half of him, but Raine doesn't seem to mind. He glides across my eager tongue, with saliva coating him and going everywhere as he works in and out. I'm overcome, turning into a sloppy mess almost immediately. Nothing but moans and pathetic noises, with my fists clenching and unclenching in the sheets and my abused lips wrapped around his cock. He tastes so goddamn perfect, fresh with that faint hint of soap from the shower and the potent masculinity that I'm sure just clings to him permanently.

As he gently pumps in and out, I become vaguely aware that he's stroking my jaw. His hands roam over the front of my neck, cupping the side of my face with those calloused fingers I can't get enough of when they graze my skin.

"*Fffffuck*. Your mouth." He pushes even harder now, spiraling my ecstasy. Somehow, I'm able to relax into it and not gag. "*Unghh*. That's good." That grunt of approval he gives me has my cock leaping back to life. Ready and thickening against my abs.

I think I make a muffled noise of agreement. Trying to encourage him to give me more, to feed me more of him. I love that his heavy balls are right there. What I would give to see if he likes them being played with at the same time as receiving head. Are they sensitive? Would he shudder with desire? If this is the only time I get to experience sex with Raine, then I don't want the watered-down version.

"Go on . . . wrap your hand around yourself. Feel how hard you are for having a dick in your mouth." He starts taunting me, and fucking hell, my wiring must be faulty because another shot of pleasure races along every vein. "Touch yourself and see just how much this turns you on," he commands, and of course, my palm is there before he's hardly even finished grinding out his words.

His cock keeps pumping in and out of my mouth, and I'm spinning out of my mind with that sensation combined with the feel of tugging on myself—of being fully exposed for him to watch me grow more and more swollen with furious need.

"I don't have to do more than stuff your holes with my fingers, and you're spraying cum. What kind of mess do you think you'll make when I'm filling you properly? What kind of a noisy slut will you be for having my cock deep inside your tight little ass?"

Raine's heated words damn near do me in. Wetness leaks from my eyes, spit has collected at the corners of my mouth, my balls tighten, and my dick is starting to weep all over again.

Just as I think he's going to keep on with this until he explodes down my throat, he pulls away, leaving me gasping, and spun the fuck out. The world is still tilted upside down, and every ounce of blood has surely drained to my dick.

"Such a pretty thing for me, aren't you, snowflake?" Raine's words fill my awareness as I blink and try to focus on what's happening. He leans over me and lets his lips meet mine again while caressing the front of my throat with the kind of hold that feels incredible. Strong hands help guide me to ease upright, so that I'm not simply dangling off the bed, hoping for a mouthful of cum to swallow.

He crosses to the bathroom, leaving me for a moment. As I regather my bearings and reposition myself, a sudden moment of panic rises. This is it. He's about to fuck me properly, and oh, god, I don't know how this next part works. Am I supposed to get on all fours while he rails me from behind, or what? I'm all frantic heartbeats and hot cheeks when he reemerges with something in his hands.

Lube. He's got a bottle of lube, and as my eyes tick down to his fat cock I can't help but bite my lip. That thing looks ready to split me in two, given how hard he is after all that we've done so far, added to the fact he's yet to find relief.

My pulse races as fast as the wind when he comes back to join me on the bed and he doesn't pause, doesn't stop, just climbs over me with lust flaring in his eyes like an inferno. He's so imposing, so in control, he tosses the lube to land beside us and crawls over my body, maneuvering so that he fits between my legs, and I'm shoved back until my head hits the pillows.

I'm so relieved he's quietly taking charge like this, while still experiencing that continual rush of worry about doing something he doesn't enjoy. Am I going to be good enough for him? Will he like doing this with me? What if I'm no good at sex with a man?

His onyx eyes glitter as he crawls up my body, plants one hand beside my head, and uses the other to pinch my jaw. Raine studies me so damn carefully, letting his gaze flicker across my face as if he's tracing something, committing it to memory, before he brushes his thumb across my puffy bottom lip to drag it out from where I still had it trapped under my teeth.

"I'm in the kind of mood to ruin you." His velvety words dance across my skin, leaving shivers in their wake. "Is that what you want, my sweet boy?"

Gulping down all my nerves and trepidation, I nod. "You know I do." The confession comes out as barely more than a whisper, which Raine seals with another of those drugging kisses.

Then his hands are moving. He reaches across me, and I'm transfixed, watching his face as I hear the click of a cap and feel him push my legs wider. I'm in some sort of pleasure-soaked daze, with my length bobbing against my stomach as he rearranges my limbs. Giving himself the angle he wants my body positioned in.

Nerves flurry around as heat continues to build low in my belly, and I suck in a gasp when he drizzles lube generously over my seam. Raine slowly works me with his fingers again, this time with the kind of added slickness that makes it feel so good. The small amount of burn, the same as I felt earlier in the shower, quickly dissolves and morphs because he just knows how to make something that I was so goddamn nervous about feel incredible.

"*Umphhfff*. Holy shit." My eyelids droop, and my lips tremble with all the whines and whimpers I'm so close to letting out as he scissors his fingers. My body rocks a little against the mattress, and I'm so conscious of not being loud. Even though I know we're away from other people, it still feels hardwired in my brain that we're certainly not supposed to be doing this, and yet I can't stop. I don't want to stop. This doesn't feel wrong in any way.

"Just breathe. I'll take it slow." Raine's voice is right there, dragging my focus back to him, pulling me back out of my head. "Keep those blues on me, snowflake." His voice dips into a lower register and I feel it rumble straight through into my chest.

Another nod, another feeble noise of need, another shift of my hips to encourage him to stop treating me like I'm going to shatter.

And then it happens. His fingers are gone, and my knees are being pressed higher. The intense vulnerability chokes me by the throat as I lie there, splayed out for him. But that feeling is quickly scattered and replaced by bold, raw neediness when the slick tip of him, hot and swollen, nudges at my ass. Raine fists himself and starts to ease forward. The entire time, his dark, hooded gaze remains drilled into mine. He holds me secure, and I don't dare look away because there might be only silence and thudding heartbeats filling this bed, but unspoken reassurance flows from his gaze.

I can't help the series of shudders and gasps and the way my hands fly up to run over his form. Greedily tracing his chest, I map his biceps, his shoulders, all while he pushes my knees back, and the tip of him slips inside.

"*Unghhh. Oh god. Fuck,*" I whimper, and my fingers claw his shoulders.

"You good?" He holds there, letting me get used to the feel of him, and that stretch that burns so good starts to ease a little. "Stay with me. Just breathe." He gives me another of those low, rumbly commands, and I melt beneath the safety in his tone.

"It's—It's good. I'm good." My throat works down a swallow. "Please don't stop."

The faintest hint of a smile ghosts across his lips and creases at the corner of his eyes, and he dips down to roam his tongue over my nipple. I nearly fucking vibrate off the bed with how unreal that feels. I'm so distracted by his mouth that it's a blur as he's still working forward, gradually easing a little deeper. All I can think as I relax more for him is how I'm addicted to the scratch of his beard against my skin, and *holy shit, his tongue is doing that swirling thing.*

I find my fingers tangled in his damp hair, threading and tugging and shuddering beneath the way he works my body so masterfully.

"Raine. *Fffffuck.* I need more." I'm an incoherent disaster of begging and moaning and trying to shift my hips, coaxing him to push further inside.

"Goddamn," he chokes out. "You're like a fucking fist. Just stay relaxed for me." His teeth tug on the stiffened peak of my nipple; then he licks a wet trail over my chest. Tracing the planes of my pecs and up to the undulation of my collarbone. He's everywhere and feels so overwhelming, but in the best kind of way. "It's so good. Too good." Raine breathes heavily and I melt in an instant.

At long last, he sinks all the way inside, and we both let out a groan when he fully seats himself against my ass. I can't help the way I'm shivering and panting, not because it's anything but incredible, but because he really does feel *huge*, and my body absolutely lights up at having him fill me all the way to the hilt.

"Please. Let me have more." I cling to his arms, begging with my eyes. My cock throbs between us, already primed with that familiar pool of tension forming low in my spine.

"*Mmm*, those lips suit begging a little." His gaze locks on my mouth as he slides back and then gives a subtle nudge forward. It's enough to have me seeing stars with just that first slick glide.

I give him more whimpers. Garbled words and reckless, mindless curses. Which Raine obliges by starting to thrust properly now.

It's incredible. Nothing like I could have imagined. He's so strong and assured, looming over me with his tattoos and dark eyes that absolutely eat me alive. It's intimate. So much more than I thought it would be. So much more than I thought it could be with someone like him, who oozes sex appeal and confidence and has a long line of company keen to spend a night being treated like this.

I have to shove any of those bubbling up jealousies aside, locking them away, because right now, he's here with me, and this is beyond anything I could have imagined.

Raine's dark hair falls across his eyes while he fucks me deep and slow, with a rhythm that leaves me crumbling fast. He sees it, and a wickedness descends over him. There's a look, a glint that catches, and I know it spells trouble for me . . . in the best possible way.

He shifts the angle of his hips and pumps forward again, and that spot—that fucking spot—lights my body up, searing sparks fly to every corner, and my balls thud agonizingly with the need to come. I'm pretty sure I start outright pleading, lips shivering, as I gasp for him to do it again, and again.

Those rolling pulses, each shift of his weight, and the thickness of his cock, hit that magic place that unravels me. Heat flashes straight down my spine, my balls draw up, and I'm straight up gulping for air as my climax roars in.

"*Ohgodohmygodrightthere*," I moan and feel the pressure barrel through, low in my stomach. My dick throbs, hot and needy and desperate. The need to come erases everything, and my vision blanks.

Thick ropes of cum shoot all over my abs, making a filthy mess between us as I lose my entire mind.

I've never experienced anything like it, and I'll surely have left bruises on Raine's arms with how tightly I'm clinging to him as he rides me straight through it. With hips slapping against my ass, his grunts grow harsher. Chasing my orgasm with his own, his jaw is tight, eyes fierce the whole time.

"Christ. *Unghhhh*. Fuck. Fuck you feel too good." He bites out the words, punctuated by dark groans, and drives into me, thrusts faltering. "This ass. You're fucking addictive." The next moment, he buries himself deep, and that's when I feel it.

His cum floods inside me, filling my ass, searing hot and so fucking good it makes my dick jerk even though I'm still coming down off my own high.

We're lost in that space where everything is floaty and glowy. All exploring touches and lips brushing over one another's. He stays inside me until he starts to soften, and I'm under absolutely no illusion, entirely aware that I'm not the same person as when I walked through that door tonight.

Raine has just given me something I could never have imagined.

And as I stare up at him, I want to do it again. With him. Possibly only him.

But that's the kind of thinking that I'm sure comes with having two mind-blowing climaxes in quicker succession than I ever thought possible.

So I swallow down the chaos of heightened emotions and feelings, and give over control. I cede any thoughts of what tomorrow might bring. As he eases out of me, we both let out a hiss at the sensation.

I can't be thinking too much about why I hate the feeling of him no longer being seated inside me.

Who knows what comes next from here. I'm going to have to figure that out at some later stage.

For now? I let myself be led back to the shower by Raine.

I'll gladly continue staying out of my head. That's the last place I want to be.

CHAPTER 30

Kayce

I've been staring at the same photo on my phone for the past twenty minutes.

The scene is snow-covered, a soft, rolling carpet of fresh powder. A good ten inches looks to have accumulated, and the shot is framed to show a clearing amongst dense pine trees.

No footprints. No animal tracks. It's an unblemished canvas. A microcosm frozen in time. The sun has just burst over the horizon, showering everything in drops of gold, and while I'm standing here looking at it on my screen, my tongue can taste it—the below-freezing temperatures, the ice crystals hanging in the air.

What does a snapshot like this represent for Raine? Why would he choose to post *this* particular picture on his social media when the man only has about half a dozen posts? It's not recent; he shared it last winter, but it's the last thing he's posted. Other than that, his social media is as barren as a rocky mountain. There are a couple of still images from his competitive years as he demonstrates exactly why he won so damn frequently—with chin tucked low, arm thrown high overhead, and fringes of his chaps swinging with the momentum of the bronc beneath him. They're images taken by a professional photographer, from events that I recognize where he won big. Then there's one of a dog and a horse by a river.

But that's it. The only peeks into my stepbrother's life. Nothing to give any clues about where he's been or what he's been doing all these years.

I really shouldn't be hovering in the kitchen at this time of the morning, sipping my coffee and stalking his Instagram. But unfortunately, I left my willpower to stop thinking about him twenty-four-seven back in his bedsheets somewhere.

My thumbs hover over the keypad to compose a message. It's driving me to distraction that up here on Devil's Peak, texting or calling like a normal person is out of the question. So, I'm doing the agonizing dance of whether to reach out to him—in the way that I'm evidently hanging by a thread to do—or if I should play it cool.

You know . . . because I'm pretty sure what we did can't ever be allowed to become anything more than just sex. Even if it wasn't that way for me, I'm certain that's all it'll ever amount to for Raine.

Oh, god. This is absolutely the reason I cannot be trusted with anything; because I destroy it. I take something perfectly good and normal, and I smash it to pieces, every time without fail. Now I've probably broken my stepbrother, who I keep imagining has high-tailed it back north of the border to put as much distance as possible between us.

Puffing out my cheeks, I close my eyes and give in to the urge, that incessant voice inside me wanting to contact him. Because even though it wasn't exactly awkward when I left the other day, it was almost dawn by the time we had both showered and recovered from the intensity of falling into bed together. When I drove back up this mountain, bleary-eyed and running on nothing but blissful post-sex hormones and cold coffee, it was about five in the morning.

We weren't really in a state to have a big ol' heart-to-heart about the fact he'd just turned my entire world upside down, and so we did what we do so well. *We didn't talk about it.*

The only problem is, I'm like a balloon ready to explode under the pressure of all the unspoken things dangling between us.

Fuck it.

I tap on the innocent little icon, the button that might spell my misery and ruin. Being ignored will be nothing new where he's concerned. If I send this message and never hear from the guy again, well, at least then, I'll know where I stand. It'll be done, and I won't have to walk around carrying any more stupid notions—no more *wondering* what any of this all means. This faulty, broken compass inside me can be patched up and, hopefully, eventually learn to be directed elsewhere.

Except, when I finally man the fuck up and brace myself to begin typing, my heart stops dead in my chest.

There's already a message there, waiting for me. Sent the morning after I left his place.

A message.

From him.

> RAINE:
> Did you get back to DPR safely?

A flurry of jitters and bouncing balls and flapping bat wings occupies the place where my stomach should be. I read and re-read the single line of text with eyes pinballing back and forth. Is there subtext here? Why can't Raine spare the use of a goddamn emoji like a sane person to let me know his intended tone? Are those words scolding, or caring, or indifferent?

My mouth is bone-dry, and I gnaw on the inside of my cheek while trying to figure out what to say in return.

If there was any doubt as to my *feelings* where my stepbrother is concerned, seeing one solitary message from him—unexpected and unprompted—has got my legs ready to buckle underneath me right where I stand in this kitchen.

I'm so fucked.

> Hey.
> Yeah, I'm back in one piece. Thanks.

Holy shit. I type the most boring, mundane of replies, promptly delete everything, and then my thumbs fly across the screen to say exactly the same thing again, before hitting send.

As I do, an anguished groan leaves my throat.

Could I sound more pathetic?

I'm not in one piece at all. I'm nothing but squishy, melted marshmallow goo on the inside, and my head is spinning. What the fuck? He wasn't supposed to message me first. He was supposed to be the uncaring and unreasonably gruff asshole.

That's how we are, and that's how things go between us.

Not this . . . I don't know what *this* is.

Raine doesn't send messages, and he certainly isn't the type of cowboy to initiate simply *chatting*. Oh my fucking god. I think I'm going to pass out with the rate my heart starts pounding, seeing that familiar row of tiny dots begin bouncing immediately. He's already typing a reply, and I'm caught between being unable to decide if seeing what he has to say is anything I can handle right at this moment, and bringing myself to walk away from my phone right now.

So, I'm left staring slack-jawed when his words arrive.

> Thought you ghosted me, snowflake.

The tips of my ears burst into flame, and my pulse does a swan dive in my neck. I can't stop to overthink this, if he's willingly replying —and not berating me for being a complete idiot like usual—I'm too far gone to put up a fight or pretend to be aloof.

I'm the least cool, most over-eager cowboy to exist.

> Sorry, I really didn't mean to.
>
> I hadn't checked my inbox . . . I promise I'm not trying to play games or anything.
>
> Honestly, I'm a little surprised you know how to use social media.

As I press send, my teeth sink into my bottom lip. Am I out of my mind? Am I allowed to be a tiny bit flirty with him? How will he take it if I tease him just a fraction? Oh, Jesus, I'm going to overthink this to death if I'm not careful. Those little dots I'm so damn rabid for all of a sudden start to flutter in front of me as I wait there, eyes glued to the screen, not daring to exhale.

> I would say come here and front up with that smart mouth . . . but I think you might enjoy that a little too much.

Oh my god. Flames lick across my cheeks, and I fully glance around my empty goddamn kitchen while clutching the phone to my chest. As if there's anyone within a hundred-mile radius other than horses and cattle to witness my simpering little meltdown at Raine's message.

I do. I like that idea all too much, I fear.

> Bet you're blushing for me, aren't you, pretty boy?

I blink, mouth dropping to practically hit the floor at the sight of his follow-up message.

Why the fuck do I feel like I want to hurl myself at him every time he taunts me like this? Christ, I don't understand it. If it were anyone else, I'd have laughed in their face and shrugged them off. But with Raine, I start squirming immediately. Wanting more of those little hints that it maybe pleases him . . . that maybe I could please him.

> No.
>
> Cowboys don't blush.

I bite my lip again. Knowing the absolute opposite of what I'm saying is true. Fuck, I've got work I gotta head out and get done around the property, and I really can't afford to spend time flirting with my stepbrother like a grinning lunatic.

> Ahh. My mistake.
>
> But they certainly do beg for my cock, oh so politely.

> Jesus . . . you were already too smug for your own good.

> I aim to please.

> Aren't you too busy for chit-chat? Thought you were Mr. Serious Rancher. All work and no play.

Raine sends a photo in lieu of a reply straight away. It's taken on horseback, looking down at the dark mane and almost bluish hue of Mist from his spot in the saddle.

That sends a bolt of bright sparks straight through me, that not only is he spending time talking with me like this, but he's carrying his phone around checking notifications immediately, even though, from the looks of it, he's riding out to check on the cattle at this very moment.

Which is what I should be doing, but it's pointless taking my phone with me.

A sudden thought of how much easier it would be if I dropped him off one of our spare radio units slides in . . . and I have to quickly shake off that ridiculous notion. What the hell would Raine want that for? He's not gonna be carrying around a radio just so he can hear my voice. Christ, I really have plunged into dangerously besotted waters and need to abort mission immediately.

> I'm excellent at multitasking.

As soon as I see those words, my cock stirs, and my stomach clenches. Because all I can think of is how it felt in the shower when he was cleaning us up after setting the charges to detonate my entire world apart . . . after fucking me senseless and watching me disappear into an orgasm the likes of which I could never have imagined was possible.

He'd insisted on being the one to do everything in the shower *after* and I was nothing more than a boneless thing propped up against the wall, watching him from behind heavy eyelids, with cartoon hearts floating in woozy circles around my head.

He kept batting my hands away if I tried to help with the soap or to make a feeble effort to clean him in return. Instead, growling at me with that sinfully sexy command to his voice. All, *let me do this for you* and *turn around, put your hands on the wall*. Before I knew it, he was indeed multitasking until I couldn't stop shaking, with strong hands stroking me from in front and behind again, and oh dear fuck, I want more of everything with him.

I'm stammering, even here on my own, unable to form words. Completely lost in the way he can have such an impact on my body despite all the distance between us.

Maybe that's what prompts me to say what I say next.

> Would you want to come up here . . . to Devil's Peak, I mean.
>
> If you can get time off work.
>
> The forecast is supposed to turn kinda soon, and if you wanted to come before this next front is due to arrive.

God. I've never suffered from nerves like this. The apprehension is so overwhelming, like I might actually crawl out of my skin if he turns me down. It's awful. The worst kind of sickness to be standing here with my heart in the back of my throat, shifting my weight at the prospect of a few words appearing on my phone from him.

That night, I told him I wasn't gonna run away—I wasn't disappearing like I have an awful tendency to want to do—but we both knew I had to get back to the ranch. There was an unspoken line that we'd accepted, one that meant I was going to leave, and we weren't exactly gonna be discussing what had just gone down between us. Or, at least, not in the immediate aftermath. So, I'm really not sure where we landed on the whole 'can I see you again' issue, or if he'd even contemplate actually coming back up here without a solid reason that doesn't involve my needing his help around the ranch like before.

I'm a microsecond from flinging my phone across the room, because I don't know if I can bear seeing him turn me down after putting myself out there to ask him that. Fucking hell, I'm such an idiot.

> You want to see me again, snowflake?

I swallow hard, fiercely trying to cool my jets and not type back the world's fastest and most over-enthusiastic *yes*. Surely, there is no greater shame than practically crawling through your phone screen to beg for your stepbrother's cock.

As I let my thumb hover over the keyboard, the thought of him, freshly out of the shower and towel-drying himself, is front and center in my mind's eye. I couldn't do much more that night than stand there, dumbstruck, while watching him, because he's just so damn nice to look at. As he wrapped the towel around his waist, highlighting that v pointing right at his dick like a beacon, Raine had caught me staring.

The deadly smirk on his lips at that moment quite possibly marked the final stage of my complete ruination.

Every scalding second of his intense focus had stayed on me, before he arched an eyebrow. *"Don't look at me like that, or I'm gonna have to take that mouth of yours again."* His tattooed hands had tucked the towel in on itself, before reaching up to tousle through his damp hair.

I didn't even have an answer before Raine stepped forward, grabbed me by the hips, and kissed me roughly. The type of branding that left me starry-eyed and struggling to remember my own name.

With all that fresh in my mind, I hit reply.

> Do you?
>
> Do you want to see me?

> I shouldn't.
>
> But it turns out I seem to keep forgetting those kinds of rules.
>
> When it comes to your pretty little mouth, I'm in the mood to ignore words like "should" or "shouldn't."

Ok, it's official. I'm grinning at my phone, and floating. Totally *not* playing it cool.

> This weekend, maybe?
>
> I feel like we need to talk.

> I'm sure I can make something work.

> Although, I'm not gonna come all the way up to the top of that mountain and turn around five minutes later. If I agree to this, you can't run away or try to kick me out in the middle of the night, pretending like it never happened.

> I won't.

> You gotta know, I'm sorry. That's not what I meant to do at all . . . I just got caught up with everything here.

> And, well, you know how phones are almost useless around this place.

It feels like he takes an absolute eternity to respond this time, with those little dots bouncing and then pausing, time and time again.

Finally, his next words come through. My eyebrows pull together immediately.

> Well, I won't take it personally next time you ignore my texts then, huh?

That makes me pause. *Ignore him?* My stepbrother doesn't talk to me, let alone text me, so I have no idea what he means.

Like a fiend, I dive into my messages—seeing there are a slew of unopened ones from that night. Between doing my best to avoid my mom and not wanting to talk to Chaos, I had tossed my phone aside while driving and didn't think to go back in and check for anything else that might have arrived. All I'd done was keep going, operating on autopilot, until I found myself slumped on his doorstep, waiting in the dark for him to return.

My next breath stalls halfway to my throat. There are texts there. From Raine. Every single one I'd ignored that night was from Raine.

What I'm seeing before my eyes . . . none of it seems real.

Even before I turned up on his doorstep, without me knowing, he'd been trying to get in contact.

Raine had been checking on me.

CHAPTER 31
Raine

By the time I pass under the hanging sign arching over the entrance to Devil's Peak Ranch, it's long after dark.

This moment right here feels like either the stupidest thing I've ever done, or the most completely *right*, and I still don't know the answer. The whole day, I've been left struggling with turbulent thoughts, an uproar running through my mind. What does agreeing to come up here mean?

Beyond sex and rampant desire and all the implausible ways the two of us aren't supposed to keep being drawn together . . . we still seem to give in.

Kayce is at the door before I've even crossed the yard, and his eyes look like they're going to fall out of his head with how wide and round they grow. He can't help himself from looking me up and down as I reach the covered porch that wraps around the impressive house. Even though he hastily swallows and tries to keep his attention fixed on my face, I see the brief flicker lower to that spot below my belt.

It shouldn't stir my blood the way it does to have his attention, but then again, there are a lot of shoulds and should-nots I've crushed beneath my tires while making the drive up this mountain. I don't know that any of my boundaries are still intact where he's concerned.

That notion alone should terrify me. It would have been the very reason a past version of me would never have considered coming in the first place.

And yet, my feet keep moving forward. Toward him.

"Hey," he says, in a voice that makes it sound like he's just run the length of this ranch. "I made dinner, but wasn't even hungry. There are plenty of leftovers if you want some?" His chin ducks low, and he slips away inside the house, leaving me to follow.

"I'm good. Ate earlier." Shutting the door, I take a moment to shed my outdoor layers, before padding after him to where he's vanished into the kitchen.

"Are you sure?" He uses the fridge door as a shield, hiding behind it, pretending to look for something. "Need something to drink? I'm not sure what we've got . . ." His words are interspersed by things clanking as he rearranges the shelves.

I have to bite back a chuckle, leaning one hip against the kitchen island. Folding my arms, I let him keep rustling around for a moment. "A soda will be fine."

When he emerges, it's with two drinks, a can clutched in each fist. He lets the door swing shut, sealing it with an elbow, before extending an arm a little hesitantly my way. As if I'm about to lunge forward with punishing steel-trap jaws and snap through bone. Those blue eyes of his waver, not meeting mine. Instead, they hover somewhere around my jawline, and he nibbles on the swell of his bottom lip.

"Thanks." Reaching out to take the soda from him, I use the opportunity to trap his fingers beneath mine. That brings his startled gaze flying up real fucking fast, widening at the unexpected contact and pressure from my hold. "Just breathe, snowflake. I'm not gonna bite."

His lip curves a tiny fraction on one side, and the faintest hint of one of those golden boy dimples makes an appearance.

"Unless you want me to, of course." I drag the can from him and click my tongue.

That seems to extract Kayce from getting caught in an internal tailspin. With a shake of his head, he slides onto one of the stools. Cracking open his soda, he tips it back and the strong curve of his Adam's apple bobs as he downs a few swallows.

I let myself just openly watch him for a moment. I mean, that's why I'm here after all. I've been drawn to these glowing embers, and there's no sugarcoating the fact that I effectively answered a booty call from my stepbrother. There are a hell of a lot of things in my life that haven't made sense, but being here with him like this doesn't feel like it falls into that category. Unlike so many of those pieces of unwanted, bitter debris that still float around inside my head, this feels . . . easy.

Strangely, unbelievably, it's as if I'm meant to be in this very spot. A natural thing to be doing on a random weekend in the middle of fall. Even if Kayce does look ready to climb the walls at the prospect of what this all might translate to.

He sets his can down, and those blue eyes dart back my way as he ruffles a hand through his hair. It's kind of adorable, really. Which is a word I never thought I'd use for anyone, especially not another cowboy, but here we are. Dropped right in the middle of a place where everything I thought I once knew has now been undoubtedly reconfigured.

"You doing ok?" I take a long sip of my own drink, bubbles tickling my nose as I swallow.

"Jesus. No? Maybe? I don't even fucking know." A hesitant laugh bursts out of him. "Why am I so nervous?"

Pushing my tongue against the side of my cheek, I let my fingers press into the aluminum for a moment before sliding it onto the countertop. There are only a couple of feet between us, and I step up to his seat at the kitchen island.

"You wanted to talk." Reaching for the front of his stool, I turn him to face me—not missing the spark that crosses his eyes, the way he hastily gulps. With one leg, I push forward between his thighs to part them. Tilting my head to one side, I drop my gaze to the place where he might be in pain. A quick check-in that it feels ok to spread his knees wider like this.

Kayce nods, not daring to breathe or take his eyes off mine. "It's—it's ok."

"Good," I murmur, wholly fixated on his mouth. "Because I don't think I could stand not doing this any longer." As I speak this time, my voice is much lower, thick with arousal.

Stooping a little, I hook a finger beneath his chin and give him one last look, with lust and anticipation scorching a blazing trail straight through my body. Lowering my head, I kiss him with all the conviction that he needs to taste coming from my mouth.

That familiar sweetness clings to his tongue, my pretty boy with sugar on his lips. As our mouths glide together, it's entirely unhurried. Not frantic, or claiming, or a kiss borne out of desperation. This time, it's languid and gentle. I press my tongue forward, and as I slip past the seam of his lips, those gorgeous little noises he makes bubble up to meet me.

Kayce slides his palms up my shoulders to circle around the back of my neck. So much more confidently than during any of the other times we've been like this. Instantly weaving his fingers into the mess of curls at my nape, he drags me down to him even more, sealing us tighter together.

I lose time in that kiss. It feels like an entire conversation, with those slow glides of exploring tongues. The sweep of my stubble rasping over his skin. Each tiny hum of relief that he delivers straight to my senses.

When I pull back just enough to search his eyes with mine, Kayce's pupils are blown out. His eyelashes flutter heavily, and I just want to splay him out on this fucking table right here in the middle of the kitchen when he looks at me like this.

"Gotten clear of all that mess inside your head now?" I let my lips remain brushed against his, wet and inviting. Famished for more where that came from.

His fingers scrape a little against my skin. With a nod, he tries to hide the cautious smile that threatens to climb all over his face.

"Then, talk to me, snowflake." Keeping my weight braced on the back of his seat, and my thighs wedged between his, I give him a moment to find his words.

That curve of his throat works, and he shifts in place a little. His touch feels so damn good. Something about having his strong fingers wrapped around my nape is far too enticing, so I drop our foreheads together and let him keep toying with the strands of my hair.

"I don't know what we're doing. Or what *I'm doing* with any of this." The words are raspy, quietly spoken with a soft gust of his breath against my skin. "But I don't want to stop, either..."

Kayce's confession hangs in the quiet room, and my heart suddenly feels incredibly fucking loud.

"Maybe I'm a little bit addicted to you. Even though I shouldn't be." He shudders as the whispered admission finally drifts between us. The pink of his tongue swipes out to run along his bottom lip, and I'm fighting the urge to chase after that motion. Wanting to pursue his mouth with more nips and bites on that plump curve of flesh.

"Well, considering I just drove to the top of a goddamn mountain..." My lips quirk as I feel him smile beneath me. God, he's so very pretty when he smiles. "I don't know what this is, but maybe that's not for us to figure out right now."

His chin moves in acknowledgment. "I can live with that."

"This is . . ." I search for a way to describe any of this goddamn confusing situation.

"Fucking complicated." Kayce finishes my thought for me.

That makes me chuckle, and I straighten up. Not to pull away from him, but so I can now slide my hand around the back of his head in return. As I seek out the warmth of him beneath my calloused fingers and palm, I see the way he softens, his shoulders drop away from his ears, and he melts beautifully at that point of contact.

"To the outside world, yes." I let my hold flex, curled around the side of his neck. "But there's nothing complicated about the fact I'm here, ok?"

Kayce stares back at me, eyes bouncing back and forth between my own. "Do you . . ." His Adam's apple dips with the effort of a heavy swallow. "Doing this—is it enjoyable for you?"

The way he stammers, all hesitancy and hopefulness, makes my cock twitch.

Letting my head tilt to one side, I study him. Perfectly cut cheekbones and freshly shaved jawline. That unruly blond hair makes him look every inch the charming golden boy.

"Is it for you?" My focus narrows on his heavy-lidded gaze.

Kayce once again does a terrible job of hiding the way a smile wants to appear. Maybe it's nerves, or maybe he's still worried about how to explain this thing between us.

"I like it when you take over," he admits. "How you just seem to understand what will feel best . . . you know?" The way he ducks his chin and says it out loud comes accompanied by a fresh wave of blush hitting his cheeks, the color deepening on those soft lips I absolutely want to see wrapped around my cock again.

When I take his mouth this time, it's possessive. A kiss filled with need, the restraint of moments before, falls away as I haul him to his feet. Hearing him confess it out loud erases any more waiting or dancing around this. We're both needing each other, and maybe it's not exactly the *talk* we should be having, but I get the feeling Kayce needs the reassurance that I want this with him more than he needs us to sit down and spill our feelings.

Neither of us are good at that shit.

But this?

Our bodies certainly know how this ride plays out.

As I fist the front of his t-shirt, he's back to being a completely flustered mess for me. And that only drives me more out of my head with craving the sight of him dissolved into a whimpering puddle. Goddamn, I love the taste of his sweet little submissive side.

"Purring for me like a slutty little kitten." I walk him backward, letting my mouth rain down a trail of hot, biting kisses along his jaw. My lips seal with his once more as we reach the lounge, and he shudders in my arms. Clinging on tight, telling me with those strong fingers that he wants everything.

"Oh god. How does that work on me every time?" As we stop in front of the massive fireplace, I ignore his protests, letting my mouth start working the side of his neck.

"Does that feel good, hmm? My golden rodeo boy likes being treated roughly," I whisper gritty words in his ear, flicking my tongue over his skin.

The groan of pleasure he gives me in return is addictive. Enough to have me keep pushing for more. "You make me want things . . . the kind of things I didn't know I could ever dream of."

"*Mmm.* That pouty little mouth has a lot of secrets you haven't dared to share, hasn't it?" Yanking his head back just a little, I steal another kiss before looking him over.

Kayce's pupils bloom immediately.

"Well, here it is, snowflake. You make me want things, too."

His breathing is shallow, chest rising and falling in quick succession against my own. "You do?"

"I shouldn't." My jaw works, knowing just how hard we both are, with our cocks straining and impatient pressed between us. "But you make me crave your perfect, sweet lips. Driving me crazy at the idea I could fuck you whenever I wanted to. To be able to slip inside that impossibly tight little hole of yours and play with you until I leave you slick with my cum."

"Oh, fuck." He gulps.

I dip my head and run my teeth up the front of his strong throat, dragging a soft bite over his Adam's apple. "Then, once you're nice and messy . . . I wouldn't stop there. No, I'd slip two fingers inside, just so I could feel how I'd owned you and marked you."

Kayce squirms against me, which only serves to ramp up the thunderous heat and billowing, carnal wanting surrounding us. The fireplace cracks and pops as his hips thrust into mine, chasing after the tiniest bit of friction.

My lips keep working his neck. I continue kissing him right over that sensitive pulse point just below his ear and feel all the vibrations his gasping moans of pleasure make. "You know I'd find that spot you love so much within seconds. It would be so easy to have you fucking up and rutting against nothing but thin air, because the feel of me stroking that sensitive little part of you . . . yeah, that would keep you on edge and swollen for me."

"Christ . . . Raine . . ." He lets out a deep groan when I suck on his earlobe.

"You'd look like an absolute dream, with my cum dripping out of you and stuffed full of my fingers, humping the bed, begging like a pathetic little thing. You know I'm an asshole, and you know I would absolutely have you whimpering. That's all it would take, and you'd give me permission to tease this beautiful body all night long."

I fucking love the way he visibly melts for me. He eats up every single one of my filthy promises, as if no one has ever had such an appetite for him—hasn't spent the time to coax him into such a panting, desperate state. I'm guessing he's never been with someone who would let him hear it, who would work him up, feeding his lust until it's dizzying and all-consuming.

Little does he know, I'm ruthless enough to leave him on edge like this, because it satisfies a twisted little part of me to know that I've got him squirming this hard, moaning quietly, and flushed using only my words.

"Is that what you want tonight? Do you want me to treat you like the needy thing you are? The rodeo star who wants to be filled with cock and pumped full of cum?"

My palm comes up to idly massage that column of his neck, the place where I love to hold him, to command him. The spot that I know makes him squirm whenever I let my fingers curl and tighten. I fucking love the way his throat works beneath my touch and the vibrations his voice makes when it's all gritty and desperate, hoarse with how turned on he is.

He hastily licks his lips, all glassy-eyed and parted lips, looking beautifully rumpled. The picture of depraved innocence.

"*Please*. Please, Raine."

I seal the moment with a bite of his bottom lip, before sucking down on the point of the sting. "Here? Or in the bedroom?"

His eyelashes grow heavy as he almost floats out of his head in front of me. "You decide."

Something swirls, hot and demanding down low in my stomach knowing that he wants to hand it all over to me like this.

"Don't move."

I make like a damn shadow, leaving him for a short moment in order to fetch my bag from my truck and returning within a few thunderous beats of my pulse inside my ears. Kayce hasn't shifted position, but his back is turned to me as he leans one elbow up on the mantel, gazing down at the fire.

He looks fucking gorgeous, swathed in shadows and firelight, and even though I know we're just indulging in something that feels good, there's also a tightening sensation inside my chest. Thoughts of where

I might be heading after this, after my time in Crimson Ridge is done, get rapidly cast aside. None of that matters right now.

Coming up behind him, I let my palms glide up his torso from behind, settling my figure against his spine. Kayce lets out a soft sound of relief, his stomach caving ever so slightly when I reach the hem of his t-shirt and drag it upward.

"You have such a stupidly pretty body." My mouth brushes over his ear before I nudge his arms to lift up, pulling the shirt free of his head. "And such a nice ass, too." Tossing the material to the floor, I guide his hands to grip the mantelpiece again. My palms roam down his front, taunting as I descend, by first flicking at his nipples and then dragging a rough touch along the hard planes of his body to reach his waistband.

"Fuck. I don't think I can take much more teasing." His head drops forward between his shoulders, and the needy thing he is, pushes back against my groin.

That makes me chuckle, and I slip his sweats and briefs down his legs, dragging them at the same time. His cock springs free, desperate and demanding attention when I crouch down and guide the bunched fabric clear of his legs.

"Do you have any idea how gorgeous you are?" I say as I shift my weight to kneel behind him.

Feeling me right there, hearing my voice come from that place beside his thigh, undoes Kayce further. I get treated to a side-on view of his toned stomach bunching and flexing as another one of those purring sounds I'm absolutely gone for rumbles out of him. His length pulses, precum coating his swollen tip.

"I—I need you." The mumble he lets out is a throaty little noise. Not anywhere near as shy as he was that first night, but just as keen for this new discovery about himself.

It's a head rush that he's trusting me . . . of all people. That he wants this with me, even after everything we've been through.

Shifting my weight forward, I drag a hot, wet line of kisses up the back of his leg. Over that dusting of hair and the indentations of muscle wrapping his upper thigh. When I reach the sensitive stretch of skin just below the globe of his ass, he flinches. A strangled noise comes out of him, and it's a sound that drives me straight over the cliff edge where Kayce is concerned.

I flatten my tongue and run a stripe along the underside of that curve, devouring the way he shudders and then lets out a feral noise when I reach his seam.

"Such a pretty little hole you have. And you just love when I tease you like this, *hmm*? Bent over like a good, obedient plaything." Kneeling behind him, I grab hold of his hips, use my thumbs to part his cheeks, and cover him with my mouth.

As I swirl my tongue over that ring of muscle, Kayce descends into a mess of curses and pleading noises. The more vocal he becomes, the more it spurs me on to work him harder. His musky scent is goddamn everything as he arches back to give me better access and lets out a string of unintelligible sounds.

"So damn sweet for me." I run a hot, seeking line of wetness over his ass, relishing the shudder it draws out of him. "Does that feel good?"

"*Ffffuck*." Kayce groans when I press my mouth forward, pushing against his entrance and massaging him. The strokes of my tongue and beard turn him from a hardened rodeo cowboy to a soft and pliant thing above me, sounding like a wet dream with all the ways he's struggling not to start incoherently begging. But I can sense it with the way he keeps shifting his weight, opening his legs ever so slightly, tilting his hips. His body chases each glide and swirling lick.

Getting to my feet, I have absolutely no right to be as pleased as I am to hear him bite back a whimpered protest. It absolutely shouldn't bring me a burning hot satisfaction to hear him respond that way when I take my mouth off him, but there's no way I'm gonna be able to hold back.

My dick is absolutely aching to feel him clench and squeeze around me again.

"Please don't stop," he pants and tries to turn around, but I nip at his shoulder, warning him to stay positioned as he is.

"Keep your hands where they are," I growl and begin ridding myself of my shirt, quickly followed by my jeans. At the sound of my belt buckle clanking and the rasp of my zipper, a flurry of goosebumps flies across those strong shoulders.

"How is it so good?" It's a soft admission, filled with open vulnerability. Craning his neck to watch me undress and grab the lube I collected from my truck. "I still can't get my head around how it can be *this* good."

His eyes are hungry, lust-blown pools, glowing with the flames reflected in their midst. As I flick the cap and pour a generous handful into my palm, the sight of each quiver in those defined shoulders of his is delicious. My strong, golden boy looking so ready to take me is an absolute headrush.

"I like seeing you exposed like this," I tell him, and those spots high on his cheeks deepen a shade at the praise in my gravely words. "So sweet, aren't you? Giving me access to do as I please with your tight little body."

When I step behind him, to start running my touch over his ass, spreading the gel around, he lets out a sigh of relief. Now, I get the view of his shoulder blades, the long lines of muscle on either side of his spine, the golden hairs covering his nape that glint a little with each flickering orange glow before us. All those dips and hard outlines shift in a delicious rhythm as his body lets me in.

With one foot, I nudge his ankles wider, encouraging him to open for me. Working slowly, I spread his ass and ease over his entrance. With a slippery touch, I stroke and fondle him, and each time I explore a little more, he shudders.

"*Ummppphhhhfff.*" Kayce makes a ragged, muffled noise once I breach him with just the tip of my finger. His teeth embed in his forearm to stifle the neediness racing forward.

"Is that alright?" I let my mouth fall to the back of his neck, sucking gently on his overheated skin.

"More." He nods. "It's—more than ok."

A dark, satisfied hum escapes me as I keep gently encouraging him to unfurl for me. First, just that fingertip, followed by a knuckle, then eventually adding another finger.

By the time he's stretched around me, letting my hand rock back and forth to work him, I can taste the saltiness of sweat coating his skin. He's blissed out, confessing all sorts of whispered words of how good it feels. Asking for all of me. Telling me he's ready. Demanding in the softest, raspiest little voice that I fuck him, to stop treating him like he's something delicate.

Bit by bit, his body relaxes. The way he still grips my fingers is unreal, especially when I graze his prostate, and he lets out a pained noise of delight. Goddamn, he's about to erupt with just the stroke of my fingers massaging him from the inside. But this time, I want his release to come at the same time as my own.

There's plenty more time to push Kayce, to see what his limits are if I try to wring him dry.

"Oh my god . . . so good," he moans, and I'm battling how painfully erect I am, how impossibly hard and downright desperate I am to fit myself inside him.

But I don't want to do anything that might add to the injury he's already dealing with.

"You gotta tell me what you can handle." I slowly fuck him with my fingers. "Can you manage on all fours for me, pretty boy?"

Kayce makes an urgent noise of agreement. "Please. Goddamn. Right fucking now." He gasps when I hit that spot that turns him inside out again.

"If it's too much, we'll change positions." Removing my hand, I guide him down to the carpet. We tumble together, all limbs and muscles, and he fits so damn beautifully beneath me. I still can't get over the perfect sight of us together like this, how it happens so naturally.

"Just—hurry." Kayce sounds like he's about to combust. All eagerness and begging rising to the surface when he makes a needy sound. And that does me in.

I lube myself up and fist at his entrance. There's a tremor that consumes both of us in time with the press of my tip forward. A low noise of relief escapes both our chests when my tip pushes just inside, slipping past that tight ring of muscle.

Fuck my fucking life. He's so hot, a furnace, as I slide forward ever so gently into his channel. Working deeper and telling him how good he is for me as I feel his body relax and adjust, allowing me to ease in gradually.

A hiss bursts out of me. "Jesus. Fuck. You're the tightest thing."

"*Ffffuuuck*. Fuck me, Raine. I need you inside."

I stroke a feather-light run of my fingertips down the length of his spine, nearly goddamn giving in—almost buckling to the need to drive forward, to ram my length all the way home. It's so tempting to succumb to his begging and pleading because it's all I want.

"Just breathe. Take a deep breath for me." I guide him through a clenched jaw, and as he follows my words, Kayce bears down.

That movement slips my cock deeper, another ravenous inch, leaving us both groaning loudly.

"Are you ok?" My brain has just flown straight to my dick, which is now fully seated inside his tight little channel, and holy fuck, I didn't know it could feel even better than before. But somehow, each moment with Kayce just keeps getting even more unbelievable, and the way he grips me is absolute torture of the best kind.

"Oh fuck," he grunts. "I need you—need you to move."

I swallow thickly and make a ragged noise. "You're squeezing me like a fucking fist. You gotta relax." With one hand now planted near his head, I let my fingers sink into the carpet to brace as much of my weight as possible. When I lean over him, it reveals firelight dancing golden streaks across his skin, and he looks so achingly beautiful.

Trembling and tempting and absolutely the kind of exquisite feeling I shouldn't be chasing after, and yet here I am, fighting the urge to start driving my hips forward.

Using my other hand, I slip it beneath his ridiculously toned stomach, splaying my fingers wide. I don't care how fierce my hold on his body might be, but I brace my weight and try to make sure he's secured against my front.

Kayce feeds me another one of those needy, panting curses. "I won't fucking break."

That's the final green light I need from him. Giving an experimental shift of my hips to slide back before pushing forward, it's not quite a thrust. Not yet. But it does leave me barely hanging on with the all-consuming need to let my dick take over.

"Yes. *Oh, ffffuuck. Yes.*"

"Like that?" I do it again, and again, and the subtle slap of our bodies together leaves me burning up from the inside.

My blood is on fire as I hold him impossibly tight, feeling every flex of his abs. We're both groaning with each rub of my length and pulse of my hips. It's not as fast and possessive as I so determinedly want, but this feels incredible. He grips me harder and begs louder, and I lose myself in fucking him with the kind of rhythm that totally erases time.

"You look so good when you shake for me, baby." I bite the bulge of muscle on his shoulder and soothe the sting with a lick.

"God . . . oh my god . . ." That quivering in his muscles intensifies, and he clenches around me tighter and tighter.

"No. *Raine.* My name is the one on your lips when you're taking my dick, snowflake." I hiss and punch my hips a fraction more forcefully.

"You feel so . . . so much . . . it's so much more this time." He's virtually whimpering; all those greedy, pleasured sounds disappear into a sequence of soft groans.

Reactions that do wonders for my ego.

"That's because my cock gets really nice and big for a little slut like you. With such a perfect ass."

Kayce moans long and low, and I slip my hand down to wrap the base of his dick. He trembles and jerks as my fingers close around his shaft. The feel of him, rock-hard, leaking, and impossibly swollen with need, turns me frenzied.

"*Fffuck.* Yes. There you go." I stroke him ruthlessly, pulsing my hips in time with each demanding pull. He dissolves into his climax with gasps, breathy little grunts, and curses. Beneath my hand, his cock pulses, spraying hot ribbons of cum. His slick release coats my fist, and he shoots everywhere while sobbing with relief. Ropes of cum hit the carpet, leaving a depraved goddamn mess.

"Look how you're taking everything. Swallowing every inch. Such a good boy for me." Dampness lines my brow, and it takes a monumental dose of self-control to see him through every last second of his orgasm first, before my own claws its way to the surface.

His body tries to arch, tries to seek out more, and I grip him tight in my cum-slicked fist as it all rushes in. My cock swells, and I vaguely hear myself biting out my own stream of curses as I begin unloading. Cum jets out as my hips stutter and bury deep, as deep as I can fucking go, because he feels unreal.

Everything is so filthy, so hot, and the silent gasp rockets through me.

"Fuck, it's too good with you." My mouth seeks out his neck, nipping and sucking and just needing the taste of him on my tongue while I'm still buried inside his body, simply unable to move. "It's always too fucking good with you."

CHAPTER 32

Kayce

Sounds of Raine banging around the kitchen drift my way. He's making coffee and breakfast for us since we both showered—reluctantly on my part at least—knowing the day wasn't going to wait. What I wouldn't give to linger under streams of hot water with his tattooed hands on my body.

There's every chance I'm not here at ground level. Instead, I'm floating around somewhere high up in the skies over Devil's Peak. Drifting along on the breeze, surrounded by the softest wisps of cloud. Ultimately hoping I don't come crashing back to earth with an awful thud.

Somewhere, somehow, I like to think there is a universe where we could rewind time to last night and drag that experience out. I certainly know my brain is struggling to think of anything except for my growing obsession, my sneaky infatuation with my stepbrother, of all people.

I'm trying my best to focus on a sequence of boring, mundane tasks. Checking emails. Picking up the radio to the Sheriff's office. Weather reports.

When really, my pulse flutters harder in my neck each time I detect a sound or movement from outside this tiny office—a cramped space filled with the debris of my dad's life here on the ranch. Each time I hear something, it further proves that Raine is *still here* . . . and while I know it doesn't mean anything, the notion that he was willing to stay long into the daylight hours, well, that sends my heart pitter-pattering a whole lot harder.

He hasn't given me any indication of what this might be for him, beyond ruining me for life with how perfectly he plays my body. Can majestic fucking be considered a thing? Pretty sure Raine owns that crown.

Jesus. I'm standing here daydreaming about whether my stepbrother wants more with me than to just fuck me senseless. Of course I am. Those words from that day down at Rhodes Ranch, the seed Brad planted, keeps blooming.

A deeper connection with someone.

What the hell is the matter with me that I've fallen for the one person who none of this can ever make sense with?

How on earth am I supposed to explain this scenario?

More importantly . . . what if I decide I do want to confess everything to the people I'm closest to, but Raine doesn't?

Tossing the radio handset back in its cradle, I scrub a palm over my face as a yawn takes over. A little bleary-eyed, I check my Instagram. The usual string of messages wait for me from my dad, which I reply to as briefly as possible while keeping him updated. He'll be a rottweiler with a bone if he thinks something might have happened at the ranch, and that's the last kind of unnecessary stress I want to cause him. A massive part of me doesn't want to let him down in any way, especially when it comes to this place. It's been his entire life. He dedicated himself to being a guardian of this land, so I'm quick to make sure he knows everything is in order.

Neglecting the part where my personal life is a complete shambles. An Etch A Sketch shaken to smithereens.

Of course, seeing Chaos's beaming presence online is unavoidable. He adores the camera, and it loves him right back. The guy knows exactly how to play the game, to put on the public persona, and turn the dial up on the brand that he's built for himself. *Daring. Breathtaking. More than a little reckless.*

It certainly helps that he's on such a hot streak of wins. I swear to god, every time I glance at his profile, his follower count has jumped up.

The latest clip he posted earlier today shows event footage from this weekend. Damn, amongst everything, and with my world being kind of entirely consumed by Raine, I'd forgotten that there was a rodeo stop nearby. Not one of the bigger ones, but still an opportunity to get out in the arena and compete for prize money nonetheless.

Seeing him soar on the back of a bronc is one thing—hell, I'm always gonna be right there being the rowdiest goddamn supporter he could ever need—but it doesn't erase the pang of all I've lost. With rodeo now being scrubbed off the chalkboard of my life, it makes it hard to come face to face with evidence that he's out there in the arena... and I should have been there too.

Pinging him a message—keeping it partly congratulations, but mostly giving him shit, because that's what we do—that familiar feeling creeps in. The sight of him doing well is a reminder of what life might have been like if I had grown up here. Chaos Hayes has always had the support of his family in doing what he does, even though I know he works impossibly hard to repay them for all they've sacrificed to help him get where he is with rodeo.

It still nags. The silent questions.

What if my mom hadn't taken me away? What if I'd grown up here in Crimson Ridge? What if I wasn't raised by a parent more interested in a bottle of pills?

But that's where it skids to a halt in my mind's eye. There are endless 'what ifs,' and dwelling on them isn't gonna do anything for me.

Also... the part whispering a little louder these days reminds me that if not for being stuck with my mom, I never would have stumbled into Raine's life.

It's only natural that thoughts of my childhood, and Mom, bring her recent efforts to get my attention slamming right back into me. As if I've summoned her, I'm just about to set my phone aside when an email notification pops up. It's an old address that I never use, and can't remember the last time I checked.

My throat tightens seeing her name on my screen. This time, it's impossible to ignore her pleading, and when I tap to open her message, the words on my screen are largely disjointed and rambling. Sent while she's high, from the looks of it. And maybe it's because I'm feeling some kind of way after the events of the past day and night, perhaps it's because Raine is only a few feet away in the kitchen, or it could just be the fact I want to shut her up for good.

I send her money.

I don't ask how much, or what she needs it for.

I refuse to be sucked into this latest round of terrible, awful circumstances she's landed herself in, because she'll only drag me down with her.

The amount I send should be more than enough to cover the type of debt I know first-hand she's capable of racking up. The kicker is that it also clears out my savings account in one fell swoop, and that's like taking a bronc hoof straight to the gut.

But what am I using it for now anyway? Those dollars were savings I'd scraped together to put toward future rodeo events I might need to travel to. Now? That dream has gone up in smoke. So I swallow down the bile and send my mom the money she in no way deserves.

I'm left standing there gnawing the inside of my cheek, with a guilty conscience that wants to take hold. Should I be a better son, go find her, check to see if she's doing alright? Is transferring her money in a cold, simplistic, transactional nature the best way to handle her addiction?

Fuck. I don't know, and it's so hard to think clearly about what might be right for her. Helping my mom doesn't always equate to a nice, neat, straight-line solution.

"Eat something." A plate is shoved under my nose, interrupting my daze of worry. My trepidation around how to best manage the woman who, beyond a doubt, is supposed to know how to take care of herself. You know, since she's an adult and all.

Raine's tattooed hands deposit the meal on top of a stack of invoices beside my dad's ancient computer. A breakfast wrap.

I feel like throwing myself into his strong arms, but there's every chance that might be the final clingy straw that breaks the mystical enchantment holding firm for now. Currently, we're co-existing in a world where we spend a night falling into bed together, and he cooks breakfast for us.

"You need to go grocery shopping," Raine reminds me. "I'm gonna go take care of the cattle; you deal with the horses. I'll catch up with you at the barn before I have to get going, ok?"

I'm a wide-eyed foal offering a speechless nod of acknowledgment. A wordless agreement to his instruction before he leaves the office as quickly as he entered. He's so good at just taking charge and doing what needs to be done. That capable nature he wears so effortlessly is something I'm finding myself attracted to more and more the longer we spend time together. A deep, shadowy place inside my heart, a crevice that hasn't ever seen the light of day, sends up another little whisper. The sort of barely-there, ethereal, crystalline shell of an idea. Delicate and fragile and forever terrified of being destroyed.

Trust him. Let him take care of you.

EVEN THOUGH I could easily get lost in the routine of daily tasks that need to be done with the horses, I've got one ear out for when Raine will make his appearance.

I've lined myself up a nice little row of poor decisions in my life—and while asking my stepbrother to have sex with me doesn't exactly feel like it should be labeled as such—I'm also chewing the inside of my cheek, unsure if he feels like it might be the worst mistake of his life.

Winnie gives me a nudge, to remind me that I shouldn't be slacking on paying her attention. Dropping my forehead against hers, I scratch a little harder up the side of her neck.

While he and I haven't exactly had a lengthy *talk* about any of this, I also can't exactly blame us for not plunging head-first into treacherous waters where *conversations* are concerned.

I'm too new to any of this, fumbling around while discovering what constitutes my sexuality. And Raine, well, he's just the type of man who isn't gonna be forthcoming with words on the best of days.

So, I focus on stupid little things like mucking stalls, cleaning water buckets, and restocking horse feed.

Because that's evidently all I can control. Who am I kidding ... there is no scenario in which my stepbrother would leap enthusiastically into a heart-to-heart about feelings and the complexities of two cowboys suddenly finding out they fit really, really well together—especially where orgasms are concerned.

Pretty sure he'd sprint for the nearest airport within seconds if I tried to put a label on this. And maybe that's all I need right now ... to stay in the bounds of *the undefined*. Perhaps being ok with enjoying hot as fuck sex, without the complications of a title or established boundaries regarding a *relationship,* is what I need. To keep it casual in order to figure out who I am in the wreckage of my former life as the smartass screw-up and bareback bronc rider.

Except as soon as I even think about my connection with Raine being nothing but meaningless fucking, my nose scrunches up.

Winnie stamps her hoof and dramatically shakes her head with a snort.

"Yeah. I hate that idea, too." I chuckle.

"Snow's here." That deep rumble of his fills the barn and sets all those wings in my stomach kicking up a notch, or ten.

When I take in the sight of him, I see tiny flecks of white clinging to the brim of his hat as he leads Peaches inside the barn.

"Sheriff Hayes reckoned it would only be a light flurry today." As he talks, I try not to outright stare at the sight of his hands running over the neck of a horse. Well, I try but fail miserably because there's something entirely hypnotic about the way his veins stand out with that sexy ink, and oh god, I really am so fucking swept up in him.

"Need anything else taken care of out here?" He makes quick work of Peaches' tack, running through the motions with a quiet, confident ease that is so immensely attractive.

I also hear it. That silent *before I leave* hovering unspoken on the end of that sentence.

"Nah, I'm good." Clearing my throat, I walk across to help out with removing the saddle and carry it to the tack room. "Thanks for the help ... you know, getting everything done today."

As I let the calming scents of leather and hay swirl around my senses, I can hear Raine's boots over the hammering of my heartbeat. Even though my eyes aren't on him, my awareness has got a laser-lock on exactly where he is at all times.

It only takes a moment, barely a second after I step back out into the main aisle of the barn, that strong hands seek me out.

Raine swoops a powerful arm around my ribs, catching me off guard, and pushes me up against the stall. His eyes glitter at me with that fierce look he gets, the one that disarms me without having to even say a word.

"*Mmm*, you didn't answer my question." The tone of his voice dips into that deeper, more raspy octave, and I feel it reach right through the layers I'm wearing. I feel his heat in more than just the places he's pressed against my body, pinning me against the wooden wall at my back.

"I didn't?" I swallow hastily, with my cock springing to life at the prospect of wherever this is heading.

"What *else* do you need taken care of?" That all-consuming gaze wanders from my eyes, down to my mouth. When he settles there, I have to fight the urge to buckle on the spot because his pupils blow out into two endlessly dark pools of night.

Gaping at him, I'm unable to form any kind of coherent thought or words. He surely cannot mean what I think he means, and why does he look ready to consume me alive right here in the middle of this barn?

"I'm about to get in my truck." He cocks his head to one side, and torrid intensity erupts in his stare when his focus lifts to the place where my cap sits underneath my hood. "So now's your chance to ask for what you need, pretty boy." With one of those strong hands, he reaches up to push at the soft material, pooling it around the back of my neck, and the sudden flow of cold air leaves a track of goosebumps peppering my skin.

A supreme level of confidence rolls off him, like he knows exactly how securely I'm transfixed. That I couldn't flee this if I tried.

He flips my cap onto the ground, then does something that leaves my body lighting up from head to toe.

Raine lifts his hat off his head, and settles it on mine.

The warmth of the felt and scent of him claims me, triumphant and powerful, just like the look of satisfaction that twitches on the corner of his lips, and he firmly presses the heel of his palm into my torso. A silent command. *Stay.*

Jesus. I've always laughed at moments when I've seen other cowboys drop their hat onto the head of a pretty girl while out at bars. I've always rolled my eyes at the clichédness of it all.

Now? Sign me the fuck up for having Raine put his hat on my head while looking at me with a special kind of depraved wickedness.

Just when I think there's no possible way I could be any more at his mercy, the unimaginable happens. A sight that will forever be written upon my psyche, further completing my utter ruination at his hands. Raine starts to move, and I realize in that split-second that this man is about to drop to his knees. For me.

I'm gasping, reaching out to fist his jacket before he can properly start to lower to the ground. My efforts stop him as I grip his collar tight. My eyes must go comically round, I'm sure of it. "Oh my god. No —you—you don't have to do *that*." Christ, I'm a stammering mess. Immediately feeling like this is supposed to be the other way around.

"Why wouldn't I?" He gives me one of those piercing looks. The kind that feels a whole lot like being scolded and yet, leaves my dick leaping to attention at the same time.

"But . . ." I wet my lips, ransacking around for the proper way to explain this. "You fuck me . . . like, isn't there some rule about who does this to the other person or something?" God, my pulse is a blur of thrumming hummingbird wings in my throat.

"There are no rules." Raine leans forward, letting his lips and stubble graze the side of my neck when he hovers right over that sensitive point. "And what if I enjoy knowing that I can make you spill cum like this, too? What if seeing you lose your goddamn mind like a little slut is the thing that gets me off hardest?"

It's official. I'm dead. Buried. Six feet below this barn.

"Holy fuck. You can't just hit me with stuff like that."

Leaning his body against mine, his weight presses our groins together, and my length rapidly hardens at all his delicious bulk covering me. My own personal Raine-blanket.

"Why? Does it make you squirm, snowflake?"

It absolutely does. His hot words leave me panting and horny, and asshole that he is, he knows it too.

"Look how flushed you get." He muses, while drawing back to study me from beneath a hooded gaze. "I bet this cock is nice and thick, greedy for the idea of being in my mouth, *hmm*. When I undo your jeans, am I going to find you weeping for me? Making a mess of yourself because you're craving my tongue to lick you all over?"

"Raine. Jesus." There is absolutely no stopping the way my hips lift off the wall and grind against him.

He leans in closer again. Voice wickedly low and tempting when his breath fans across my lips. "I wonder if you'd drip cum when I push my tongue against your tip, flick it a little until you lose your mind?"

"You're killing me." I'm already losing my mind.

"Are you aching, my sweet boy? Could I just keep talking to you like this? Maybe all I gotta do is tell you to hump my leg, and you'd blow your load all over yourself. The only thing I need to do is whisper in your ear, and you'll fall apart."

A fevered groan of desperation escapes me. Words bubble up before I can do anything to stop them. "I want—"

"*Mmm*, there you go. Tell me what you want. I like hearing you get a little extra nasty when you're horny and impatient."

"I want your mouth . . . *please* . . . let me have your mouth." Fuck me sideways, is there anything else I've wanted more than to know what it feels like to sink past his lips?

"You're such a hot-blooded little thing when your dick wants to be played with. Because that's what you like, isn't it? Someone like me, with a man's touch, with a scratch of a beard and sharp teeth, who can bruise you and suck on you properly, until your eyes roll back in your head."

Holy fuck. I nod. Rendered voiceless.

"Yeah. You don't want a soft, tender, sweet cunt bouncing up and down on your cock. You want to have your ass eaten, and balls licked, and you want to be pounded into so hard you see stars all night long."

"Raine, you're gonna end me right here. You're such a fucking asshole."

He goes in for the kill. Dusting his mouth over my pulse point. "How hard are you right now, *hmm*? How fat does this perfect," *Kiss* ". . . pretty boy cock of yours," *Lick* ". . . get when you've got a real cowboy to look after you?" *Bite*. "How desperate are you to fill my throat with cum because you know it'll please me?"

"*I am—I want—ohmyfuckinggod—*" Raine slips one hand between us and cups my erection through my jeans.

His other hand takes my jaw in a pinching hold. Shoving two fingers in my mouth, he presses down on my tongue and watches with rapt fascination as my eyes drift back with pleasure.

"That's it, feed me all those horny little sounds, snowflake. You drive me insane with the way this mouth looks, you know . . . always so ready to wrap around my cock and suck me down. Walking around with that greedy stare, like the only thing you want is for me to unbuckle my jeans and feed you my dick. To give you something to choke on until you're a drooling mess."

As he owns my every brain cell, he rocks back and forth against my tongue while using the other hand to squeeze my cock until I'm a writhing, lust-filled wreck. "Yeah, I can take this throat until you've leaked cum all over yourself, because you'd get off with just the feel of me heavy on your tongue, wouldn't you?"

My only thought is him, and how intense and dazzling and fucking hot everything feels. I make a muffled, pleading sound around those thick fingers I know can do such devious things to my body. All I can do is give him eyes that absolutely, unashamedly *beg* for him to make his next move.

If he doesn't let up, there's every chance I'm going to burst inside my jeans. Heat swirls and coils low in my stomach, and my balls throb with each of those devious words he lavishes on me.

Raine tuts at me, taking in the sight of where saliva has pooled around his knuckles, then gives me another of those silent commands. The one that keeps me pinned to the wall, putting every ounce of my focus into not crumbling to a heap and begging him to fuck me right here right now.

His hands drift down, hooking beneath the hem of my hoodie to find my belt. Impulsive passion and desire pour forward as soon as his fingers scrape my bare skin and work my jeans loose. My brain stalls at what happens next... even though I knew where this was ultimately going.

This man, with all his dark, unruly hair and sexy-as-hell tattoos, sinks down in front of me, and I'm struggling to believe we're in this position. I don't know what to do with my hands, and they end up drifting to settle on his broad shoulders as he roughly tugs my jeans low on my hips, dragging the waistband of my briefs with them.

My already hard dick fills rapidly as soon as it's freed. The sight of myself flinching and thickening while Raine's mouth is right fucking there... it leaves me more than a little lightheaded. Never in a million years did I think he'd be into this. I don't know what I expected, but I didn't understand that giving me pleasure would bring him pleasure, too.

He doesn't waste any time. Keeping his eyes fixed on mine, drilling straight through me, he wraps one hand around my length. That rough touch, the way he takes hold of me like he damn well owns every single one of my climaxes, does something to me I'm unable to explain. A wretched kind of noise drifts up, and I'm painfully aware of the way I barely hang on, narrowly avoiding starting to shoot cum everywhere from one single brush of skin-on-skin contact.

On reflex, I can't help but dart my eyes around the barn. It seems so exposed. We're right out in the open, and it feels reckless. But at the same time, I have zero interest in anything but giving him exactly what he wants. I couldn't stop this if I tried.

Raine spilling all those filthy words and winding me into a mess, leaves me ravenous to come. My orgasm claws at the base of my spine, already locked and loaded. The porny little noises I hear myself make evolve into something deeper and more primal when Raine takes me into his hot, wet mouth.

"Oh my god. Oh my fucking god."

I'm babbling straight away. My nails dig into his shoulders.

There's no stopping my hips from leaping forward. I'm embarrassed, flushed, and out of my mind with how incredible it feels. To know what a man's mouth actually feels like. Impossibly heated and able to take all of my cock in a way I've never experienced before.

Raine slaughters me. I understand now. I know, with each skilled suck and swirl of his tongue, that this isn't about me. This is absolutely something that hands over the keys to my goddamn soul so he can have that power. With each hollowing of his stubbled cheeks, as he swallows me deeper, he's ruthless in the pursuit of my climax.

That glorious sensation runs riot in my veins. Boiling, sizzling, tracking everywhere as the pressure builds down low in my stomach. I'm cut-down, no better than a shaking, incoherent stream of curses and groans. Each time his throat closes around my tip, it's accompanied by my abs clenching and my fingers scrabbling for purchase. I'm vaguely aware that I tug on his hair too hard. I push my hips forward too frantically. I say things that make absolutely no sense.

He's a bastard who set about dragging me to the precipice of my orgasm with his hot words and dirty talk, and now he ruthlessly shoves me over the edge. The seductive skill of his mouth overwhelms me.

"*Ffffuck. Umphfff.* Raine. I'm gonna—" My words of warning die on a loud, pathetic gasp.

He seals his lips around me, and hollows his cheeks, and I fucking lose it. He demands my climax, and I'm hopelessly lost in the need to be good for him, to hand everything over without a second thought. My dick throbs, swells, jerks, coating his tongue, and I'm left nothing more than a panting, moaning mess.

Raine swallows my cum. Sucks down every last drop. It's heaven being in his mouth with his throat and those swirling licks to clean me up . . . and oh fuck, the way he makes such a sexy, deep groan of pleasure vibrates right through to my balls. Before I've fully come back into my body, he's on his feet, this time taking my mouth.

Kissing me fiercely, passionately, he treats me to that hold around the front of my neck that I can't get enough of.

I'm pretty sure there isn't any part of Raine I *can* get enough of.

CHAPTER 33
Raine

My sweet boy is a pliant little thing as I draw back. Starry-eyed and looking the picture of rumpled, satiated bliss.

Wearing my hat, no less.

Exactly how it should be if I'm about to walk away from whatever is going on between us.

We're not together, which means that leaving should be easy, in theory. Ironically, it feels the absolute opposite of that. Fooling around out here in the barn, making him lose his goddamn mind, yeah, that's me being selfish.

I want to drive through that gate with the taste of him on my tongue, knowing without a shadow of a doubt that Kayce won't be thinking of anything else except what it felt like to feed me his climax.

The worst part of me wants to imprint myself on him. A notion that makes absolutely no goddamn sense considering who we are to one another. Yet, I can't deny that I'm feeling all sorts of weirdly possessive where my *stepbrother* is concerned. As if Kayce is gonna walk straight out of here and find some other cowboy to mess around with. The kind of thinking that immediately grates on my nerves, because he can do as he pleases, and owes me nothing.

Except, every fiber of my being hates the idea of him giving those eyes, that mouth, to anyone else.

While at this particular moment in time, things between the two of us worked out, after I leave it's all gonna change. I know that our lives are largely going to return to how they were before. Especially once I leave Crimson Ridge.

"*Umm* . . ." Kayce blinks slowly at me, looking like he's only just found his way back to his body.

"Cowboys don't blush, huh?" My lips twitch as I take in the sight of the bright red spots on his cheeks.

His blue eyes are damn near shimmering in the light filtering into the barn, and he bites down on that bottom lip.

Plucking my hat back off his head, I set it on my own and catch that faintest hint of his scent that comes with it. As he tucks himself away, I walk over to where I'd tossed his cap aside, allowing myself a wry hidden smile since he can't see my face. Handing it back to him, I manage to suppress that curl wanting to cling to my lips, but kinda enjoy how floaty and light I feel on the inside right now.

Even if I'm goddamn hard as stone after how hot that was.

"You don't need . . ." His words drift off with a lingering question as he looks at the outline of my dick straining behind my fly.

At the feel of his eyes on me, my length kicks, but I ignore it. "As tempting as that prospect is . . . I'm ok." Shaking my head, I readjust my hat. I don't need him to reciprocate anything right now. Remembering how he came undone for me will be a particularly pleasurable memory to replay later on when I'm alone.

"But . . ." Kayce is the picture of confusion.

"Trust me. I got what I needed."

His lips twist, still looking uncertain as all hell, but he at least gives me a little acknowledgment. "Ok."

"There were only a few light flakes of snow when I was coming back in." I duck a glance at the open doors down the far end of the barn before looking back his way. "The mountain crew checked in with you this morning?"

He nods at me and clears his throat, blinking away the fog. "*Uhh.* Yeah. They said the snow wasn't gonna be a problem today."

"Alright." Dipping my chin, I know I gotta get my ass back to work, and this is just how this has gotta be. "Remember, you need groceries.

Don't let me catch you forgetting and finding out you're stuck up here living off nothing but fucking instant noodles for weeks."

Something flickers across his face for a brief second, but then his lips curve into a grin, followed by a shake of his head. "Promise. I'll make a trip to town."

With a jerk of my chin, I let him know I'm starting to walk to my truck, not exactly sure if he's gonna follow, but it makes something glow a little warmer in my chest when he falls in step with me.

"So . . . I'll see you at the thing Hayes is putting on?" I venture as we cross the gravel yard. While I don't know if he has thought about the fact we're still going to be running in the same circles, it feels like I gotta rip the bandage off. No sense in pretending we won't be seeing each other in public, where I can't exactly pin him to the wall and nibble on his ear until he starts squirming.

"The Halloween party at the Hog?" Kayce laughs, and he's still got a dreamy kind of grin on his face when he pauses and watches me walk around the other side to the driver's door. "Please tell me you're gonna dress up. Do they make delicate little fairy wings and a tiara to fit someone your size?"

I let my tongue run over my lower lip and study him from across the roof of the truck. "My size, huh?"

Kayce's blush deepens.

Waving his hand in my direction, those long lashes of his flutter and he shakes his head before tucking both hands into the front of his hoodie. "God, you are too smug for this time of the day. I don't even need to know what time it is to know I haven't had nearly enough coffee to deal with you being cocky."

As I open the door, I watch him dig the toe of his boot into the gravel, then dart a hasty look up to meet my eyes.

"Thank you for coming up here." His shoulders slump a little, and I know he's dropping back into that uncomfortable place—the one where talking about events and the Hog means that we've suddenly collided with the reality of the outside world. "Even though I know..."

It sure as shit looks like he's backpedaling now on all those sentiments about enjoying how *good* it feels to be together.

"We don't have to call this anything, Kayce," I say. Keeping my focus narrowed on him.

Kayce gnaws on his bottom lip. "I think the only thing we can call this is *complicated*."

"You sure got that right."

"Raine—when we're down at the Hog—"

My brows knit together. Yep, there it is. Kayce once again realizing he's in limbo where opening up about his sexuality is concerned. There's nothing I can do; it's gotta be his journey. "Don't worry. It's fine. I'll keep my distance. You don't have to stress out about any of your precious rodeo friends finding out anything." Yeah, that probably comes out with more snarl to it than I intended, but I never promised I was good at *talking*.

"Wait . . . you're upset with me." Big blue orbs stare my way.

A heavy sigh leaves my chest. I should have known that he'd freak out before I'd even left the ranch. "I'm really not. But I have to go. And I don't need to be caught in the middle of some dick-induced crisis you've got going on."

"You know I didn't mean it like that."

"Then what, Kayce?"

His Adam's apple dips. "I just . . . I don't know if I'm ready to tell anyone about *anything*. I haven't even properly told Chaos, or Brad, or even my dad about my knee. What am I gonna do, drop a bombshell that I'm finished with competitive rodeo, and then tack on the end that I'm gay?"

"Well, I'll make it real easy for you," I grumble.

"Raine . . . please, it's not that I'm embarrassed or anything."

"Sure seems like you might be." I raise an eyebrow at him.

Kayce is already on the move, crossing to my side of the truck. "Look . . . can you just put yourself in my shoes for a moment? I'm trying to get my head around a lot of really big fucking changes right now." There's the faintest hint of a tremor in his voice, and I hate that for him. I hate how similar we are in that regard. We've both been fucked up from day one when it comes to learning how to trust others.

Tilting my head to one side, I reach out and cup his jaw. Lifting his focus to meet my own, I give a little shake of my head. "You're right. I'm sorry."

He goes completely still. Lips parted.

"Don't act like that's the weirdest thing to ever come out of my mouth." It's a rough grunt I offer, doing my best.

"You just apologized. Just like that."

"Yeah, and?"

"You never . . ." From how shell-shocked he looks, it certainly puts into perspective how long we've been out of each other's lives. He doesn't know the version of me who has had a chance to do a little bit of healing. There are still a lot of scars there. I'm still the world's worst person at knowing how to put crap into words . . . but I'm better now than I used to be.

"When we were younger?" Lifting one shoulder with a shrug, my chin dips in acknowledgment. "No. I certainly wasn't good at anything except being an angry asshole. I'm still not good at shit like this, either," I add.

Kayce works down a swallow. "Ok, but I just need you to know, I'm not ashamed. Especially not when it comes to you, or what we're doing."

While he might be saying those words, with all that golden boy sincerity, I saw the way his eyes flickered along the length of the aisle when I was undoing his jeans. I saw the fear lingering there. Still nervous that someone might see, even though we're on the very top of a mountain, and miles from any other people. It doesn't piss me off, but I'm still not sure if Kayce is ready to actually embrace himself.

If he's worried about someone catching us together all the way out here in the wilderness, he's gonna be crawling out of his skin, even being in the same room as me at The Loaded Hog for a fucking Halloween party.

Maybe that's what drives me to push him just a little harder. One last reminder of the fact he asked me to come up here. A not-so-subtle nudge to point out that *he* was the one who turned up on my doorstep in the dark that night. "Oh, so you're not ashamed, huh?" I pinch his chin harder. "Not even when you're pleading with me to pump you full of cum? Not embarrassed by all the slutty, needy little noises you make for me?"

That gives me the prettiest version of Kayce. The one where he flushes all over when I give him a whole extra dose of sternness in my voice.

"N—No." His stammering protest is met by a smirk that, yeah, is definitely smug, knowing how easily I can affect him.

And that's what I'm gonna have to hold onto. Because the next time we see each other, there's every chance that he'll pretend I don't even exist.

Angling my head, I brush our lips together. It's a soft press against his mouth, a hint of wetness coating his lips, a last taste of his sweetness before I let him go. Before I slide into my truck and start the engine.

"Bye, snowflake."

CHAPTER 34

Kayce

"Slutty vampires?" Chaos points between me, Brad, and Flinn as we come up to the bar.

Halloween at The Loaded Hog is in full swing, with nearly everyone wearing some kind of costume. They've gone all out on the decor, with pumpkins stacked outside, fake spider webs hanging from almost every surface, and a smoke machine puffing gusts of vapor illuminated by red lighting.

"Slutty *eighties* vampires . . . to be precise." Brad gestures at our outfits, which are a loose collection of leather, chains, and fake earrings. He leans a forearm on the bar, then pokes at the place where bright crimson spills down Flinn's chin—the same as we've all painted on for tonight. "Fortunately for your little pork chops, we already stopped for a snack before coming."

"That hair needs its own postcode." Chaos snorts at the hairband-worthy long, curled wigs the other two are wearing, then smirks at my spiked-up hair. "Always a pleasure to have the Lost Boys in the house."

"How the fuck did you stuff Knox into a pig onesie? Did you have to tranquilize him?" Flinn barks out a laugh when the other member of the *Chaos Twins* makes an appearance carrying stock from the chiller. He's in a suit to match, with the hood including floppy ears pulled over his head and everything.

"I'm very charming. Not to mention, I make the cutest piglet you ever did see, huh? Who wouldn't want to be hog-tied by this tonight?" Of course, he jumps and spins around in order to shake his ass in our direction, wriggling his hips to reveal the sight of his little coiled tail.

"You're something, all right." I shake my head at his antics.

"Good to see you in the land of the living . . . or maybe, non-living tonight." He winks back at me. "How's the knee?"

"Strong enough to chase you down and empty out those sweet piggy pig veins of yours, no problem." With a flash of a smile, I really fucking hope that tonight isn't gonna be endless questions about topics I'm not yet brave enough to go public about.

Which makes the back of my neck immediately flame underneath the high collar of the jacket I'm wearing, because I haven't seen the one person I've been on high alert for since walking through those doors.

"What's your choice of poison tonight, bloodsuckers?" Chaos asks, as he slides a tall glass of soda my way. He makes a show of adding a flourish of red syrup to it with a cheeky grin.

Flinn ticks off one finger. "We need something 'fruity and strong as shit' for the two fairies. Their words, not mine."

"They're witches." Brad shoves at his shoulder. "And the fact Briar has gone to the effort of all that green face paint, means that I'm sure she'll kick your ass if she hears you disrespecting her witchy powers."

"Sorry." Flinn huffs and rolls his eyes, before ticking off a second finger. "Fruity shit for the pink witch and the green witch."

Chaos is already starting to mess around with making something, then looks across the room at the bar leaner where Briar and Sky look like they've hijacked a pair of flying monkeys for the evening and taken a direct flight straight out of Oz.

"Jesus. You'd have never thought old man Rhodes would put in an appearance at something like this." He starts shaking up a potent concoction. "What the fuck is he meant to be?"

Brad smiles and steals some candy from the pumpkin bucket set out on the bar. "Angry ice hockey player sent to the penalty box." As he pulls the wrapper off, he gestures a circle at his face. "Hence the black eye . . . the permanent scowl is just *au naturale*."

To be fair, Lucas Rhodes dressing up for anything would mean the entire world was probably about to descend into an apocalypse. For him to even set foot in here tonight, speaks volumes to exactly how down bad he is for the woman swathed in pink and glitter tucked at his side.

"And Stôrmand Lane mugged a pirate and stole his outfit, I'm assuming?" Chaos grabs Brad and Flinn's beers when they point out what they're after.

"Something like that. All I'm hoping is that none of us have to listen to him making dumb jokes about *plundering* or Briar's *bounty* . . ." Brad pinches the bridge of his nose and shudders. "Otherwise, I'll put out a distress signal for you to shut this place down immediately."

Chaos shakes his head with a wide grin splitting his face. "Deal. No one needs to be scarred for life by him going full method acting tonight. This shall remain a horny pirate-free safe haven." He swirls a finger in the air, encompassing the room. Then gets called away to serve other customers waiting.

As we carry the drinks over to the bar leaner we've settled on for the moment, the two witches have somehow worked their magic and convinced their cowboys to join them out on the dancefloor.

It's almost a relief, even if temporary, to be able to avoid unwanted conversations. I'm grateful for Brad, that he's kept our conversation private. Even though Flinn is his everything, he hasn't brought up my revelation about being attracted to men, or being gay, and he's not pushing me to talk about it either until I'm ready. That's just the type of friend he is. I swear, the guy has a sixth sense for knowing what others need.

But the lingering unease still sits there. My knee. My rodeo career. It all resembles a tangled ball of twine coated in spurs, and even though I'm not straight up lying to my friends . . . am I?

By avoiding telling them any details, does that amount to the same thing?

And right there amongst all of that is the even more precarious truth of how far things have changed between me and Raine. The fact I'm so swept up in him. Even just the thought of his name and whether I'm going to come face to face with the subject of my ever-increasing adoration curls something low in my stomach.

"Wanna head outside with us for a bit?" Brad leans closer to lift his voice at me over the top of the music.

"Nah, you two go. I'll stay here and keep an eye on their drinks." I shrug the two of them off. As much as Brad and Flinn are always the first to include others—not to mention that Brad is a social fucking butterfly and would probably wither away without having the opportunity to be surrounded by people—they could use some time for themselves.

I tell myself it's not because I'm on the lookout for Raine. I try to play it cool, and not feel a certain kind of way that he hasn't been in contact since leaving Devil's Peak the other day. What was I expecting? To have a steady stream of messages from him? He probably got back to work and had god knows what waiting for him to handle.

Don't I know it. Ranching equals endless problems. If it's not the horses, it's gonna be the damn cows, and where Sunset Skies Ranch is concerned, they've got guests to accommodate on top of all that.

So, I sip my drink and lean on my forearms to people-watch.

Definitely *not* studying every broad-shouldered, tall guy with dark hair and trimmed stubble who might possibly be my stepbrother beneath their costume. I'm absolutely *not* glancing at hands and forearms to see if I can catch a flash of his tattoos to let me know it's him hidden behind a mask.

Christ, is he even gonna actually come tonight? The longer I'm here, the less it seems like the type of shit Raine would willingly put up with, not without a good reason to. Honestly, he's no different than the likes of Luke and Storm, who would never have been caught dead at a Halloween party in all their years living in Crimson Ridge. And now here they are, in the middle of a crowded dance floor, with their girls wrapped up tight and hearts in their goddamn eyes.

An unfamiliar feeling stirs deep in my chest, a flicker like a candle that might get snuffed out with one false move. Maybe that's what I want... or could let myself believe that I deserve?

For too long, I've been caught in a place where I didn't think I could ever truly let anyone in. Why risk it? Why voluntarily put yourself through heartache when, at the first sight of my painfully cracked edges, they'd want to leave? Hell, my own flesh and blood didn't want me around—the one person who was supposed to, but chose a different place to focus her twisted brand of love—so surely no one else could ever find me worthwhile of the effort to keep close.

That's when I feel the fine hairs on the back of my neck stand on end. It's incomparable, the knowledge that Raine's eyes are on me, and it might sound like madness but it's as if every cell in my body can *feel* him before I even see him.

Scanning the crowd to take in all the costumes, the flickering lights, and the billowing red smoke weaving around people's ankles like mischievous ghosts... I don't find him.

Until I turn toward the furthest corner of the bar.

Our eyes lock, and goosebumps fly. When I finally spot him, the man is enough to make me feel like I could damn near float across the room, drawn to his magnetism rippling through the crowd. An alluring, hooded stare is accentuated by face paint—giving him darkened black pools around his eye sockets. It's a devious look, straight from the underworld, and as I wet my lips, still staring, I notice he's wearing those faded black jeans that seem custom-fitted to his body, with a black collar shirt.

Holy fuck, he's hot.

I've never been struck immobile, floating in time where the sight of a man has taken my breath away at first glance. I mean, I've come to realize I'm finding Raine endlessly attractive, forever being sideswiped by how gorgeous he is. That in itself certainly isn't a new revelation.

But this?

I'm transfixed. Glued to the spot. Mesmerized at the sight of his frame hugged by all that midnight black and how he looks capable of stopping my heart at will. Simply seizing it from my chest with a single glance.

Raine watches me for a moment, but it's hard to see the exact expression on his face between the pulse of lights and people getting in the way. Something knowing twists on his lips, and he turns back to lean both forearms on the bar. It's an open invitation, laid out for me to either take it or walk away, and I know right there in that thud of my pulse and tightening in my chest what my decision is.

Glancing back at the bar leaner, then over at the dance floor, I catch Luke's attention. When he nods, I point at the drinks waiting for the four of them. He bends to speak into Sky's ear, before she shoots me a bright smile and waves. Once they're headed over, I make a show of my empty glass and slink my way to the bar. Feeling his penetrating stare with every step, utterly helpless to resist his allure.

Right now, I'm the rabbit willingly stepping into the snare.

When I get a few steps from the bar, I dart a glance at the *Chaos Twins* in their pig onesies, both of them too busy slinging drinks to notice us. I hate that this is the first thing I think of, that I hesitate rather than feeling like I can stroll right up to Raine and be with him.

I'm tongue-tied and fumbling around inside my own head before I've even gotten close. Which is ridiculous; I gotta shake this off because it's just talking, and that's something I do easily whenever I'm here.

My eyes do a quick once over, just a tiny, brave look as I close the final few feet to stand by his side.

Goddamn, does he have a nice ass.

I clear my throat, feeling like a skittish foal when I set my glass onto the bartop, slipping in just close enough that we brush shoulders. At that point of contact, it's like my blood starts damn well singing beneath my skin. Everything goes tingly and bright upon catching a glimpse of his scent.

"Demon?"

"Archdemon, actually." Raine tilts his head my way, voice low and gritty. "Here to collect your soul."

My dick is already starting to stir as that masculine hit of how good he smells weaves through my senses. Curling a wisp of a finger beneath my chin and placing an invisible hold around my neck. He's gotta damn well know that he has me in a chokehold already, turning up here, looking like *that*.

"Ah, well. *Vampire*." I touch my tongue against my incisor, before gesturing up and down my body. "So, you're out of luck . . . I don't have one."

His lips twitch as his gaze rakes over me, and damn him, that leaves my pulse jittering. I could never have pictured Raine at a Halloween party, but goddamn, I can't get over how unbelievably sexy he looks.

"This is..." With one hand, I swirl around my eyes, imitating the face paint he's got on.

"All Tessa's doing." He makes a groaning noise. "Apparently, I'm here so she can live vicariously through me while being at home pregnant... or some shit like that."

Before I can reply, just as I'm opening my mouth, our little bubble is unceremoniously burst.

"*Hiiiiii.*" A loud, tipsy voice slides between us. We're overrun by a group of girls sporting crooked halos and fluffy wings, all in various stages of undress—or maybe that's the entire point of their translucent-white costumes—and long eyelashes framed by a thick caking of glitter bat my way. The majority of her friends crowd the bar, giggling while I hear one trying to get the attention of a *little piggie I'd like to fuck* as she presses her tits together. On the other side of the girl swaying in front of me is a matching outfit of minuscule proportions belonging to a girl who is her clone.

Both blond. Both sporting heavy fake tans. Both one shot of vodka away from a nipple-slip.

Raine turns, leaning his elbows back on the edge of the bar, and lifts an eyebrow my way. There's absolutely nothing I can discern in his gaze. Does he want this? What would he normally do on a night like tonight when there's a girl confidently rocking up to him with lust in her eyes?

Obviously my expression, or lack of ability to form words, must give him a signal that I don't think I intended to give. But also, leaves me stranded in a place where I can't do anything right here right now. This is a disaster, and once again, I've fucked everything up because he turns that handsomeness to focus on the girl wearing little more than a bikini.

She's overtly hitting on Raine. Reaching out to touch his arm while nibbling her lip. And I don't know how to handle any of it, because we're not together.

Fuck this. Jealousy slithers up my spine. A wild unspoken protest swirls hot and demanding inside my chest. Bitterness lines my throat as her fingers slide higher to play over his bicep. I'm not giving an ounce of attention to the girl in front of me who is still yelling over the music, far too many drinks in, to notice that my eyes are fixed elsewhere.

Raine must surely feel me watching?

He can't possibly go back to being the aloof, cold-hearted asshole who ignores me?

Not now. Not after everything we've shared.

However, my collision of thoughts and inability to know what to do at this moment are sideswiped. A soft hand slips into mine, tugging to lead me into the crowd. The drunk angel skips ahead, dragging me to follow as she shouts over her shoulder at me.

"C'mon, sexy. Dance with me, and then maybe I'll let you bite me later."

CHAPTER 35
Raine

I'm not interested, and Kayce should know better.

Those eyes he's giving me. Blue pools muddled with confusion and bitterness at the prospect I might be giving my attention to some girl who is too busy hiccupping to hold a real conversation.

Only, that's where his whole problem starts and ends.

Kayce doesn't know how to get from the place where he's stuck right now, hiding from the truth about so many things, to feeling safe enough to take the plunge into the unknown.

It's almost poetic really, that he's found himself being dragged into the middle of a crowd by a girl—the likes of which most dudes in here tonight would be drooling after. The type of head-turner, stepped straight off the pages of their fantasies. When all of two seconds ago, he had that curiosity and eagerness fixed on me . . . us. For a fraction of a moment it seemed he might take another step forward, to finally move toward his true ambitions in life.

Which is why I have to grip my soda and let the girl hanging off my side blabber on. It'll serve him right to get a little wake-up call in the form of a trashy buckle bunny, the exact type he should know not to get accosted by. A girl dressed in . . . fuck knows what you'd call it, but it looks like she lost the majority of her dress on the way to this party, but there's a crooked halo involved, so I suppose it counts as a Halloween costume.

Not that I'm judging any of them for what they wear. They can do as they like, just take it somewhere that doesn't involve brushing against me under the misguided notion that it'll *stimulate* my interest in this conversation.

Over the top of my drink, I see the blond swing around his neck. Trying to tug him down to her, and Kayce is still pretending to be the cowboy who does shit like this. The guy who dances with *girls* and dates women. All those invisible strings are pulling on his limbs, puppeteering him along into this charade of grinding together on a dance floor, and as she turns around to start rubbing her ass all over him, guiding his hands to settle over her bare stomach... yeah, that's enough.

I'm done watching him flounder.

This was always gonna be our biggest hurdle. Kayce has never been able to face up to reality, even when it's staring him right in the face.

So he's gonna let that girl push her ass against his cock, he's gonna put on a performance that makes it seem like he's interested, and I'm the only one who knows he won't get hard for the likes of her.

Convincing the drunk friend beside me to bug somebody else isn't difficult. So, after I've sent her twirling away, I make my exit and find a clear path to escape outside. The place is packed, which, in a lot of ways, makes it easier to ghost into the crowd. Especially since almost everyone here is wearing costumes that would involve doing a double-take to figure out who lies beneath the disguise.

Slipping into the shadows, I vanish around the back of the building, pulling out my phone as I do so. Out here, it's staff parking and stacked beer kegs, and I'm almost surprised there aren't already more than a couple of people in this spot getting busy.

As I swipe open my texts, I drag my palm over my stubble. This is gonna be the real litmus test, and I'm exactly the kind of asshole that wants to see how far he'll go in denying who he is.

With full knowledge that Kayce has to make this decision—he has to be the one to take the leap—I give him just enough of a push to see how flimsy those cords holding him back might be.

> She's got a pretty mouth.
>
> Bet it won't get you off, though.

Leaning up against the wall, I watch as it only takes a few seconds for the message to be read. And only another breath for Kayce to start replying.

SNOWFLAKE:
Where did you go?

> Does it matter?

Of course it does.

> Doesn't seem like you need me to hold your hand in there.
>
> Already got yourself a nice pair of tits, horny and revved up to take care of a rodeo star.

His reply takes longer this time. Starting and stopping. There's a little quirk wanting to hijack my lips as I imagine him trying to discreetly text me. Attempting to hide the words on his phone screen while he's still dancing with a girl he has zero interest in. All because that's what Kayce Wilder, the perfect little Crimson Ridge buck, should do.

God. Just, don't be a dick.
I didn't want to be rude to her.
Besides, it wasn't like you were saying no to that girl with her hands all over you.

Ahh, so he was jealous. That possessive creature lurking inside my chest boasts a little louder, knowing his first reaction was to see red.

> So what are you gonna do about it?

> I could be out the back in the dark with a pair of those angel wings already tossed on the ground and a sweet moan in my ear.

> Does that bother you, snowflake?

His response is immediate.

> Yes.

> Sure seems like you're not worried.

> Like I said, I won't make things too difficult for you.

> So this is me, keeping my distance, just as you asked.

> Where are you?

> Just . . . don't leave.

> Please.

My chest squeezes, seeing that word come through. I really, really should be hardening myself against this. There are a million other places I could be right now, and I absolutely shouldn't be trying to force some sort of admission out of Kayce. But then again, when he's sweet and gives me this side of him, it tugs on something that has no right to exist in my stomach.

> You didn't go, did you?

> I'm still here.

The text has barely been sent when I hear a corresponding ping. Kayce hits me like a whirlwind, bursting through the night, grabbing hold of the front of my collar.

He's got a wildness about him, a glimmer in his eyes that looks even more feral than the creature beneath my ribs. Shoving at me, he lets out a little growl. A frustrated, gritty noise in the back of his throat.

"Fuck you."

Before I can say anything in reply, he slams our mouths together.

Kayce's fists tighten, holding me in place as our tongues slide against each other's, a hot, wet, desperate chasing of that connection. Everything seems to crackle in the air around us. I don't know what the fuck it is about kissing him, but there's a special sort of electricity to it, the kind that makes my pulse spike as high as these mountains and blood thrum like thunder.

Spinning us around, my bulk slams him against the wall. Shoving one hand into the back of his hair, I use the other to hold his jaw. There's nothing but a sloppy, hungry urgency to take his mouth and meet his frenzy with my own.

"Gonna be a reckless little slut?" My voice is raspy, heavy with need. "Right here, out in the open, pushed up against the wall?" I bite his bottom lip to the point it'll definitely sting. Tasting that cherry sweetness on his tongue and a slight tang, the chalkiness of face paint, as I suck on that spot.

"If that's what it takes." He breathes choppily. Still clinging to my shirt.

"Don't know what you're talking about, pretty boy." I lick at the pouty curve of his bottom lip. "Thought there wasn't anything... that we weren't gonna be anything."

"Well, maybe I changed my mind." His face is hidden in the shadow, but I see the way his eyes are heavily lidded. There's a certain kind of resilience in his voice. A far cry from the wavering I've noticed there in the past.

"How do I know you're not gonna flip on me again." My fingers descend to flex against the front of his throat. As I shift my hold, a delicious vibration comes through beneath my touch.

In that split second, he hums out a noise. Part demand, part relief at the feel of my mouth covering his, then I feel him start to slide down the wall. I'm dumbstruck for a second. Kayce wants to blow me out here?

"What are you doing, snowflake?" I study him, letting my hand cup his jaw. Watching as he lowers himself and slides his hands down until they hit the top of my belt.

"I want to—to prove to you. I'm not ashamed of being with you."

His throat sounds thick with lust, and there's something more meaningful behind those words.

He's prepared to get down on the hard gravel and give this to me, and that in itself means more than any endless weakness I might have for his lips to be wrapped around my cock. "Your knee," I warn.

The cowboy he is, Kayce's jaw tightens with determination. "It's fine."

Oh, my sweet boy. I see it, and feel it in his energy, just how sincere he is in wanting to demonstrate his willingness, once and for all.

I follow him down, crouching in front of his face, hooking his bottom lip with my thumb as I do so. He makes one of those tiny whimpering noises of frustration at me, and I'm about fucking ready to get this over with.

"You want me to take this throat where *anyone* could see? Want me to use you like my personal little fuck toy? Thirsty for a belly full of my cum?"

His breathing grows ragged.

After a few seconds of panting breaths echoing in the darkness, the momentary battle Kayce wages behind those blue eyes finally calms. He nods against my hold.

"I know I'm fucked up for saying this out loud . . . punch me in the face if you want, but . . . I want *this*, not in a way that's hidden. I want us. And I want what we have to be more than just a random hook-up."

Hauling him back up to his feet, I have him pinned against the wall with a knee shoved between his thighs in a heartbeat and absolutely fucking devour him. Every single one of those words feels like they burst into crackling, soaring flames, and I slant our mouths together so I can taste each moan and savage noise my boy gives in return.

Kayce brings his hands up to tangle in my hair and lets me have every ounce of that confession as it bursts onto my tongue.

Behind us, I hear some high-pitched giggling "*Shhhhh*. Oh, shit. I think this spot is taken."

It happens as quick as a bolt of lightning. Kayce tenses up, turning rigid beneath me.

I keep on slowly kissing him, easing up on the intensity, but tighten my hold on his neck and the front of his shirt. As I leisurely make out with him now, in between strokes of my tongue, I give him the reassurance he needs. "Don't worry." A soft kiss drags his bottom lip so I can suck on it briefly. "They won't be able to see you." Another kiss covers his jaw. "All they would have seen is the back of me."

"Ok." He lets out a shaky exhale.

A satisfied hum rumbles out of me. "Did you drive?"

"Yeah."

"I'll drop you back here to pick your truck up tomorrow."

"Wh—" I shut him up. Cutting off his words with a deep kiss, one that I could so very easily get lost in. The kind of pleasurable hit of *him* that reaches straight down to my toes. Once I've temporarily satisfied my craving, I pull back and swipe my thumb over his wet bottom lip, giving him a stern look through the darkness.

"You're coming home with me tonight."

CHAPTER 36

Kayce

"Come here."

Raine's voice is a low-pitched command filling the front seat of his truck as we pull out of the parking lot.

My heart is in my mouth, and I'm almost certain my brain has melted completely.

I glance at the length of bench seat between us, illuminated in a slow-moving strobe effect of streetlights as we drive by. My eyes tick up to him, filling the space at the opposite end, with one hand leisurely caressing the steering wheel. He has an arm hooked up high on the back of the seat and looks every inch a rodeo king.

Raine wants me to nestle there at his side.

For some reason, that sends shivers flying everywhere.

His eyes remain on the road, but he adjusts his weight and clicks his tongue. "There ain't a question mark on the end of that. Come. Here."

The truck's engine purrs into the night as we drive away from town, headed toward the ranch, and it feels like my chest is vibrating at the same speed, caught someplace between being so lost in him and not being used to this sort of treatment. I huff out a little protest, half-heartedly grumbling as I inch my way over to join him.

"I'm not a girl." My complaint is wafer-thin. I like it far too much for my sanity as soon as his warmth and big, strong arm becomes a safe place to curl into.

"Oh, that's right. You're a cowboy who absolutely, definitely, under no circumstances would ever blush... because that's not *manly*."

I pinch the side of his stomach as he treats me to the faintest hint of his dry sense of humor.

"Shut up." Wriggling around a little to get more comfortable, I hook one foot up on the seat and let my body sink into his. Reclining against him, while he drives, and music plays through the stereo. It feels like we've done this before. And, of course, there have been countless times we've been stuck in a vehicle together; if anything, I have too many memories to count of us driving somewhere while trapped in silence.

Yet, this particular moment feels... comforting.

I mean, my blood is still on fire after that kiss outside the bar. I'm a riot of need and hunger running rampant through my veins. But I also wouldn't trade this, being tucked in this spot right here, in the crook of his arm, for the world.

There's an allure hidden in this scenario, the front seat of his truck, of enjoying being with Raine in the quietness. As much as the times when he steals my breath and torments my body in the most delicious and enthralling of ways.

When we pull up at his place, that hammering of my pulse, a flurry of strikes against an anvil, has intensified to the point I feel giddy. Have I ever felt this way? This incredible? With this kind of liquid gold pouring straight into my veins?

I can't believe this is happening, and it's as if Raine can read my mind. When we move to get out of the truck, he's right there waiting for me. Not only does he move like lightning, but without any preamble or explanation, he reaches for my hand.

I'm securely anchored by him—our fingers threaded together—and I shiver at the warmth of his touch intertwined with my own. My eyes fix on that spot as we walk up the steps, and with every passing second we climb higher; my heart races into the starry night sky above us. Captivated by the sight of the place where my hand joins with his... the veins, his ink, those corded muscles of his forearm revealed where his shirt has pushed back. It's a possessive kind of hold on me, one that leaves an internal battle going on to avoid a bashful little noise escaping.

That calloused, working man's hold wraps me tight as he unlocks the door and pushes inside, dragging me behind him. It's only once he turns on a soft light that our focus flicks in a series of rapid-fire bounces between each other's eyes, lips, cheeks . . . we simultaneously digest the other's appearance, and it's impossible not to burst out laughing.

Red and charcoal is smeared everywhere, coating his mouth and cheeks. There's no doubt I'd find the same if I looked in a mirror.

We're a pair of messes.

Raine shakes his head and plucks at my jacket, reminding me to take it off. I'm thoroughly addicted to the way his lips quirk as he takes in more of the details of the outfit. Leaning a little closer, he flicks the dangling gold cross earring clipped on.

As he does, the pad of his finger grazes my jaw and sends a thud straight to my balls. I could never have imagined the smallest, faintest hint of a touch from this man could have such an impact on my body.

"Can I take a shower to get all this crap off?" Pulling at my hair and all the stickiness gluing it to stand on end, I grimace.

"Can you help me figure out how the hell to get rid of *this* while you're at it?" Raine scoffs and circles a palm in front of his demon-eyes.

Trapping my bottom lip under a biting hold, I nod. This time, with a racing, skittering pulse, I reach for his hand. He doesn't pull away. Instead, allows me to lead him to the bathroom, where we end up chest to chest in his shower, scrubbing at costume paint and, in my case, washing my hair to get rid of the gel.

Raine needs a few attempts at the layers coating his eye sockets until all the black has washed away, remnants swirling the drain at our feet. As he does, I'm slowly doing the same, but mostly find myself trapped in a daze, checking him out from behind my fingers.

God, he's stunning. All those slopes and planes of his muscles become more defined, perfectly highlighted by running water. I love the way his body isn't for show, but is strong all the same. He's not training for a certain physique, and if anything, the way his stomach holds a little softness while slightly indented at the sides, just makes him even sexier.

I want to run my hands *everywhere*. So that's what has me damn well tackling him against the wall with soap.

"Let me do it this time?"

Raine lets his hands drop, then devastates me with a twitch of his lips while leaning back. Those onyx eyes are heavy-lidded as I start to lather over his chest, tracing the path of his broad shoulders and down to those biceps honed by years of ranching.

"You're really hot," I breathe as rivulets of water trace over my lips. "Do you even know?"

I can't look him in the face as I say it. The whole notion of telling my *stepbrother* something like that out loud is the kind of madness that should have me snapping out of it. Hearing those words pass my lips should be the incantation that clears my haze, freeing me from this unhealthy fascination with someone I can't possibly be so pulled under by, can't possibly feel such a strong urge to be with.

Yet, nothing approaching that occurs. If anything, all it does is make me want to erase the words step and brother and replace them with something else. Boyfriend, maybe? I don't even know. Gnawing the inside of my cheek—watching my hands descend his stomach, following the path the water spray maps out for me—I realize that even that word doesn't feel right to describe what we are. It feels too immature, too fleeting, too easily forgotten, as girlfriends and boyfriends tend to be over the course of a lifetime.

"You like my body?" Raine keeps his shoulders against the wall but drags the backs of his fingers up my stomach, starting from the spot where the dusting of hair thickens just above my erection. We're both rock-hard but haven't touched each other properly yet. I guess knowing that we've got all night to indulge our yearning allows me the freedom to explore, and generously adore other parts of him.

Dipping my head forward to kiss the tattoo of the wolf sitting above his heart, I hum softly. "Insanely gorgeous." The truth of that confession probably isn't loud enough to be heard over the running water, but I keep my lips pressed against him.

Raine lets his fingers slide up to curl into my washed hair, running up my nape, leaving a scattering of goosebumps flying across my skin in the wake of his caress. It's perfectly him, with just enough firmness there to drag me up to his mouth so he can kiss me, while also staying in this gentle place we've paused in . . . until this moment.

"Aren't you cute when you're horny." He draws my bottom lip into his mouth to suck down and turns the shower off.

From that point on, we're ravenous for each other. Towels are only a cursory thing. Hardly stopping to bother with anything like properly drying ourselves, it's just him and his mouth on me as we stay connected through a hurried stream of passionate kisses, tumbling onto the bed.

When he takes hold of the reins, it's unquestionably my favorite thing. I'm spread out beneath his bulk, staring up at him as he kneels between my thighs and works my body. With expert hands, he preps me, all while keeping that glittering, hooded gaze locked with mine.

Raine tells me how pretty he thinks I am. How much of a good boy I am. And with each gradual slide of his lubed-up fingers, each time he pushes my knees higher, my body comes alive . . . just for him.

"Oh fuck. *Fffffuck*." I writhe as he finally, fucking finally, closes a fist around my swollen length. He coats me in lube and treats me to long, drugging pulls from root to tip, before reaching lower to tease my balls. I'm too easily begging, far too quickly feeding him all the pathetic sounds that I didn't ever think I would make. But where his compelling touch is concerned, it always feels mind-altering.

"No girl can give you this, can they?" Something fierce takes over his voice as he strokes me harder from both inside and where his rough handling of my cock works me in slick glides up and down. "No one else can give you what you crave, will they?"

My eyes squeeze shut, and I let out a garbled noise as he grazes that spot inside me that lights my body up within a blink. The sensation is made almost excruciating when he cups my balls at the same time and tugs lightly on them. "*Only you.*" Clawing at the sheets, I feel my length jerk, and I just want him buried deep, to take what he wants and fuck me all night long.

"Christ, you're too tempting," he murmurs hotly, and even though

I'm lost to the rhythm of his skilled touch, the intensity of his stare scorches across my nakedness, watching me start to tremble for him.

Then he moves, and when he eases away, I moan a little at the loss of his hands. Peering out from behind my lashes reveals the arresting sight of his tattooed fist running a generous amount of lube over his cock. Holy fuck, from this angle, he looks like he'll definitely split me in half this time. The sight of him, flushed and fat and veined, is enough to make me shiver with anticipation.

"Raine," I plead, not wanting him to keep taunting me—or maybe I do, I don't even know. But the sound of my voice groaning his name, while that big hand shuttles up and down seems to give him an extra glimmer of depravity.

Searing me with a look that compels me to watch, he takes my cock in his free hand. Wrapping me tight, holding onto both of us, one in each palm, Raine then shifts his weight forward ever so slightly. Keeping me strangled with those two dark pools, staring down at me splayed out in his bed, he lets a long line of saliva fall from his mouth to land on my crown. It's filthy and unbelievably hot and has me bucking off the bed, rutting up into his fist, letting out a stream of curses and whimpering noises.

That's when I feel it, the flood of relief as his tip nudges against my ass. I don't even care that he has to let go of my length; I just want him to hurry up and fuck me. The head of him slowly slips inside, and every muscle in my body sighs with the pleasure of being connected like this.

Raine takes his time, as he always does, allowing my body to adjust to him. Slowly easing past that resistance with careful, gradual movements. All while talking me through swallowing his cock in that gruff voice that's so unbelievably sexy I could die knowing those words are all for me.

"You're mine."

Biting down on my lip, I nod. "*Mmm* . . . I am."

"Did you miss me, snowflake?"

"*Yes*." Of course. I did, and always do. I miss him every second of every day, and I didn't even realize that was what this gaping hole in my chest had been caused by.

"I missed having you in my bed." His muscles strain with the effort to hold himself back. "This ass . . ." I'm definitely in trouble, because I would do very questionable things to hear that noise rumbling from deep inside his chest, to hear him reveal exactly how good this feels for him.

My lips shiver as he plants both palms beside my ears, starting to pump his hips properly now. "*Unghhh*. I wanted to be here. So—*ffffuuck*—so badly." I gasp as my body rocks beneath the force of him moving on top of me.

"These sugar lips. Did you know you always taste like candy?" Raine dusts kisses over my mouth and then scrapes his beard along my jaw. He licks and sucks a slow path down to my pulse point, the curve of my throat.

"*Umphfff*. Fuck . . . that feels . . ." Chills sheet my body.

"I know, baby. I know." His breathing is more ragged now. This is affecting him just as much as it's turning me inside out, and that propels me closer to the edge.

"Oh fuck. Oh fuck." The way my cock is rubbed between our bodies combined with that spot he keeps nudging each time he withdraws and then slides forward, I'm only just hanging on.

He knows. He knows I'm close. And Raine is nothing but ruthless when it comes to demanding that I fall apart.

"My." *Thrust*. "Sweet." *Thrust*. "Boy."

The tingling in my spine intensifies and I let out a gasp followed by a groan. Tipping my head back, exposing my throat.

"That's it. You're doing so well. Gonna give it all to me, aren't you? Gonna give me that thick cock spraying yourself with cum while I fill you up."

That's what ends me. I'm done. He does me in with that visual.

My dick swells, and I outright sob with pleasure as my mind blanks and a relentless blazing surge pours through my groin. I'm a pulsing and throbbing mess as ribbons of hot cum spurt all over me, all over him. It's so intense that I'm only vaguely aware of Raine falling apart, too, as he slams forward and starts to unload. His climax chases on the heels of my own, and we're both panting into each other's mouths. Damp with sweat. Slick with cum. Falling in too deep, too fast, or maybe it's just how it will always be when it comes to us.

A blissful place to disappear into, where all that matters is letting go with him.

I don't know what time it is when I wake up from a deep, peaceful slumber, cocooned in Raine's arms. Everything is dark; it's still the middle of the night, but his hands dragging up my side and over my abs are soothing. His big frame blankets me from behind, and I fucking love the weight of him, with a leg slung over mine, holding me down and secure. This right here is the first proper glimpse I've had of a hopeful, wishful sort of feeling curling inside my chest. The kind of moment that makes our connection feel real . . . as if we're actually *together*.

"Are you sore?" His mouth finds my ear. A sleepy rasp as he places a kiss against my neck.

"No." My head tilts, giving him better access to keep doing that thing with his mouth that melts me into a puddle of bliss.

"Good." His whisper is velvety and oh-so-delicious. "Because I need you."

I'm right there with him. Desperate and arching my spine and unashamedly opening for him to do anything he wants when that familiar glide of something cool and slippery runs over my ass. My cowboy taking perfect care of me.

"God, I'm gonna need this every day," Raine groans deeply as he presses forward. My blissed-out body hardly puts up any resistance, welcoming him in as his length gradually slips inside.

Those calloused fingers caress my spine as we lie together cloaked in darkness, while the haze of sleep and earlier pleasure he wrung from me all combine to make my toes curl.

"Good boy."

Oh god, hearing him say that does something to my entire soul. Every time without fail.

He holds tight to my hips and fully seats himself inside, hips flush against mine. "You're so good for me. So perfect."

I'm limp, defenseless, categorically consumed by bliss at his hands. The way he keeps pouring more of those words over my heated skin in that raspy, quiet confession spirals me up into the sky. It's enough to leave me breathless and soaring, softly repeating his name.

This time, it doesn't feel like sex. It feels like making love.

Raine fucks me slow. He claims the fragile, bruised thing inside my chest. It's heaven, right here in his bed and his arms, and there's no doubt my heart is fully his when his lips seek out my ear once more.

"You belong right here. I'm not letting you leave me."

CHAPTER 37
Raine

"You're gonna give me a complex staring at me like that." Kayce grins and rolls his eyes at me. "I mean . . . I know you're obsessed and all . . ."

Shaking my head, I keep swiping the brush over Ollie, who I'm almost certain has gone to sleep on me mid-grooming. If a horse could start snoring on demand, this one would achieve that feat at any time of day.

"I looked into options for your knee." I try to keep my voice as even as possible. Knowing full well that it's a topic Kayce still hesitates to talk about, having more or less accepted there's nothing more to be done. While that might be the headspace he's in, I hate that there isn't something tangible to still explore.

"Oh." He concentrates on the bucket he's filling up real goddamn hard. "You don't have to do that, you know." One shoulder lifts and that spark that was in his tone from a second ago deflates like a flat tire.

"I know I don't. But that's for me to decide, and I want to help if I can. It might not be anything, but there are specialists out there to talk with."

He stays quiet, and the only sounds come from horses munching hay and the trickle of water running into the bucket.

"Thank you." I can already hear the *but* that will be coming. "There are still a few things I gotta get my head around with it. Doesn't change the fact that I won't compete in rodeo again, no matter what I do."

"It hasn't been too painful?" Kayce is pushing himself hard around the ranch. Preparing for winter and all that entails. He thinks I don't see the occasional wince, or way he absently rubs it while he's sitting on the couch at night scrolling on his phone.

"Nah, it's feeling strong."

"Those exercises are helping?"

He nods and shoots me a sly grin.

"You *are* doing them, aren't you?"

Kayce signs a crisscross over his heart and then gives me a wink. Little shit. That isn't exactly an answer, but I'm not gonna push him either as he turns and walks off in the direction of the tack room.

I've been up here at Devil's Peak Ranch with him for the past few days. Ever since Halloween, after our night together, it's been hard to let him up and leave. While Kayce slept tucked against my chest, I lay awake listening to his soft breathing and realized there would only be a matter of hours before our lives would be back to the cold reality—dropping him off to his truck before dawn, to the day-in and day-out of taking care of cattle and horses and all his other commitments up here while Colt is away.

While I fundamentally hate the concept of calling in a favor and felt like shit for sort of lying about the reason I needed a few days off, Storm and Briar are covering for me at Sunset Skies. Of course, Beau had already been nagging me non-stop about taking a break, so he pretty much fussed over me like a proud mother duck when I called to let him know what was happening.

"*Take all the time you need.*"

God, but if it doesn't just feel so damn right to be here, and that goes some way to assuaging my initial reluctance. It's given me and Kayce a chance to just be together in a way that has an ease to it. The sort of daily flow that isn't rushed or secretive or fraught with impending knowledge that one of us has to go.

Getting to actually wake up together that first morning, when I could turn my head and see his disheveled blond hair on the pillow next to mine, with his thick lashes settled over those perfect cheekbones, almost felt like I was still dreaming. So much so that I had to tug him in close, just to feel his warmth and inhale a long drag of his scent; to let myself believe that he was truly there. *Not two seconds from running away.*

We've been able to cook meals and watch movies and just . . . I don't even know what you'd call it, but it's about as close to being in a relationship as I've ever been. There hasn't been anyone I've ever felt called to spend this much time with, and I still catch myself occasionally in awe that it's Kayce. That he's the one I'm doing something as simple as pouring a cup of coffee for, so that he can take it out to the barn with him.

Storm and Briar are looking after things under the vague premise that I needed to help Kayce out with some jobs up here on Devil's Peak. Not exactly a lie, but not the whole truth about why I'm here by any stretch of the imagination. As for when he might get around to telling anyone or letting himself fully open up to his friends, his dad—I'm not pressuring him to do anything right now.

Would it be preferable if we didn't have to act like there was something wrong or shameful about the two of us getting together? Sure. But I know, even to the most liberal-minded of people, the fact they've only ever been introduced to us as stepbrothers, it would be a hell of a thing to turn around five minutes later and hit them with the double-whammy surprise that Kayce prefers men. And to add to that, well, apparently, I prefer *him* to anyone else on this planet. Yeah, it makes my head spin off its axis . . . so, I can't imagine it would be simple to lay out on the table for anyone else to understand.

Occasionally, I catch Kayce with that look in his eye, the one that tells me he's thinking hard about what that moment might be like. Even though he told me that Brad already knows the tiniest fraction of detail, about discovering himself sexually, that's a long, long way from the rest of the chips that have fallen into place over recent weeks.

As I watch him walk toward me, I can't help but slide my attention down to the length of his stride. It's become something of a habit, to watch for any subtle hint he might be favoring his leg in some way.

Trying my hardest to discern if the golden boy I'm finding myself so consumed by, with all his jokes and playfulness, is suffering underneath that facade he puts on so well.

"My eyes are up here, you know." Kayce snaps his fingers at me and lets out a low chuckle. "Keep looking at my junk like that, and I'll start to suspect you're only after my body."

He leans a shoulder against the wall and coos away to Ollie. She flicks her ears and gives her tail a swish in a *hello* to the person she reserves hearts in her eyes for. Kayce really is so in tune with all these horses, and I can't help but feel my chest swell with a whole lot of pride whenever I see him at work out here.

The kid might have a mom determined to shit all over his life, but he's managed to keep his heart . . . that's what these animals know. They can pick up on the faintest of subtleties.

A horse is a better judge of character than damn near any other creature I've come across.

"I know you're secretly planning away over there." His blue eyes crease just a little at the corners when he watches me from beneath the peak of his cap. "Guessing you've looked at the options for a specialist in meniscus surgery?"

I dip my chin. "And I take it you've been up late at night doing enough online research to last a lifetime."

He tilts his head to one side. "You could say that."

"I'm not gonna press the matter. But you want me to take you halfway across the country just to sit in a doctor's office for five minutes . . . I'm right there with you, ok?"

An unreadable expression flickers across his face for a brief second. I catch it out of the corner of my eye, the way his throat dips, and he fiddles with his cap.

"Ollie's all done . . . even if she tells you otherwise." Time to change the fucking subject. I toss the grooming brush into the bucket, giving her a disapproving look. She bobs her neck to nibble the arm of my jacket in the usual way she tries to goad everyone to do her bidding.

"C'mon, girlie." Kayce leads her back to her stall, and as he walks the length of the barn, an idea rushes in. Except, it's something I don't want to move too fast on. In the times I've seen him since his accident, he hasn't once mentioned riding.

And even though I haven't been here to know for certain, I can't help but wonder...

"Hey, so I was gonna head down to the cattle. But I want to do another check on that fence that looked like it needed fixing." I scuff my boot and tuck my hands in my pockets.

Big blues meet mine from across the barn.

"Ok, cool. Well, I think we're about done here." He looks around before turning back to me. "Do you want to take Winnie out... and I can head up to the house to get something ready to eat..."

Kayce trails off as I close the distance between us and grab hold of Winnie's halter. I stop in front of him and reach out to hook his chin, tipping it up a little. My eyes search his, and I can't help but notice the way his breathing hitches.

"Ride with me," I offer.

"I haven't—I don't think—" he stammers, eyes going wide.

Bending to kiss him softly, a quick reassuring press of my lips, I hand him the halter. "I know."

I think it's the first time Kayce has contemplated being back on a horse since his accident, and every single messy thought of *what if* is written all over his face. A flurry of nervous energy comes off him straight away, but I can see this is also something he wants.

Kayce lives and breathes horses. This is something important for him, among so many difficult and life-altering things he's in the middle of right now.

So I move to join him at Winnie's side and nudge his shoulder with my own until he gives me his eyes.

"I'm right here. I've got you."

CHAPTER 38

My eyelids struggle to crack open when I stretch and roll over—to dare a peek at the place beside me where I know I'll be met with the sight of tattooed skin and a wild mop of dark hair.

Raine looks younger when he sleeps. Those years of being gruff and unapproachable and downright surly all vanish when he drops into a slumber. Something I don't always know that he's able to do peacefully, considering his past.

But as I blink the fog away, expecting to make out the shape of him lying on his stomach with an arm tucked beneath his pillow, I jolt awake. Normally it would be a murky gray light in here. Usually the bedroom is all shadows and a grainy sort of haze with how early it is.

"Fuck. We gotta get up," I groan, slapping an arm in the direction of my phone on the bedside table. Crap. The alarm didn't go off, and if there's one thing I know about this property, it's that the days your morning doesn't start on time, are usually the ones when problems snowball. Those days where everything that can go wrong, will go wrong.

It's the cattle ranch equivalent of Murphy's Law.

I fucking hate it.

Though, try as I might to flounder around and find my phone, strong arms snake around my stomach. I'm hauled back against Raine's broad chest, and as hard as I squirm, he's entirely uninterested in letting me go.

"Seriously. What's the time?" I rub my eyes and halfheartedly try to shove his hand away, which is now splayed across my abs. Despite all the ways I know I need to haul ass this morning, my stomach caves, and god . . . he's just so warm. So inviting. So damn delicious to wake up next to.

I really, really fucking like waking up with him right there.

There are a lot of things I've come to discover that I like about having him to myself like this—all day and all night—but the clock is ticking on this brief escape we've managed to buy ourselves, the ticket we've managed to steal where we can just enjoy being together and the rest of the world gets put on pause.

It's as if nothing exists beyond the entrance to Devil's Peak Ranch, and we've been able to remain hidden in this perfect bubble. One that is liable to burst the moment Raine has to leave.

I don't want to think about it.

Letting out a frustrated sigh, I push at his hold on me, trying and failing to dislodge him from wrapping me tighter, nuzzling into my shoulder. Goddamn him, because if there is one move that guarantees I become all kinds of slutty and yearn for him without restraint, it's when he kisses my neck. "We have to go."

"Not a chance." His morning voice is rumbly and gritty with sleep, right at my ear.

He ignores my efforts, continuing to pin my back against his torso, and something about the way he's keeping me here because he wants to—as if he doesn't give a single fuck about anything beyond the need to touch me—well, that turns my world on its head as we lie here tangled in bedsheets and the complexities of our connection to one another.

"Who would have thought I'd be the Boy Scout today." I let out another little huffing noise. "But . . . as much as I wish mornings could be lazy . . . you know as well as I do that concept doesn't exist around here."

"Already done." As he lays another sweep of spine-tingling kisses up the side of my throat, I feel the hard length of him grind against me from behind. "I got up and dealt with the stock early. The horses are fine, too."

I go still, heart pounding against my ribcage. "What? You would do that? Why?" He would go to that sort of effort without telling me?

"You looked too dreamy. Fast asleep and twitching." He runs his nose along the side of my jaw, then nips at my earlobe. "Too much like a sweet little thing I selfishly wanted to enjoy."

"I feel bad." Clearly not bad enough, because my dick is flinching and filling rapidly with the way Raine keeps working me with wet glides of his mouth over my ear and that temptation of his erection pressing into me.

"Figured you needed to sleep." He shrugs it off, which is so typical for him. I've come to realize that Raine will always downplay the things he does. This man is so quick to shoulder the load for others, and he'll gladly do it all without anyone being any the wiser.

"So what, we get to have a cute morning and I get to be little spoon, huh?" I tease him, letting my body relax fully against his now.

"Something like that." There's a wickedness in his tone. An edge of raw sensuality coloring his words that immediately has me grinning like a lunatic. To the point I have to keep my face turned into the pillow in a valiant effort to disguise just how giddy he makes me.

I notice both of our phones, sitting beside each other on the bedside table. It's certainly not where I left mine last night. Which puts Raine at the scene of the crime, being the cause of my *missing* alarm this morning. I grunt and stretch to catch them with my fingertips, reaching for both devices at the same time.

One look at my screen confirms that, yes, he'd turned off the alarm. My heartbeat starts fluttering away in a pitter-patter—feeling all sorts of upended that he went to all that trouble to let me stay sleeping. I can only imagine what he must have looked like, creeping around in the dark so as not to disturb me.

That's when my attention drifts to his phone. It's an older model. Complete with scuffs and scrapes and a cracked screen. The thing looks like it's seen a hard life.

"This brick still works?" I wiggle it so that he'll be able to see it in my hand. "Kinda looks like something that belongs to a fifty-year-old."

He grunts a muffled curse while biting my neck.

"C'mon then. Let me see what cobwebs you've got all up in here. Is there a steam-powered engine we need to start up in order to get it going? A landline extension we need to plug it into?"

"Always such a smartass," he grumbles and drags my hand holding the phone closer to his face so that it unlocks, then pushes it back my way.

I'm left gnawing on my lip, ever so curious about what Raine might have on his phone. But at the same time, if his social media is anything to go by, it's probably nothing but mundane, work-related stuff. Screenshots of horse feed brands and shit like that. I'm almost bursting out loud with laughter when I see that his camera roll is exactly that. An assortment of boring things he's obviously had to take care of around the ranch and send to Beau, like photos of a broken fence and, sure enough, a pallet of horse feed.

Swiping out of his camera roll, I swerve past the icon for his Instagram. As much as I'm a little bit anxious as to whether there are other cowboys and cowgirls dropping into his inbox, that's the kind of territory that is certainly none of my business.

So I go into our text thread, and see the icon with just a K for my name on display.

"You don't have a photo for my contact in your phone." I pretend to pout.

Behind me, I feel him shrug. "What do you want it to be?"

My stomach swoops as I think about it for a brief moment. Then decide to unapologetically be the guy he's currently got his arms wrapped around. I'm the one he's in bed with. I'm who he's pre-planning ways to enjoy spending a cute little morning sleep-in alongside.

So I rearrange Raine's hand on the comforter, fussing with it until it shows off the sexy tattoo of the vintage rose covering the back of his hand. All those veins sticking out in the gorgeous way they do. I slip my palm beneath his, thread our fingers, and take a photo of us—just our hands with fingers interlocked.

"There." I nibble on my lip and show him the image on-screen. "Better?"

Raine lifts the phone from my grasp, and the next moment, there's a soft thud when he tosses it aside to hit the carpet. He doesn't say a word but pulls me closer.

That hand, splayed wide across my front, moves down to cover my hip, and he drags me tight against his cock. I feel every inch of him like a steel bar as he shows me exactly how this is gonna go from here.

I'm shuddering with anticipation, without a single word needed. Every part of me hums to life, and my blood quickens as his other hand explores ravenously. His strong fingers slide around to the front of my throat, and his beard scrapes the sensitive patch of skin above my pulse point as he resumes kissing up and down the slope of my neck.

All I can do is tilt my head and open that invitation to him. I want him to take everything. Take every part of me.

His lips brush over the shell of my ear as he whispers in a dark, gritty voice. "I fucking need you."

My reply is a soft, greedy sound. A barely there whimper. I'm so goddamn done for, every time without fail, and my dick smears precum against my stomach as he rearranges himself at my back. A click of a cap is followed by that cool gel coating his firm touch.

It's bliss. Heaven. The most idyllic of moments being wrapped up in him. He fucks me from behind, reaching around and stroking me in slow, punishing twists of his hand to match the timing of his thrusts. He absolutely owns me until I'm on edge and panting before pushing me to roll onto my front. I'm face down, sobbing into the pillow as he torments me with deep, languid rolls of his hips. My aching cock is squashed between my stomach and the bed while he rides me, slapping our bodies together.

Each time I think I'm done for, that I'm one second from bursting, he eases back. All while whispering filth and praise, and mixing it all together in a way I can't get enough of.

It's not until he flips me onto my back and dives into me with my ankles locked around his hips—not until our mouths are fused together in an unhurried kiss that he guides my hand to stroke my dick while our bodies rock together.

Moaned curses unleash, along with the rawest noises of pleasure, straight into Raine's mouth as I come. It feels like it goes on and on as my cock empties itself all over our stomachs, and the slide of our bodies is so damn hot. I've gone blank. Washed away. A fluffy cloud. Hoping like hell I didn't just tell him I've fallen in love with him as his climax hits and he spills deep inside me. It's so exhilarating, so gorgeous to watch his face contort that I feel my cock jerk and release a little more.

And I realize—as I stroke his face and pull him closer to wrap my arms around the back of his neck so we can kiss more intimately in that glowing comedown—that I do love him. It's a painful, awful thing to finally admit. To fall in love for the first time, with Raine, of all people, is probably the stupidest thing I could ever do.

Yet, here I am. In a place where I've never been before, and I just have to hope beyond all hope that he maybe feels a fraction of what I'm feeling.

I know he tells me things like he's not letting me go . . . that I'm his.

But the nagging voice in the back of my head says *beware*. He'll wake up one day and see all those broken pieces and decide I'm not worth the effort.

"*Hey*." With a soft hum, he looks down at me. Still fully sheathed, branding me in the way that I'm obsessed with. I can't get enough of these moments when he lingers and lets me have that closeness, that connection afterward. "Where'd you go?" His fingers brush across my cheeks and up to push my hair off my damp forehead.

"I'm right here." I swallow and blink up at him, taking in all his handsomeness.

"You're thinking awfully hard." He gives a tiny thrust of his hips. "Too hard for someone with my cock still filling them." A faint hint of a smile tugs on the corners of his mouth, and I press my fingers there, as if I can seal it permanently in place or steal it to hide away in my memories.

"Just . . . I guess this is it . . . the part where it feels too good to be true." I wet my lips and smile back a little shyly. Not wanting to say the whole truth of it.

But Raine is who he is. It's like he can see straight through me and always knows there's something more that I'm not saying.

"Let's shower, get some food into you, and then I'm gonna go down to Crimson Ridge to do a supply run." He feathers a kiss over my lips before slowly drawing back, gazing down at me with soulful, calming eyes. "I'm right here with you in this. All of it. Don't forget that."

CHAPTER 39
Raine

This has gotta be the strangest place to realize you've fallen for someone.

Standing in the middle of the grocery aisle, contemplating which cereal to buy, and the only thought in my head is that I know Kayce prefers to eat the pink charms first. He doesn't eat it for breakfast, either. It's some sort of weird evening snack he has.

Which then leads me to running through events of the recent nights we've spent watching his top ten movies because, apparently, me not having at least one favorite is a *disaster for humanity*.

Truthfully? I don't give a shit what plays on the screen. It's the fact he enjoys it and can quote me all these stupid facts about the making of it or other interconnecting events in full flight. That's the part I secretly enjoy.

It's him.

So, as I knit my brows together and toss his favorite cereal into the cart, I consider what that means for the two of us. It's odd to be without him, after spending so much time together in the past couple of days, and knowing that I've got to go back to work tomorrow feels like a kick in the balls.

Each time we have to go our separate ways stings worse and worse. Normally, it wouldn't be anything to worry about. Two people getting to know each other and alternating spending nights at each other's places. All a very mundane and standard *dating* concept.

But when it comes to our situation? If there isn't a sudden shift in the weather bringing a storm through Crimson Ridge, which might cut him off for weeks on end... then there's the fact I'm circling closer to a decision about where I go next. My time at Sunset Skies Ranch is almost up, and while I don't doubt that Beau might be kind enough to give me an extension on my contract, I know there are other ranches who want me back again.

And then there's the inherent worry; if I stay here, eventually, he'll follow. Foul bastard that he is. My father won't stay, he never does, but he likes to turn up wherever he's not wanted just to stir shit and cause hell—he gets a kick out of fucking up my life a little bit more. Always in small ways, since he knows he can't physically hurt me anymore.

When he first started doing it, things were hardly noticeable. The properties I worked on might have equipment stolen or vandalism occur. It was once he got bolder that was when I fully understood what was happening.

It all came to a head when I found out he'd been harassing the teenage daughter of one rancher I'd been working for. Cornering her in town. Being a leering drunk. Following her from a distance. Nothing that would get him arrested, but it was enough to leave her shaken up.

I resigned that night and left the state. Sure enough, a few months later, he tracked me down again. At first, I couldn't figure out how he knew where I was. I've never really used social media; my phone is always for work, but then it clicked. *Rodeo.*

As long as I was still competing, he had easy access to a way to keep tabs on me.

So, I quit that, too.

He's been a shadow lurking in the corners of my life for so long; it's become deep-seated in me now. An inbuilt response to keep endlessly moving. If I stay anywhere too long, it becomes more and more likely something will let slip, and he'll figure it out. The guy comes back on shore from the rigs and has nothing but time and money on his hands. A pathetic excuse for a man with a stained fucking soul.

Part of me is worried he'll catch wind that I'm back on this side of the border. A bigger part of me is fearful that if Kayce is part of my life, that leaves him the easy target.

I blow out a long breath. This is the internal battle I've been waging since Halloween. In the past, I refused to contemplate letting someone in. Not one single time did I feel compelled to allow a person into my life long enough to be considered a relationship.

With Kayce? Now things between us have evolved? I can't imagine doing any fucking thing without him.

As I'm standing in the parking lot, loading groceries into my truck, our conversation from breakfast this morning rolls back through my mind. After noticing his expression while we were in that floaty, blissed-out place, still coming back into our bodies, I saw it in the blue of his eyes. There was a moment when he disappeared on me, and I hate that the first thought I had was that maybe he didn't want this, or us, anymore.

That's why I had to tell him. I had to blurt it all out right there, in the middle of frying up breakfast, so he could keep hold of that certainty.

"I'm sorry for always being so hard on you back then," I grunt, pushing the sizzling bacon around the pan. As I say the words, there's no hiding the fact that Kayce's eyebrows just jumped into his hairline. *"I just wanted you to be as strong as you could be, you know. I wanted you to be tough enough to survive without me there. I needed you to be able to survive."*

Kayce's arms wrap me from behind, and he rests his cheek against my spine.

On reflex, I snatch up his hands and hold them tight beneath my own, pressed to the center of my chest.

"After you left..."

"It was shit. I know."

His nod is subtle, the faintest of scratches against my shirt.

"She stayed in that house when we both should have left. I got out at the first opportunity, too ... but she wasn't strong enough to leave him, or the pills." His words vibrate against my spine. *"Maybe that's why I keep helping her, even now, when I know I shouldn't. The guilt gets to me."*

I take the pan off the heat and turn around, cupping his face in my palms.

"You did everything you could. Her shit isn't yours to carry."

"But I ended up with too much of her in me. Too many of her weaknesses." He winces.

With a long exhale, I wrap him in a firm embrace, pulling him flush against my chest. I know he's struggled with his own path, fumbling through making shitty choices that an outsider might be quick to judge him for. But I get it. I understand. Hell, none of us are perfect.

"I wish I'd been here sooner," I confess, speaking into his damp hair, inhaling the scents of soap and shampoo.

"You wouldn't have liked who I was." Kayce's fingers flex against my ribs. "I'm glad you got to know me now."

I feel him toying with the fabric of my shirt and give him a moment to collect those words he obviously wants to say.

"I prefer this version of me. He's the guy I want you to know."

My heart feels ready to burst. It aches for how little he thinks of himself, and at the same time is so proud of him for everything he's achieved against all odds.

"I'm here for each version of you, snowflake," I confess into his hair before clearing my throat. "C'mon, you need to eat before all of this gets cold." Running my palms over his back, I squeeze him a little harder before releasing him, reluctantly. We start throwing food onto plates, and Kayce fusses with the coffee maker.

When he slides onto the stool opposite mine, his blue eyes narrow and pause on me for a moment as he slowly reaches forward and hands over a mug.

"What?" I stop with a forkful, hovering just in front of my mouth.

"You . . . you don't drink when you're around me. But you do around others." He chews on the inside of his cheek.

"So?"

"Why would you do that?"

Setting my fork down, I tilt my head. "Kayce, your mom struggles with addiction. I know I might seem like a heartless asshole, but I'd be a real selfish prick not to respect your needs."

He's got a strip of bacon pinched between two fingers, forgoing silverware completely like a heathen, and stalls with it midway to his mouth. Gaping back at me with something flickering across his eyes.

I pick my fork back up and keep my attention on him as I chew slowly.

Kayce sets the bacon back down and wipes his hands on a towel, swallowing hard. "Well . . . uhhh . . . you don't have to stop, you know. Not because of me or anything. I'm used to being around the others when they're having a few cold ones." As he says the words, he starts squirming. My golden boy who has no idea the lengths I'd go to if it meant keeping him protected. And now, in this new connection between us, to support him in being happy.

Pushing off my stool, I've already finished my last mouthful as I cross the kitchen island. Walking around, I step into him.

With one hand, I brush a few strands of hair off his forehead. "If you think I would choose a drink over you, snowflake. Then you're sorely mistaken."

Those pink spots on his cheeks deepen, as he stares back at me. Then, a faint little smirk plays on his lips as he watches me get ready to go into town and do a pick-up run for supplies that both he and the ranch will need.

"Never not *obsessed with me,* huh?"

I can't help the way a smile makes an appearance when I recall that mischief in his voice. The sight of him sipping his coffee and the glint of turquoise flickering back into his eyes, with those blond strands of his all ruffled after showering together.

He's managed to retain a brightness to him that many people growing up in his circumstances would have lost—myself included. I mean, I don't know if I ever had the humor and the personable nature he so effortlessly possesses. I've never known a time when I wasn't *the quiet one.* It just got bashed into me over and over that I needed to stay that way. So I guess, I never got the opportunity to find out whether I liked to crack a joke, or laugh from somewhere deep in my belly.

Being with Kayce? He shows me a different way of being.

Something brighter.

I've loaded everything and slide my ass behind the wheel when my phone starts buzzing. To be honest, being up at Devil's Peak with no cell service has been a dream for someone like me.

What I'm expecting to see is Tessa or Beau's contact. I'm anticipating them getting in touch about something urgently needed at work, or to confirm what time I'll be back tomorrow. However, when I glance at the screen, there's no name. *Unknown Number.*

I decline the call straight away. While the chance is only slim to none, there's every possibility it could be my father, and I'm not ever gonna take that risk.

While I've got my phone in hand, I quickly check to see if Kayce has messaged me, but there's nothing new there. He'll be out with the horses, and hopefully will have gone for a ride like I encouraged him to today. No doubt in my mind, I'd prefer to be there with him like yesterday, but knowing he can do it on his own will settle that inherent tinge of worry.

Especially since I won't be there.

I fucking hate thinking about it. Not just that I won't be at the ranch with him, but any thoughts of the future and how this is going to work between us. All that mind-chatter blasts me the second I give it a chance to rise to the surface.

As much as the sense of relief washes over me when I start the truck and begin making my way back to the Peak, I still don't know how this is all going to work out. With Kayce unsure how to tell anyone, and in the longer term, there's only a matter of time before Colt and Layla come back. It's not like I can stay here indefinitely, and if he's not willing to open up to others about *us* . . . then that leaves everything up in the air. We can't stay secluded away on top of this mountain wrapped up in each other in secret.

How is life gonna look?

And more importantly, how will this delicate thing we have together learn to survive when it's no longer hidden in the shadows?

Will it flourish, or wilt?

CHAPTER 40

Kayce

In no world did I think I'd be picking up takeout from The Loaded Hog, carefully sidestepping conversations about why I'm walking out of here with enough food for a small army, and giddy at the prospect of a sleepover with my stepbrother.

The guy, I've come to realize, I want to wake up next to every morning.

The cowboy who owns my heart . . . even if I'm too shit scared to admit that to him, or anyone else.

Not one single part of me is ashamed, or worried about coming out. In fact, that feels like the least of my concerns within my group of friends. I'm so thankful I've got incredible people surrounding me. What absolutely petrifies me is the notion of opening up my fragile heart. There's a very real risk that if I do finally dare to step out onto the wafer-thin ice—allowing Raine to get close enough—he could decide to abandon me.

A soul destroying moment, when the other shoe might drop, sending me plummeting into the deepest, darkest of waters.

Yeah, that word strikes a nerve most ruthlessly of all. *Abandonment.*

Jesus, even just sounding it out inside my head, as I juggle the cardboard box full of food out to my truck, makes a chill run down my spine.

I'm so fucking terrified he's gonna leave me that it's left me frozen as if I'm stuck in the middle of a white-out. My body goes rigid, and my veins turn to ice, and the grim reality is that I don't know how to do any of this.

I don't know how to be a guy who loves someone this deeply. Knowing I'd do anything just to hear him grumble in his sleep when he turns over and doesn't realize that he tangles his legs with mine. There's this feeling, a yearning to be close to him at every opportunity. Not only a passionate confession of love, or chasing lust, but also the simplicity of being *with* him.

Having a secret part of Raine that he doesn't allow anyone else to see.

To the rest of the world, he's so gruff and surly, but I get his sly grins, his dry humor, his gentle care and attention. All the stupid, meaningless, quiet moments. The kind of random Tuesday night where we can lie on the couch and share inside jokes that no one else would understand.

When I get into my truck, my head is spinning. I've been ransacking my brain all day to make a plan on how to tell the people in my life who need to know. Who deserve to know something so important. Fall isn't going to stick around much longer, time marches on with a steady drum beat calling winter in to take hold of Crimson Ridge. I should really tell them before I get stuck up the top of that damn mountain for weeks at a time, rather than being a shitty friend prolonging keeping my vault of secrets. And I know that I need to stop dancing around confessing the truth—to let them in on the extent of my injury.

If I ran into Chaos right now, right here in this parking lot, would I have the courage to open up and confess to him? Would I have the guts to look him in the eyes and let him know I've been hiding so much?

Or would I brush it off with a joke and a smart remark and be the version of *Kayce* they all only really know the surface-level of?

I turn the key in the ignition and then pause with both hands on the wheel. Right now, there is about one person in this world who I feel could give me some advice on what to do. Because I'm certainly not bugging Raine about how to make decisions where all of this is concerned, but there's one particular friend who promised me that I could talk to them if I ever needed to—even if it feels like a lifetime ago.

The first person to see me clearly, when I hardly knew myself.

> Hey, so I know you're probably sucking face with Heartford . . .

SAGE:
> Oh, look. It's the rodeo starlet himself.
> To what do I owe this pleasure?

> You got a minute?

> For you, Wilder? I can make time.
> Hit me.

> Do you remember that day when the Chaos Twins put on the big opening at the Hog?

> I certainly do. Was very memorable.

> And you know how you kinda spotted something that we'd never spoken about before?
> But you told me I could always talk to you if I needed.

> Is this about the cute blondie in the impossibly tight wranglers?

Sage hits me with an entire row of eyeballs, eggplants, and water spurts. I groan and pinch my brow. Here goes nothing.

> It's not about him.
> But in a way, it kinda is.
> . . .

> So, I've realized I'm gay, but not in an "I like all guys" kind of way. It's more of a "there's one very specific person," and I don't know how to tell people about him because I'm a walking disaster.

> Anyway, I could really use someone like you who is good with words to help me figure out how the fuck to handle the fact I've been avoiding telling anyone.

Sage reads the message, and nothing happens. As I'm chewing my thumbnail, waiting for some words of wisdom to appear, my phone starts ringing.

"Um. Hello?! Do you want to run that bombshell by me again? My eardrums weren't quite obliterated the first time..." Sage screeches at me down the phone. "I thought you just told me you're gay?"

I can't help but chuckle. "Hi, Sage."

"Don't you *Hi, Sage* me, Wilder. How is this the first you're mentioning anything to me, and what in the actual fuck, and please tell me every single detail about your boyfriend immediately."

"Ok, don't go planning a wedding or anything—"

"Oh my god. You would look stunning in a blue suit. STUNNING." She gasps.

"Sage." I scold her. But the grin is there, widening across my features in the face of her enthusiasm for said imaginary wedding she's already planning.

"And, of course, you'd have to have it at Devil's Peak. Photos on horseback? I can just picture it all. The barn spruced up. Late summer. Divine. Book it in right now."

"You're ridiculous."

"Now, for the cake... do you prefer dark chocolate? No, knowing you, it'll be something layered with extra sugary goodness." She makes a squeak. "One of those cakes where the middle is hollow and filled with candy?"

"Ok, let's just rewind here."

She coughs and puts on a serious, stern voice. "Oh yes. Sorry. We're here to discuss the matter of Kayce Wilder, newly anointed cock aficionado."

I let out a groan.

"How's your blow job game? Need some tips?"

"Don't make me regret this phone call."

"You know if you do this thing with your tongue—"

"SAGE."

"Sorry... I just want lover boy to be left with his toes curling each time you worship his schlong."

I chuckle.

"Is it big? What kind of girth are we working with here?"

"Can I talk to Beau instead?"

"Alright, alright. I'll behave." She whines and puffs out an exaggerated sigh. "How very booooring."

"If I told you I'm running late to go over his place, would that satisfy you?"

I can hear the stifled glee from the other end of the call. "Immensely. Are you guys *serious-serious*? Or is it a *we're keeping it flirty and casual* kind of deal?"

My teeth sink into my bottom lip.

"*Ohmygodit'ssoseriousIdie.*" She breathes, and I can practically hear her jumping up and down.

"I mean, I'm not exactly ready to start shouting from the rooftops. But I also want to tell certain people. And well, I just feel like I don't know how to blurt it out and start *telling* them." I gulp hard as I say it. "It's dumb. I know."

"Not at all, Kayce. And all joking aside, I'm gonna be shedding a tear when I get off this call over the fact that you chose me, of all people, to ask about this. I feel like a proud mama lioness."

"Thanks, Sage."

"Ok, but before I answer, I gotta ask... do you want me to give you an opinion, or do you just need a listening ear right now?"

I pause for a moment. "Definitely hit me with any pearls of wisdom you've got. I know you and Beau were a different set of circumstances... but I figured you'd understand about feeling like you couldn't tell people, even though you might've wanted to."

Sage hums as she thinks. "My advice is you're better off not hiding things. Just take baby steps. Start with one person, then go from there.

That sneaking around shit isn't healthy. And I hate to bring up the hard, but very necessary, truth—that it's much better to make the tough decision now, which sometimes turns out to be the positive solution needed in the long run. A new relationship is difficult enough as it is. One built on a foundation of hiding who you are and your sexuality, on top of keeping your relationship a secret? That's gonna be super tough going kiddo."

Letting out a laugh, I guess I kinda already knew the answer. But to hear her say it out loud, well, just reinforces that fact.

"You haven't just withered away on me, right?" Sage croons in the way she does.

"Nah, I'm here. Thank you."

There's a noise in the background, and I hear a deep voice talking quietly which I'm guessing must be Beau.

"Shit, I feel like the world's worst agony aunt right now . . ."

"Please don't. You go. I've got a hot date to get to, remember"

She sighs wistfully. "Can I at least text you my tip about the tongue thing?"

"Bye, Sage." I smirk.

"Ok. But your boy toy will thank meeeee." She whisper-shouts as I end the call.

After quickly texting Raine to let him know I'm on my way, I set my phone aside, with a grin firmly on my face. Of course I could count on Sage to somehow give me wise advice while at the same time also making me laugh about something that had felt heavy only a few moments ago. Her words just gave me a confidence boost, the exact type I needed in order to make a plan. I can do this, even if it's just one person at a time, as she suggested.

I don't have to shout it out to the world—don't have to holler from the rooftops about Raine. But I can at least start opening up about who I truly am.

That part of me . . . I don't want to hide anymore.

Figuring out how to explain more than that can come later . . . maybe after we've had more of a chance to be together.

Just as I shift into reverse, my phone bursts into life. I swipe it up without a second thought, assuming it's Sage calling back. I'm half expecting her to be coming in hot with another outlandish tip for my sex life.

But the voice on the other end of the phone is clipped. Functional. And there are all too familiar sounds in the background making it clear this is a call I really, really don't want to be receiving.

"Am I speaking with Mr. Wilder?"

CHAPTER 41
Raine

His footsteps sound different tonight. Before I've even opened the door I can already tell that this isn't *Kayce* bounding up with takeout to spend a night together.

When I wrench the door open, light spills out onto the small landing at the top of the stairs.

Red-rimmed eyes. Mouth turned down. Jaw tight.

He's carrying a box that I immediately take from his hands and put it down before it tumbles to the floor.

"I need you." The words come out in a cracked whisper, and I barely catch him as Kayce slumps into my arms.

"Hey, I've got you." I swallow hard, arms banded around him. We stay right there, with Kayce buried in the crook of my neck. Emotion ripples off him, thick and heavy, as he winds his fists tightly into the back of my shirt. Tension fills each one of his muscles, it's almost like hugging a block of concrete at first, he's rigid from head to toe.

"You're safe." My mouth moves against his hair. Fuck knows what happened between him texting me and stumbling through the door. A multitude of possibilities fly around my mind. Did something happen at the Hog? To be honest, I know he trusts himself and doesn't mind being around other people drinking, but I can't help feeling uneasy on his behalf. Or, even worse, did he run into someone, try to maybe come out to them and they weren't supportive?

Fuck. If that's the case, I'm gonna have to use every bit of self-restraint I can muster not to go do something reckless.

"Wanna come inside?" After a few minutes, sensing the moment his muscles unclench gradually, his body sags into mine. Those ragged breaths he draws begin to ease a little, and he nods against my shoulder.

Kayce clears his throat, but his voice is strained. "Sorry."

"I don't see anything that needs apologizing for." I squeeze him a little tighter, before easing back. "Unless that box doesn't contain dinner like you promised." Cupping his nape, I softly bump our foreheads together.

That makes his lips twitch a little, even if his face is still contorted with the impact of the shock he's evidently suffered.

"You're such an asshole." He shakes his head and lets his hands slide up to rest at the back of my neck, holding me there for a few more seconds. On a deep inhale, he squeezes his eyes shut, and those fingers I'll gladly have on me any time of day or night play against my skin. It's almost as if he's testing to check I'm really here before carefully releasing that breath.

"Tell me something I don't know." Lifting my chin, I drop a kiss onto his brow and really fucking wish he wasn't going through something so distressing. The way I want to be able to lift those hurts, to carry his pain, to be the one who can take the blows on his behalf. "I've got those shitty slasher movies you wanted to watch loaded up, but if you don't feel—"

"Sounds perfect." Kayce cuts me off and gives me the kind of smile that doesn't reach his eyes. It's the hollow expression you compel your face to twist into when your mind is anything *but* a good place to be.

We make our way inside with the food and quietly go through the motions of getting settled on the tiny couch. I'm not gonna bother him about talking. I know how hard it can be to open up, especially when it doesn't come naturally to speak about the heavy stuff. So, if the only thing I can do is be here by his side, even if it's gnawing away inside me to know what's wrong, I'll be right here for the second he finally finds the words.

It's not until we've eaten and we're in the lull between finishing the first movie and starting the sequel, that he tucks himself into my side. I drag him closer, making sure I can lie back and have his head resting on my chest. The opening credits roll on the screen of my laptop, and I thread my fingers of one hand through his, with the other I sift my touch through his strands of hair.

When he speaks, it's right over my heart. His voice is low, measured, as if he's been silently rehearsing what to say this whole time.

"My mom overdosed."

I squeeze his fingers tighter. *Shit.* He told me they spoke occasionally, but I didn't even think they had much of a relationship, if at all—not after all these years, with her being so far away.

"The hospital contacted me as I was on my way over." Kayce's muscles ease just a little bit more with each word. It's like the act of finally allowing them past his lips gives him the ability to sink a bit deeper into the way we're lying together.

We can stay exactly like this all night if he needs to.

I'd do anything to bring him a sense of relief or calm.

"How is she?" With my hand still threaded in his hair, I continue softly stroking over his crown.

"They'll keep her in for observation for the next couple of days." His voice cracks a little before he swallows heavily, and I feel his throat work as it dips against my torso. "It's all my fault."

Kayce keeps his face turned away from mine, but I tighten my hold on him. "Well, I know that's not true."

"You don't know how much of a fucking terrible person I am." His head shakes ever so slightly from side to side. "It *is* my fault. I was the one who sent her money. She kept bugging me, and eventually, I just dumped money in her account because I wanted to shut her up and stop harassing me . . . now look at what I've done."

God, I hate the way he's so quick to blame himself for her addiction.

"Firstly, giving your mom money isn't the same as handing her pills." I run my thumb in slow circles over his palm. "Secondly, did she tell you that's what she wanted the money for?"

He doesn't answer. There's nothing but the sound of the movie fading into the background now, and my heart thudding slowly. I hope he can hear it. I hope Kayce can hear that surety that he's not alone in this.

"But what if I caused her to do it?"

My chest tightens, hearing all that pain in his voice. He's trying so hard to disguise it, to not let a single crack show as to how much this is fucking killing him on the inside.

"Did she owe money again?" I ask.

His head tilts in a subtle nod.

"Then, if anything, you helped her more than she deserved by trying to fix a different problem in her life, one that she brought on herself."

He stays quiet for a moment before speaking. "I can't be responsible for her forever . . . I feel like it's always one step forward and two back. She makes it seem like I can't ever get away from her shitty decisions."

Now, more than ever before, I just want to take him away from all of this. Before he arrived, I'd been pacing up and down my kitchen, bursting to share the news with him—something entirely new for me to want to do. A glimmer of hopefulness lit me from the inside. I had wanted to greet him the second he walked in that door with a surprise. But now's not the time, he's not in the right headspace to even think about it.

But one thing I do know is that Kayce deserves to know a life where he's not haunted by his mom's demons. She's an adult, she's had decades to get help, refusing all the opportunities presented to her.

He's been a better son than most would ever bother to be.

"She's got medical help right now. Being in the hospital is the best place for her." Running my palm down his arm, it's hard not to be taken right back to a time so many years ago. A flood of memories of our strangely intertwined past in that poisonous house. Two toxic fucking people who should never have gotten married and who certainly fed each other's addictions.

"What happens when they discharge her, and inevitably, she goes back to old habits? What do I do the next time she starts calling?"

I lean forward off the couch a little so that I can drag his hand to my mouth and brush my lips over the pads of his fingertips.

"We just take it one day at a time. And I'm right here with you."

SLEEP COMES RESTLESSLY FOR KAYCE. When he does fall into a patch of heavier breathing, and his limbs droop, it's only for short stretches at a time.

Keeping him curled against my chest, I lie there in the dark holding him, listening to his shallow breathing. I've never been much good at sleeping, there are too many corners of my mind that lurk waiting for the moment when my guard drops.

Although having Kayce next to me, I've found more and more nights have been dreamless. Waking up almost with a start to realize that I've slept for hours undisturbed.

Maybe that's why I feel like I need to watch him, to make sure he actually gets some rest—or if not, I want to be here if he's awake and struggling with the intrusive thoughts laying siege at two a.m.

He turns into me a fraction more, his fingers pressing firmer into my bare chest, and I hear a small hum of a noise in the back of his throat. It's so faint, but my heart stills, trying to figure out what might be causing him to cry out in his sleep. The next second it comes a little stronger, but still muffled. A wordless plea.

Jesus. I'm no stranger to the horrors the mind can conjure up at night. I've spent years waking up in cold sweats and thrashing so hard the sheets dislodge off the mattress.

I shift my weight a little, not sure whether he'll settle back into a deeper sleep, or wake up.

Kayce's body jerks, and he makes a grunting, guttural noise. His head lifts off my chest when he startles out of the dream. It takes him a moment, head swiveling around as he must be coming back to the here and now, then blows out a breath before sinking back down.

"Are you ok?" Keeping my voice low, I watch carefully as he nods and then readjusts to nuzzle closer. My entire fucking heart is ready to explode when he immediately places a kiss against my chest. The first thing he does when waking up from a bad dream is to curl into me. To feel safe enough to give me that. If I didn't already know that I've got both feet in this thing with him, that just sealed it for me.

I love being at his side. I love being the person he can turn to.

I'm in love with him.

Kayce rubs at his eyes, then makes a sleepy noise that vibrates into me. "Yeah. Just crappy memories coming back."

"I'm right here. Try to get some more sleep."

He sighs. "You were in my dream, too."

"I was?"

"It was more of a memory really. A night you didn't think I was awake . . . you didn't know that I heard you outside my door." His words are punctuated by a yawn, and he twines our legs together.

My mind ransacks through times that I've tried so damn hard to forget—a lot of them have been eliminated, hardly a foggy recollection anymore. It's like my brain has taken a whiteboard eraser to so many pieces of my past, swiping things away and leaving a blank nothingness where they used to be.

"It was a time when you blocked the door. I could hear you refusing to let your dad in that end of the house because he was drunk and mad." His voice is thick with sleep. "It was like he was right there. All the horrible shit he was slurring about me. That I was just a skinny little runt. A piece of shit who would end up a whoring little bastard. *Just like his momma,* he was saying it over and over." He shivers against me, a brief tremor rolling through his muscles, even though it's toasty warm in here.

"Just a dream." There's a rock lodged in the back of my throat that I struggle to swallow down.

"You never knew I found you sleeping on the floor outside my bedroom the day after that." Kayce sighs, words dragging a little slower over his tongue as sleep starts to reach for him again. "When I asked you about it, you said it was just because you'd been out with friends. That you'd had too much to drink, so you crashed out and didn't make it to your room."

My heart thuds harder. I can remember slumping to the ground that night in front of his door, with a bruise forming around my eye as I stayed there on guard for hour after hour.

"I knew you were lying." His next yawn makes the words elongate, as he starts to drift off.

Stroking his spine, I reveal the raw truth, freeing it into the darkness—not caring if he'll hear me or if he's already asleep. Because it's the fierce reality, and it's been that way since long before I cared about Kayce in the manner I do now. Back then I did it for entirely different reasons, but now those words feel even more powerful with the depth of my feelings for him sneaking up on me.

"I'll always be here to protect you."

CHAPTER 42

Kayce

"It's early . . . way too early for you to be cooking for me." I rub one eye with the heel of my palm as a full-bodied yawn and stretch combination takes over.

Raine rolls his eyes in my direction and continues cracking eggs into a bowl before whisking them.

Outside, there's only blackness to be found beyond the crack in the curtains, and the dawn chorus has begun, those faint chirps when the earliest of birds first wake up.

"I gotta eat before work anyway, and I'm not letting you go all the way back up Devil's Peak on an empty stomach," he grumbles at me.

Am I protesting that my *maybe-kinda-sorta* boyfriend is making breakfast in nothing but a slutty pair of sweats and a sexy scowl? Not in this lifetime.

I'm still processing the events of last night, but certainly having him here to hold me and just be there—without judgment or turning me away for being such a terrible fucking screw-up like I was terrified he'd do the moment I told him about my mom—that helped me more than he could ever know.

No one could ever possibly judge me harder than I already do. And even with the black fucking headspace I'd been in when I got here, he didn't think of me that way. God, I don't know what I've done to deserve this man. Or to earn a place in his bed... wrapped securely in his arms.

It's overwhelming in a wonderful, unbelievable sort of way.

"You want extra cheese, or a normal amount that won't clog your arteries?" He rummages in the fridge while the giant omelet for two starts sizzling. Goddamn, that buttery, caramelized smell is insanely mouthwatering. Ok, maybe he was right about the whole eating before driving back up the Peak situation. If it weren't for this, what he's making, I probably wouldn't stop to eat anything until dinner time.

"Just make whatever you want." I drag a hand through my hair and have to hide a mile-wide smile when he lets out a heavy sigh, secretly rolling his eyes in an adorable way. He promptly adds double the amount of cheese I know he would normally have if it were his own.

Raine flips the omelet and clears his throat. "Take a look at this." He picks up his battered phone and swipes something open. When he slides it across the wooden table so that I can read what waits for me on-screen, it's an email. "See what you think." His voice is all rumbly and extra gravely with sleep, and I raise an eyebrow at him before he turns his back on me to plate up our eggs.

My focus flies back and forth across the few short lines of text. It might be early, I might still be feeling rough and barely half-awake, but what is written there—plain and simple and devastating at the same time—makes my heart lurch into the back of my throat.

"What do you reckon?" Raine hands me a plate. His expression is unreadable, as it so often is, and the only hint of anything I get is the way his eyes flicker briefly between the phone and my gaze.

I swallow the massive fucking lump that just appeared out of nowhere.

"This looks like a job," I croak.

"It's the ranch I used to work for." He hovers, not sitting, not eating, and I'm feeling that flopping sensation in my belly. Not the good kind. "They've asked me to come back urgently."

"I can see that." My tongue feels numb. He was in Canada before coming here. God knows how far away in the back of beyond. That's ranching for you.

"The pay is too good to turn down. Besides, Beau will be back any day, and I was only ever on a temporary contract here."

I push eggs around my plate, now having zero appetite, even with how amazing this looks and smells. Because all I see when I look at that perfectly golden omelet is that I'm never going to have Raine making me breakfast again.

"What do you think?" He slides into a chair opposite mine, but I can't look at him.

"It doesn't matter what I think."

He scoffs. Out of the corner of my eye, I see him shake his head. "That's bullcrap."

"You need to do what's best for you." I run my palms up and down the thighs of my jeans.

Raine chews a mouthful thoughtfully, eyes boring into my skull the whole time. Meanwhile, I sit here feeling about two inches tall. Like all the wind has been let out of my sails. I've been left flattened and discarded by the side of the road.

"And what if that involves you, huh?" His voice has got just enough bite to it that I flick my eyes to meet his, and my pulse kicks up. "What if my first thought was to ask them if there were other positions available, because I want you there with me?"

Ringing intensifies in my ears. I feel more than a little lightheaded.

"I—I can't go anywhere. I gotta stay here. You know I can't let my dad down." I'm ransacking my brain, trying to find words that fit the feelings coursing through my veins. I don't want him to go; that's what my brain is screaming, but at the same time, that murky, dark recess of my mind shouts at me gleefully. *Told you so.* This is what was inevitable. He's too good for me, and the truth was always going to come to light that he deserves better.

I've still got shit to make up for. I owe my dad, and I can't hold Raine back.

Everything feels hot and prickly and I can't believe this is happening.

The love of my fucking life studies me with his usual quiet steadfastness. "No. I don't believe that's the real reason." He's calm and assured when he speaks. Not giving me a single clue as to whether this feels as tumultuous for him as it does for me.

Flustered words tumble out of my mouth. "What do you want from me, Raine?"

"I want you to start thinking about your future. Your life. What is it that *you* want?"

"Maybe I don't know what I want."

"How about you stop running for five minutes and think about it properly."

Is his voice cold? My pulse is thudding so hard, I can't tell for sure. But I swear to god he's closing up, freezing me out, because that's exactly what I deserve. He's already written me off.

He would have every right to. Who wants to be with someone as messed up as me?

That hot and clammy and nauseous feeling sets up camp in my stomach as I struggle to find words. When I do, they're clunky, awkward, not anything approaching what I actually want to say. But that's what falls out, and I'm unable to bite them off or swallow them down. "Look, I can't be the reason you get held back, ok? You don't need to be responsible for me and how much of a mess I am."

"Kayce . . ." He sighs heavily.

"No. I think you should take the job. You should go." I'm on my feet and moving toward the door with my keys and my phone and needing to escape right fucking now. "They're giving you a great opportunity. I think you should take the chance to do this, and do what's best for you."

His shadow looms large at my back as I shove into my coat and boots.

"And where does that leave you? What's best for you?"

"I'm ok here. I'll be fine." *Lies. All lies.*

Raine inserts himself between me and the door, arms folded as he studies my spectacular meltdown in real-time. Yeah, I'm such a fucking loser, and this is the precise moment he'll see all that. He'll realize that by leaving Crimson Ridge, he's dodged a bullet.

"That's not what I mean, and you know it." The way his voice dips into that low hint of warning makes my pulse race. "Quit dancing around the thing you wanna say, and just say it."

"Don't you see? This is how I break things." I spread my hands wide, gesturing around the room and then between the two of us. "I take something good, and I fuck it up every single time...so...so...I think you're better off without me."

A noise like a warning comes out of him. "That's not your choice to make. You don't get to decide what's best for me."

"Maybe not, but maybe I can decide for both of us." Jesus, the acid burning the back of my throat is impossible to swallow down, and I want to sprint away, hide, throw myself off the cliff edge that I'm racing blindly toward just so I can plummet into freefall and not feel a goddamn thing.

"I know what you're doing," he says quietly.

"Well, that's wonderful."

Raine steps into me. And I hate this. I hate that I'll never again get the side of him, the man who cares and heals the parts that have remained wounded for so long. What the fuck is wrong with me? I've ruined everything and managed to destroy the only bright spot in my life.

I've fallen in love and successfully made him hate me, all in one fell swoop.

"Go on then." His brows furrow together. "Push me away, snowflake. Make sure to really light the match and set it all on fire. All because you don't believe you deserve anything, when you actually *do*."

"Raine...don't..." I can't stand here any longer with him looking at me like that. Giving me those beautiful, dark eyes that pierce me like a hundred arrows with just one glance. I'm too weak. I'm too pathetic. "You deserve so much better." When I finally get something out, it's a feeble effort, and I see his lip curl.

"It's ok. I'm hearing you loud and clear with your *maybe we should just end this* bullshit routine."

"It's probably for the best... I'm messed up, and you don't need to be dragged into my crap. Look at last night. I came in here with all my shit . . . ruined your evening . . . dragged hell after me once again. You keep on having to take care of the mess I cause. But I won't do that to you anymore. There's no way I could live with myself constantly being this fragile goddamn thing exploding like a bomb all over your life." The words keep on coming, pouring out of me, and I just want to shove them all back down. Somehow swallow them, hide them away, and rewind time to a few minutes ago when I hadn't detonated the charge right in the middle of everything.

"I'm nothing but bad news." Stepping around his bulk, I can't look him in the eye. There's no way I'm strong enough to endure what I might find there. Knowing he can't stand me is one thing, but seeing it in his gorgeous features—witnessing that deadened look as he takes in the sight of my pathetic state—leaves me crumbling to pieces.

My focus stays lowered as I reach for the door handle. This is for the best. I'm doing us both a favor. I'm helping him more than anything by telling him to take the job, to move on with his life. He'll realize that. He'll thank me.

"I'm the fuck up you don't need to worry about anymore, Raine. You and I both know you'll be far better off without me weighing you down."

CHAPTER 43
Raine

Slamming the truck door behind me, it closes with such ferocity there's every chance the damn thing might buckle inside the metal frame.

I know he'll be with the horses.

My strides are long and determined as I round the hood and step into the barn. Large iron letters spelling *DPR* set against cedar planks loom overhead.

Sure enough, Kayce comes into my line of sight immediately, barely two paces inside the entrance. He's carrying a shovel, wearing his usual faded hoodie with the hole in the bottom hem, cap pulled down over his blond hair, boots looking as if they're going to fall apart any day now.

"No one else is ever going to treat you the way I do, and you know it." I bark at him as my steps chew up the short distance between us.

Kayce's big blues grow wide as his head whips around to see me advancing on him.

"W—what?" he stammers. Eyes bouncing all over me, taking in the sight of my clenched jaw and shoulders stiff with tension. The whole way here, I was trying to figure out what the hell to say to him. How to handle such a violent tempest of emotion, the likes of which I've never experienced before. I'm crawling out of my skin, angry at him, our circumstances, our pasts that have broken him so badly that he can't see a good thing when it's shoved right under his nose.

"Fuck you, Kayce." I stop short of reaching out for him. I can't bring myself to touch him, even though that's all I really want to do right now. But there's not enough time for that. I've barely got enough time to make a detour all the way up this godforsaken mountain. "What are you playing at? You don't talk to me for nearly a week? Wanna be with someone else, or what?" Folding my arms across my chest, I feel my nostrils flare as I give him both barrels.

"Of course not." Those words are quiet, hushed. Anguish colors the flecks of turquoise in his eyes. The line of his throat dips, his Adam's apple working as he wets his lips. "I don't want anyone else."

My chest rises and falls as I barely stop myself from grabbing him by the shoulders in an effort to rattle some sense into him. I shake my head, throat tightening. "Well, you don't have to worry about whether we're together or not. No more stressing about where I fit in your life."

"Raine . . . I'm . . . I don't want to lose you." He goes a little pale.

My eyes narrow. "I'm gonna make this real fucking simple for both of us then."

"Wait." Kayce steps a little closer. A muscle tics in his jaw. "I didn't say I wanted to end things."

"Didn't you? Thought that message was pretty self-explanatory when you said you weren't interested in coming with me. Then kinda doubled down when you went all zero contact straight after." And it's too fucking late now, anyway. I've got to leave, and honestly could've saved myself a lot of hassle today by not coming here. But like a goddamn magnet, I was drawn to this road, this place. Almost as if I didn't have a choice, my truck brought me all the way up here for one last opportunity to see him.

"No. That's not what I—"

The laugh that comes out of me is a thin disguise for the crack forming in my chest. A chasm splitting wider all week long. Each passing day after he left my place and didn't make any effort to be in contact sliced deeper. "You didn't mean it like that? That you couldn't come with me? Sure, Kayce. Except, we both know the truth. We both know there are other people who are capable of running this ranch for the winter. You told me yourself that Colt has offered to bring help in if needed. So *this* . . ." I gesture a forefinger between the two of us. "This *cutting me off* nonsense has nothing to do with letting your dad down . . . and it has everything to do with you hiding from yourself."

His mouth opens and closes, staring back at me with the blue of his eyes starting to shimmer like ocean pools. "I just need time." It's a broken admission. Hearing the agony in his voice is a fucking knife to my gut. This could've all been so much easier.

"Yeah, and that's what I'm giving you. Time. Space. You've got as much as you damn well need."

I lose the battle with myself. It hurts so fucking much.

Lunging for him, I roughly cup his jaw and crash our mouths together. Kayce makes a gasping sound against my lips. I've been desperate to taste him, to feel him, yet he's kept himself locked away up here—punishing both of us with this stupid goddamn routine where he doesn't believe he's enough.

So, I kiss him, and put all of that emotion into the way our mouths move together. Because no words will ever fucking convince him. I could put it into poetry and song and write it in the goddamn sky, and Kayce still wouldn't believe me. All I've got left to give . . . all I can do is show him this. To hand over something tangible and real.

It's my only option before I go.

As I slip my tongue into his mouth and feel him melt into the kiss, I'm filled with so much damn regret. Not about him, not about us, but for all the possibilities we could have had. That morning in my kitchen, I'd foolishly thought Kayce might be excited by the prospect of starting fresh. After everything with his mom? A new town, a new country, an opportunity to have the time and space to get to know himself away from all the pressures of other people's opinions. I thought he'd see that. Had imagined and damn well hoped he might understand that was what I was offering him.

Instead, here we are. Kayce, stuck with both feet glued to his present, roots he refuses to pull up and plant elsewhere, while trying to outrun his past at the same time.

When all I wanted was to give him a future to look forward to.

Pulling back to break the kiss, I squeeze my fingers against his nape. With a heavy exhale, I rest my lips against his forehead. "I'm leaving. So you don't have to worry about figuring anything out."

Kayce makes a choked noise. He knew. He knew I was going. It's not exactly a surprise, but it must catch him off guard—no doubt stings like a bitch hearing me say it out loud all the same.

"I'm sorry for being broken. I'm sorry for breaking us." He eventually whispers.

"Snowflake, you didn't break us." Drawing away, I keep hold of him, and let our gazes lock. "There's nothing wrong with having cracks and broken pieces. But you gotta work on healing the scars still in here . . ." With one finger, I tap his temple. "And here . . ." I shift that same hand down to place my palm over his heart. "The parts of you that won't let you move on."

"But I'm ready to move on." His eyes squeeze shut.

"Are you? If I asked you to go in that house and pack your bag right now, could you do that for me?"

Kayce swallows hard, before opening his eyes, and the vibrant gaze I'm so used to seeing is dulled by that weight of inner torment.

"No, I didn't think so. That's your answer right there."

There's a war clearly raging inside him as he tries to form words. "I hate myself right now. How can you even stand to look at me?"

A ragged noise escapes my throat, and I press our mouths together again. Taking his soft lips, I hope like hell this will imprint both my loyalty, and the connection we share, upon him. To be strong enough to withstand following paths that will take us on separate journeys for now. "You're right here in my goddamn heart, baby." I give in, dragging him against me so that I can tuck his head into the crook of my neck and brush my mouth against his ear. "This is where you are. No matter whether you piss me off, or leave me ready to toss you over my shoulder, or be so goddamn in love with you I don't know how to breathe. That's who you are. You're better than this, and I believe that you'll figure out you're worthy of being loved by someone one day. Trust that I'm gonna be out there hoping like hell you might want that guy to be me."

Kayce makes a strained noise and wrestles out of my grasp in order to be able to look at me. "You can't possibly be in love with me." He shakes his head, renewed pain slashes across his handsome features, everything drawing tight in his expression.

"You're telling me I don't know my own mind?"

"No . . . I'm just saying it's not possible that it's me. You're meant to love someone else."

This fucking cowboy. Determined to fight me to the bitter end.

"Am I? Who am I supposed to be in love with then, huh?" I narrow my gaze, and my voice dips into a low warning. Like fuck I'm gonna fall for anyone else in this life.

Once again, my golden boy, with all the charm in the world, is speechless.

This time it's the last. This time, when I kiss him, it's the final one. It's all too brief, and I wish everything could play out with a different melody. I swallow back the pained groan that threatens to rise up when I gently brush a goodbye over his wet lips.

When I step back, it feels like a clamp seizes my heart, putting so much pressure there my chest is going to damn well explode. "It's you. I don't know if you'll ever trust that. But I guess I understand a little too easily why you wouldn't. Those walls are hard to let down, which is why I also know how hard it is to hear me . . . to believe me, when I say that I love you."

With my confession hanging in the crisp fall air, I turn on my heel. That's all it'll be. It's all it can be for us until Kayce figures out how he intends to move forward.

As I open the door, I pause and level him with a look across the truck roof. "Maybe one day you'll let me love you the way you deserve."

Getting back into my truck, I start the engine and watch him through the rearview as I pull away.

I wish he didn't let me leave.

CHAPTER 44
Kayce

My days have a wretched, despondent emptiness to them, the likes of which I've never known before.

There were times when I would get wasted, blackout drunk, and avoid reality for weeks on end. Even then, it didn't ache deep in my bones like this. Not having Raine in my life feels like the worst kind of hollowing out, a gaping cavity in my chest that used to be filled with the warmth of his presence.

Every morning when I look at my phone, when I check my messages, there's a hopeful prayer lingering on my lips where he last pressed his against mine.

Please remember me. Please come back to me.

I re-read back over the messages I sent him in the days after he left. After I pretty much crumpled in on myself and felt like a ghost floating around the ranch, lost and drifting along aimlessly. It took everything to put it into words and tell him, because it felt all too little too late. If he hadn't already blocked me, it felt like he'd take one look at what I was saying and laugh. Carelessly casting me aside after seeing me send a stupid little message. Why the hell would he care, when I should have been bold enough to say it to his face and out loud.

There are so many things I should have done differently.

> I've thought about what you said every day.
>
> I'm a better person because of you. Because you taught me how to fall in love.
>
> I didn't know how to tell you at the time, and I'll regret that moment for a fucking lifetime. That day, I was an idiot and I froze, so here's me saying it now.
>
> I love you with everything I've got to give.
>
> It's selfish of me to expect you to ever come back, and that's the kicker. Maybe I'll just have to love you from afar.

Blowing out a shaky exhale, I swipe out of the message thread—a deserted place where he hasn't read or replied to my words—and dial the number I've been putting off reaching out to this entire time. Someone I haven't spoken to in what feels like forever, yet is undoubtedly who I need to have this important conversation with.

One person at a time.

The line is filled with static, as I sit in my truck with the hot air blasting and a coffee cradled in one hand, parked up on the side of the road in the dark.

I've driven down into Crimson Ridge under a carpet of stars and a moonless night, but it's only as far as needed in order to reach cell phone coverage, then I'll be hauling ass back up to the top of the mountain as soon as this shit is over and done with.

"Is everything ok?" My dad's voice is gritty with sleep when he answers after half a dozen rings. "Are you alright?"

"Look, some of us are out here putting in a full day's work, alright? And you're still snoring."

"Excuse me for nearly having a goddamn heart attack because you're calling me out of the blue. What's going on?"

I hear the line jostle, and mumbling in the background. My dad must cover the speaker, because I hear him rumble a quiet reply—something about *going back to sleep.*

"Sorry for waking Layla up." I wince and take a sip of my coffee. Probably shouldn't be having another cup this close to midnight, but I don't sleep much these days anyway. I'd rather be alert driving back up the mountain road in the dark, especially considering the weather due to roll in.

"That storm is supposed to hit soon," he mutters at me, in the Colton Wilder fashion I'm all too familiar with. "Why are you hanging about down in Crimson Ridge? The safest place for you is to be on the ranch."

He gives it to me sternly, but I also hear the unspoken question there. My dad knows me well enough to understand that this is something big if it warrants an international phone call.

"Yeah, *uhh*, about that." I clear my throat. "Promise I only needed to put in this call. As soon as I get off the phone to you, I'll be heading straight back while the roads are still passable."

"Good. You don't need to be messing around or taking unnecessary chances."

"Don't worry, I won't be." Normally, I'd have something smart to say in reply. The old version of Kayce Wilder would be rolling his eyes and doing the whole 'yeah, Dad, tell me something I don't know' routine. But tonight, I'm just sitting here with my knee bouncing and trying to figure out how on earth to spit out what I gotta say.

On the way down here, I had it all planned out. Now that he's on the other end of the phone line, I feel clammed up, like I don't know how to pry that shell open.

I hear him close a door with a soft click, then begin making himself a coffee in the background. Pretty sure it's around four in the morning over there right now.

"Do I need to do this by guesswork or what?" He chuckles, still sounding sleepy, but it's kind of a relief to hear that he's not pissed off even though I've woken him up. "Does it begin with the letter A? One word or two? Movie or a book?"

"God . . . stop . . ." I shake my head and tilt the air vent on the heater. "That sense of humor of yours hasn't improved while being away."

"Alright. So hit me with it." A faucet runs briefly before cutting off, followed by the sound of rummaging around in cupboards, a chink of ceramic, drawers rolling open and then closed.

Sucking in a deep breath, my thoughts are spinning as fast as a roulette wheel. Clattering and whirring, they're in there somewhere, but the thought I actually need has gotta land in place before I can get the words out.

"Kayce, you know I'm not one to jump to worst-case scenarios. But right now, you're beginning to freak me the fuck out. What's wrong?" My dad's voice firms up. Somehow, hearing him admit that—hearing the concern front and center in his tone—snaps my focus in place. Just like all the times I've been in the bucking chute, ready to compete and dialed in every ounce of attention on the horse beneath me.

It drops me out of my head, and I just start talking.

I tell him *everything*.

My knee. The fact I'm no longer going to be in rodeo anymore. How I'll maybe need surgery, but that wouldn't fix anything, and actually might be more invasive than healing naturally and continuing with regular rehab.

That somehow flows into telling him about Mom. About her latest overdose. About the money I gave her. Not all the grimy details of my childhood, but enough that I touch on the reason for so many of my shitty decisions in recent years. Stuff I should have told him before now, but honestly, never knew where to begin. So I just avoided doing so.

The kind of man Colton Wilder is, he listens. My dad just fucking listens, and it's the most cathartic thing ever to let this all finally fly free into the night.

It's like I've got a second wind. Hardly pausing for breath, I launch into the next part. I step off the ledge and plunge headfirst. First, starting by telling him about kissing that random guy way back on New Year's Eve, then continuing through to realizing I'm attracted to men. Finally, with a thud, I crash land on the scariest admission of all.

I tell him about Raine.

The waterfall of words keeps on pouring. All my confessions about these monumental goddamn things in my life, laying out all the worries that have been eating away at me.

By the time I've unloaded so much more than I ever imagined I would tell him, I feel like I could float out the roof of this truck like a feather on the breeze. At the same time, I'm also unsure where we go to from here.

My dad and I don't exactly have heart-to-hearts.

"Sorry. I kinda just trauma dumped twenty years worth of father-son chats on you in the space of twenty minutes." I grimace.

Dad clears his throat with a slight cough. "Give me a second. I'm gonna drink this coffee first. Then I've got something I need to say, ok?"

I shift my weight. "Sure." As I sit there in the ensuing silence, chewing the inside of my cheek, I can't help but blurt a little more. "And yeah, I'm well aware, I should probably come with a sign stamped across my forehead that reads, *Hi, I'm a complete fucking mess; nice to meet you.*"

His deep, rumbling voice chases away any of those self-deprecating thoughts. "Kayce ... when you were younger, I backed off when I should have been trying to find you. It's a burden I'll always bear, because I deserve to carry the weight of that decision around. A forever reminder of doing you wrong. I hope you know just how sorry I am."

Christ, the way my entire chest squeezes at the sincerity of his words. "I don't want that for either of us, Dad." I shake my head. "Nah, fuck that. Please don't feel like you did anything but the best you could."

"Son, I might've only been a dumb teenager at the time, but I shoulda known better. Or at least shouldn't have let your mother so easily make it seem like everything was fine over the years, when it wasn't."

Emotion pricks the back of my eyes. "She's good at manipulating things to her favor. That's not your fault."

"I truly am sorry." He exhales the sort of weary sigh that comes with years of his own awful experiences, the way he suffered, compounding with the shit I've been through.

"I know you are. And I'm just glad I found my way to Devil's Peak eventually."

"Me too, son." Then he makes a throat clearing sound again, and I'm already internally groaning. "So ... *uhh* ... I know I might be past forty, but I'm pretty sure my hearing is doing just fine. You wanna just... *uhh*..."

His awkward stumbling around the words makes me snort with laughter. "Explain that I somehow ended up falling for my stepbrother?"

"Yeah. That bit." I can just picture him with a hand dug into his hair, phone held up to his ear, leaning against the counter of the kitchen in some quaint Irish cottage half a world away.

My cheeks burn, followed quickly by the pit sinking in my stomach at the thought of Raine. Fuck, I miss him so much. Just pausing to think about his name for the briefest second plunges me right back into all those awful feelings of yearning to have him back.

Worrying my bottom lip, I pull my phone away to briefly check the time. Fucking hell, it's almost midnight. I really do need to get my ass moving.

"How did you know Layla was the one?"

He stays quiet on the end of the line for a long pause. "That day I first met her, and we got to talking—when I didn't know who she was or her name—I felt something I'd never felt before. Then things played out the way they did, and I tried to forget her, honest to god, I tried." My dad's voice softens when he talks about her, and all I can think is that I'm so fucking happy for him that he's been able to find that kind of love in his life. "Except, there was no forgetting her. There's no other way to describe it. It's like she was there in my blood; all it took was a brief conversation. None of it made sense, but there was a connection there. The kind of unmistakable attraction... pretty sure I'd still be carrying that around with me a hundred years later, even if she'd never come back into my life again."

Is it awkward talking about my ex with my dad? Maybe on a certain level, but in all honesty, it feels like we're speaking about two different people. A different life completely. Back then, I was an asshole drinking away my problems, and she walked in and out of my life in such a short span of time.

"I think he's my *one*." My mouth feels dry as I say it out loud, hardly more than a coarse admission into the emptiness of my truck.

"Then that's all that matters." It's so calm, so sure, hearing my dad just take everything in his stride like he does so fucking well. "But it's gonna hurt like hell in the meantime."

"You think he'll come back?"

"After everything you just told me? The fact he said he was giving you time and space to figure things out? I have no doubt."

My breath wooshes out of my lungs. "I'm gonna have to get going." A few slushy droplets start hitting my windscreen as I peer out into the darkness. *Snow.* "Thanks for understanding . . . for not being weirded out, or flipping on me . . ."

The steadfast man he is, Dad further reconfirms with his next words exactly why I'm here doing what I'm doing to help him, even though it might be breaking my heart not to be with Raine right now.

"I'm here for you, Kayce. Anytime. Anything you need. All you gotta do is say the word. I'll get on a flight tomorrow if you need me back there."

CHAPTER 45

Kayce

The first winter I spent here—when the snow arrived and grew thicker by the day—I cursed it endlessly.

Along with so many things in my life at that time, I hated what it represented. Being isolated. Stuck up here with nothing but my own dark thoughts and terrible places my mind was liable to go. If I didn't have the constant buzz of alcohol simmering in my veins, and company to waste days away with, I would have to confront what was going on inside my head. I'd have to see all those broken pieces laid out.

Now, I've learned how to make peace with the mess. I've learned how to accept the parts of me that aren't pretty, that certainly aren't perfect, but can still be loveable all the same.

Or so my therapist tells me.

We do online sessions. After starting out twice a week, we'll aim to eventually work our way down to a biweekly check-in. Something I've done a hell of a lot of lately . . . *talking*.

Only, it's not to the one person I actually want to speak to. What I wouldn't give to hear his voice after spending these frozen winter months apart. To feel his touch cupping my jaw after all these miserable weeks on end without him. Burnt golden leaves of fall seem like a distant memory; an eternity ago when I look at the calendar and see how we're crawling closer to spring. Hell, I'd do just about anything to even be on the receiving end of one of his stupid scowls, as long as I was able to witness it in person.

Staring out over the ranch, the place is an endless expanse of white. Sugary powder dumped over everything after last night's fresh snowfall. It's beautiful, that much I can appreciate for what it is now. In this new season of Kayce Wilder, man who is learning how to *love himself*. When in the past, I might have stood in this exact same spot with my coffee and wanted to hurl the entire thing against the wall because all I could see was a cage made up of winter's icy touch.

At the conclusion of each session, I've been given homework. To find a way to open up to one person, about one thing. To take this monumental pile of crap that I've been terrified of being buried under in a landslide, and pick it apart piece by tiny piece. So today is the day I know I'm ready to talk to Chaos.

Honestly, I've left him until last. By now, I've pretty much worked my way through everyone I'm closest to, letting them know about how different my life is going to look once I'm no longer snowbound on this ranch, after winter vacates and the weather turns warmer.

So many things are going to be different, and yet there are also some massive fucking unknowns.

Namely, if I'll be able to find Raine. Will he want to see me? Would he even consider returning to Crimson Ridge?

I take a quick photo through the kitchen window, showing the snow coating the view, remembering the times I stood here with him and took it for granted. When I rambled on about some stupid show, a series we should watch together, never once assuming there might be a future point in time when we wouldn't get the chance. There's no avoiding how much of an idiot I feel at times, the foolish naivety I had, presuming we'd be blessed with endless *time*.

Now I know more than ever how true the sentiment is that time is precious. It's never guaranteed.

So, I send Raine the photo. Something I've started doing lately, even though I'm pretty sure he'll never check his Instagram—or worse, he'll outright ignore my messages, as he has every right to do. I add a little text with it. Hoping against all fucking hope that maybe there will be a day when he appears back in my life again.

> Snow's here.
>
> I wish you were, too.

With a sigh, I leave my phone plugged in at the kitchen counter, then gather up my mug. I'm gonna possibly need this entire coffee pot for this. As I make my way to the office, each step is punctuated by me quietly hyping myself up. Being my own one-man fucking marching band to get the words straight and my head in the right place.

I'm at peace with this decision. If anything, once I was able to open up to a professional—someone who had nothing to do with rodeo or Crimson Ridge, or any of my life here—it was easy to look at what I'd achieved with some perspective. There are a fuckload of people out there who will never get to ride a bronc, let alone compete, and I've been a lucky enough son of a bitch to do both.

Hell, I can still spend the rest of my days on horseback if I want to.

I'll take that as a fucking win.

Settling into the rickety chair my dad keeps in here, it squeaks and protests when I sink down. I pick up the handset for the radio and flick onto the right channel before speaking.

"Hayes Ranch, come in. What's your twenty?"

The line crackles and pops while I take a sip from my mug and wait.

"Go ahead. Wes, here." The familiar deep voice of one of Chaos' older brothers, Westin Hayes, comes through.

"Eyes on Chaos?"

There's a pause. "Kayce. Good to hear from you, man. You good?"

"Toasty warm up here on Devil's Peak. You know how it goes."

"I'll check his status. Stand by." I smile to myself. Wes is about as grouchy as my dad. The two of them are more similar than they'd ever admit, except in this case, the second oldest of the Hayes brothers has taken over running their family ranch. He's not that much younger than the eldest, but Cam has been Sheriff for years now. So, the mantle to take charge of their family property fell on Wes' shoulders, with help from the others.

"Shit-for-brains is out covering the south pasture. Hit him on channel forty-two."

"Copy." I flick the receiver over and ping Chaos.

"Fuck face," he answers, voice slightly distorted by the crackle of the radio.

"Miss me?"

"Heartbroken. Tormented. Every day is a tragedy without you in my life, Wilder."

"As it should be." I let go of the handset button for a moment and gather my thoughts. It's not ideal doing this via radio, but it's not like I can pick up the phone and call him.

"What's up? Cam's the one doing welfare checks on your ass, so I know this isn't about the roads or shit like that."

"You sittin' down?" I grumble, before taking a deep breath. "I'm not coming back to rodeo after winter. Or ever, actually. My knee is too fucked up. Also . . . in some more recent developments, that I don't know how to explain without just going ahead and saying it . . . I'm gay."

The words rush out before I let the static hang in the air, filling the tiny office with the anticipation of his reaction. I'm not worried as such, but I kinda hate that it's taken me this long to tell him.

In my fist, the radio unit hums and whines before bursting back into life.

"Say again? Did we just transport to dueling banjos territory? Dueling dicks? Where the fuck you been hiding this juicy detail, sweetheart?"

"Yeah, turns out, I'm into guys now." I'm laughing to myself, wishing I could see his face. "And apparently my gay compass has been broken since day one . . . because I kinda only want Raine." As his name passes my lips, I wince. It hasn't gotten any easier to say it. Even after telling Brad and Flinn, Sage, my dad—no matter how many times I tell the people who mean everything to me, it still stings that I can't tell *him*.

The line stays quiet, and I suddenly feel like I need to add on the next part hastily.

"It's not as if I'm out here secretly obsessed with *you* or anything. You don't have to worry about that."

There's another long goddamn pause before Chaos' voice echoes over the radio. "You aren't? I'm kinda disappointed. This is me pouting."

"Of course you are." I drain the last of my coffee.

"Don't you think I'm pretty?" he whines.

"Oh my god." A laugh chokes out of me so suddenly I nearly spit my entire mouthful all over my dad's ancient computer. "You're gonna make this about you, aren't cha?"

"Tell me I'm pretty right now, or I'll never speak to you again, Wilder."

"Jesus. Yes, you're very pretty alright."

"Thank you." He huffs. "Now rewind to the fact you slipped and fell onto Raine's—what I'm sure is very impressive—dick. I coulda been coaching you through every trick I've got for sucking cock."

"Why does everyone keep telling me I need coaching?"

"Well . . . you ain't gonna be deep-throating a monster like that your very first time."

"Ok. I'm not having the rest of this conversation over a radio channel. I just wanted you to know and hold all questions for the next time I can get off this mountain."

"So what . . . are you two like kissing cousins now, or what?"

"Jesus." I scrub my hand over my mouth.

"What does a stepbrother-flavored blow job feel like?"

"Bye."

"Negative. Don't you dare end this transmission, prick. Didn't Raine leave? Heard he fucked off back to moose country."

"Yeah. I'm not sure where we stand, ok. But if I didn't completely mess it up, I wanna be with him. As in a serious, proper relationship, go all-in kinda deal. Is that enough spilling my guts to keep you happy?"

He pauses and takes his sweet time before replying. "For now. But you bet your perky, firm ass cheeks I will hunt you down as soon as that snow clears and expect the full story. Copy?"

A wry smile settles on my lips. "Loud and clear, Chaos." *Loud and fucking clear.*

THE REST of my day goes by uneventfully. Cattle get fed. Horses take up too much of my time. It's a familiar loop around the ranch while the place is coated in fresh snow. With such a significant fall, the mountain road will be shut for a while. I've heard from the crew who work to clear access as fast as they safely can, but there's no promise it'll be open until next week at the earliest.

So here I am, in my little bubble. With cows and horses for company until things clear a little and the weather settles. Once the forecast looks good for a few days in a row I'll ride out and check some of the fences and further parts of the ranch for any damage. But today all I need to do is the basics and make sure all the animals are safe, with access to food, water, and shelter.

Winter has a strange sort of rhythm to it. Up here, you're at the mercy of the elements, so much more so than down in Crimson Ridge, with the extreme of added altitude to contend with. So you can make plans, you can prepare your ass off, but ultimately you just gotta play the hand you get dealt.

Sometimes, it's a royal flush, a winning streak to leave you grinning from ear to ear, and at other times, it's one that makes you immediately want to fold.

Right now, it's not the ranch making me feel that way. It's the messages waiting for me in my inbox. An email address I wish hadn't made an appearance, and yet here she is, once again.

I hurriedly scan the contents of her email. Apologies and flurries of chaos from her life. She was discharged from the hospital straight away; somehow, the doctors who evaluated her didn't consider her to be a risk—they never do. And it's no big surprise she's once again turned up asking for something.

SAVING THE RAIN

The cycle she's stuck in keeps on repeating itself.

I'm fucking done.

I keep thinking about that night and how strong Raine was for me. He made it seem possible to actually have a life for the first time, one that exists beyond all the ways she continually keeps on trying to wreck mine. The days of her dragging me into her mistakes are over.

As I read her email again, my skin feels a flush of warmth. It's almost like his hands are holding me tucked against his chest, just as he did on the couch that night when I was a fucking mess. I feel him stroking my hair in that gentle and tender way he does. A careful touch that seems impossible for a man like him, who is so gritty and rough around the edges. There's a soft rumble, a vibration of his voice; even though I can't hear the words exactly, I can *feel* the energy of him giving me the strength to do what I should have done years ago.

I start typing.

Mom, I'm going to help you this final time, but it's not what you'll expect from me. Or, maybe, it's what you've been begging me for this whole time, and I just couldn't hear your cry for help.

I apologize for giving you money last time. I should never have done that. The guilt I feel for what happened is something I really struggle with, but this time I will do the thing we should have done in the first place.

I'm booking you into a rehab facility. The details are attached. I'm gonna send a car and a driver to pick you up tomorrow. It's up to you whether you take this step for yourself, but this is the last thing I'm going to do.

I love you. I wish you the best of luck with getting clean. But I can't keep picking up the broken pieces of your addiction.

A shaky exhale leaves my lungs as I press send straight away. The information that she needs is attached. With the help of my therapist, we had already put together a plan for what I would do if this very moment reared its ugly head again.

So here I stand, doing the hard, uncomfortable thing, and the relief I feel is immense.

What takes me by surprise is that she responds straight away. I didn't expect an immediate reaction, if at all, in all honesty. If anything, I fully anticipated to discover tomorrow that she had disappeared, or turned down my offer, or never arrived at the facility.

God, no. Kayce, please understand it wasn't your fault. I promise, I didn't do anything with that money you sent, except to use every cent of it to pay back the debt.

Ezekiel gave the pills to me. He handed them to me, and I took them because I'm always too weak to say no. I'm not well, and you've given me an incredible gift, you have no idea.
I'll go tomorrow. I will.

This is more than I deserve, and I wish I could hug you right now, Kayce. Those pills are my personal hell, and I never did enough to protect you when you were younger. Not like Raine did. I'm so sorry for all the trouble I've caused you in your life.

The sight of his name is like a beacon. A burst of light that obliterates anything else. I hardly notice all the other lines of text my mom has written. What does she mean? My entire chest tightens as my fingers type a reply so fast I fumble over nearly all the letters.

What are you talking about? What did Raine do?

God. She takes forever to reply. I'm chewing my thumbnail, pacing up and down the kitchen with my phone in hand. Each time the screen dims, I tap to keep it awake, eyes fixated like a hawk on the space where a notification will drop down. Please. *Please.* Don't let her wander off and not continue what she was saying.

All those cuts, the bruises. It was awful to see every time.

He was so determined to keep us safe that he used to provoke Ezekiel before he got to the house.

My heart is pumping so hard that it feels as if the entire thing climbs straight out of my chest. I'm growing more and more dizzy as I hit reply.

Mom. What the fuck are you talking about?

I need you to be straight with me. What did Raine do?

—

It seems impossible that such a good kid came from a terrible man.

I'm so sorry I ever married him, and that I stayed. Raine didn't want us getting hurt, so he used to make sure he took the beatings. Made sure we would be left alone. Then, when he was old enough, once he was bigger than his father, he made sure to turn it back on Ezekiel. Threatened him to never touch either you or me again before he moved out.

God, it was so long ago now. He was only a teenager when it all happened. I remember it was sometime around when you fell and broke your wrist.

My body slumps down the front of the kitchen cabinets until I reach the cold floor. The back of my eyes sting as I struggle to read through my blurry vision.
All the times Raine came home a mess.
All those nights, his face was cut to shreds.
All the black eyes. Split lips. Bruised cheekbones.
I thought he'd been fighting other teenagers. This whole time, he

led me to believe that he'd been some angry guy getting into scraps just for the hell of it.

When the truth is that he'd been using himself as a shield. He put his body on the line time and time again.

A wave of nausea threatens to consume me.

No wonder he didn't want to stick around. He's already sacrificed so much for me. Raine has been there to protect me in ways I didn't even know or understand—doing it all in secret.

Maybe this is all I deserve, to follow in my dad's footsteps and spend years up here in isolation. At least that way, I can't hurt anyone anymore. I can't hurt him further if I stay here and leave him alone.

Sinking my fingers into my hair, I tug on the strands until it stings. I miss him, and I ache for him, and I'm so in love with him. With shaky hands, I open the messages I've sent, my insides feeling torn to pieces. I'm contemplating deleting everything. To fully erase all those pathetic attempts to tell him how I feel because I want him to have a future that isn't contaminated by my poison.

No. Oh god. By the time I get there, it's too late. The blood drains from my face. He's read all the messages I sent, yet there's no reply. Of course, there's nothing because I've been a goddamn burden on his life ever since our worlds first collided.

Except, I see something new. Raine has posted a new image on his page—the first one in who knows how long . . . at least a year, maybe more.

And it's us. It's our photo. His tattooed hand covering mine, with our fingers interlocked and resting on top of the bedsheets.

Beneath it sit five words that rob me of every breath and bring my heart stuttering to a halt, clattering against my ribcage.

"Never not obsessed with you."

CHAPTER 46

Kayce

The snow keeps coming, day after day, seemingly unending. I know it's only inevitable, and enduring these sorts of moments in time, where the sun rarely puts in an appearance and the night comes around all too rapidly . . . well, such is the reality of winter in these mountains.

Even so, it's tough mentally.

Particularly so on days like today when it feels like iced tendrils have been whipping at my face nonstop, and I'm weary. I'm so fucking weary.

How my dad has done this year upon year, I can't fathom. He did all of this, without another soul to check on him or care for him. I might not have anyone here to physically help me out with the chores and the mundane routine of taking care of our stock, but I've got constant support.

Whenever I pick up the radio or find pockets of time when the internet is working strongly enough in the morning and at night to look at my phone, someone is always there to see how I'm doing.

Winnie jostles beneath me, her ears and mane are flecked with a dusting of snow, just as I am too. As I ride, I keep returning to the knowledge that it's foolish of me to feel like it's not enough. But I can't fucking help it. The weeks have drifted on, and that glimmer of hope I had when Raine read my messages and posted the photo of us holding hands feels like a distant memory now.

I don't know what I expected, but he's typically distant and impossible to read. Of course, he is. This is the man who owns my heart from a million miles away, and he's the absolute worst at communicating at the best of times.

So I gotta put up and shut up, and deal with the fallout from my own stupid mistake of pushing him away.

For all I know, he's working in some similarly remote and inaccessible location. There's no question . . . he's undoubtedly going to be gone a long fucking time, and it's on my shoulders to become the man who is worthy of him by the point when our lives cross paths again. Although, I hate not knowing when that might be.

This right here is all I can do. Focus on me. Do what he told me to do, and continue healing a little more each day in the meantime.

Even if it means doing so while balls fucking deep in snow and ice, cut off from the rest of the world.

Winnie tosses her head from side to side, which is her way of letting me know she's just about had enough of being out in the elements. At least we've had a reprieve from the storm fronts battering the ranch. Today's conditions aren't due to deteriorate in the way they can so dramatically turn on a dime, but there's still an ever-present drift of snowfall dancing little twirls and flourishes.

Those puffy clumps stick to my lips as I sink deeper into my high collar to shield against the wind. I lean forward and give her a pat on the neck. She's been good to me today, so I promise extra treats and a night tucked up warm in her stall as thanks for being out with me in the bracing fucking chill while we made sure the cattle were fed.

Once we're just outside the barn, I swing out of the saddle and give her a good dust-off. Her big liquidy eyes blink at me, and those clever ears twitch as she damn near runs me over in her enthusiasm to get back inside.

"Yeah, me too, girl." I laugh. Fuck I spend a lot of time talking out loud to these horses. They've probably heard almost as much as I've unloaded on my therapist. Except for where that's concerned, I've had to find someone who can do everything via messaging. The other fun part of our antiquated goddamn WiFi up here is the fact it isn't strong enough for calls or anything that the rest of the world would be able to do with the power of the internet at their fingertips.

Now I can safely say, I'm in a hell of a better place.

Mind... relaxed.

Confidence... strengthened.

Sexuality... discussed at great length.

"At least it's something of an improvement," I mutter as Winnie clops beside me, and the two of us make our way toward the doors.

"Did you really mean what you said?" A deep voice reaches out from the shadows at the entrance to the barn.

Dark eyes lift to meet mine. The strongest of jaws, covered in a slightly thicker beard than when I last saw him. He leans back against the wall, with arms folded and boots crossed at the ankle.

The goddamn love of my life is waiting there, staring right at me.

I drop the reins and rush him. My balled-up fists collide with the front of his jacket, and I shove at his chest. With a desperate snarl on my lips, my pulse absolutely howls in the side of my throat.

"How could you? Putting yourself in danger like that?" I shove him harder. "I know everything. How could you not tell me? All this time, I thought you were the meanest asshole to ever exist and that you hated everything about me. You leave me to find out by pure chance that you put your damn life on the line? He could have fucking *killed* you. A grown man beating up a teenager? All for the sake of me?"

I'm panting. My skin prickles as I keep wailing on his chest, and something hot and wet rolls down my numb cheeks. "I didn't deserve to be given your protection. I've been nothing but a worthless, piece of shit burden to you. Why the hell would you ever do that?" My arms feel like they weigh ten thousand pounds as I slam my fist into the front of his jacket with a guttural noise.

Raine traps my glove against his front. Pinning me beneath a secure hold and equally firm stare. "Have you ever stopped to think that I can't stand to see you hurt, or suffer? Maybe I didn't always know how to show it. I probably fucked up too many times to count, but I'm here now, doing the only thing that makes sense—not leaving you." His voice is like velvet. A mirage from my dreams. Anything he says in that low, rumbly tone, I swear to god, I feel right down in the depths of my soul.

Snow keeps trickling from the sky, dusting across our shoulders, eddying between us to cling to my damp lashes, melting against my lips.

I'm speechless. Limp. Suddenly sideswiped by an onslaught of fatigue—I've been so tired, trudging forward for this long without him—and now am so impossibly relieved that this is real, and he's here. This is all so surreal. I can't do anything but stare at him while my heart zooms laps inside my chest.

Studying my features, Raine traces them slowly, like he's re-learning every single angle and slope.

"Hey, snowflake. I missed you." The corners of his lips twitch, before his brows crease. ". . . wait, what's that look for?"

"I don't know how to feel when you call me that. I used to hate it."

"Why?"

I sniff. Am I fucking crying? Is that what this is? I can't remember the last time I cried. If ever. "You know why. That I'm weak and all that."

He shakes his head, and being locked in the high beam of his gaze is a feeling I'll never get used to. "Not in my eyes. I mean, I used to call you that purely because I knew it pissed you off . . . and I'm sorry." He reaches up and brushes a thumb over my cheek. "But I don't think of it as reflective of being weak. A snowflake is a thing of beauty. An infinitely unique pattern. It melts, yes, but that depends on its circumstances. When it transforms into water, you and I both know, that's one of nature's most powerful forces. Able to flow and bend and fucking move mountains. A life-giving substance."

Yeah, I'm crying. Full, fat, rolling tears make their way over my cheeks, and my eyes swim with the impact of everything he's saying in that calm, anchoring way he does.

"You give me life, Kayce. You've shown me there's a way to move on from the hurts of a past we shared . . . you're stronger than I am, because you got back up each time. I'm so proud of you, and I didn't always know how to say those words."

Raine dips forward and takes what belongs to him. He tugs his hat off his head and seeks out my lips. A soft, yet intense, reconnection where all the ways he's the center of my goddamn universe crackle and explode into a roaring bonfire. His mouth presses against mine, and I breathlessly dissolve into him. I can't help but be reeled in by him and all the ways I'm longing for his rugged, gorgeous protectiveness.

"Snowflakes are beautiful," he murmurs against my mouth.

"You think I'm . . ." It's mostly just choked-up noises, rather than words coming out of me.

"Beautiful?" He hums. A rich, life-giving sort of vibration that pours forth to fill my veins. "Of course I do. You're so goddamn beautiful, my sweet boy."

Feeling Raine smile against my lips is everything.

In that moment, the cracks heal, the chasm closes over, and I'm more whole than I've ever felt before.

RAINE LETS ME GO, but only long enough to tend to Winnie. The entire time, he's by my side, tracking me like I'm his willing prey, as we make sure she's settled before he collides with me again.

My brain and body are screaming for him. With every drop of blood thrumming in my veins as we crash inside the house.

It's unspoken between us, that need to be reconnected physically. I don't think, just act. My hands are everywhere, pawing at him, pushing him ahead of me while tugging on his clothes with frustrated whines.

He matches me the whole way. Doesn't pause for more than enough time to discard winter gear—boots and hats and jackets are tossed haphazardly—before he's taking me by the hand and dragging me into his body so he can kiss me senseless once more.

Fuck, I love him so much.

Threading my fingers into his hair, I meet him in pure urgency. Our teeth clash, tongues slide together, and mouths angle to fully indulge the hunger roaring low in my stomach.

"You didn't answer me before." Raine bites down on my bottom lip so hard it stings, and I want him to do it again. "You meant everything?"

"Every word."

"Fuck, I hate that it took so long to get here." He keeps walking me backward in the direction of my bedroom, with a gravely timbre coating his words.

"Wait..." I pant into his mouth, fumbling with his shirt. "How did you get to the ranch? The mountain roads are under ten feet of snow. No vehicles can get past." I'm barely able to form a coherent string of thoughts as Raine draws back enough to do the rest of the job for me, shucking it over his head, and thank fuck he's finally bare-chested.

"More like three feet in places." His fingers curl beneath the hem of my top, and the stroke of those rough fingertips against my skin sends a riot of goosebumps flying everywhere. "And I rode here. Horses don't mind a bit of powder." Tearing at my thermal, he drags it roughly up over my head.

"I can't believe you're real right now." My eyes bounce everywhere in a rapid-fire devouring of the sight of him, before I launch myself forward. I just want to taste him, lick every inch of his body, and show him just how much I missed this, us, being together. Pushing my tongue and lips against the stubble covering his throat, I breathe out a whimper of pleasure across his warm skin. I love the rough edge to him, the scratch, the scrape, and the way he smells.

"I love you." Sliding my hold up the wrap back of his neck, I seek out his hair and tangle my fingers there, whispering the words against his throat. "I missed you so fucking badly. I'm sorry I fucked everything up for us."

Raine's unwavering, strong hands roam across my back, dragging his calloused touch and brightening a path everywhere he maps the contours of me. "You needed space. You needed time. It wasn't fair of me to drop that on you and expect you to know how to handle it." He drops kisses along my temple, down to my shoulders, laying out a trail of hot, wet reminders of just how good it feels to have his affection. "I'd been so used to only ever needing to think about myself. I'm sorry for being selfish."

SAVING THE RAIN

The backs of my legs hit the bed, and Raine pushes me down. As I land on my elbows and gaze back up at him, the sight steals my goddamn breath. He's so fucking magnificent and has that sexy hooded look to his eyes. The darkness in those obsidian depths tells me he's in no mood to be anything but in command.

"I'm yours, snowflake. I'm so fucking in love with you. Got it?" As he speaks in that deep, gravelly voice that makes my stomach swoop, his hands work at his belt and jeans.

I'm officially gone. Dead. Buried. My cowboy half-undressed, ridding himself of his jeans while telling me he loves me in a voice that sounds like pure sex? Game over.

Swallowing hard, I nod. Greedy eyes remaining fixated on his hands—those sexy fucking veins popping up beneath his ink, the strong hands I want to have wrapped around my dick and my neck as soon as possible—until the moment he's naked. Standing in front of me, thick and erect, the impressive sight leaves my mouth watering for him.

The overwhelming intensity of his gaze, as he strokes himself from root to tip, has me gasping, pinned to the mattress by nothing more than just a look. Even though I want to push up off my elbows. Even though I want... "Please, I need to taste you, just for a moment." I bite down on my bottom lip.

Raine shakes his head, and I feel every place his eyes rake over my body. He sets me alight with that onyx stare, calculating his next move before he strikes. Those strong hands of his reach for my hips, yanking me closer to the edge of the bed before they hit my waistband. As he works my jeans loose, my stomach caves, and I have to clutch at the sheets in an effort to ground myself into the here and now and not immediately float away.

The sound of my pants hitting the floor is like the moment that bucking chute crashes open. Raine shoves my knees wide, stoops down, and before I can think, or react, his mouth is there.

It's so heated and slick, and at the same time, his beard scratches to leave sparks of pure adrenaline-filled pleasure replacing my blood, as he runs his tongue *everywhere*. The noises coming out of me are feral as he lavishes attention on every exposed part of me. It's a struggle between letting my head drop back to hit the sheets and staying like this so I can watch him.

He's fucking hypnotic. So powerful. Muscled shoulders and corded forearms frame my body. Raine reduces me to rubble and dust and cursed moans. Sliding his tongue over my balls, followed by long lines up to my weeping crown and then back down to that unbelievably sensitive patch of smooth skin in behind. His hold on my body is wicked and delicious, bruising me with demanding fingertips all while I'm manhandled into the exact splayed-out feast he demands me to be for him. He keeps licking and grazing his teeth over all those delicate, begging parts of me until I'm reduced to a writhing mess.

"*Ummphfff*. God. Raine. Don't stop. *Ffuuuuuck*."

My cock smears precum all over my stomach, rock-hard and aching for so much more of his mouth than he's given me so far. And the gorgeous asshole he is, Raine knows it, too. With a final tormenting swirl of his tongue tracing the veins along the underside of my shaft, he braces himself over my body, giving me those hooded, darkened eyes as he wraps his lips around just the tip. It's enough to have me lifting up off the bed to seek out more, but I feel his mouth curve into a smile, recognizing my desperate attempt to go deeper. God, I just want to sink deeper.

Letting me go on a wet pop, he hums a deep, primal sort of noise and then crawls up my body. "My sweet thing. Eager for more?" Along his path, there's a moment's pause as he stops to torture my nipples, alternating between sharp nips and swirls of his tongue, before sinking against my mouth. Offering another branding, claiming kiss.

"Please. Please, I missed your cock." The weight of him on top of my body is absolutely everything. I'm almost sobbing with relief, making muffled pleas onto his tongue all while his bulk blankets me.

"Goddamn, I missed this pretty mouth." He groans. A vibration that sends tingles and sparks straight down my spine, from hearing how much I affect him. I love knowing that I can have such an effect on the strong, usually stoic man that he is. He crawls up over my face, and my heart lurches when I realize what he's doing.

Hastily licking my lips, a torrid flood of heat pools in my groin when Raine lowers himself slowly. The fat head of him is right there, and he proceeds to ease past my waiting lips. I straight up moan around the velvety smooth weight of him sliding onto my tongue, and simply refuse to have him keep treating me like some fragile thing.

I grab his ass with both hands and pull him deep, stuffing him into the back of my throat. A muffled, garbled noise of pleasure rises fast and needy, as the muskiness of him fills my senses. Heady relief floods through me at finally having him, tasting him.

Raine shudders above me, and over my hammering pulse, I hear him curse violently, his body clenching as he struggles not to start fucking my throat. I'm pretty certain the way I'm squeezing the globes of his firm ass tells him that's what I want. I want all of him. I want to be owned by him. I want everything he has to give.

He showers me with all sorts of ravenous words. Letting me guide him deep as I choke and slurp and concentrate on relaxing my throat. Hearing his perfect mix of filthy wickedness and smooth praise sends me spinning out of my head.

My perfect little hole. Jesus Christ. Listen to yourself. You're made to choke on me like a dream. Is this what you needed, baby? Gagging to be face fucked until you soak yourself with cum. Does that make it all better?

I swallow around his tip, and the way Raine's dick swells and his hips jerk is everything.

"That's..." He groans out a rough, ragged noise. "That's it. *Unghh*. Get it nice and sloppy for me." His hips pulse, and I taste the hint of tangy saltiness burst onto my taste buds as he leaks all over my tongue. "You feel so good. God, you don't even know how perfect you are."

When he pulls out, I'm in a daze. There's no way that I don't look a mess. Wetness coats my chin and streaks down my face from where my eyes have watered.

Raine dips to run his tongue across my cheeks one by one. "So perfect, my pretty thing." Hearing him call me that, while licking away those tears is enough to ruin me forever.

"Fuck me. I need you inside me. So bad." I don't even care that I'm begging over and over now.

"Rub us together. I need to see you come for me." There's so much hunger and desire in his voice that it strips me of any thought but to please him. As he reaches across to the bedside table, I'm caught up in how powerful he is. The strength of him. His perfect body and the sexy ink covering him. How I just want to be connected at all times. Drifting my touch over his lower stomach, I trace that v shape, following the dusting of dark hair below his navel.

This is real. He's actually here. Every stroke of my fingertips reminds me that I'm not dreaming any of this.

Raine is the perfect mix of demanding and careful. He pushes my knees high, settling himself onto one forearm so that we're pressed together, and I can wrap us both in my palm. Hooking my leg to give him access, he goes about driving me insane. Gliding a generous amount of lube over me, teasing my back entrance, and slowly working thick fingers into my ass. We make out with sloppy, biting kisses, and he alternates that with sucking down on my pulse point. Those bites and nips along my throat, over my Adam's apple, it's all consuming as I do my best to squeeze our cocks together. The weight of Raine alone creates more than enough exquisite friction, leaving me gasping, groaning loudly as my spine tingles and my balls draw up tight.

"Oh, my—fuck." He finds that spot with precision. Repeatedly grazing over that secret place until my body turns into an explosion of light and color. "*Fffuuck. Unnghhh.* I'm gonna come. I'm gonna come for you." Searing, pulsating pressure roars through and combusts at the base of my spine. I'm not even ashamed at how quickly I lose my mind. Erupting in hot, desperate pulses of cum, my cock jets all over us both while I moan his name.

"That's it, my good boy. So good for me." Raine's grunts are filled with drugging pleasure against the side of my neck. He kisses me all along that thumping pulse point while I see stars, and he keeps massaging me from the inside, leaving me jerking and flinching with the intensity of how hard and fast he just made me come. "Make a goddamn mess, and I'm gonna fuck you until you forget your own name."

Too late. I already have. He owns me. Plain and simple. There is nothing but Raine and how much I need him to be inside me.

It's love and lust and everything perfect in the precision of how he knows to treat me. Raine eases his fingers out before notching his dick there. He's covered in my cum, and that thought drives me out of my goddamn head.

He fucks me slow and steady. It's worshipful, without any sense of urgency or hurry. As if he has all the time in the world to leisurely work his way inside, not like the rampant oversexed mess I was. Damn him for the way he's able to slow everything down, to take his time savoring my body. Each measured, careful glide forward builds my carnal appetite back up gradually, until my dick has somehow filled once more. Infatuated as always, with his unique brand of pleasure and torment.

"I'm so proud of you. Taking me so well." His groan is the best sound. Listening to him enjoy the way we fit together is everything. "*Fffffuuuck*. This ass is so perfect, I don't ever want to lose you again." Strong hands push my knees against my chest as he sinks forward and fills me completely.

My body flushes from head to toe. The weight of him, the pleasurable burn of my body accommodating his thickness, followed by the intensity of having him fully seated inside, leaves my toes curling.

"I fucking love you." I gasp. Not caring about anything but telling him that on repeat.

Raine makes a sinfully hot noise as he pulls back, then sinks forward so wickedly slow it makes us both groan at how insanely good it feels. "Fuck, you're such a dream. There you are, swallowing every inch like you were made for this."

Boneless. That's all I am. Ruined. Whittled down to nothing more than a puddle of bliss as Raine fucks me into another whimpering, moaning climax. He pours the depth of his connection to me straight into my veins. *I love you*. With each time he says it with his actions, with each thrust, with each moment he rocks us together—those words bury deep in my chest, swelling my heart to bursting.

"Give me your eyes." His voice is ragged, the effort of holding off long enough for me to be with him. When I focus on his face, I cling tight and stay right there, trapped in his scorching gaze as he lets out a dark groan and his rhythm falters. "*Fffffuck*. I . . . fuck, I love you." Raine drops his forehead into the crook of my neck and buries himself to the hilt, pulsing with the sexiest grunts and pumps of his hips. And I fucking feel it. The overpowering heat of him. The slickness. How incredible it feels as his cum shoots forward and he unloads as deep as possible.

I blindly seek out his mouth, his lips, holding him there as we melt into each other.

As I fall even deeper in love with the man I don't ever want to be parted from again.

CHAPTER 47
Raine

So this is peace?

This is what it feels like to find your sanctuary in someone else . . . and learn to live wholly in the moment. To fall deeper every day now that I've allowed my heart to crack wide open to being with Kayce.

I willingly lose myself in the act of loving him.

We've had weeks of seclusion here on Devil's Peak, hidden away together, getting to reconnect and find our path forward. Having long nights in front of a roaring fire to figure it out *together*.

For two people who spent so many years on opposite pages, facing each other down across acres of torment and struggle, this feels like coming home. I've never known where I'd land in this life—after spending so much time continually moving and endlessly uprooting myself—but quitting my job and returning to him was the easiest decision I've ever made.

Do I wish I'd seen what he wrote to me sooner? Perhaps. But having heard how much progress he's been able to make in my absence, makes me think the timing was right . . . or something approaching that. Kayce wouldn't have been able to take some of those vastly important steps that only he could take by himself—setting one foot in front of the other each day as he climbed that personal mountain. If I'd turned up to disturb that, I'd regret not allowing him the opportunity to feel that he'd achieved that feat and learned to trust himself.

To learn how to face down the parts of himself he'd fled from all this time.

I'm endlessly proud of him. I try to remember to tell him as often as I can.

The snow barricading us at the top of the Peak has cleared—the roading crew having arrived late yesterday and confirmed safe access has been reinstated to Crimson Ridge. Not that I was hoping for a reason to be trapped here longer, but what should have been good news also seemed a little hollow.

Selfishly, I've relished having this time without anyone else interrupting. While I usually thrive in a life that most would find lonely, having Kayce at my side, all to myself, has been incredible. Something warm and comforting seeps through my bones, knowing he's never far away.

We need to go into town for supplies later today, a fact that had Kayce just about bouncing out of bed this morning, while I was grumbling that it wasn't anywhere near as exciting as he seemed to think. He pretended to pout and reminded me that he's basically been stuck up here in the winter equivalent of time-out for way too long.

So I couldn't resist the temptation to remind him why it wasn't a bad thing to have to spend a little extra time between the sheets.

His flushed cheeks and disheveled hair are always a delicious sight first thing in the morning.

I like that he's gotten bolder with asking me things every now and then, talking to me when he's starting to flip out inside his head a little. While we were showering earlier, he gave me that *look*.

"You know I still get caught by these moments. Like my brain wonders why you came back. Am I really worth all this hassle?" Kayce nibbles his bottom lip and darts a quick glance at me while he lathers up.

"I was used to doing things on my own for so long. I never had anyone else to consider before now. Always being able to pack up and go whenever, wherever. Without needing to think about somebody else, you know?" I rinse my hair off under the shower spray, then scrub the excess wetness off my face, feeling his eyes drilling into me the entire time.

"And yet, while I was gone, all I could think was, what if I've done the wrong thing? What if walking away from you was the biggest mistake I ever made and would come to regret."

"So what made you..." He falters, mid question.

"Snowflake, as soon as I realized you'd sent me those messages, that was all it took. I just needed to know your head and heart were in this as much as mine are. Because I couldn't do it for you."

"I still feel like shit it took me so long to get up the courage."

Shaking my head, I step out from under the water and drip my way across to where our towels are stacked on the vanity.

"You needed to trust. Yourself. Me. Your friends to be a safe place for you to open up. All of that takes time." I dry myself off as he finishes in the shower and then joins me.

God, I love that this is what our mornings, our days, our life looks like.

"Wanna know something? I've always trusted you. I've always felt safe with you, and I never knew it. You were my protector, and I had no fucking clue because you were a stubborn idiot and hid all that from me."

Wrapping my towel around my waist, I rake my fingers through my hair and study him. Kayce still hits me up about that, and it's hard for me to put words to that time in my life. I'm guessing I'll be due for my own round of therapy at some point.

"Why did you do it?" He steps into me, a small, ever so curious smile hides in his blue eyes.

"Back then... I don't know. I hated that I had to. It wasn't like I took one look at you and felt things as a teenager." I swallow hard. "Can I be really straight up with you about that? Believe me, I was just an angry guy who felt like he couldn't watch someone else go through what I'd been through. My dad's bastard side, I knew how to handle it, knew how to take it. You and your mom would have ended up in the hospital, so I got in the way because I didn't want your blood on my hands."

He wraps his arms around me, and the way he lets our damp chests press together, to indulge in feeling each other's steady heartbeats, is everything.

"Then I left, and things evolved over time. I don't know. It was like you stayed with me, and I couldn't shake you following me around. Like you were in my bones, and it wasn't until I saw you here in Crimson Ridge . . . that was when I realized I wasn't feeling this way because I hated you or hated our life. That connection evolved into something deeper."

"Something deeper." He hums against my chest, his smile broadening, that soul-stealing sensation of his lips curving with happiness against my skin.

I just want to hold tight to him like that for hours.

I'm still deep in that memory, going through the motions of sorting out saddles and tidying the tack room, when a commotion pricks my hearing.

Not the usual sounds of the ranch. Not the horses kicking up a fuss or cattle bellowing.

Voices.

Raised voices.

Setting the saddle down, I make my way in the direction of the barn entrance, hearing Kayce's words echoing loudly, but I'm unable to see him.

"I don't know where the fuck Raine is. He's not here. Last I heard, he was in Canada."

There's a harshness to his tone. With hackles up, I can immediately tell the response isn't friendly. In an instant, I'm on edge, ready to speed to him and stand my ground, to handle this intruder.

"You never were any good at lying."

My steps freeze. Every muscle locks up, and my blood turns to ice.

That voice.

That goddamn voice.

"Yeah? If he is, then where's his truck? Christ, I don't know where he went after leaving town. He's been gone since before winter."

My heart kicks into overdrive. Kayce is acting like I'm not here, and I know without a doubt why he's talking as loud as he is. Fuck. *Fuck.*

"Nah, I can see straight through you. You got those same eyes like your momma. A dirty, good for nothing liar livin' behind those eyes."

The slithering words of my father spread foul tendrils the length of the barn from where they're standing off with each other outside. In between the racing of my pulse and numb sensation crawling through my limbs, I crouch low and move as quietly as possible to the left, avoiding being in a direct line of sight through the partially open doors.

Jesus. There's nothing within reach to use as a weapon. And I don't want to leave Kayce to stand up to that psycho alone. Even if he is foolishly trying to protect me.

"Go on. You wanna rob me? Search the house? Take what you fucking want and piss off."

As Kayce keeps arguing, I duck around the side of the building, keeping as low a profile as I can while carefully navigating to the shaded area at the back of the barn. There's excess wood stacked back here. Debris from the ranch. Machinery. Nothing fucking useful for me to defend us with that I can see as I inch forward, doing my best not to make a sound.

Each carefully placed footstep through the remnants of snow and ice lingering beside the barn feels like an eternity. I just want to sprint—to race out there. But in my gut, I know that's the worst thing I can do. Since the asshole has followed me here, he's found a way to connect me to Devil's Peak. Now that he knows Kayce is here, I hate to think what shitstorm he's brought with him.

My heart is in my mouth, hoping like hell that Kayce will just keep him talking. Don't be a fucking hero, Kayce. Just talk and buy me time until I can get there. Please don't try anything with him.

Just hold the fuck on until I can get there.

As I draw nearer, their muffled voices sound curt, growing more agitated, and my entire heart is damn well pumping in overdrive. I'm terrified—colder and more sick to my stomach than I've ever felt before—that there's gonna be the worst before I can get there in time.

Please. Kayce, I promise I'm coming.

I'm not leaving you to face this alone.

Inching as close as I dare to the corner of the barn, I remain partly hidden by a pile of timber stacked beside the wall.

I see him. I come face to face with the monster himself.

The most miserable and pathetic of men. Witnessing my abuser in the flesh. His hollowed face and sallow skin. Countless years of alcohol and drug abuse are present in those sunken, beady eyes.

And as I shift my weight, trying to control my breathing, trying to make a fucking plan—my entire world tilts on its axis. A vile, hideous trick of fate.

My stomach plummets through to the soles of my boots as the asshole steps forward, revealing the worst possible scenario. All my fucking fears have come to life.

With a gun in one hand, he toys with a lighter wheel in the other. A five gallon gas can sits at his feet.

"I'll put a bullet straight through the eyes of every single one of these horses. Fuck me around, Wilder, and I'll show you just how serious I am."

Oh, Jesus.

No. No. No.

Kayce shields the horse with his body. My fucking beautiful man is protecting Winnie as she shifts her weight and her nostrils flare. "I don't fucking care if you shoot me. You so much as put a scratch on one of these animals, I won't be held responsible for what happens next." His voice is low, deadly serious.

I know exactly what he would give for these animals, and if I was terrified before, now I'm doubled over with the painful realization that he'll absolutely do something stupid if he thinks it'll protect Winnie.

"That's ok, boy." My father sneers and gestures with the barrel of his gun. "How about I shoot you first, put a bullet in both knees real easy like, then set fire to this place. You can lie right there in the dirt and watch your precious horses burn."

"Fuck you," Kayce spits. "Piss off back to the hole you crawled out of."

"Ah, but you stopped playing along nicely. You didn't give me any choice."

"Mom deserves to be rid of you. She should've kicked your rank ass to the curb years ago."

"You shoulda kept your nose out of it. The hospital was mighty helpful in letting me know who's been paying for my wife's rehab. Certainly didn't take long in a small town to find out where you were hiding these days."

"You don't care that she left you. All you care about is the money."

Fuck. I see the way my father keeps readjusting his grip on that gun, and I edge another step closer. What if I can only stop Kayce from getting hurt, but not Winnie? I don't know if he could handle that. He'd lay down his life for these horses; that's how pure his heart is, and it sends a chill straight to my core, realizing the precipice we're dangling from.

One wrong move, and I might lose him in an entirely different way. Not to a bullet, but to guilt—to demons he's done so much to come back from—if he feels like he failed to protect the most vulnerable lives on this ranch it'll end him.

My father clicks that lighter wheel again and gestures with the gun. "Damn straight. I couldn't give a shit where she goes. But I ain't gonna be walking away without the money I'm owed." He takes a step forward. "Money *you* now owe me, you little shithead."

That's all it takes. I see him cast his attention toward the interior of the barn. I catch his focus wandering for a split second, and I burst forward.

It happens in the blink of an eye but stretches on and on, dragging out into slow motion.

As I rush him, cannoning into his torso, I wrap my arms to pin his at his sides. Tackling him to the ground.

I don't register the kick of the gun.

I barely hear the shot go off. The echoing pop sounds far, far away.

I hardly feel the white-hot, searing pain.

Adrenaline blasts a path through my limbs. Undiluted blind rage, a brutal fury, grants me the ability to overpower him. It's rapid fire. The act of wrestling the gun from his hands and slamming the blunt end into his nose over and over and over. Then crashing the butt into the side of his head.

With a roar, I twist sideways to jam the barrel against his kneecap. I don't pause, letting off two rounds in quick succession.

Red mist coats my vision.

My father's screams of agony are deafened by the thundering pulse in my ears.

His face is pulverized into a mess of red and split skin as he garbles in pain. I don't fucking care. I spit straight in his fucking face.

Words won't form. Everything grows heavy. Lead weights pull my limbs toward the center of the earth.

Hands are on me. Grabbing my shoulders, tilting my jaw.

Kayce's face swims in front of my eyes.

I can't hold myself upright anymore.

It's too hard to fight it. Slumping over, I clutch one side.

Warmth oozes, a track of something liquid seeps from my stomach. When I bring one hand up in front of my face, there's bright red glistening all over my fingers.

It's not his blood. It's mine.

My blood.

CHAPTER 48

If hell had an image, it would surely be reflected in my bloodshot eyes. It would live in the burn that lines the back of my throat.

This place is nothing but a prison, a hellscape I'm trapped in because there's no way I won't stay by his side. Not when he's lying in that bed covered in tubes and equipment, and I don't fucking know if he's going to make it back to me.

Machines beep, and fluorescent lighting burns my retinas, while Raine remains in that terrifying post-surgery void where even the doctors simply *don't know*.

Abdominal trauma. Risk of sepsis. No exit wound.

I've hardly been able to concentrate on anything other than studying his slack features. Searching for a flicker of an indication that he's gonna wake up. There's hardly any capacity to take in the information doctors give me during their rotations through the wards. They talk to me like I'm a child. Attempting to spell it out for me in the simplest terms possible, I can tell.

"*He's stable, Mr. Wilder. However, a projectile from a firearm can damage anything in its path. The severity of a gunshot wound like Mr. Rainer suffered may vary according to bullet caliber or the trajectory of the object. Below the skin, those layers of tissue can be inflicted with trauma that is harder for us to identify.*"

Then there are other snatches of conversation that I honestly feel like I'm gonna hurl every time I hear their whispers. *Rapid response time. Blood transfusion. CPR administered en route.* And possibly the worst of all... *Luck.*

The fate of the man I love beyond all reason cannot fall to luck. There's no way that someone as strong as him, who walks this earth like he's my goddamn steadfast, solid rock, could be lingering in a place where only *luck* is gonna successfully bring him out the other side.

Squeezing my fists into balls, I dig them into my eye sockets and lean forward on my knees. Sitting here, I feel more useless than ever, clinging onto hope with all the desperation of every bronc I've ever ridden, rolled into one. Raine is my rope, and I'm doing everything I can to keep him secure inside my grasp. All while stuck in this stupid chair at his bedside. Watching him, waiting for him to find a way to return to me, while we linger in this holding pen of doom. I feel like I've been pacing the same three feet of linoleum for endless tortured hours.

Waiting.
Waiting.
Waiting.

It leaves me replaying events in my mind's eye. Unable to escape the horror of that moment when Raine burst out and played the goddamn hero. Hearing that fateful shot, a sickening pop and echo like the whole mountain was about to crumble beneath my feet.

I knew it had hit him. There was no way it could miss at such close range.

The medevac arrived after I was able to get a radio call out using the handset in my truck. I didn't want to leave him for even a split-second to make that call, knowing that the more blood he lost, the worse his chance of survival might be. But it was either watch him die in my arms or get an emergency signal out.

I had to go into survival mode. To put that onslaught fear and of emotion to one side and do what needed to be done. For him.

What followed was a blur, but the helpless misery of *waiting* for someone to arrive still tightens my throat and strangles me with tendrils of panic. The minutes spent hunched over his figure, that agonizing trickle of time, not knowing how long it would take for the air ambulance to get to us. I don't know how many times I told him to just hang on a little longer, to be as strong as I know he always is, to stay with me. Applying as much weight as possible in an effort to stem the bleeding, covering the site of him hemorrhaging beneath my fingers, soaking through every bit of fabric I could tear off my body and use along with the first aid kit from my vehicle. My shirt, my thermal, my hoodie, gauze—maintaining pressure over the wound while he bled out in the middle of the yard.

The rapid whomp of that helicopter cresting above the tree line has never been more of a relief to hear. Still, I didn't know if it was too late.

God. He was so pale by the time they took over.

As quick as they landed, he was gone.

They had him loaded onboard and whisked away amid rotors whirring and the efficient bustle of flight doctors. Taking him from me before I knew it.

Having to watch on while they loaded him on board was gut-wrenching. I didn't even have a chance to hug him or kiss him or tell him he'd better fucking fight this because I don't want to consider a world where he's not in it.

All that was left to prove he'd been there was his blood covering my hands and clothes.

Sheriff Hayes wasn't far behind, arriving with his team and the EMTs to handle the man who I couldn't fucking care less about—couldn't have given a shit if he'd passed out from blood loss in the meantime.

Everything was numb, a waking nightmare beyond that. My statement was taken. An arrest made. Evidence collected. The entire time, all I wanted was to get in my truck and start driving. To get to Raine as fast as possible.

As for his father, Ezekiel Rainer is gonna be behind bars without bail. With any luck, he'll lose that leg in the process, too.

There were a number of outstanding warrants against Zeke. He turned up at the ranch, coming after the money he claimed my mom owed him. *His cut.* After feeding her addiction for god knows how many years, he'd been profiting off her sickness and forever mounting debts. Evidently, he'd been associated with the same dealers who my mom was always getting herself into trouble with, and when she finally paid those assholes directly and checked herself into rehab, he lost his shit.

A rotten maggot of a human, through and through.

My shoulder is jostled, and when I blink at the person swimming into focus through my bleary, exhausted vision, I see one of the nurses. She gives me a sympathetic look. "Go grab yourself a coffee. Try eating something. He's not going anywhere, and he's stable." Then she carries on her way.

Shifting my weight forward, I lean on the edge of Raine's hospital bed and link my pinky finger with his. The deepest, darkest ache settles inside my chest when there's still no response. But I hold on to that small glimmer of hope that he's in recovery, he survived surgery, he's in the best place possible.

"Don't leave me. Don't you dare," I whisper and keep our little fingers hooked. "I've never known what it's like to love this wholly. Every part of me is attached to you. If you go somewhere without me, I'm coming straight after because I don't want to do any of this without you."

I swallow the painful lump in the back of my throat and place a kiss on his knuckles beside the drip line in the back of his hand. Then unfold myself from the chair, proceeding to make my way through the maze of corridors and hospital levels until I reach the cafeteria. I'm like a zombie. I don't know what time of the night it is. I don't know anything beyond this no-man's land we're stranded in.

As I load up a shitty coffee with sugar and creamer, I can hear his steady voice. That day when he convinced me to get on the back of a horse for the first time since my accident, the memory of it barrels into my awareness.

"Ride with me." *He repeats those three little words, taking in the sight of my immediate hesitation. That onyx gaze dances, with gentle creases forming around the corners of his eyes. He's so breathtaking. So handsome. I* don't know how to handle it when he offers me that sort of tenderness that is so uniquely his to give.

My stomach lurches with unease. Getting on the back of a horse feels unfathomable, impossible. It's such a huge part of my life, but at the same time, this one thing I've always done without a second thought now seems like yet another thing I've ruined.

Once more, Kayce Wilder breaks something good.

"What if—" Swallowing hard, I have to wipe my clammy palms on my jeans, juggling the halter he just handed to me.

"You won't. I've got you. I'm gonna be right by your side the whole way." He steps closer, all masculine scent and security in his warm presence. "This is you. Riding horses is as much a part of who you are as being the rodeo cowboy, snowflake. I'm not gonna let you fall."

God, it felt so good. Riding with him at my side. I was able to shed so many doubts, finally ridding myself of the terrible cloud of dark thoughts I'd been smothered by.

He gave me something that day I wish I'd been able to thank him for.

Raine showed me I could trust myself. That I was strong enough to do something on my own, and he wanted to be there to see me do it.

I absently rub over the center of my chest as my footsteps lead me back to the room he's laid up in. As I reach the doorway, a low voice pierces my awareness. Blood drains from my face; at first, I think it's Raine, and I'm riddled with guilt for not being at his side the moment he woke up. But in the next frantic heartbeat, I realize it's not his voice. It's not him at all. On reaching the doorway, I stop dead in my tracks.

". . . you looked after him when I wasn't there. For that, I'm forever in your debt."

"Dad?"

Colton Wilder. My dad. He's here. There's no possible way he's here in this hospital, when he's supposed to be damn near on the other side of the world. With jet lag and sleeplessness clinging to his expression, his broad frame strides over to me without pause. He encircles me in a fierce hug.

I fucking lose it. I'm shaking, leaving sodden tracks of silent tears on his shoulder.

"What the fuck are you doing here?" I croak. With my head turned to the side, through the wetness clinging to my lashes, I take in Raine's figure where he lies dreadfully still. Unmoving. Machines surrounding him, monitoring his vitals.

"Hayes got in contact. I got on the first flight I could."

"You didn't have to." But as I say the words, it hits me like a landslide that I'm so unbelievably grateful he did.

"There has been so much of your life I haven't been there for. Times when I should've been a parent and wasn't." He rubs one palm back and forth between my shoulder blades and cradles the back of my head with the other. "I'm gonna be there for every fucking thing you need, son. And I know it might be too little too late, but tell me what I can do, whenever, and I'll be there."

CHAPTER 49
Raine

The first thing I see when my eyes creak open is blond hair set against the stark, utilitarian hospital sheet. Kayce's scruffy, mussed strands rest on the edge of my bed. His face is ashen, creased heavily with sleep, or maybe lack thereof. He's leaning forward in the chair at my bedside and must have drifted off while resting alongside my arm.

When I try to move my hand, to stroke his face, I realize his fingers are hooked through mine.

He's here.

Apparently, I'm still here, too.

"Hey, snowflake." My voice is rusty. A faint rasp.

Those big blue orbs fly open, blinking rapidly. His eyes are red, with deep purple shadows framing his wild gaze, as he stares back at me in disbelief.

"Oh my god." His words come out hoarse, still addled with sleep, but he launches out of his chair and softly grabs my face in both hands. "You ever do something like that again . . ." The rest doesn't come out. It's a broken, raw thing that he struggles to put words to as his breathing hitches.

Wetting my lips, I stare up at him, still foggy but it doesn't matter.

Nothing else matters. Because all I want right now is him filling my vision.

"You saved me," I croak.

All I want is Kayce filling my entire life. No matter what I have to do to make that happen.

His fingers trace my face, gingerly mapping across my brow, my cheeks, my beard, and he bends forward on a shaky exhale to drop the softest of kisses against my lips. He's so warm, so soft, I know he's being careful to avoid all the tubes and shit attached to me. I can't exactly feel any pain, but I also don't feel like I can move either.

Kayce shakes his head, letting his nose ever so gently bump against mine. "No. You saved *me*. In so many ways. You turned my life inside out, and I've never been so scared about losing anyone . . . someone . . . *you*." Hearing him, feeling him, and getting a second chance at having those whispered words brushing up against my lips is the best thing I've ever experienced.

"Are you ok?" I reach up and catch his hand. Or at least try to. I'm so fucking uncoordinated, thanks to the cocktail of painkillers I must be on. It takes me a couple of attempts before I manage to drag his fingers to my mouth so I can kiss those fingertips I don't ever want to let go of.

"I thought I'd lost you." Kayce's throat dips, and his exhausted eyes glisten. "Please don't ever fucking do that to me again. My heart won't be able to take it."

"He's awake?" A loud whisper cuts across the room from the doorway. When Kayce turns, I blink a couple of times. There are a fuck load of people standing just inside the door to my room. "Oh my god. You're awake." Tessa waddles toward me with a look on her face that dangles somewhere between wanting to smother me with a pillow and immense relief. Wetness tracks down her cheeks as tears roll freely, and she stops on the other side of my bed.

When she bends down to give me a quick hug and kisses my forehead, I rub a thumb over the dampness there.

"You're a fucking moron. And I'm so glad you're ok." She shakes her head.

"Don't go wasting tears on me."

"Such a grump." She swipes at her cheeks with the heel of her palm and sniffs.

I look over toward the rest of the figures starting to appear. For someone who has been on his own this entire time, who has gone it alone, my brain can't fathom what all these people are doing here.

The drugs kind of blur everything, but there's a steady stream of familiar faces. Like half of goddamn Crimson Ridge is here. Right behind Tessa is Beau, and I'm introduced to Sage, who wraps me in a hug as if we've been friends for an eternity. The crew from Rhodes Ranch is all here, with Storm and Briar hot on their heels. After they've all managed to squeeze in for a mix of hugs and gruff teasing about the state of me, the Hayes boys appear, too.

What leaves my chest squeezing is the way they're here, as much for Kayce as anything. Which means they're obviously more than aware of who we are to each other. Looking down, I see that Kayce still has our fingers interlocked. He hasn't let go of my hand this entire time.

There's no mistaking the final visitors who come through that door. Colton Wilder might have dark hair and doesn't have blue eyes, but there's more than enough of Kayce that I see in him immediately. At his side is a woman with copper curls who rushes straight up to Kayce and gives him a massive hug, before doing the same to me.

It's all kind of overwhelming, and most of the chatter goes over my head. But I feel the sensation filling the room—that undeniable care, that love in here is palpable.

I'm so goddamn proud of Kayce for everything. The way he's been strong enough for the two of us. Because he's the one who has done all of this, brought all these people together.

"Ok, we're getting a bite to eat down the road." Tessa flurries her hands at everyone. "And to be honest, you assholes all need to move before we get kicked out for breaking visitor rules." She hisses, then turns to me with a small smile.

"Thanks . . . you know . . . for coming." I manage to get some coherent words out. Kayce is doing most of the talking as I lie flat on my back, still kind of stunned that all these people made the effort to be here.

"Don't you need to eat something? You're not going with them?" I say to Kayce as the last of them waves and vacates the room.

He shakes his head. "Dad is gonna come back. He'll drop something off for me after."

"Isn't he supposed to be in Ireland or some shit?" I squint one eye, trying to make sense of any of this.

Kayce chuckles. "Yeah, he gave me a hell of a shock turning up." Then he settles back at my side, dragging the chair closer before pulling my hand up and laying a kiss on my palm. "I'm done with shocks. No more. None for the foreseeable future. Please?"

"Deal."

He lays his cheek against the heart of my palm.

"Everyone knows. I just want you to know that I—"

"I could see it. I could see that you'd spoken to everyone." My lips curve into a grin. "I'm proud of you."

He blinks rapidly at me. Looking every bit the man I want to spend every fucking minute of every day with.

Clearing my throat, I press my fingers against his cheek, feeling the warmth of him embedded beneath my touch. "You told me you're a better person because I taught you how to love. Well, I'm better because of the way you love. I'm out here wondering how a guy like me could ever get so lucky . . . or ever deserve to have someone like you looking my way twice."

"I'm not special. I'm nothing special," he whispers.

"To me, you are. To me . . . you are magnificent."

His lips quirk. "I think you're high."

My heart damn near swells ten sizes inside my chest, seeing him smile like that, and this time it reaches his eyes. "Nowhere near high enough for the fact I'm pretty sure I've got a chunk missing from my stomach." As I gaze at him, I use my other hand to gesture between the two of us while holding onto him. "But this? I know *this* for certain."

"I love you." He kisses my palm again, before leaning up to press his lips to mine.

"So fucking much." I reach to cup his jaw and take a deep inhale. "You don't even know all the ways I love you, baby."

"Never not obsessed?" His lips form a hesitant little smile over my mouth.

"Never *not* obsessed with you."

EPILOGUE

Gathering around a bonfire with friends, high spirits, and laughter is nothing new. I've lost track of how often I've spent nights exactly like this.

But right now, I find myself secretly smiling, basking in the moment as I take it all in. Recalling a multitude of evenings under a starry sky that acted as a mirror image to this one—with a grill sizzling, soft music, and lively chatter floating on the night air—except there's one major, life-altering difference now.

He's here.

He's here with me.

All it takes is for the briefest lift of my gaze, to raise my chin, and I find Raine. Those dark eyes of his are right there, and I'm kinda addicted to the way he's forever watching me.

Seeing him now, as we lock on each other for a brief moment, I can't stop a grin from completely taking over. My wide smile is met with his cute scowl. He's got his usual stern demeanor going on, but it's just a front.

He's found his home at long last.

His contentment is a tangible, beautiful thing to be in the vicinity of.

Besides, it would be impossible to ignore the way he's been

welcomed into this group of our friends and family. The way he's damn well adored to pieces by all these people makes my heart swell to bursting.

I'm quite honestly the luckiest son of a bitch to ever exist, knowing that he's mine, and I'm his, and that we're together in everything that might come our way.

All our friends are here, along with my dad and Layla, of course. Summer bonfires at Devil's Peak Ranch are becoming something of a tradition... and as I glance around at the people gathered in front of the flames, it hardly seems possible that just over a year ago, we all stood in that hospital waiting and hanging onto nothing but hope.

Twelve months since I sat by his hospital bed, praying he'd come back to me. And I've never been more relieved to hear his voice than in that moment when he finally woke up after surgery.

A year ago, he and I were still finding our feet in the aftermath of Raine being discharged. Safe to say we're both very happy to see the back of medical staff and emergency wards.

Raine gives me the kind of look that hooks into my stomach, drawing me to him in an instant. Just like I unknowingly found myself drawn to him the first time I saw him from across a bonfire when he arrived in Crimson Ridge, here I am sauntering over, trying to at least attempt not to give him moon-eyes and a goofy grin.

God knows he already has enough evidence that I'm a fool for him.

He's sitting a little further away from the bonfire, with his ass resting against a hay bale. The fact he's over here on his own makes me feel even more alive, knowing that I can have him to myself for a little while, even though there are others here enjoying the night.

Who can blame me for wanting to corner my extremely hot boyfriend alone in the dark at every opportunity?

"I've got something for you." His voice is all velvety and deep.

"Oh yeah?" My eyebrows lift, and that smile I'd been attempting to dial down breaks free. As it stretches to take over my face, my point of focus drops.

"Christ. Not in my pants." He groans and tilts his head back, exposing the stubble coating his throat.

"That would be an excellent choice of present though, just saying."

Raine tugs me to stand between his knees, giving me one of those reproachful *that'll cost you later* looks. "Cheeky. No... but this is it right here..."

His big palm unfurls, and in the center sits a smooth, round stone.

"Oh my god. Where did you find this?" My eyes pinball between his face and his hand, then I grab it from him. It's warm from his touch, and I melt a little that it has something of him infused into it. Except my initial excitement over a silly little fucking rock makes way for my brain to catch up.

Narrowing my stare, I look at him for a long moment while rubbing the surface with my thumb. "Have you had it this whole time, or what?"

Of course, Raine gives me absolutely nothing. An unreadable expression sits there as he watches me closely.

I shove at his shoulder. "Seriously? I thought I'd lost it. Figured it was gone forever."

"Don't pout." Now he finally gives in, allowing a twitch of his lips as he teases me ever so softly.

Rolling it between the pads of my fingers, I shake my head and find myself speechless. This is such a tiny thing, such an insignificant little fragment of rock, yet it holds a lot of memories for me.

Raine clears his throat. "I kept it... and didn't understand why at first. Maybe guilt? Part of me thought I'd somehow been responsible for you getting injured. Probably would've carried it around for a long ass time... a reminder that I was the last person you spoke to before your accident."

I'm already shaking my head. "If I didn't have my own shit going on—stuff with my mom that day—you'd have never gotten to me that easily. It was all on me that I carried on competing when my head was messy."

His gaze softens, and my insides go all gooey. "After a while, carrying this stupid stone around, I realized it kept me grounded." He takes my hand in his own. "Kept me centered even when I was away from you all that time. I wasn't ready to give you up... so it was like carrying a little piece of you with me."

"Completely obsessed, huh?" The words might be playful, but

they're thick with emotion surging at me unexpectedly and I have to blink fast. "How'd you end up with it?"

"That day at the hospital, when I first arrived, the nurse handed it to me. Said you'd been mumbling on and on, bugging them non-stop to make sure it was kept safe."

He runs his thumb along the inside of my wrist and swallows heavily.

"Honestly? That day, I shoved it in my pocket. Didn't give it a second thought. When I went to Canada . . . I found it again. All that time later, I pulled on a jacket, and in it was your fucking stone." His eyes glitter, reflecting a flurry of bonfire sparks. "You'd snuck away with me, without knowing it."

My pulse thumps harder, emotions stinging behind my eyes.

"You kept me with you?" The words are hoarse as my throat tightens.

He hums in agreement. "I did. *Right here.*" Wrapping my hold in his own, he places both our hands over his heart. As he does so, I feel him use his free hand to tuck something else into my fingers, closing my fist around something small and velvety—a tiny box.

"I'm never going to walk away from you ever again. I need you to know that. I'm in this thing with you, snowflake, where you own my whole goddamn heart. So I'm asking if you're ok with me taking care of you forever, baby?"

His eyes hold mine. Secure and rich and layered with so much softness, reflecting back to me the love that we share. *Our love story.*

I'm trembling as I turn my fist over, swaying, growing more and more lightheaded. Absolutely giddy with the prospect of what is happening right now.

I can already sense what lies inside.

Swallowing thickly, I fumble with opening the lid, but Raine's strong hands come up to close over mine when he sees me struggling. Of course, he does. My man demolishes me with the kind of soul-eating smirk on his lips that should be illegal as he takes over where my fingers are clumsy with rising emotion.

A choked-up sound escapes when he plucks the two metal bands from inside, and lays them in my palm on top of the stone. They're gorgeous. Ruggedly perfect. Brushed metal, with an engraved mountain range on each of the wide-set bands.

"What do you think?" he hums softly.

As of this moment, the rest of the world has evaporated, dissolved; transformed into nothing but mist and shadow. I'm so captivated by the sight of his fingers against mine, the two circles resting in the middle of my calloused palm. The very hand I've trusted to hold on for grim death throughout countless bronc rides. His is the same, has gone through so much of the same life as me, and not only that . . . it's his hand he used to defend me with all those times I knew nothing about.

Now, that same touch is reaching out. Allowing me to cling tight to him.

My future. My cowboy. My love.

"Fuck, yes." Air rushes from my lungs as I throw myself around his neck. My fist clenched tight to keep the rings safe.

"You're supposed to let me ask?" Raine chuckles softly, his words muffled against my shoulder.

"I don't need to be asked. I already claim you." I grin, tilting my face against his throat, a high beam smile now firmly in place when I draw back so that I can kiss him fiercely.

"I love you . . . so goddamn hard it hurts," he mumbles against my mouth, and it's that low, delicious tone of voice that makes me shiver with pleasure and so much relief that he's still here by my side.

"You already know I'm stupidly in love with you." I dust another kiss over his lips, then pull away a fraction. "Wait, can we put these on? Like right now?" I'm already pawing at his left hand and grabbing his knuckle, ready to slip the band on my boyfriend's ring finger . . . or, I guess, my fiancée's finger.

He rumbles with laughter. "Just wait, Mr. Over Enthusiastic."

A petulant noise and associated pout are busy making their presence known when Raine spins me around and stands up behind me. His big arms wrap tight to band me against his chest, and his short beard scratches my ear.

"Watch for a second."

"But I wanna wear the r—" The rest of my efforts to say anything disappears in a blink because a hundred tiny lights are glowing and glimmering against the night sky. When they flick on, a festoon of tiny bulbs resembling fireflies, all hanging from trees just beyond the bonfire, are revealed. My eyes bounce everywhere, widening rapidly as I see all our friends here tonight have moved away from the fire and are now gathered beneath the lit-up grove of trees.

"Oh my fucking god." My voice is a shaky whisper.

"Marry me." Raine's quiet, steadfast rumble is in my ear, and I go weak at the knees.

It's not a question. It's a promise, a gift of his heart, and I couldn't believe it possible to love him more. But here I am, nodding and gasping a string of words along the lines of *Yes. Of course, I will. Fuck, Yes.*

"Then, we'd better get over there. Don't want to keep our wedding guests waiting."

His warmth and powerful arms leave me briefly, only for him to stand at my side, threading our fingers together. Dragging my hand up to his mouth, he kisses my fingertips gently and keeps those onyx eyes securely on mine. A hidden smile dances in his gaze, as he sweeps me away with words I never knew I wanted to hear, but are complete perfection when coming from his lips.

"Ready to be my husband, snowflake?"

THANK YOU FOR READING

These angsty lover boys crept in and took over my life, in the best way possible. I hope you enjoyed Kayce and Raine's love story. You'll be kicking your heels to know the epilogue's little cliffhanger has a delicious completion . . . a Devil's Peak Ranch wedding *(and wedding night)*. The extended epilogue from Raine's POV can be found here + settle in for a sneak peek at where we will be heading next beyond the Crimson Ridge series.

KEEP READING HERE:

https://www.elliottroseauthor.com/bonuses

Loving the Crimson Ridge world and don't want to leave? Me either . . . Make sure to come and join my reader group - this is where all the announcements and first peeks will be happening on any future bonus content:

https://www.facebook.com/groups/thecauldronelliottrose

—

INSTAGRAM | TIKTOK | FACEBOOK

ACKNOWLEDGEMENTS

Crimson Ridge will forever be the series to completely change my life. Not only professionally as an author—with the originally indie published books moving to find a home with Kensington Books—but in bringing me so much creative joy telling these stories. The completion is always a little bittersweet, but this certainly won't be the last you see of your favorite Crimson Ridge cowboys and cowgirls.

First and foremost, I have to thank every single reader who has taken a chance on stepping into this world and adding these books to your TBRs and bookshelves. Without you, the opportunities to be in bookstores everywhere could not have been possible—this is one giant love letter to you, wrapped in chaps and adorned with a cowboy hat.

To my ever patient and wonderful Mr. Rose, I love you endlessly. Never *not* obsessed with you. Thank you for being there for the immense pressure of this deadline and being the absolute rock for me on the days when I simply didn't do anything but eat, sleep, and breathe this book.

Lazz, you are my champion, listener, first reader, support Queen extraordinaire... ILY. ILU. *I'm so happy we finally have given your cowboy crush his long overdue HEA.*

Brandi, Sam, Colby, Lib, and Jenna—you ladies are the reason the

ACKNOWLEDGEMENTS

Elliott Rose-verse keeps spinning. THANK YOU for all the ways you've allowed me the breathing room to focus on bringing this book to life. I'm so deeply grateful for everything you do behind the scenes.

Sandra, your covers leave me swooning each and every single day. I'm so grateful for absolutely everything, and still get a little misty eyed thinking back to the very first time you had Chasing The Wild's concept in hands and said 'trust me'. *In Sandra we trust.*

To my editors—a million thank yous for being with me on the journey as we wrapped up four books in the space of a year (and in particular, for being able to help turn this one around on a dime).

To my incredible supporters on Patreon, thank you for taking a chance on an indie author and hanging out in my world month to month! You have no idea how much it all means, and I adore the lot of you! Getting to read your reactions to the goodies (and art!) each month gives me fuel to keep the words flowing.

Of course, bringing a book like this to life takes a village behind the scenes. To my alpha, beta, and early readers, you are absolute magic and thank you for pouring so much love into these two. Thank you for being accomplices in my mischief, the chaos of chapter drops, and putting up with my endless questions.

Jen, you have been there from day one. I am eternally thankful for all your time and enthusiasm for these books and my mad flurries of chapters.

Matt and Phil, your help with this book means the world. Kayce and Raine are all the better for having your thoughtful feedback and input. I can't say a big enough thank you for being so willing and available to dive in to this story.

To the amazing teams behind the scenes at Kensington, THANK YOU for giving Crimson Ridge such a warm welcome and fantastic home to find readers all over the world.

To my agent Nikki Groom, I am so grateful for all your time, effort, and enthusiasm for my books along with supporting my steps in this whole authoring business. It's been one heck of a wild ride this year, and I'm so excited for what is to come!

My Creator Crew and Crimson Ridge Riders, you are EVERYTHING. I send all the gruff dirty talking cowboys your way. To everyone who

ACKNOWLEDGEMENTS

has shared about this book, hyped, *gently* insisted on a bestie reading it, you are just so damn wonderful.

To every single person who has helped promote one of my books, I am besotted with you, and swoon with heart eyes every time I get to see your creativity and excitement for an Elliott Rose character or story.

From the bottom of my heart, and from Kayce and Raine . . . we send you all our love.

xo

LEAVE A REVIEW

If you enjoyed this book, please consider taking a quick moment to leave a review. Even a couple of words are incredibly helpful and provide the sparkly fuel us Romance Authors thrive on.

(*Well, that and coffee + HEAs*)

Also by Elliott Rose

Crimson Ridge

Chasing The Wild

Braving The Storm

Taming The Heart

Saving The Rain

Also from the Crimson Ridge world

Bouquets & Buckles (Novella)

—

Port Macabre Standalones

Why Choose + Dark Romance
Where the Villains get the girl, and each other.

Vengeful Gods

Fox, Ky, Thorne, Ven - HEA Novella

Noire Moon - Prologue Novella

Macabre Gods

—

Nocturnal Hearts

Dark Paranormal-Fantasy Romance

Interconnected Standalones

Sweet Inferno

(Rivals to Lovers x Novella)

In Darkness Waits Desire

(Grumpy x Sunshine)

The Queen's Temptation

(Forbidden x Shadow Daddy Bodyguard)

Vicious Cravings

(MMF x Vampires x Enemies to Lovers)

Brutal Birthright

(Academy Setting, Teacher x Student)

About the Author

Elliott Rose is an author of romance on the forbidden and deliciously dark side. She lives in a teeny tiny beachside community in the south of Aotearoa, New Zealand with her partner and three rescue dogs. Find her with a witchy brew in hand, a notebook overflowing with book ideas, or wandering along the beach.

- Join her reader group *The Cauldron* for exclusive giveaways, BTS details, first looks at character art/inspo, and intimate chats about new and ongoing projects.
- Join her Newsletter for all the goodies and major news direct to your email inbox.